Oh the feels! What an emo
well-written story. The charact.... .......... ......., ...., ....
Ollie. And I liked that there was a Jane Austen loving dude as opposed
to a girl, and that he was the one who liked to read and not her. So
many sweet moments and sad moments and moments where I just had
to keep reading to see what happened next. Just perfect.

**-Katie Kaleski**, author of *A Fabrication of the truth*

I wouldn't change a single letter! I loved this book so much, it was
so emotional. I couldn't stop reading. I knew I would suffer, but I
wanted to keep reading anyway!

**-Alina**, tea-books-lover.tumblr.com

This is too perfect. First Sentences, First Impressions. . . It's like all
[M.C. Frank's] books are gifts for Austen fans. I love that Ari is a stunt
girl, it adds a spin to the story and puts her in a unique position- close
to celebrity but not a part of it, physically powerful and yet confronted
with dangerous situations. I love the settings so much, they set the
mood incredibly well. It's like watching a film. And Wes is so yummy!
This book is doing dangerous things to my heart.

**-Claire Palzer**, velutluna.tumblr.com

This book made me tear up and broke my heart. I absolutely loved
it.

**-Izabella**, thepagesfullofstars.tumblr.com

I really loved this story! I read it so fast. It had me laughing and
crying the whole way through. I felt connected emotionally to the
characters, and the turmoil they faced broke my heart. I thought it had
very witty dialogue, and I loved the writing style -from the quick banter
to the snippets of magazines/tumblr accounts . . . it was all very clever!
And definitely, the lovey-dovey stuff was exquisitely swoonworthy!

**-Christina Fong**

What I loved about this story was that I was emotionally drawn in. I
found myself totally loving the damaged and believeable Ari and Wes.
Emotionally, I was so connected to them loving each other at their most
damaged. I'm a total fan of Lose Me., it gave me all the feels

**-Angie Taylor**, author of *Twists in Time*

This is such a beautiful piece.
**-A.E. Cummings**

Absolutely adorable.

**-Raven Desroches**

I'm absolutely in love with the protagonist. We're not at all like each other, but she just feels relatable and so cool. It's kind of weird to see yourself in the shoes of someone absolutely different, but it's also kind of the purpose of storytelling, and [Lose Me.] really did great on that.

**-Miriam Mitsume**

I adored this story! It was absolutely beautiful and heart breaking.

**-Hannah B.**

I loved it. It was a clever, modern spin on a classic trope. The writing flowed beautifully, and the characters all had clear, recognisable voices throughout. I felt very emotionally invested in Ariadne from the beginning, and it didn't take long for other characters to follow. I would definitely recommend this to people for good, romantic reading! It's quite unique, in a lovely way, but I would compare it to ***Pride and Prejudice*** *by Jane Austen*, and ***The Fault in Our Stars*** *by John Green*.

**-Lorna George,** author of ***The Redwood Rebel***

Addictive.

**-Flisstea**

Lose Me. was a fun and exciting to read! It's cool that the characters are making a modern *Pride and Prejudice* film while experiencing it in their love lives. And I like how the story is set on a Greek island, very lovely.

**-Chen Yan Chang**

Wes and Ari forever. I loved reading this, loved it. It made me lose sleep, laugh, cry and scream on the inside. It caused me pain and joy. I connected with both of the main characters, as well as several others. I loved it!

**-Charlotte W.**

Absolutely loved this! I loved all the twist and meaning of this story. Wonderfully written.

**-Lyric Weldon**

# LOSE ME.

M.C. FRANK

Title: Lose Me.

Author: M.C. Frank

ISBN: 1542519500
ISBN-13: 978-1542519502

for the boy with the scar

on the back of his head

who fell in love

with a girl with a scar

on her heart

# PART ONE

First Sentences

First Sentences

First Sentences

## emails

To: Ollie <olivercromwell@gmail.com>
Fr: Wes <therealwes@wesspencer.com>
Re: L&H

Dude, that's sick! Not funny sick. Sick sick. Are you actually planning to stay on the boat for the entire shoot?! On MY boat, I may add. Sure, it has your name on it as well, but I'm the one who has to bring her. As far as I'm concerned, she'll only be there for a swim or two, I'm not staying the entire month on a stinking boat, even if it is the L&H, not while working at least. . . But it's your call, man. I know you hate living in a trailer since that unpleasant incident with that stalker chick, but anyway I hear that Tim's gone nuts on this one.

Low budget, have you ever heard anything more vile?

Who DOES low budget films anymore? And on a stupid Greek island no one's ever heard of?

I'm telling you, I almost backed out of this one, only I really need this project to get into the Academy in October. If they decide that I'm not too old or too Hollywood for them anyway, and that's a big if. FS is going be one of those indie, deep ones, right? Well, they adore those. Damn Tim, he seems to be their darling, although I don't see how he could be anyone's darling. Self-important prick.

Ok, enough with the venting.

The boat and I plan on arriving at the Corfu main port no later than 5 pm on Tuesday next. Be there, or else.

Give my sincerest disgust to that bitch your lovely mum. I'll crash now. Tomorrow I'll regret writing to you after a drinking spree, but tonight I'm king of the world! Not to mention king of the dystopian pirates. And Mr. Darcy.

Sweet dreams, my dear Bingley.

W.

To: Wes <therealwes@wesspencer.com>
Fr: Ollie <olivercromwell@gmail.com>
Re: Re: L&H

If you say 'my dear Bingley' one more time you're dead. Just because we're filming a modern version of some stupid English lit book by Austen, you don't need to out yourself in front of girls and everybody. I'll support your inner bookworm as long as it remains where it belongs, in the closet. If word gets around you're a nerd, I'm done. I'm so done.

Just kidding.

You may call me Binge. But that's it.

Get over yourself and get over here. The L&H had better be waiting for me in dock as soon as my plane touches down, 'cause I'm not staying on that damn island for a second more than I have to. Best stay on international waters while we're not shooting.

Has Tim finally snapped? Low budget?! Dude, you don't need this for school! You're freaking Tristan from THE WATER WARS. Although I do see why a Hollywood teen TV series wouldn't impress those theatre Brits so much.

It's gonna be one month, tops. You, me, Laurel and Hardy. And after that the world is ours. Just promise me you'll be sober when I see you next. I'm asking you as Bingley. Seriously, dude.

I remain Mr. Darcy's faithful sidekick LMAO.

Binge

To: Ollie <olivercromwell@gmail.com>
From: Wes <therealwes@wesspencer.com>
Re: Re: Re: L&H
Eff off Binge

# O N E

*Today is not the day I die.*

I'm not even breaking a sweat as the road curves steeply upwards, and I continue to jog, my trainers slapping the cobbled stones in an even rhythm. My right hip flexor, which I'd strained a while back, isn't even tender. Sweet.

At the very top of the road I take a right, my mind at peace as I focus on my breathing and the flexing and unflexing of my leg muscles.

I repeat the phrase over and over to myself, like a mantra. I say it in every language I know, which is three, and turn it over in my head, until the words mean nothing, until their repeated rhythm soothes me.

Until I believe it.

At least I think I do.

It's stupid really. Stupid and silly and totally useless. As though by merely thinking it I could keep disaster at bay—if it's about to happen, that is. Normally it's not about to happen. Not when I'm the one doing the stunt. I'm good and I know it.

Coach taught me the mantra, back when it had no meaning for me, at least it didn't mean what it does now. It was just a few words strung together, nothing more. He said I should repeat it during especially dangerous and complicated stunts to calm and motivate myself. I told him that was bull and he drew his eyebrows together. So I said okay and started repeating it after him like he wanted.

The man has me wrapped around his little finger.

I reach the school in two minutes, just as the bell is ringing for recess. I don't have to stand for more than a couple of seconds outside the huge, brass doors on the cobblestone street of the little town of Corfu, before kids start flooding out of the school gates. Behind the herd, dad jogs towards me, his hair a sweaty mess.

"Am I late?" he asks me, squinting against the midday sun.

"You're filthy," I answer as we take off towards the car.

He runs a hand through dark wavy hair that still makes every woman in his vicinity swoon like a schoolgirl—not to mention the actual schoolgirls that imagine themselves madly in love with him every day. "I had class until. . . " he looks at his watch "about three seconds ago."

"Why don't you let them do their warm-ups alone?" I say, not for the first time. We've had this conversation before. "Two PE teachers passed me as I waited, and not one of them had a hair out of place. Why can't you just yell orders and watch from afar like a normal person?"

Dad puts on his serious face, but his eyes are laughing. "Cause I enjoy it," he answers switching in English, as we cross *Leoforos Alexandras*. "'Sides, *I* need to be warmed up, the other PE's don't. All they're gonna do is go home and sit in front of the TV." He lifts his arms and cracks his elbows in a smooth, elastic movement, bringing them in front of his face. He sighs in satisfaction. "Are you ready, Ari?"

I look down at my tattered cut-offs matched with a simple dark blue tank top. To look at me, anyone would think that I was one of the leftover tourists from summer. Only my blue New Balance running shoes, worn out and sturdy on my feet, hint at the athletic nature of my job.

"My swimming suit's in the car," I answer and bend my head back to look at the clear sky. No hint of any clouds yet. "You'll tell me the truth, right?" I ask my dad, as I slide behind the steering wheel in my dad's old Ford Fiesta, which he gave me as a questionable birthday present two months ago when I turned eighteen.

He immediately starts messing with the buttons, turning the air-conditioning on full blast and wiping his sweaty brow. I slap his hand away.

"My car, my rules," I say, adjusting the seat to fit my height. I am not what you would call short, not by any chance, but still I am a bit shorter than my six-foot-one dad—although not by much.

"Oh, who are we kidding, Ari?" he says, his voice tired but playful. "We're going to wear this thing down if we keep passing it between us like this. We can't share a bathroom, much less a *car*! I think I'll call your mum," he mumbles, mostly to himself, after a small pause. "You're a grownup now, and a professional, you need a car. That would be the adult thing to do."

Although I had just pulled into the trickling, midday traffic, I slam on the breaks.

Dad turns surprised eyes to mine and my heart squeezes at his anxious expression. He quickly bends his head down, but he can't conceal how he feels from me. I have lived with this struggle against his personal guilt for all my life.

"No," I say simply.

He swallows and turns away.

And that's that.

At least I hope it is.

We arrive at the beach about twenty minutes later. That's the beauty of living on an island. I love the feeling of being surrounded by water, even during the winter months, when the streets are quiet and most of the shops in the great tourist markets close down. I don't mind. This is my home.

Most years I am glad to see the tourists board the ferry that leaves the port of Corfu every half hour. I love the quiet and the space they leave behind. I feel safe in my daily routine, which I've kept since I was little with very small variations: school then gym, practicing my stunts with dad and, in the last two years, with Coach as well. Working at grandpa's shop on the weekend and going out with girlfriends on Sunday evenings.

That's all I need out of life, at least all I needed until a few months ago.

At the beginning of the summer, my academic career at the Greek primary educational system ended. I graduated from high school, and suddenly I had to face the very real dilemma of what I would do with *her*.

Oh *her*.

It always boils down to that, doesn't it?

Well, not this time.

I snap my hair out of the tight band that kept it securely in a bun at the top of my head. I jog over to the little white beach cabin at the farthest corner of the tourist parking lot, under the fig trees, to change into my Billabong spring wetsuit. Coming out, I toss the car keys to my dad and run on the burning sand towards the water.

"Hey!" he calls behind me, "your car, *your* responsibility!"

As I dive in one swift movement into the clear water, behind me I hear the beep of the car doors being locked. Dad runs after me, calling my name in frustration, and I dip underneath the surface, blocking out all sound except the water in my ears.

I resurface just as the sea becomes really deep, its color darkening slightly under the sparkling rays of the September sun, and take a few deep breaths, only to discover that my dad, damn him, has almost overtaken me.

"Will you stop doing that?" I yell, frustrated.

He seems to hear me even though he was underwater, because he lifts a wet head next to mine. "What?"

I splash him and we race each other towards the huge rock rising from the water far into the distance. He visibly holds back, and we arrive at the same time. "Ars, are you okay?"

"Just fine," I gasp in return.

"You *did* warm up, didn't you?" his eyebrows meet and he lifts a hand to grasp the lower part of the rock that sticks out and hoist himself up. "You would have told me if you didn't, and we'd do it now."

To listen to him talk anyone would think that I was an irresponsible teenager, out for a swim with her daddy, instead of a trained stunt actor, getting ready for her first gig on a low-budget film featuring the famous dystopian pirate Wes Spencer.

Which I totally am. Not a famous dystopian pirate. The other thing.

"We can't all be like you," I say through clenched teeth.

*I'm not struggling to catch my breath*, I say to myself.

Yeah, like that would work.

Dad waits until I'm ready for the climb, and turns around to stare at the impressive villa perched high atop the cliff that drops straight into the sea, right ahead of us.

Rumor has it that the illustrious film director, Tim Something, is planning to evict the family that owns the place, in order to use it in his new film, *First Sentences*. I see some kind of movement through the dark green windows, but it is too far high above me to see if it is indeed the film crew already at work or if its occupants have refused to leave it.

And suddenly it hits me.

I am so incredibly lucky to have this opportunity.

I mean, it's like this film practically fell into my lap. Of course, I know that *she* arranged it all, but still, it is the greatest opportunity in the world. People like me don't get breaks like this. And even with the coach *she* hired for me two years ago straight from Hollywood, and with all the interminable hours of practice—*torture*—that I put in, I know that there have to be hundreds of better-trained and well-connected stunt actors out there, far more eligible for this role.

*You can't blow this, Ari,* I say to myself.

Dad watches me from his perch with something like amusement in his eyes, as though he can sense the struggle within me.

"Shut your face," I tell him and start climbing.

"Nice way to talk to the guy who raised you."

For once, I beat him. I reach the top first, quick as a cat, and dive headfirst into the water. When I surface, he is still watching me from above.

"How was it?" I shout.

The rock is more than twenty meters high, and although the sea is absolutely calm right now, still he has to bend down to hear me.

"A bit slanted," he shouts back. "I think your concentration was off."

I am already climbing back up, my tangled hair dripping down my back, cooling my skin.

I take a deep breath and concentrate. I close my eyes and focus on listening to my heartbeat. At the last moment, I open my eyes and dive, my body a straight line, arms outstretched before my head, toes curled tightly so that there will be minimum splash.

"Perfect," my dad whoops. "Again."

The sun is in the middle of the sky.

It's going to be a long day.

. . .

My dad raised me all alone; it's been just the two of us for as long as I can remember. He gave me his mother's name, Ariadne, which I quickly abbreviated to Ari, especially when he tried to start teaching me to speak English before I had a chance to master my mother tongue, Greek. He later explained to me that English was my mother tongue as well, or at least my *mother's* mother tongue, and that he felt I should be brought up with the choice of speaking it as well as Greek, should I want to.

Turns out I do want to.

As for *her*, well, I know little about her and care to learn even less. Not that it's easy to forget about her, with her face showing up in every gossip magazine almost once a week. But anyway, that's all I know about the woman. I've never met her, if we don't count the one time I came out of her womb. If I met her even then, which I very much doubt.

I've lived on the island all my life, and not regretted one moment of it.

There isn't a more precious place on earth. I love Corfu, with its fragrant olive branches, brown cliffs that drop into sparkling blue waters, narrow winding roads and salmon-colored houses at the harbor. It's home.

...

We're driving home at about five in the afternoon, when I get my first glimpse of the 'star'. The first time I see Wes Spencer, he's climbing down from his obnoxious yacht.

I know yachts don't have personalities, but this one certainly does. I mean, who names their boat 'Laurel&Hardy', for crying out loud?

Or L&H, as Young People magazine's column calls it:

Kept very much under wraps, Tim Hall's new project is said to be in production as we speak at some unnamed destination in the Mediterranean, where one or two of the stars will be arriving on Weston Spencer's yacht, the *L&H*, named after celebrated comedians Laurel & Hardy.

The working title has been announced as **First Sentences**, a play with words on Jane Austen's *Pride and Prejudice*'s original title, *First Impressions*, is a modern-day remake of the famous literary work.

Elle Burke, the actress who is set to portray the modern-day *Elizabeth Bennett* next to Spencer's *Mr. Darcy*, has been romantically linked with him in the past, mostly during the years of their costarring as Tristan and Kat in the TV series that made them both famous, **THE WATER WARS**, where Burke was playing Spencer's love-interest in seasons 6 and 7. Though rumors as to whether these two lovebirds are still together differ, we did hear from a source that an engagement *(?!)* isn't far off in the future for these two.

Yep, I read it.

I had to, Coach—smirking—said it was part of my training. How I kept from gagging I'll never know, but now I am more than sufficiently up-to-date with who my fellow-actors will be. Although I'm pretty sure I won't be acting in fellowship with any of them, because I'm not a real actress. I'm just the stunt girl.

My part is anything that is too dangerous, unpleasant or unnecessary for the real actors to do. Exciting, isn't it? If it weren't for the kickboxing and climbing and snorkeling and diving and driving around in fast cars I would be the saddest person on earth.

But the truth is, I am the luckiest.

So let Wes Spencer climb out of his yacht with his white college sweater wrapped around his manly shoulders and his Ray-Banns balanced on top of his golden curls all he wants. Give me my rock any day over having to talk to him in front of a camera with a crowd of curious fans around.

A few hours later, it's time for the first 'event' with the film crew. It's supposed to be an informal meeting, just so that we'll get to know each other. Everyone is dressed to the nines, cocktails and canapés are being served on the roof garden of one of the most expensive hotels on the island, and you can only get in with an invitation. Informal my ass. Anyway, I meet the director and producer, among others.

The famous Tim Something.

He didn't look as intimidating in person as he does on TV, but still, my knees were wobbly the whole time. He's this eccentric, incredibly rich man, who loves his job, so he has all this energy emanating from him, like a live wire. He's short and twitchy, a bit ordinary really, or he would be if it wasn't for his clear-blue stare that can stop your heart if you've done something to annoy him.

He says we will try to fit in the relevant stunt sequences along with the actual filming of the actors, because he doesn't want the lighting of the water or the sky to change, which would make the scene appear unrealistic. He wants me there every day at six. In the morning.

So basically my work will have to be squeezed in-between the shoots of the actual actors, and I'll have two directors over my head instead of one. Easy peasy.

Now I get why he is so successful. The guy is a complete control freak. I suppose he has to be, if he wants his film to be 'perfect'. I've never heard of anyone doing things quite like he's planning to. *If it's not chaos on day three I'll take my hat off to him.*

Then he takes me aside and tells me that his star, Elle Burke, doesn't do water.

"I beg your pardon?" I say and he winces. Uh-oh.

"I know," he shrugs.

His thin, suntanned face, gleaming under the lights (he has no hair, like not even one) takes on a what-can-you-do expression. "You'll have to film all the water scenes for her. But don't worry, Wes always does his own stunts. You'll be with him, he'll show you the ropes."

Wes 'does-his-own-stunts' Spencer walks by right that second, and Tim Something is kind enough to try to introduce me.

"Mate, are you going to introduce me to every gaffer in this place?" The actor dude says to Tim, looking right through me as if I wasn't there, and turns to ask the person next to him—Elle Burke—in a bored voice where the nearest 'pub' is. He's dressed in a white shirt over tapered trousers. Damn him, I'd swear he was a fashion model, with his golden locks swept back from his forehead and those chiseled cheekbones, but the expression of utter disdain on his face makes him look the opposite of charming.

Tim just laughs and tells him not to be a word that I'm not sure what it means, but it can't be good, and then Wes curses even more colorfully and asks again about the pub.

Elle Bourke, who is indeed stunning as far as looks go, smirks—and believe me, that *is* as far as her looks go, because immediately she looks like a weasel. And Oliver Sikks, Wes Spencer's best friend who, apparently, who will be playing Charlie Bingley in the film, gives me his hand and asks me to call him "Ollie" with a sunny smile.

I look up and the dreamiest pair of blue eyes meet mine. I suck in a breath. How are these Hollywood guys so gorgeous in real life? You always see them on screen and think, well, he'll be too short or too skinny or too pimply in real life. But this guy isn't. He is too perfect in real life. He has a fop of dark hair hanging tantalizingly over one eye, and as he runs his hand through it to clear his vision, a muscle bulges on his arm and I can't take my eyes off him.

He sends another heart-stopping smile in my direction and asks me to 'join them'. I mumble something intelligible, and then Tim brings over the stunt coordinator and everyone leaves us alone to chat.

I take one look at the guy. And that's it. Everything is a blur after that.

All I remember is my mouth hanging open and my eyes bulging out of my head. I must have turned beet red, my cheeks flaming, my hands trembling, staring like a complete idiot. The coordinator looked less than impressed. Much less. Not that I blame him.

But . . . I mean it's *him*. He's my idol. I've been following his career for years.

His name is Matthew Lee, and he's been described as the Brad Pitt slash Jack Nicholson of stunt actors. Every single actor, producer or crew member here treats him with so much respect, even though he's much younger than my dad. But the guy's a prodigy.

He gives me his hand, and introduces himself as 'Matt'. *Are you for real?* I want to say. *Am I supposed to work with my idol, and on top of that, just call him 'Matt'?*

Not that I can say any of it out loud. My brain has totally frozen.

He looks impossibly tall, now that I meet him in person, that's all I can think. He's towering a head and a half above me. His face doesn't show in any of the movies he's been in, but I've seen it online in articles. Up close, though, he looks so extremely hot, which is weird. I've never thought of him as anything but stunt performer goals.

But this is totally the opposite from how I'd fantasized meeting him. He purses his lips as he looks down at me, and his face is expressionless, observing me in silence. He must not be very happy with what he sees, because he stands patiently next to me for a few seconds, and then, with an abrupt flick of his glossy black ponytail, he's gone.

I knew he was Korean, but actually he's Korean American, they tell me afterwards. He's brilliant, that's what he is.

Tim Something certainly didn't skimp on the stunt coordinator, let's put it that way. Matthew Lee has won everything but an Oscar, since they don't nominate stunt performers for them. He's now in his mid-twenties, but he's been working since his pre-teens, having performed some of the most famous stunts of all time.

That action movie with the blonde guy who jumped on and off trains to rescue trafficked children? Yep, that was him. And the other with the water Olympics where an outbreak of some disease breaks out and they have to be isolated in the stadium? He's in practically every stunt in that movie, doing just about everything that can—and can't—be done. Somersaulting, diving, swimming, jumping, holding his breath for ages below water to support the actors who didn't know how to swim. The film practically shows more of him than of the star. And it won about a billion Oscars.

And now he's a director.

No, he's *my* director. He'll be directing my stunts.

I can almost see the words forming in his brain as he walks away: *'Ari Demos, the girl who lost her tongue. My new stunt girl. Can't wait to start shooting.'*

Great.

...

The next morning, I find myself again at the rock. I'm alone this time. Officially, on the map of Corfu that the tourists buy, this beach is called *Glyfada*, and the tiny village perched on top of the mountain that overlooks the bay is *Pelekas*. But we just call it 'Rubble'.

So the Rubble and I have been having a lot of alone time this past summer, and something tells me that we' re going to have to get to know each other even more intimately.

The beach is empty as far as the eye can see, because it is still early in the morning and the few left-over tourists of the season will not yet have woken up from last night's parties. No yacht on the horizon either, which is also a plus, since I would prefer to do my training without an audience, drunk and indifferent though it may be.

Thankfully, none of the crew members are here today.

Bored with the warm-up, I turn on the volume of my iPod, because I know I have to finish it no matter what. Today's not one of my best days. My muscles feel stiff and there is an annoying headache drumming in my left temple—I wonder if it's going to build into one of the blinding migraines I have been getting lately.

*Not today*, I inwardly yell at myself, *get it together!*

I climb up the rock with slow, steady movements, and when I reach the top, I sit down on the sharp rocks for a moment to catch my breath. I lower my aching head in my hands. Across from me, the villa is almost at eye-level from up here, and I notice for the first time the intricate hedge that conceals its huge terrace from the beach below. The doors and windows are all done in Grecian style, with little elegant columns, and the walls are painted a very light yellow, which gives to the whole place the appearance of perpetual sunshine.

Below me the sea is calm and blue, almost effusing peace. I lift my arms and fall, feet-first, the cold water burning my calves and thighs almost soothingly. Then I begin to swim in a powerful front crawl towards the open horizon with no intention of coming back until the coolness of the blue-green waters has calmed me.

# LOSE ME.

I am tired even before half an hour has passed.

I try to keep my strokes contained to preserve energy, and turn back towards the beach. A slight hint of panic starts at the pit of my stomach as I see that I can barely discern the outline of the shore.

Maybe that's why I'm so tired? Did I go too fast, trying to outswim my frustration? I check my watch again and yes, that's right, no more than thirty minutes have passed.

*Okay, don't panic, start treading water slowly and calmly, and you'll get there. You're fine. You're fine. You're doing good.*

I try to conjure up Coach's voice in my head, but my breath is coming short, and it's all I can do to just float and try to catch my breath.

And then I see it.

I can't believe I missed it; apparently I was concentrating so hard on my movements that I did, and now it's only a dozen strokes or so away.

It's the boat. The stupid M&M or whatever it's called yacht—I don't remember its name right now, but it sounded like the candy for some reason. Great.

Man, it looks huge close up. I read that it's got twin Volvo Penta IPS600 diesels and it's over fifty-six feet. I have to admit, it looks impressive up close. Pretentious or not, the guy is rich, so why shouldn't he buy a beauty like that if he can? I know I would. Imagine how it would feel to cruise that baby in open sea.

Its hull is the most elegant thing I've ever seen, massive, but still gorgeous. You can see a bit of the wooden floors on deck if you look up, and the rest of it is silver, not white like you'd expect. It looks endless, gleaming in the dull light as though it just came out of the marina. I float on my back and start a slow backstroke, keeping it in my sight, and then I can see a few heads popping above the railing, and that decides me for good.

*'Mate, are you going to introduce me to every gaffer in this place?'* Wes Spencer's words from our 'introduction' yesterday still ring in my ears. Because looking through me and asking for a 'pub' wasn't enough for him. Oh no, he had to humiliate me with his Oxford accent in front of Tim and everyone.

With his stupid, condescending, mocking voice in my head, I turn around and swim as fast and hard as I can towards the shore.

*You just need them for this, you just want to catch your break. Then you'll never have to see them again.*

I am concentrating so hard on giving myself a pep talk, that when my head ducks beneath the surface, I'm taken by surprise. So much so that before I realize it, I've swallowed some water.

I try to lift my head above and take a deep breath, but another mouthful of water chokes me. A sharp pain shoots up my leg and I double in two. My whole body stiffens in response to the cramp, and dark spots dance in front of my eyes.

In one huge effort, I push myself to the surface, gagging and gulping in air at once. My heart beats crazily and I can't catch my breath, and before I know it I'm sinking again. I fight with all my strength, but my brain is fuzzy with pain.

I surface again and force myself to keep my legs moving past the pain of the cramp, just to stay afloat. And then something sharp pierces my head, my headache reaching its peak, and I must black out for a second, because the next minute I'm choking on water and sinking in darkness. The surface is nowhere to be seen.

*Today is not the day I die*, I think, dazed, as my lungs scream for oxygen.

*Well, if it wasn't today, it would have been tomorrow.*

I feel myself slip further down into the water.

The thing about drowning, Coach always used to say, is that it doesn't look like drowning from afar. You might be visible on the surface, your body vertical, looking like you're just floating there. And in an instant, you could slip down, out of sight, without warning. That's why you must always be on your toes, and get to safety or ask for help at the first sign that something's wrong, especially if you're training or competing. Or doing a stunt. No one will be expecting you to need help, so you might just quietly slip under and no one will be able to get to you in time.

*You must never cross the line of your own endurance, do you understand? You mustn't wait to ask for help.*

But there wasn't time. There wasn't any warning. I wasn't quick enough, I wasn't strong enough. I wasn't vigilant enough.

A last breath escapes my lungs, and more water comes in as my vision goes black. I didn't know it would hurt so much. Dying. I didn't know my chest would constrict until my bones would ache. I didn't know there wouldn't be enough energy left to open my eyes.

I didn't know the water would be so calm, so utterly still, embracing me as I fall.

I didn't know—

Suddenly the water around me is filled with bubbles and a dark shape swims powerfully towards me. My lids have almost drifted closed, but I try to peer at the silhouette with one last effort.

Brilliant shining eyes, filled with panic, meet mine and a hand grasps my chin, lifting my face towards the surface. The face in front of me is yelling something, but I can hear nothing above the whoosh of blood in my veins. Hands encircle me, supporting me, and I shoot upwards, towards the surface. I'm being shaken roughly as though someone's trying to wake me up. I would like to tell them, whoever it is, that it's too late.

I can't, of course. That's what too late means.

Everything turns to black and I feel myself slipping away from the hold of these strong arms that had grasped me, sinking downwards.

*My dad will die when they tell him*, is my last thought. *Today is not the day. . .* Oh, never mind.

# LOSE ME.

wherever
I'm
going
I'm
not
there
yet

.

#spencerstumblr   #queue   ◊TRENDING

**1,713,029 notes**

## T W O

"Breathe, dammit, breathe! Don't die on me, come on!"

A rough voice blasts commands in my ear, but I can't answer because something is pounding on my chest with so much force that almost all the water I had swallowed comes out in a rush.

"Okay," the voice sighs loudly. It sounds like someone is panting heavily. "Okay."

"Is she alive?" another voice asks.

"Shut up," the first one answers sharply.

I gasp and choke some more, trying to breathe in enough air to stop my lungs from burning.

It takes a while to register that I'm alive. But then again I'm shaking violently and I'm so cold it hurts to breathe and rivulets of water are running from my turquoise swimming suit. So maybe I'm not entirely alive after all.

I open my eyes to blurry shapes all around me and pain hits me with a force that knocks the breath out of me. My head pounds, my leg muscles scream in agony, my armpits hurt as though I was dragged with force.

I am on a hard, uncomfortable surface that hurts my ribs. Strong hands grab my back and lift me to an upright position, and I throw up more water. Fingers brush my dripping hair out of my eyes and I curl into a fetal position trying not to go crazy from the pain in my head.

Then a soft, gentle, slightly mocking voice, whispers in my ear with a really superior English accent:

"Don't move, you idiot."

I try to push whoever is talking away, but even that movement is enough to send my migraine over the edge and I black out again.

The next time I come to, someone is yelling into a  phone, right above my head.

I am lying in a bed now, which is a great improvement from before, but everything, from my body to the bedclothes, probably to the mattress underneath, is soaked wet.

"Are you kidding me, mate?  What do I have to dial around here to get an ambulance? What? You want me to ask you in Greek? How should *I* know? WHAT are you saying? Come on!"

The voice fades into silence, defeated, and then an infernal tapping begins.

"Please stop," I try to say, but it comes out all choked and croaky.

"Oh, you're up," the voice says again next to my ear.

And then I get it. Oh no. *Please don't let it be true.* I turn and look at his face. Sunny blonde curls and green eyes swim into focus. Yep, it's true. It's *him*.

"Are you all right?" he asks, and suddenly my vision field is full of his green eyes.

The tortured look is pretty hot on him.

"Fine," I croak. Wait. Did I just think that the pirate looks hot? The one who just called me stupid? These headaches are messing with my head.

"What a moron—," he goes on, mumbling a string of curses.

"Yeah, you said," I interrupt. He looks surprised, as though he didn't expect an answer.

"Since you can speak now, can you tell me how to call an ambulance?"

I try to raise myself on one elbow, but my head swims again and I lean back, everything turning black again.

"Hey hey hey," he says, his voice going gentle. He runs over to place a hand beneath my neck and lifts me up, since I landed in an awkward angle like a stupid infant that can't hold up its own head. "No more fainting, we've had enough for one day. Just hold on a bit longer, they'll be here in a moment, yeah?"

"Why d'you need an. . . ? Are you hurt?" I ask, slurring my words, and for a moment he doesn't answer, because a hacking cough shakes me again.

He's also soaking wet. Which would have been sexy, judging from the photo-spread on the Young People magazine I was reading the other day, except he's fully dressed, in a white button-down rolled at the elbows, and a fancy pair of dark boat shorts. His shirt has gone transparent, and it's clinging to his stomach and biceps.

"What?" he asks, watching as my gaze travels all over his waterlogged clothes. Then his expression changes. "What are you, stupid? Don't you get it? Don't you understand what's happening here, you almost—"

"Stop yelling at me!" I protest, before I start coughing some more, and he makes an exasperated gesture with his phone-holding hand.

"It's for *you*, you twit."

I clench my teeth against the pain and get up slowly and dizzily. He doesn't move to help me but he doesn't leave either. He keeps watching me with this faintly mocking, detached stare that makes me want to punch his blond locks right out of his stupid English forehead.

"I don't need one," I say.

He shrugs. *Shrugs.*

"You should probably change." I have already turned my back on him, and I lean a trembling arm to the wood-paneled wall to steady myself. And now it dawns on me. I am on his boat. His M&M yacht.

The room I'm standing in is an extravagantly luxurious tiny bedroom, with a huge flat screen embedded on the wall and a wide, modern-design bed covered with a white bedspread that right now just lays there limp, wet and wrinkled. I feel my cheeks burn and turn to try to tidy it up.

The next second, five long fingers are wrapped around my wrist and my chilled skin tingles as it comes in contact with his warmth. "What are you doing?" He looks down at me, his eyes turning to ice. "You need to go to the hospital. Or wait. . .*is* there a hospital in this hole of a place?"

And he's back to his usual self.

"Did I say thank you?" I ask, suddenly realizing that I didn't.

"You did not."

"Well, thank you."

"Listen, if we're not going to call an ambulance, would you mind getting out for a sec? I need to change." He's already lifting his clinging shirt over lean, well-sculpted back muscles. They would have impressed me much more if he hadn't just thrown me out of the room. But I can't even care about his rudeness right now.

I'm terrified.

I don't think I have ever been more scared in my life.

What happened out there? Was I really dying? I *would* have died. I almost did. There is of course no question of a hospital, but. . . well, what am I supposed to do? Just wait until the next migraine actually succeeds in killing me?

Am I still slowly dying, even though I was pulled from the water?

Hot tears burn my lids but I refuse to let them fall.

There are six people watching me curiously as I emerge on the upper deck. Five girls—one of them is Elle, the only one I recognize, and she looks like a bikini goddess, a long cigarette resting lightly on her scarlet lips—and a guy are sitting by a hot tub. The guy—it's Ollie—jumps up as soon as he sees me and rushes to my side, taking my elbow, swearing.

"What are you doing up?" he says, his blue eyes dark with concern. "Hey, get over here. Sit down before you fall over."

I sit on a wide lounger and lean my head between my knees until the wave of dizziness passes. He swears some more, kneeling next to me, while the girls snicker.

"I'm fine," I say, "so sorry for. . .everything."

"Sorry? Wha—Dude, I'm freaking out right now," he says. "I can't even begin to think of what might have happened. I mean, we were all facing the other way, we hadn't even seen you. Next thing I know there's a splash, and Wes has dived in after you in his clothes and in his *shoes*." He says this as though it's a big deal. And, I suppose, if you're Spencer the Tristan pirate, it is.

He gazes out to the sea. "He lost them, too," he adds incredulously. "Josh, he's with the crew, he jumped in after him, and helped bring you on deck. But even he wouldn't have seen you if Wes hadn't. . .How are you feeling?"

"I think I'm good."

He turns to look at the fast approaching coastline. "Well, how long do ambulances take around here?" he asks eventually.

"Uh. . .I said not to call one," I say to Ollie, shivering. He looks at me, surprised, and I have the strange feeling that he, too, thinks that I'm an idiot. Although he's too well-mannered to say so. "I'm fine, really."

"Are you cold?" a soft voice to my left asks.

A slim girl gets up walks over to sit down next to me, offering me a cardigan of sugary white fabric that gleams in the sunlight. She is dark-skinned, with rich brown hair and dimples on her cheeks. I like her immediately.

"I'll get seawater on it," I hesitate, as another cough shakes me.

"Just put it on," she says easily and drapes it over my shoulders. "It's for the cleaners anyway." She smiles. "I'm Anna."

And then I recognize her. She's Anna Dell, the famous British actress of the popular teen vampire TV series, the one who always walks around with a pint of blood smothered all over her plump lips.

"Thanks," I tell her as I furrow into the warmth of the sweater.

"No prob," she answers. "You're the stunt girl, right? Ared. . . "

"Ariadne," I say, smiling back. "But everyone calls me Ari."

"Right, Ari," she gives me her manicured hand, laughing, and then she leans close. She's petite, shorter than me, and a light, fruity perfume wafts from her skin with her every movement. "I have to tell you, I'm so excited to work so close to a stunt actor! I haven't ever before, so I might fangirl a little."

"But I thought. . .with the vampires. . ." I say lamely, thrown by her enthusiasm.

She shakes her head. "That was TV, doing a film is completely different, you'll see."

"Well, judging by today," I say dryly, "maybe Tim should have picked a different stunt person."

She laughs, her dimples twinkling, and slides her palm in mine, as though we're best friends already. "Hey, accidents happen," she says, turning serious. "Thank God Wes spotted you before you went down again. Oh, that's him now."

He's changed into a striped V-neck sweater and a pair of long white shorts, which are showing off his long, tan legs.

His still damp hair sends droplets all over the wooden floor as he walks, but he strides forward carelessly, ignoring the seven pairs of eyes that are fixed on him. He flops onto a chaise-longue, crossing said legs at the knee and puts on his headphones, gazing coolly into the distance while sipping from a bottle he's holding in his left hand.

"Dude," Ollie says to him under his breath, "where's the ambulance?"

Wes shrugs. "She said she didn't want one." He still doesn't turn to look at me—nor at anyone else for that matter.

"She did?" Ollie asks a bit uncertainly, glancing at me. "Still, I think we should call one. What if she. . . ?"

Wes cuts him off impatiently. "What can I do."

His head sways with the rhythm of the music slightly.

"Look," I interrupt, feeling my temples begin to throb again. "We are a lot closer to the shore than we were. Do you think there's a way I could get out? I've my car parked on the beach."

"Why don't you swim to the shore?" Wes says, with a glance to Elle and the other bikini girls, who start laughing as though he said the most amazing thing in the world. "You seem to be so good at that."

That's it, I've had enough of this.

I get up, but a hand on my arm stops me. I turn and meet Anna's warm brown eyes. She shoots me a warning look beneath her bangs. "Come on, we're dropping anchor. Do you mind if I come with? I want to go to town today."

"I'll come too," Ollie says, looking at me, "just to make sure you're all right."

Wes lets out a snort and Ollie shoots him a murderous stare.

I get up on sore legs. "Thank you," I say again, although Wes is looking the other way. "Although I think you should be the one to thank me," I mutter under my breath and his eyes snap at me behind his sunglasses.

"You think what?"

"I think *you* should thank *me*," I repeat. "I clearly saved you from the most boring morning of your life."

His lazy pose doesn't change. He bothers to answer me, but he isn't even looking at me. "You think you did me a favor by almost drowning next to my yacht? You know, you really are st—"

"Stupid?" I interrupt, tired of hearing it. "Yeah, I am the stupid one, not you, sitting here in your college sweater in the scorching sun, chugging your whiskey in the middle of the morning, just killing time in your M&M boat"—here a loud snort interrupts me, but I'm on a roll, can't stop now—"missing all the beauty of one of the most gorgeous islands of the Mediterranean. . .Yeah, that's not stupid."

He gets up.

That's new.

"M&M?" is all he says.

"Whatever," I answer, and the coolness of this answer is completely destroyed by a hacking cough that doubles me in two. I'm not sure, but I think a bit of seawater may have come out as well. I stumble and Ollie catches me.

"That's it," he says, "let's go." Then he turns to Wes and his blue eyes darken. "And you, Darce, please dude, no more diving until you're sober."

"Eff off, Binge," Wes says without turning around, and downs the entire bottle in one swoop.

...

I spend the afternoon in bed, hiding from my dad and dozing off with my earplugs in. This groggy feeling is far from unfamiliar to me; I've swallowed too much water while training so many times, it's nothing new to me. I usually know what to expect: there will be coughing up water and a clogged nose for two days, tops. But this time, it's different. There's a dark feeling at the pit of my stomach that says this is way worse than a stunt gone wrong. Every few minutes I wake up to cough up a bit more saltwater—which is also coming out of my nose and ears, nice—while piling up the painkillers.

At about eight I call Coach.

"Yo there, Ars," he says around a mouthful of chips—these days he's binge-watching the 1994 FIFA World Cup USA, from the qualifying rounds to the Final. "How's it hangin'?"

His name is Ben, but I've called him Coach since I've known him—he insisted on it. He lived in Pasadena before he started working with me, but these past two years he's kind of relocated in Corfu, on account of *her* hiring him as my coach. At first I was dead-set on refusing her, because it was *her*, but as soon as I saw him, I knew he would change my life.

And he has.

Kids at school didn't take me seriously when I said I was training to become a stunt actor, but as soon as they saw this huge black dude following me around, forbidding me to stay up later than ten at night and forcing me to the gym straight after school, they began to get it.

Coach is pretty intimidating. He looks like one of those really ripped athletes you see on the TV during the Olympics, with his fierce stare, his buzz cut and a deep voice that can scare ten years off your life.

"Not good," I croak.

I hear a sudden movement as though he is sitting up, and I know I have his full attention. "What's up, honey?" He goes all protective-dad on me.

The fact that he already suspected that there was something going on with me drives me nuts right now. I clear my throat, which hurts like there are razors being dragged across my skin on account of all the coughing.

"It's the dive from the Rubble, I don't think I can do it."

"Oh, dude, is that all?" Coach asks, relieved. "I'll take you out there and we'll knock it out of the park."

"Well, I appreciate your enthusiasm, but I went there today and yesterday with dad, and I can tell you my performance left a lot to be desired."

"Don't get all technical, judge-y on me, Ars, you can do it, I know you can."

"Maybe it's because the pressure is on, you know; after all I got this job because of. . ."

"No, Ars, don't give me any of that." His voice gets fierce. "You auditioned for this part fair and square. You don't owe anyone anything, all right?"

"I know."

"Besides, I saw you owning that dive last week."

"I *did* own it then, but I don't anymore. I just. . .I know that this will be one of the scenes they're gonna film me in, maybe I'm just not. . ."

"Ari, Ari, stop honey, breathe. Listen to me." I hear him sigh, and then a crinkling sound, as though he'd putting down the bag of chips. I imagine him leaning forward to rest his elbows on his knees, his eyebrows drawing together like they do whenever he's concentrating. "You got this, okay? I haven't seen anyone with more passion and energy at this job. Believe me, I know. You have the technique, you have the talent, you've got the determination. I'm proud of you, Ars. And I don't say that easily."

"No, you don't," I agree quietly. "Thanks, Coach."

"Anytime. Now go get some sleep, yeah? I'll see you tomorrow."

I turn my phone off and sleep like the dead. Which wasn't such a great idea after all—the shutting off of my phone, I mean—because the next morning when I wake up and turn it back on, I have a mini stroke.

...

So, of course, I call Katia.

Katia has been my best friend ever since I can remember myself. My grandma used to work as a seamstress back then, working in a small alterations shop in a tiny street just behind the busy tourist market. Katia's mom came in one day wanting to let out a skirt, and I was playing soccer in the street, just outside. Naturally, just as Katia—five years old then, same as me—appeared, sucking on her thumb, I sent my ball flying in an ambitious assist. It landed on her head. We have been best friends ever since.

This is the first time in fourteen years that we've been apart. She's gotten into the National and Kapodistrian University of Athens, and she had to move there. She's been going back and forth all summer to find a flat and so on, but classes start a few days from now, so she's finally moved to the city.

"Hey, dude, guess what!" I shriek as her face pops up in my phone.

"Do I need to sit down for this?" she asks.

She looks the exact opposite from me. She's curvy when I'm full of angles, and she dresses all girly while I'm almost always in sneakers and shorts. Her hair is wildly curly and black, her eyes large and usually shining with mischief, as they do now. She can see it in my face that I've got something big to tell her.

"You do."

"Hold on a sec," she answers and goes into the next room, coming back immediately with a huge towel draped around her wet hair, towering above her face. "Hit me."

I tell her, and, even seated, she almost passes out. Then she starts screaming and my phone buzzes with static.

"...so much!" her voice exclaims as soon as my headphones start working again.

"What?"

"Right now I hate you so much," she repeats.

"No, no you don't understand," I reply, "it's the worst thing that could happen! Me and parties? You know that's not a good combo."

"Yeah, it's the worst, I feel so sorry for you," she says heartlessly. "Wait. How did you meet all these actors in the first place? You never told me. Wes Spencer? And Anna Dell? I mean, will Benedict Cumberbatch be popping out of a box anytime soon?"

I cover the screen with my palm, and she swats it away impatiently.

"Tim Halls introduced me to everyone the first day," I tell her, keeping it simple. "I don't have to tell you how *that* went!" There is no chance, of course, that I'll tell him—or much less anyone else—about our second 'introduction' yesterday.

"Apparently it went better than you thought it did," she answers.

"Oh man, when I think of that stuck-up rich kid, Wes, it's enough to make me stay in tonight."

"Listen to you, casually dropping names all over the place," she laughs. "First it was Tim Halls, now 'Wes'... Okay, promise me one thing. Promise me you'll have a crazy hot fling with him."

"*You're* crazy hot."

"No, come on, it's just one tiny little thing for your bestest friend in the whole world... Please?" she is using her cute voice again, pursing her lips and blinking like a crazy person.

"Katia, the dude is freaking Weston Spencer!"

"Yes, and you already call him 'Wes'. So you're half-way there already!" Her voice goes low, like it used to when she was trying to explain Algebra to me, and all I wanted was to go outside and play soccer. "Or I'll send you a pic of me wearing my new safety goggles in the physics lab. I'm warning you, it's not going to be pretty."

"You are so sending me that photo anyway," I laugh.

"Deal. And you'll consider having your first Hollywood kiss?"

I snort. *Yeah, right.* Then I think back on Weston Spencer's green eyes locking with mine through the mist of water and the blackness that was enveloping me like a sinister charm from a fairytale as the sea was swallowing me up, and that memory sobers me up quickly.

"I've got to go, Katia," I say. "Thanks for the support, you're the best."

"Wear cute clothes," she begins shouting directions. "And lipstick. And try to be bubbly and witty and entertaining... And... "

"I know, I'll try to be like you."

"Exactly. Fake it till you make it. Only in a less curly dimpled way, more in a freakishly tall, tomboyish way. You know, like a really athletic model," she adds.

"You're going to be a really dead curly dimpled physics student if you keep this up," I say.

"Oh, you know what I mean."

"I have no idea what you mean. Plus, you owe my future kids free tutoring lessons, just for calling me freakishly tall."

"I owe you that anyway," she says and begins unfolding the towel from her hair. In the background, I hear the TV turn on, and a girl's voice shouting that the bathroom is free—must be her roommate. "Okay, gotta go," Katia dimples, leaning down from her perch on her desk. "Gosh, I can't wait until I can buy a proper phone with a camera and we can skype all the time, like normal people. Bye. And, Ari?"

"What now?"

"Pics or it didn't happen. Tag me."

I lower my phone with a sigh, and flick back to the recent texts I received. And there it is, at the top, the text from Anna Dell, the one that started my day in a panic. I sweep another glance across it, just to make sure I didn't imagine it. Yep, it's all there.

> Hey, girl. Anna here, Matt gave me yr number, hope its ok. We're having a getting to know each other party tmrow nite @this place called Drop, u know it? Be there 10ish. xx p.s. Ollie asked if you were coming ;)

I sigh and fling the phone on the bed.

I spend the day at the Rubble with Coach, perfecting my dive, and then we go for a little driving—not normal driving, stunt-driving. He proclaims me ready for anything.

I am just so relieved and thankful not to have a splitting headache today. Maybe I overreacted before. I feel perfectly fine now. It was probably nothing, I say to myself.

And then, in the darkening afternoon, as I ride my bike through the narrow cobblestone streets that will take me home, the *kantounia*, as we call them, it begins to drizzle. All my good mood suddenly evaporates like the sizzling heat of the day.

Light raindrops land on my damp, newly-showered hair, and the thin wheels of my bike skid along fresh puddles.

Then it hits me.

What if Wes tells Tim about my accident and they decide to pull me?

My heart freezes. I can't let that happen. I can't let it even be a possibility. Argh. Now I *really* have to go to the stupid party.

...

I swear, my dad is the coolest person you'll ever meet. Or he was until tonight. Tonight he spends a large part of his evening outside my bedroom door, waiting for me to come out in different outfits. I'm sure it's as much fun for him as it is for me.

Finally we—but mostly he—decide on a fitted lacy dress over a dark brown top and mauve leggings. My tan looks cool next to the light-colored fabric, which hangs loosely around my waist. I try to put on a little makeup, but without Katia here I completely mess it up and end up wiping most of it off.

I let my brown hair just hang in waves down my back, dragging a brush through its tangles and that's all the time I'm prepared to dedicate to that.

"Knock 'em dead, Ars," my dad tells me in an attempt to get me in a good mood. I think he senses how scared I am.

"Lose the weird accent and let me change the dress for my denim shorts, and you've got yourself a deal," I tell him.

"Only if you also change your sandals for a sensible pair of ballerina whatsits, 'cause the streets are wet outside."

"Fine," I say. "And it's ballet flats."

He lifts his hands in the air, in surrender. Then, so fast I don't even see it coming, he stands up and sneaks a tiny kiss on the top of my head.

"Have fun," he whispers.

"Won't you tell me to be back before. . . sometime?"

"Should I?" he looks at me seriously. I know this isn't about the party anymore, nor is it about the need of a curfew.

"Don't worry about me, dad," I say, as calmly as I can. "Everything is going to be fine."

The look he gives me fills my stomach with butterflies, and I know I haven't convinced him, not by a long shot, but he lifts his hand to tell me to go on. And that's what I do.

Drops is built right above the sea level, and as you arrive at it from the road, it gives the impression that it's floating on top of the Ionian. It's one of the most prestigious night haunts of the Town of Corfu.

Long, floor-length windows open into the dark sky, and the city lights blink from the shoreline, mingling with the stars. During the summer months, Drops is packed with people, young bodies swinging along to the beat, laughter ringing across the street, glasses sparkling with cocktails.

Today it's closed to the public, booked entirely by the crew. I slide in and find the darkest corner. I try to merge in with the walls, feeling the beat of the house music that's bouncing off of every smooth surface, and I begin to dig in my black clutch for my phone.

Then, a voice to my left. "There you are, girl, what are you drinking?" It's Anna.

She's wearing a thigh-length, white, shimmering sheath dress and sandals with incredibly high heels, and next to her I look like I just got out of the shower.

"Hey," I say, turning to her, and then my smile slips away.

Elle is with her. Of course. They both—*both*—kiss me on the cheek and insist that I join them for margaritas. So I go over to their table, which is right by the floor-length screen, overlooking the dark open sea, bathed in the moon's white glow.

"So, you're Greek, right?" Elle asks me in a husky, slightly-out-of-breath voice that tries to sound super-polite but ends up sounding weird. I'm guessing she's not as good an actor as she thinks she is.

"I'm half-Greek, on my father's side," I answer. "Although my—" I stumble over the word, but it comes out eventually. "Although I've hardly ever seen my mom. I've grown up here."

"All your life?" Elle asks, her eyes widening. Anna elbows her.

"So," I say after a couple minutes of awkward silence, "I haven't seen the entire script yet. They only gave me a list of the things I may be expected to do, and that's it. Surfing, driving, diving, that kind of thing." At this Elle shudders visibly and nods to a waiter to fill her glass again. "What's the story?"

"Like you even need to know," Elle scoffs, stretching back on the white sofa, at the same time that Anna says:

"Well, it's based on Jane Austen's *Pride and Prejudice*." Elle was right, the stunt actors aren't always given the entire script, nor do they need it. Still, Anna tries to explain it to me. "You know, the famous Darcy and Elizabeth romance, but set in the modern era. Darcy is a recluse, a writer, and Lizzie is a waitress."

And that's when it all begins to go wrong.

"Darcy who?" I ask.

"Did you say, Darcy who?" a familiar voice hisses above me.

## texts

**Wes**: Ols, where are you mate? You said you'd be on the L&H by 8. Am having girl overload here, they're getting ready for tonight, asking me all these weird questions, does this go with this and stilettos and earrings aaargh help!

**Ollie**: too busy having the world drop from under my feet

**Wes**: What?!?

**Ollie**: she's done it again. mom.

**Wes**: There's one word one never wants to hear from you.
**Wes**: What'd she do now?
**Wes:** Whatwhatwhatwhat

**Ollie**: even you won't believe this.

**Wes**: She coming here? Cause if she is, I'm getting out.

**Ollie**: no, this is something she did, 20 years or so back.

**Wes**: What kind of 'something'?

**Ollie**: She lets me know by email. Can you believe it?! 2 seconds ago. Said she has an important secret, kept it from me and stuff, and now is the time. Has something to do with Europe, she spent a summer here back in the day and did some naughty things. Reporters will be all over this place (and me) within days, or hours. She doesn't want the truth to find me unprepared.

**Wes**: What truth?

**Ollie**: She did something so. . . Dammit, I can't just  write it on a text, I just can't. . . She said she's waited all these years because of the past and the distance and blah blah blah BOMB
**Ollie**: I'll tell you everything in person. just get me out of here.

**Wes**: Where are you right now?

**Ollie**: dunno what it's called. Lots of columns and trees. Ancient greek style kinda like a palace. Kept running until I couldn't breathe.

**Wes**: ok stay there I'll find you w gps
**Wes**: got you. Be there in a few.

# THREE

I turn around slowly and he's there, in all his Tristan glory, glass in hand, tan jacket fashionably sculpted to his narrow frame, his eyes mocking me beneath their bored lashes.

"Hey," I say awkwardly.

"Hey!" a warm voice answers me as Ollie emerges behind him. "We've been looking all over for you guys." His eyes crinkle at the corners when he smiles. For the first time since I got here, I begin to relax.

"Is it possible that you haven't read Austen?" Wes lifts his eyebrows at me. "Can you believe this?" he turns to Elle. She leans into him, her white-blond curls brushing against his thigh as she's seated and he standing.

"Oh, no." Ollie laughs behind me.

I get up, taking a swig of my drink. The strong taste hits me so hard that I wobble a bit as I swallow and I grab on to the little glass table that's decorated with tiny cream tea-lights to steady myself.

Wes' eyes fly to my glass immediately. "You've never read Austen," he says. He doesn't ask, he just says it in that deep, condescending voice, his gaze looking past me. "Don't you have schools in Greece?"

I just gape at him. Is he kidding me right now? Why won't he let this go?

"Well?"

"We do," I answer him evenly, "but we mostly study ancient Greek geniuses, not English nobodies."

He goes pale.

I mean, I can't be sure, because it's dark in here and people keep pressing in on us from every side, but he visibly winces.

"English *nobodies*?" His left eyebrow flies to his hairline.

I sigh. What is his problem? "Oh, I don't know. We study Homer at school, he lived three thousand years ago. When was yours born?"

Now it's his turn to gape. His mouth actually falls open for a split second; he wasn't expecting my retort. Then he's bored again.

"Do yourself a favor," he says, fixing those green eyes on my face, "and read it asap. I mean, you already can't swim, so you might at least be familiar with the story we'll be playing out. What was Tim thinking. . . ?"

I cut him off.

"Athletes don't read," I say, trying to imitate Elle's nonchalant attitude, but without the drunk. I take another swig from my glass.

Fake it till you make it, wasn't that what Katia said?

Wes suddenly takes my arm and pulls me away from the table, as though he's embarrassed to have this conversation with me in front of his friends. My glass gets jostled around and a few drops fall out.

"What are you doing?" I shout at him over the noise.

"That's not reading," he says, "that's only the most famous work of literature to date, excepting maybe the Bible. That's educating yourself. That's opening your mind."

"With a soppy love story?" I retort. Even hearing about it a minute ago bored me to tears.

He looks surprised.

"Darce, dude, you do me proud," Ollie's laughing voice drifts over to us, but Wes looks as though he didn't even hear him, and I don't get it, so neither of us answers.

The girls begin to giggle and ask him to come sit with them, but he doesn't even acknowledge them with a glance.

"It's not a soppy love story," he explains calmly. His eyes are glowing and that bored expression is nowhere to be seen. "It's a story of misunderstanding, of overcoming one's worst faults and of social comedy."

"Okay," I say carefully, because standing here in the most prestigious club that Corfu has to show, talking about books with Hollywood's most popular teen actor is definitely not a situation I ever imagined finding myself in.

"When Darcy and Elizabeth first meet, they thoroughly dislike each other," he goes on. "But neither of them understands that this intense dislike, almost hate actually, on the part of Elizabeth at least, is in fact the sparks that fly when two people are attracted to each other. Not to mention it makes for pretty entertaining dialogue."

"Wow, you seem to have really studied this book," I say, half amazed, half wondering if this is a topic that usually interests American film heartthrobs.

Unexpectedly, he bends down his head and studies his shoes. Are his ears turning red? "I. . . uh. . . I read quite a lot." He lifts his gaze to mine. His eyes are filled with an intensity that takes me by surprise. "They don't write that about me, ever," he adds with a grin. "Don't tell anyone."

"I won't," I say, trying not to look confused. Is this the same guy who called me 'stupid' the other day? "Anyway, this masterpiece of yours, it doesn't make sense. I mean, two people hating each other and all the while they're falling in love?"

"Well, they are *behaving* as though they hate each other. There's a difference."

"Yeah, like people often stop in the middle of an argument to kiss."

He lifts a sandy eyebrow. "People don't say what they mean very often. You have to read between the lines of their behavior, of what they say, to get to what they truly feel. That's what good literature is all about—what Austen did better than anyone."

"What difference is there between calling someone an idiot and a 'twit', whatever *that* means, like, five times in a row, and actually hating them?" I ask fiercely.

"There's a difference if they say it and don't believe it. If, say, they'd been so scared, so damn terrified that their fear came out as. . . " he stops himself and takes a different tone, the one I know really well by now. Bored and slightly mocking. "Anyway, as I said, it takes a truly superior education to get what a work like that is all about, and that's why if you start reading it now, maybe in a few years you'll begin to grasp its meaning."

And that's it. I'm pushed over my limit. Where does this guy come off demeaning me every chance he gets? He knows virtually nothing about me.

"Listen here, pal," I say, trying not to cringe at the thought that the word 'pal' just came out of my mouth. All the frustration of the past few days has been looking for an outlet for so long that it comes out with a force that, frankly, is scaring me a little bit. But I can't stop. "No one, least of all you, is allowed to talk to me like that. Just because I come from a different background than you, you've no right to tell me that I'm stupid, or that I'm not as good as—"

That's when my little outburst is stopped abruptly.

His lips come down hard on mine, and for a moment I'm stunned. His tongue begins to explore my mouth hungrily, but his lips are soft and gentle. He tastes of alcohol and aftershave and summer.

Slowly, he places his hands on either side of my face to turn it sideways. I feel his body heat envelope me as he draws me closer to him, his hip leaning into mine, his chest pressed against me.

He cups my head with his long fingers and bends his body to the level of my face—wow, he must be tall, if he's that much taller than me— and then I can't think anymore because I'm kissing him back.

We sort of sink into the kiss, forgetting to breathe. His tongue is doing things in my mouth that make my knees go weak and forget to support me. He lifts me onto him and pulls me closer with his other hand sliding around my waist.

Everything goes on around us, bodies moving, rubbing against each other, glasses clinking, voices laughing, but we are oblivious to it all. I had no idea that there was this person inside of me, who would kiss a guy back like that, swept up in the moment, forgetting myself, unable to stop. I don't know who she is or what unleashed her, and I know that in a moment or so, maybe I'll regret everything she did—everything *I* did. I mean, joking about it with Katia is one thing, but this. . . This isn't safe. It's the opposite of safe.

Oh, but it's so much fun. I'm surrounded by actors, being kissed by one, and right now, what's pretend and what's real all blur together. I'm one of them tonight. I don't know how much time passes as we Wes and I are locked in our own little universe, but finally, sighing, we part.

I gasp for breath and stumble, taking a step back.

He pushes me away almost forcibly, but his eyes are still watching me as his chest rises and falls rapidly. There's a look of surprise and amazement on his face. And then I look more carefully at him, and I discover something else in his expression: fear. Just plain fear.

Fear at what he discovered, at what we both unearthed during this kiss. I raise a hand to my swollen lips and find out that my cheeks are wet.

His eyebrows meet as he, too, notices, and his lips tighten. "No," he whispers in a low rasp. Mesmerized, as though he isn't aware he's even doing it, he lifts a finger to wipe my tears away. At the last minute, he stops himself and drops his hand.

"What you said before," he says, his voice coming out hoarse. "I never said you weren't as good as me. What I think is that you're. . . Ah."

Just like that, he stops talking and turns on his heel and leaves. He lifts his head, his hair caressing the back of his neck, and drains his glass in one swift movement.

I go back to the girls and an awkward silence greets me. Ollie rushes off to Wes, and Elle and Anna keep talking, ignoring me. I lift my drink to my lips, trying to cool my flaming cheeks and get a grip.

I've never felt so relaxed after drinking just a glass of margarita. Wow, this stuff must be good. As soon as I finish my glass, Anna gets up to go to the bathroom and asks me to with her.

"Do you want one more?" Elle asks me, "I'll have the waitress refill it."

Okay, so the period of silence is over.

On the way back we run into Tim, who wants to introduce me to a bunch of people whose names I forget immediately after hearing them, because everything is fuzzy.

There's a huge man with a beard down to his chest and a thin, short lady with a weird haircut, who looks neurotic and clings onto my hand, babbling incessantly about my wardrobe. Then a guy about my age tells me his name is 'Tik' or something crazy like that, and I extend my hand to shake his and almost miss it, because the room takes an abrupt dive to the left.

Everyone laughs it off, and Anna whisks me back to Elle.

Elle is standing next to Ollie, and keeps talking and touching his arm, but Anna gives me my refilled drink and we sit down on opposite sides of the small glass table and clink. I notice in the background Wes' back twisting on top of a dark-haired girl. They are making out sloppily, drinks in both of their hands. Classy.

"What do you say in Greece?" Anna asks curiously. "Chin-chin?"

"No, we say *stin igia sou!*"

I bring the glass to my lips but before I can drink, a hand reaches out of nowhere and flips it all over the front of my dress. I try to jump out of the way, but there's nowhere to go. Laughter fills my ears from everywhere around me, and I look up to see Wes' tall form towering above me.

"Don't you think you've had enough?" he spits out.

How did he get out of that girl's face so soon?

My glass is shattered at his feet and his hand is still dripping from when he tripped it all over me. His scowl is the darkest I've seen yet, and his eyes glaze drunkenly.

I don't seem to have any fight left in me.

I get up, my seat slippery with drink, and try to move away, but my path is blocked by laughing people and Wes. I try to clear the cotton-balls from my head, but I stumble again before I can right myself. The last second before I land on the floor, a strong hand grasps mine and keeps me from falling. I'm once again pressed against Wes' chest, dripping dress and all, but before I can lift my eyes to his, I begin to fall.

I land on something cool and firm, which is another pair of hands, around my waist, steering me away from the laughing mob of people.

"Come on," Ollie says tightly, and just like that he's in control of the situation. "I've got her," he says over his shoulder to someone, but I can't see who it is, because I'm struggling to keep myself upright.

He slips off his jacket and drapes it over my shoulders, covering my dripping—and, more importantly, clinging to my body—shirt. He turns and exchanges a glance with Wes and then, his hand still protectively on my shoulder, he leads me out into the fresh air.

"How much did you drink?" he asks, supporting me as I struggle to climb up the twenty steps that will take us to street level.

"Just a glass," I mumble. Not that he would believe me. *I* wouldn't believe me. "My car is right over. . ." I begin to point with an unsteady hand.

He's trying to hide it, but he's definitely laughing under his breath. "You're hammered," he says. "Here, this way."

Long story short, he drives me home. And as if my humiliation wasn't complete after that, he waits with me at the door until I can finally fit the key in the lock and watches as I stumble inside.

"I'm really sorry," is the last thing he says to me. His voice sounds serious, maybe a bit sad.

I look back at him, confused. Sorry for what? He just shakes his head and leaves.

...

The next day is day one of shooting. My alarm promptly explodes at five thirty, splitting my head in two.

I'm hungover. Perfect. As I slide out of bed holding my pounding head in my hands I wonder how one margarita rendered me to this light-fearing, noise-avoiding, nauseous mess. I take a long shower and head to the door only to remember with sudden panic that my car is parked all the way over at Drops.

Oh no.

*No no no. It's all wrong.* This isn't how my first job was supposed to begin. Confused. Embarrassed. Scared. Late.

*Late. Shoot.*

I rush over to pick up my wallet and run to the door, gathering my still damp hair in a ponytail. The day promises to be hot today, all summer and no fall.

My home is in one of *kantounia*, tucked away in the east quarter of the tourist market. Downstairs from our two-storey apartment is a tiny bookstore named affectionately "Matchbox" by my granddad. I adore that place.

There's no time to pop in and give him a quick kiss on the cheek this morning, though, as I run through the *kantounia,* my sandals echoing as they flap hurriedly on the smooth stones, only to stop short, my breath coming in quick puffs, as I stumble out into the street.

Because right there, where I usually park it, is my car.

I approach it tentatively, and grab the driver's door handle. It's unlocked. Of course. Whoever brought it back must have broken in.

Ollie must have done it. I don't know if I should be touched or furious. I go back home to fetch my keys.

As I slide them into the ignition I notice something beside me, on the seat next to mine. It's a book. An ugly book, I might add, with no design on the cover, just a worn-out gray color, like those vintage, 1930s collector's items my grandpa has a small, precious selection of.

But this one is no collector's item. It has been read over a hundred times through the years, by the look of it.

I open it. Inside is the title:

## PRIDE AND PREJUDICE

### JANE AUSTEN

And below it, handwritten in a boyish but careful hand, in pencil, is an inscription:

*Do yourself a favor.*
*page 133*
*PS: this book was passed on to me by my maternal grandmother.*
*Please try to be careful with it, if you possibly can. Cheers, Darcy.*

My jaw literally drops. So it wasn't Ollie. It was Wes. Why on earth would he do something nice for me? After the way he treated me last night, too. Is the guy kidding me?

I fling the book back on the seat and step on the gas, trying to vent my frustration. Twenty minutes later—instead of the thirty-five it should have taken me, had I driven like a normal person and not a crazed maniac—I'm at the sprawling yellow villa on top of the hill overlooking the beach. A guy with sunglasses and a very serious gray suit lets me in—security, of course—and I push a few stray curls out of my face, trying to appear composed.

Before I can take stock of my surroundings, the thin, twitching lady I remember vaguely from last night takes my arm and begins leading me away.

"Good, you're here," she says in a clipped tone. "Makeup, now! And you should be here at six tomorrow, got it?"

I nod quickly.

# LOSE ME.

*This isn't how it was supposed to begin.*
*Today is not the day I die.*
I glance at my watch. It's barely five minutes past.

Turns out that what Tim said to me the first day was kind of an understatement. Elle really doesn't do water. Like, at all.

So, they tell me I'm to be her.

There's this scene towards the end of the film, where Will and Lizzie are sitting on their surfboards in the calm sea, talking. That's where we'll start. They put a dark-haired wig on me, because Elle will be a brunette as Lizzie in the film. It's close enough to my own hair color, but they want it to be exactly like hers, so whatever. Then they spray tons of makeup on my shoulders and back. I'm wearing a version of the impossibly white bikini Elle will be wearing in this scene.

It will be only close-ups of her face while she delivers her lines. When Wes talks, it will be the back of my head on the screen. Matt comes over quietly, as the makeup team struggle to make my really tan and toned arms look bony like Elle's, and looks me in the eye.

"I know it's too soon, but go with it," he says. "I know you can do it."

"You do?" I ask, uncertainly. I'm still dazed.

"Yeah," he says, "Ben says you can, so you can."

Ben is Coach.

"O. . . kay."

"Now, when they're shooting the back of your head, you have to react slightly to what he's telling you, right? Nod, or lean towards him. . . " He must notice my face going white, because all the blood is leaving it right now. "Here, I'll show you," he adds.

He must be the calmest, most patient person in the world.

I've never seen anyone so zen. He shows me all he can and before I've had time to think of it, we're down in the water.

We take our places the way they want us, with our bodies facing each other, our legs dangling in the sea, and someone sprinkles water on our hair—my wig—,our backs and swimming suits.

Wes looks like an ancient Greek god of the sea, the sun in his eyes, water dripping from his golden curls. He peels off his shirt to reveal sculpted, bronzed shoulders. Dammit, no one's supposed to look that good. His swimming trunks are knee-length and dark blue with small white swirls that look like Hawaiian flowers, and as soon as he's in the water they cling to his legs, accentuating the swell of wicked quadriceps underneath. A sudden realization hits me: he may not even remember kissing me last night. He was drinking, and he kissed that other girl right away. He certainly doesn't act self-conscious around me, but then again I wouldn't expect a guy like that to be self-conscious around anyone.

Wes smiles at me and I know he's trying to help me relax, but I'm totally freaking out. There are cameras, rafts, microphones in my face, next to me, all over the place. How exactly am I supposed to concentrate? This is going too fast.

31

And then Wes begins to speak.

"I do respect your family," he says, looking directly into my eyes with a green, piercing gaze full of meaning. "I really do, and I'm sorry for the things I said about them. But. . . " at this he leans forward, almost to the edge of his bobbing surfboard and takes my hand lightly in his. "But much as I care for them, everything I did, I did it for you," he says and I melt into his eyes.

"Cut!" a voice yells over the PA.

The kind, endearingly eccentric man I met a couple of days ago is entirely gone. This guy is fierce. "That was brilliant, Spencer," he calls. "Ari, honey, what are you doing? You're rigid. Get a grip. Go again."

I'm shaking all over.

For some inexplicable reason, Wes seems to have forgotten to let go of my hand. Now I feel a slight squeeze.

"Wait!" he calls to the camera crew. He turns to me. "Are you all right?" he asks me quietly, bending his head so that nobody else will hear. "Look, it was too sudden for you, I told Tim, but he says. . . anyway, you've got this, yeah?"

I nod uncertainly. He smiles. "Right. First, stop looking like a frightened chicken. It shows in your body language. Try to relax. Did you read anything from the book I left you?"

"No," I whisper, wanting the sea to swallow me up whole.

"Well, I *did* tell you to do yourself a favor. . ." he frowns. "All right, look at me. Look only at me. Nothing else exists, no cameras, no lights, nothing." I do. "Good," he smiles again, and suddenly I couldn't look at anything else even if I tried. "Now, you're in love with me. We've had our ups and downs, but they only made us appreciate each other more. I'm the best guy in the world as far as you are concerned. You are a level-headed young lady, but right now you are star-struck by me." He waits for a minute, and then, "yes! That's it!" he whispers. "Ready," he yells to the cameras. "Don't lose me," he says to me.

I don't.

The clapper snaps in front of us, but we don't break eye contact. We shoot the scene again, and Tim mumbles that it was okay. Then the cameras change positions and Wes delivers his lines flawlessly again. They tell him to bend as though to kiss me, then to hold my hand and so on.

My skin has broken up in goose bumps, even though the sun is sweating hot, and I feel my legs going numb in the water. Wes has some more lines to deliver.

"You're gonna give us a few seconds," he tells Tim.

"No way, golden boy, I'm dying here," he replies, and Wes seems to take that as a yes, because next thing I know he's grabbing my hand and sliding with me into the emerald sparkling waters.

We come up for air almost simultaneously.

"Better?" he asks.

"Thanks," I say, gulping in air.

We shoot until two. I don't know how he does it. I mean, sure, it must be more exciting to actually say lines instead of just sit there with your back to the camera, but still, the guy is tireless. Gone is the drunken stupor of the past two days, gone too the bored look and the drooping eyelids.

His mood gets even more brilliant with every passing minute, as though this whole thing makes him come alive.

Wow.

Not to mention that he has me believing him every time he says he loves me. Tim, too, seems amazed by his performance. He high-fives him warmly after every take, his eyes glowing with enthusiasm.

We stop for a meal, which I can't eat because my stomach is in knots, and Elle drapes herself all over Wes to congratulate him on his performance. The bored, haunted look comes back into his eyes and she turns her attention to me.

I'm idly twirling my plastic fork around a plate of chicken wings, fiddling with the fluffy pockets of the blue bathrobe they draped around me as soon as I came out of the water.

"You know that's an animal you're eating, right?" she asks me, her eyebrows raised. "Animals are not food."

She snickers, catching Wes' eye. He's busy stuffing his mouth with a hamburger, containing another animal's meat, as far as I can tell, and Elle sees me glancing at it.

"That's soy isn't it, babe?" she asks him quickly and he just grunts, looking out into the sea.

"Well, as long as you know water is not food either," I tell her, as politely as I can, seeing that she has only a bottle of sparkling Evian in front of her.

"Gosh, what even *is* this rubbish they've served us? They had finger food at the last set I worked." She wrinkles her nose at me. "You Greek people eat snakes and disgusting stuff like that, right?" She's rubbing her hand up and down Wes' left arm slowly. "At least now you do. It's been pretty much a third world situation for your country these past few years, I understand that, but still. . . I remember reading about Greece returning to the dark ages during this economical crisis thing and probably taking the whole world with you. I mean. . . talk about bad luck!"

I get up abruptly, leaving my plate full. I walk away, then break into a jog to meet Matt, who is coming towards me across the street with long, measured strides.

"Don't mind that," he says as soon as he reaches me, and I'm surprised to see concern in his eyes. "Some people can't realize that other countries besides their own exist. I've dealt with it my entire life. You were brilliant out there."

"Thanks," I say. "Did I look like a frightened chicken?"

His lips curl slowly around a smile, and he shakes his head. "Only for the few first shots."

A few paces away Elle is twirling her fingers at the longish hairs on the nape of Wes' neck, as he throws the wrapper of his burger in an excellent arc to the rubbish bin. I miss Ollie and Anna.

Wes leaves a sulking Elle to go talk with Tim and two other dudes and they closet themselves in a room at the villa, while Matt and I sunbathe on the immense veranda.

Soon enough, it's time to get into the water once more.

Now I'll start working as well.

We're going to surf!

I knew Wes is famous for doing his own stunts, but knowing and seeing are two very different things. He hasn't touched alcohol all day; at least he swears he hasn't.

There are no waves to speak of right now, but they will be 'added in post-production digitally'—whatever *that* means. I mean, this beach usually has really huge waves, and I get why they have picked it for a surfing scene, but right now the water's surface is smooth as a mirror. Matt approaches me and starts telling me the moves I'm going to have to make.

"Are you kidding?" I ask him. "How am I going to surf with no waves?"

He shrugs, glancing at Tim.

"We'll have to go to the other side of the island," I tell him. "I know of a beach down south, it's perfect."

"Tim is pressed for time," Matt frowns.

I go over to the assistant director and tell him. Tim overhears and he shakes his head immediately, everyone gathering around to witness our upcoming fight. But there is no argument in the end. Wes comes to stand next to me and listens to me carefully. At the end of my explanation he simply turns to Tim and says: "I'm game if you are." And that's that.

Before we pack up and leave, Tim wants a few long shots of us—Wes and me—sitting on our surfboards, just floating on the waves. So we get in the water, no rafts or cameras around us this time, only the endless Ionian sea.

Wes grabs my hand, as he did before, and looks into my eyes with an intense expression. I try to do the same with little success. "Our bodies say we're in love right now, but our lips can say whatever we want," he says in that mocking tone. "Even Tim can't lip-read at this angle. No, don't look towards them, keep your eyes on me."

Someone is on the Rubble, almost directly on top of us, and is taking a precarious aerial shoot. How can I not look?

"So you broke into my car yesterday?" I ask, abruptly.

"Ollie asked me to do it," he shrugs. Ollie? I perk up. "And you're welcome." His eyes darken. "And for the other thing as well."

I decide right here and now, that if the 'other thing' is the kiss, I'll act as if it didn't happen. I mean, my brain is too overloaded to even begin to analyze that.

"What other thing?" I ask, defensively.

# LOSE ME.

"Your drink, Ari," he says, letting my name roll on his tongue in the most delicious way. "It was spiked, didn't you notice?"

"What?"

I'm so surprised that I snatch my hands away in a hurry and lose my balance on the board. In a swift movement, almost invisible, he catches me expertly and rights me before I fall.

"Sorry!" he yells to the cameras. His touch on my warm, wet skin sends shivers up my spine. He glances at his watch. "You're cold. How long are they going to keep us here?"

"Spiked?" I ask, incredulous.

"Yeah," he replies. "Elle and Anna did it. They had it all arranged, I heard it as they were getting ready on the L&H. It's a trick they play, you know a joke on the newbie, that kind of thing."

"A trick?!" I repeat, outraged. "Do you know what... what could have happened to me...?" I stop myself. I don't even know what could happen to my head, or if it would even affect my headaches at all. But still, I'm scared at the prospect. Terrified. And that's without even considering the dangers of alcohol poisoning, rape and extreme humiliation among my coworkers—which I don't remember the details of, but I'm pretty sure it happened. On a massive scale.

"I know," he answers, his voice serious.

"Well, thanks for telling me sooner," I say. "You didn't have to dump the drink on me, either, but I suppose that was part of the plan to humiliate me as well, right?"

"No," he says, "of course not. It's just, I thought you'd realize. I took you away from them, and then when I turn around, there you are again, seated at their table. I was so mad... I had to act quickly." He pauses, looking at me. "Listen. I've been in the industry since I was a kid. The first thing you learn is to trust no one. No one. Not even your own mother."

I snort at this, not that he knows what I'm snorting about.

"Yeah," he says, "I grew up fast. Never had friends, never went to school... I hope it matured me some, although some times I think it made me a worse person than I would have been if I'd had a normal childhood. Sometimes I think it..."

"It drove you to drink," I say before I can stop myself.

I can't believe I just said that. Of course, I meant it as a joke, but something in the way he lowers his head immediately and rakes his hand through his hair tells me I touched a nerve. The billboards have never mentioned anything like this about him.

Sure, I haven't seen him without a drink in his hand before today, and Ollie said something to him about being sober on the boat the other day, but I didn't think he had an actual *problem*.

He turns to me, a haunted look on his face, and a chill runs down my spine.

"Nah, I did that myself," he says after a minute in his bored voice. "So, yeah, you should always be prepared to save yourself, always look out for yourself. No one else will do it for you. Not like I did the other night."

"Thank you," I say more calmly. "That was a decent thing you did. Anna too?" I add in a small voice.

He nods, then looks away. "I won't tell you that you're an idiot," he adds in a minute, "'cause we've established that I don't think you are. But, please be a little more careful around people like... well, me, in the future."

"I'll try," I say, looking down. The sunshine seems to have gone out of the sky.

"Hey," he says, bending close. "You did really amazing today. I couldn't believe it. And Tim was telling me something along those lines too."

"Thanks for helping me, again," I say, "I only did what you said."

He looks at me curiously for a moment. "What will you do if I tell you to kiss me?" he asks. I can't speak for a moment. He lifts a thumb to trace my jaw line and takes my hand in his lightly. "Come here, Ari," he says softly, his voice a bit rough, as though he can't contain it. He bends his head to mine and our mouths meet. A moan escapes his lips and his hands move to circle my waist, only this time there are no clothes between his touch and my skin. I lean into him and turn my head to let him deepen the kiss as much as he wants.

And he wants.

His hands are in my hair, on my shoulders, tangled between my fingers. This is a complete different person to the one who was pushing his lips against mine last night. He is so passionate and gentle at the same time, I can't help but abandon myself to the moment.

With a lithe movement, he pulls me into his arms, never once lifting his lips from mine, and sweeps us both into the sea. I taste the salty water on his lips and bury my fingers into his crunchy, sunshiny hair. I hear our surfboards flop on the sea, drifting away on the blue-green waters, and then he hooks my knees around his thighs, balancing me on his waist.

What on earth is he doing with his mou—? Oh, okay. He's biting my lower lip. Stay calm, no big deal. He's totally biting down, though, teasing it with his teeth and then his tongue does this thing...

My heart is racing and I feel myself sinking into him as though his arms are the deepest sea. I gasp, trying to catch my breath, but he doesn't let me go. He's supporting me with both hands, our legs tangled, our skin burning hot.

"Look at me," he whispers against my lips.

His eyes are intense, as though they want to tell me something that his voice can't. He buries his head in the curve of my neck and kisses me there gently. "This is no lie," he murmurs against my hair.

I look at him, a question in my eyes.

"Cut!" the PA's voice yells over the megaphone. "Frame. Now get your asses over here."

Wes dives in and starts treading water, leaving me there staring after him. Oh. So that was the Will and Lizzie kissing scene. And, man was he good at it. Then again, so was I.

'Don't lose me.' Yeah, right.

I dunk my flaming cheeks into the water and race Wes to the beach. I come, of course, first.

...

We drive to a beach in the south of Corfu, and proceed to spend the rest of the afternoon, while the sunlight lasts, shooting surfing sessions. Wes is a decent surfer, which, seriously? Is there anything this guy can't do? And I'm not bad myself, but we have to concentrate on our moves and the directions Matt is calmly giving us over the megaphone, so we don't talk anymore.

Fine by me.

As soon as I get out of this water, I'll grow up. I won't have feelings, I won't trust anyone, and I won't let my disappointment show. Today was the last time, I promise myself.

But for now, I steal small glances towards Wes' amazing moves and his sculpted body as he's swaying against the blue backdrop of a white-capped tunneling wave, wishing that kiss had been real. Wishing at least he had told me it was for the shot. Ah, never mind. I bet kissing a girl is so mundane for a dude like him, it meant nothing; he didn't give it a second thought.

He's just polite to me, nothing more, nothing less. At least he's not a complete a-hole like last night. That's something. Plus, I'll have a story to tell Katia, but not yet, or she's going to start putting ideas in my head.

"Camera left, Ari," Matt's voice calls, and I obey him, finding myself face-to-face with a camera, which causes me to fall the next minute, but the cameraman has his shot and he gives me the thumbs-up as soon as I resurface.

Wes is right on my tail, going through the same motions as me, his every movement fluid, one with the wave.

"Now just ride the wave, straight up ahead," Matt continues as I get on my surfboard for the millionth time.

Filming surfing is in no way like actual surfing, because you have to fall all the time. Anyway, I'm doing all right, I think, but I am getting a little tired, maybe because I haven't eaten since last night. Oh well, better to surf on an empty stomach.

There's this feeling I get, every time I find myself on the crest of a wave, no matter how small, as though I'll never get down again. I've been surfing since I was a kid, and yet it always steals my breath away. The waves that snatch me from the surface, rising me gently three, five meters in the air. If I look down, it seems like I'm staring at the abyss. At the bottom of the world.

When I was eight, I used to have to remind myself that I'll always come down at the other end of the wave. Always. No matter how long it took, I finally made it to the shallows. Most of the time safely, too. I'm over that fear now, of course, but it's not about surfing anymore. It's about feeling like I'm adrift in the ocean. I'm not on top of the waves anymore; I'm tossed by them. I'm sinking.

Metaphorically, of course. Unless I don't concentrate enough, in which case I might be literally tossed. But I won't let that happen.

"Excellent, Ari," Matt calls. "Wes, ride the wave from camera left to right and try to meet her in the middle there. End in a front facing shot."

It's not easy, but we do our best. The rush of adrenaline is pumping through my veins, giving me the strength to push myself to the limit. By the second take I've got the move nailed and I'm riding on a small swell towards Wes, when a sudden stab of pain in my forehead cripples me.

We've drifted towards the shallows again, as the wind is blowing in that direction. The waves get really big here, rising a full four meters in the air and crashing with a roar on the sand. It's dangerous to surf here, I usually jump off the board and swim carefully out. At this point the current is so strong, blink and you're swept under. If you're lucky, you'll resurface in the deep end of the sea, and try to catch your breath before the next wave covers your head. If you're not. . .

Well, let's try to avoid *that* happening for the second time in a week, shall we?

I bend my legs, trying to keep my balance, but black spots dance before my eyes and I can't contain my reaction to the pain. In the flash of a second, I lose my footing on the board and wipe out. I fall sideways into the water, the splash leaving a nasty burn on my skin. I surface a second later, my head splitting, and try to wipe the saltwater from my eyes, hoping a wave isn't on its way to swallow me up.

Immediately a hand is thrown before me, open, inviting me to grasp it.

"You okay there, Phelps?" Wes asks in that mocking voice, but then he sees my pale, tense face and freezes. I'm already being towed away from my board by the current, and I'm struggling to stay above and breathing. My hand reaches for the board, but I miss. My body is starting to feel weird, weightless, as I bob up and down on the waves—more down than up, if we're being honest. Something warm and solid grabs and steadies me.

"Hey, what's wrong?" Wes whispers, bending down and taking my arm in a firm grasp before I'm submerged. "Did you swallow a lot of water out there? You're not going to drown on me again, are you?"

I shake my head and, refusing his hand, I climb up on my own. But just as I do, I almost black out from a stab of pain, and he dives forward to catch me before I fall.

"I'm done, Matt," he shouts. "No more for me today, mate, I'm beat. Come on," he adds, turning to me as though he's the one in charge.

"Cut," Matt yells and calls for us to get out. We slide back into the water, paddling our boards towards the shore. The current is really strong and it takes a lot of effort to keep afloat, let alone steering a massive surfboard with me on top of it. It feels like I'm swimming in place.

"Wait, let me," Wes says, grabbing my board to tow it along with his.

"I'm good," I say.

"Well, see, now you're being an idiot again," Wes says. He doesn't sound as much insulting as exasperated. "You're wiped after all that you've had to do today, not to mention you haven't eaten a bite all day. . . someone offers to help, you accept."

"Stop calling me that!" I almost shout.

"Yeah? Then why did I have to tell Matt that *I* needed a break?"

"Cause you're the star," I answer matter-of-factly.

He tips his head back and bursts out laughing.

"Yeah, and you're Donald Duck!" he retorts. What did he just say to me?

He keeps on swimming effortlessly, as though it requires zero strain for him to go against the swells slamming against our bodies, while holding on to both our boards.

I open my mouth and spit out water, preparing a caustic answer, but he starts talking again.

"And how do you explain the fact that the other day, even though you needed help, you didn't once call out?" His voice turns dead serious. And a bit patronizing, too. "I was watching you, you know, from the L&H, and you deliberately turned the other way as soon as you were in trouble, as though you didn't even need anyone. I saw you were sinking and I jumped in after you the next second but I. . . " he swallows and grabs the nape of his neck, his Adam's apple working. "I almost didn't get to you in time."

He stops and places an arm on my shoulder, turning me so that we're eye to eye as we keep bobbing on the waves. "You could have died, Ari," he shouts over the roar of the sea. "Isn't that more important than stupid pride? Than pretending you don't need anyone? It doesn't make sense. That's what I meant when I said you were an idiot. And I still stand by it."

"Did you just call me Donald Duck?" I ask, trying not to let it show that I'm out of breath.

"I'd call you a proper duck if you knew how to surf," he retorts, rising that eyebrow. He seems to be expecting an answer to what he said before.

I was a bit scared at how he got me spot-on, but after that 'duck' comment, all I feel is annoyed. "I didn't need anyone from your M&M boat, that's for sure."

He bends his face close to mine. His lips part to reveal a cheeky smile full of teeth.

"Not even me?" he asks, and for a moment I want to be the one to push those lips onto mine.

But I don't, of course. Serves me right for thinking he was serious for a second, but it turns out he was joking all along. Very funny.

As soon as we get out, someone rushes over with a white robe for

Wes and a towel for me. My headache has subsided to a dull throb, but I know these outbursts of pain haven't ended yet. Not by far.

"Towel yourselves off, children," Tim says as we get out. "You, come here."

The "you" is me. My work is not done, apparently.

Wes is led to the shade and offered a drink, his long body wrapped inside the robe, which looks impossibly white against his tanned skin, while Tim explains to me what I am to do next. "The light is not yet fully gone," he explains. "We can save up a few hours still."

I try not to moan. *I've got this. Today is not the day I die. Today is the day I prove myself.* They say I'm just to walk along the beach, but it's never as simple as that, is it?

Lizzie is supposed to meet Will out on the beach, while running to her sick sister's assistance. She has to be a bit dirty and disheveled and sandy and wet, since she's been swimming. Will's impeccably dressed friends, out on the beach for a party, are supposed to smirk and judge her, but Will himself will be struck silly by her brilliant eyes and her devotion to her sister.

Tim doesn't know yet what he wants exactly, so we spend the next two hours, getting footage of me running up and down the beach. I run back and forth across the strip of sand where the huge waves crash and the tiny pebbles, rushing into the swells, are slippery beneath my feet. I lay down to get sand in my hair, which is my own hair, quickly twisted in a braid, and try to pretend—all with my body language, of course—that I'm anxious and worried about Jane, my sister.

When we're done I can hardly breathe, the pain is killing me, and I've got a stitch in my side. Score.

I try to get up from the sand and fall back down on my knees. A wave rushes over and I have just enough time to pull myself up and away before it swipes me into the sea again. I'm panting.

*Deep breaths*, I say to myself. *How will I ever get home?*

Wes drove his own car here, but I rode in the van with the lighting team.

Sigh. Nothing to do but start walking towards the parking lot, so I can grab my clothes, at least. The road is going uphill all the way and my muscles are screaming with the added strain, so I start counting my steps. I keep looking down, at my flip flops, totally absorbed in the effort it takes to just put one foot in front of the other, and that's why I don't notice the car that's been slowly following me.

I look up and there it is. Wes' gorgeous BMW i8 is soundlessly gliding right next to me. I recognize it from a tiny, grainy photograph I'd seen in a magazine weeks ago. Inside there was an article, and Katia said we should read it since he might be working at the same movie as me. So I'd read that the guy was crazy about cars—he even collects them, supposedly. There was a photo spread of some of the cars he's driven the last two years, and I kept looking at them, swooning, while Katia was screaming in my ear about his shirtless photo shoot by the pool. I hadn't even gotten to that page. I guess not everyone swoons at the same things, right?

Anyway, I didn't know he's brought one of them here, but thinking about it, of course he would have. I've seen Elle get in and out of limos all over the place, but few of the other actors get such treatment. Except Wes isn't just one of the 'other actors', is he? He's even brought a freaking boat with him, after all.

The car's engine stops and next thing I know Wes is rolling down the window and reaching a long, tan arm across the seat to open the passenger door.

"She'll ride with me," he tells Matt—I hadn't noticed him walking behind me either. "We need to talk about. . . stuff. Hop in, Phelps, come on."

He says it like 'c'm on', and it sounds as though he's talking to a kid. He has that eyebrow raised again, and I want to tell him that *he* looks like a patronizing idiot right now, but I don't even have the energy to argue.

"Come on," he smiles up at me, "you know you're itching to ride in the supercar." That's what the i8 is called by the reviewers, a 'supercar'.

Drat him, he's right. I get in, all sandy and salt-watery and wait for him to complain about me getting the leather seat dirty.

"Buckle up," is all he says.

As I turn to the side to look for the belt, I feel something touch the heavy braid that's hanging down my shoulder. I glance at him quickly, and he drops his hand on his knee, smoothly turning the wheel as we peel away from the pavement. I can't imagine why he would want to touch my hair, except to flick away a pebble that's maybe tangled in the stray hairs that escaped as I was traipsing around the beach like a crazy person.

"Wow," I murmur, looking around me, my fingers aching to touch the wheel. "I thought there were like, ten of these in the world."

"Yep," he says, looking smug, but he doesn't elaborate.

He's looking straight ahead, as though the empty lane demands his entire concentration. After five more minutes of silence pass, I begin to think he's forgotten I'm there and, deciding I'm going to ignore him too, I sit back and fall into an exhausted sleep.

When I open my eyes, we're not moving. Wes is watching me with a frown on his handsome face. The sun has set in the distance and the trees cast long shadows across the windshield. At first, I don't recognize where we are. Have I been asleep the entire time? It must be more than an hour. Or did I pass out?

And then I realize what's happening. Why I'm so tired, why my legs won't obey me, why I fell asleep in a freaking BMW i8.

Tears prickle the inside of my eyelids and I close them before they spill over.

I swallow hard.

Oh no. It's begun. It's here.

I'm dying.

## young people

Unidentified sources have compiled for us a juicy bit of gossip concerning our lovely dystopian pirate-turned-gentleman, Weston Spencer, and his closest friend and current co-star, Oliver Sikks. Turns out Oliver's mother, the famed and infamous actress Christina Taylor, recently sprung a bit of news on him.

Now, listen to this, you won't believe it. It seems that, back in the day, Christina wasn't the 'good girl' her recent roles would have us believe. According to an unnamed source, Taylor spent a wild, hot summer on a remote island in the south of Italy. Yum.

Well, you ask, is that all? Of course it's not. Turns out she didn't simply have a nice time, she had the BEST time. Apparently, she hooked up with a guy who rowed boats to the shore, or something romantic like that, and when she came back to L.A., she started to put on weight super quickly, if you know what we mean, wink wink. Yup. You read that right. Ms. Taylor has another kid. Rumor has it that the kid's a daughter, who was raised somewhere in Europe, by her hunk of a dad, and has never been at the receiving end of a reporter's flash until now.

Now that's a nice piece of news to spring on your twenty year-old son, isn't it? Hmmm... it will be interesting to see how our beloved star will react to it. As for us, we'll wait for the photos that will no doubt flood the media (if the story is true, after all) before we pass verdict on this mysterious mini-Christina.

What do you think?
Fact of fiction?
Mother or Monster?
Send us your opinion at **ypm@youngpeople.com**

## F O U R

Wes insists that I take a shower in his room. I start to protest, but he lifts his hands in the air.

"If you think you look better without a shower, be my guest," he says.

My mouth gapes. "Are you really saying that I—?"

He interrupts me quickly, laughing. "You know I'm not, Phelps."

Then he explains that we stopped at the yellow villa to pick up my clothes and my car, but I wouldn't wake up, so he had the skinny lady put my things in a bag and decided to bring me here. He's stopped the car in a gorgeous part of the old Town called *Kanoni*, in front of the main entrance of the Divani he's staying at.

"Didn't you just tell me not to trust guys like you?" I ask him. A shower would be a life-saver right now, it's true, but there's no way I'm letting this happen. "Sorry for messing up your lovely car," I add, as I get out of it on aching limbs.

"Don't worry about it," he answers, holding the door for me. What, is he being nice to me now? Okay. He tosses the keys to the valet.

He's wearing a black form-hugging T-shirt with a V neck and fitted jeans, simple enough, but on him the clothes look like a million bucks, as though they were tailored for his body.

His hair is all tangled and dried-out, crispy with salt and sunshine and it falls over his eyes as he takes off his sunglasses and fits them into his left pocket, turning that brilliant gaze on me for a second.

He slows down so that I can walk next to him and stretches an arm to my back, not quite touching me, but so close to my skin that I can feel the heat radiating from his body.

"You had me a little scared there," he says with a slight frown. "You were sleeping so deeply and looking so pale, for a moment I thought there might be something seriously wrong. I was hoping to let you drive a bit, but you wouldn't wake up. Maybe my ride didn't impress you as much I'd thought it would."

The thought of him wanting to 'impress' me with his car is so surreal and spot on, that I want to cry. He looks at me, waiting for a reply, but I say nothing, looking straight ahead, concentrating on putting one foot in front of the other. I barely have the energy to do that.

"Phelps?" he insists. "Are you really that tired? You're a trained athlete, aren't you?"

I turn to him, feeling the helplessness exude from my face. His expression changes; he was half-teasing before, but now he looks scared. In a second, he shrugs it off.

"Probably the hangover," he says. "Come on up."

His 'room' is the penthouse suite. The entire top floor. Of course.

"I thought you'd stay at the villa," I say as the elevator doors open and we enter a spacious living room decorated with gauze curtains and cream sofas. The entire left side of the room is made of two wide windows overlooking the sea.

"Yeah, that's what Tim said, because of the low budget nonsense. . . Not happening."

There are books everywhere. Literally everywhere. Stacked on the flat screen. Open on the dinner table. Strewn across the floor in stacks in front of a pair of dumbbells by the window that overlooks the sea. The glass doors are ajar and a breeze fills the room, the curtains billowing and falling with every gust of wind.

Other than that it's really tidy. Not to mention that an army of maids must have just been in here, for the place looks pristine-clean.

"I can't shower here," I whisper, clutching the canvas bag with my clothes and shoes—he handed it to me as soon as we got off the elevator.

"Why not?" he asks. His forehead wrinkles, and he looks at the floor. "It's clean in there, I swear. The hotel ladies are in twice a day, they'll have the place wiped of every sign of me."

This is so cute that I smile in spite of the crippling pain throbbing in my head.

"Dude, I just got sand all over your car and now. . ."

"*Dude?*" he asks, lifting an eyebrow, his eyes smiling.

"Sorry, sorry," I say quickly, bringing a hand to my aching head, "I mean you are *freaking Weston Spencer* after all—"

Abruptly, he goes all bored and quiet on me. He turns away, planting himself onto a chair and turning on the TV. A Greek anchorman appears on screen, and Wes changes the channel with a soft curse.

"You've never acted before like I was anything *freaking* special," he spits out, not looking at me. "I swear, I could almost imagine I was a real person there for a while. Go on in," he adds after a horrifying moment, while I stand mute in the middle of the room. "It's the second door to your left. The sooner you're done, the sooner I get my room back."

I have a sudden urge to run back out in the street and call a cab, bikini and all, but I know that would be childish. So I walk away, head throbbing but held high, and into the second door to the left.

His bathroom is the size of the yellow villa. Well, not *actually*, but it's pretty close. It's all covered in marble, wall to wall, with wide windows that bring the stars inside. The overhead light reflected on the marble is so blindingly white it's making my migraine worse and the sudden onslaught of pain threatens to double me over. Right. Let's get this over with.

The shower is a freaking separate room within the bathroom. I stand in this space that's separated by a wall of fake, red-colored bricks and notice that there are four showerheads around me. I turn on the tap and water starts spewing at me from four different directions at full force. I turn it back down. Oh, wait. There's buttons on the wall. How does this thing work?

The water feels so cool running on my burning forehead. Am I running a fever? I close my eyes and let it wash over me, not bothering to wash the sand grains off my skin. My arms feel too tired, my legs can barely hold me up. I turn the knob towards hot and I notice that my hands are shaking.

The desperation descends on me again and as the lukewarm water hits me with blissful force, I fall to my knees. Then the tears come.

I hate crying. I never used to cry. And I haven't really cried, not since the day I found out. . . well, I haven't. Maybe that's why it comes down in torrents now. I cry in that heart-wrenching, hiccupping way only kids do; I cry until I can't breathe anymore.

This whole crying thing does not help with my migraine, but I can't stop.

I try to get up, but everything is made slippery by the water and my feet can't find the proper purchase on the shower floor. I slip back down on my knees, and I bend my head down, letting the water slide across my back, while tears soak my knees.

I make another effort to get up and the room sways as though I'm about to pass out and for a moment I almost wish that that was it. That it was already all over. It would be so easy to slip away right now, so painless, so convenient.

Then I realize what I had been thinking and fresh sobs shake me.

*Help*, I think.

*Someone stop this. Please.*

"Ari?"

I hear pounding on the door, booming through the room like thunder.

"Ari!" Wes' voice screams. "If you don't answer me *this second*, I'm coming in!"

I try to tell him that I'm fine, but my voice comes out hoarse from all the crying and it's not enough to carry to the other side of the door. He pounds on it some more and then it suddenly opens with a crack—he must have kicked it, because I locked it as soon as I came in.

"Ari," he shouts, and it sounds like he's having a hard time breathing, "did you—I heard. . . Oh my G—"

The shower door opens, letting in cool air, as he walks around the separator with his clothes on. I can't see him through the tears and water; I just hear him inhale sharply. He falls to his knees next to me with a splash. "What's wrong?" he asks, his voice sounding all hoarse and scared. "Are you hurt?"

"Wes. . . "

"Yeah, it's me," he replies, his voice dropping to a low rumble. "Just tell me what's wrong, I'm here."

I don't know what's wrong, so I can't tell him. The caring in his voice makes me cry even harder, until I choke and gag, water falling into my eyes and nose.

"It's okay," he whispers into my hair, cupping my neck and lifting me out of the way of the water. He envelopes me in his arms and folds his long legs under him, tucking me inside his body, supporting me between his knees. He bends down over me so that his head is right next to mine, and holds me tightly as the water splashes all over him. "I've got you, baby, shhh, it's okay, it's okay."

He repeats it until my sobs subside a little and then he gets up and I whimper. It felt like his arms were the only thing holding me together, and now I'll fall apart all over again. He doesn't leave, though.

He takes the showerhead in his hand and lowers the pressure of the water.

Then he begins to wash the sand out of my tangled hair. He unbraids it with quick movements and smoothes it over my shoulders as he runs the water over every single strand, running his fingers through it. I can feel my headache slipping away with his every touch and I close my eyes, savoring the feel of him, losing myself in his nearness.

I would never have imagined it a month ago that I would be sitting in a guy's penthouse suite shower, crying on the bathroom floor while he washed my hair.

Then again, I would never have imagined other things as well.

Slowly, tantalizingly, he passes his hands all over my body, washing away the sand and salt. "Your skin is burning," he whispers.

It's not just from the fever that it's burning. I can feel his fingers trembling too as they curl around my arm, so I don't say anything. He places his palm flat on my bare back, sliding it up and down and I lean back, letting him support my weight for a second. I sigh as his calm movements drive the last of my anguish away, and by the time he has cleaned me out the tears have stopped. He washes my face last, turning me to face him, his lips puckered in concentration as his fingers linger on my lips, my cheekbones, my eyebrows.

Then he turns the water off.

"Put your arm around my neck," he says softly, carefully, as though he's afraid he'll break me merely by speaking.

He lifts me in his arms and carries me inside. His jeans have gotten wet, but he took his shirt off before he got into the shower, and droplets from his wet hair are falling on his chest.

He helps me sit on his bed—*again*, I might add, because I remember soaking his other bed, on the M&M, as well—and goes to get me a towel. I dry myself off and he closes the bedroom door behind him as he leaves me to change.

A few minutes later I open the door, only to find him on the floor just outside it, still in wet jeans and hair. He is barefoot. He leaps to his feet as I grasp the door handle, and opens it for me.

"How are you feeling?" he asks in a hoarse voice.

"Fine," I answer, hiding my swollen eyes from him. "I'm so sorry. . . I don't know what happened before, I guess I was just tired, or— "

He shakes his head.

"Don't give me that, Phelps," he says. "I know I said that thing about the duck, but I didn't mean it. I've seen you surf, remember? You were fierce. And from that to this? This isn't right, Ari. It's not normal, okay? I tried to explain it away, but. . . Now I'm beginning to think something is seriously wrong and if you don't tell me, then so help me—" his voice cracks.

"Hey," I say softly. "Thank you for today, I'm so sorry you had to see that. . . Nothing is going on, okay?"

He runs a hand through his hair. "I'm going crazy here," he whispers.

"So am I," I whisper back.

# LOSE ME.

I don't know why we're both whispering, what we are trying to hide from. Is it the ugliness he just witnessed in the bathroom, all this darkness coming out of me? Or is it ourselves?

"Have dinner with me."

"Thanks," I try to smile. "But I have this splitting headache. . . "

"I have painkillers," he answers immediately, watching me.

"It's really massive," I say.

"I have tons," he replies.

"I'm sorry. I just need to go home."

"You're not seriously going to leave without an explanation, nothing?"

"What needs an explanation?" I ask.

"Ari you. . . you keep nearly dying in my hands," he almost yells and I flinch more at his words than the tone of his voice. "Now I'm good enough to save you but not good enough to hear about it?" A vein ticks in his forehead, and his Adam's apple bobs up and down as he swallows. "Can't you just give me a chance here? I know I'm not the sort of person you. . . But I thought at least. . . Argh!"

He makes an exasperated gesture, giving up. I feel tears prickling my eyes again.

"Wes, listen, I can't. . . right now I can't even begin. . . "

"Took you long enough to say my name," he says vehemently, turning to stare at me with anger flashing in those brilliant eyes. "Too bad you won't have the chance to ever say it again."

"Wait, so you can behave like a jerk all you like, but I can't refuse to tell you what you want the second you want it?"

He freezes.

I didn't know I had it in me, to try to cover up my fear with aggression. But, there we are. It's not like this anger towards him hasn't been building up inside of me since day one. I mean, what was up with all the 'this-is-no-lie' line he fed me right before he kissed me for the cameras? He swallows and then he says the last thing I expected to come out of his lips.

"I'm sorry. For the way I acted in Drops. And for today. I wanted you to be relaxed, to make you act like the kiss was natural, I didn't think how it might hurt you. . . I'm sorry. You're right, I'm used to people doing anything to get what they want. It's no excuse, but I made the decision in that split second, I didn't think that you're not what I usually. . . "

He lifts his eyes to mine and my heart melts in a puddle around my feet. I take a steadying breath.

"I'm sorry," he repeats, taking a tentative step towards me. "Can we start over? I just want to be friends with you, I. . . I haven't cared to be friends with anyone except Ollie in a long time."

"You. . . after all this, you're telling me you want to be friends?" I ask him, incredulous.

He nods.

"Why?"

47

"Why not?" He looks down, hiding his eyes from me. I wish I could see his expression.

"Okay," I press my lips together. My head is threatening to explode and I close my eyes for a second, trying to breathe through the pain.

He smiles and turns his head aside. "So, should I order pizza?"

"No, I still have that headache, I think I need to get to bed," I tell him.

He looks down, hiding a smile. Only it's not a real smile. It's that harsh grimace people do when they are about to say something hurtful. My stomach sinks.

"Man, I *knew* you didn't like me," he says. "Not that you know me enough to not like me already, but I just thought you were different, you know? The good kind of different."

His words cut me. "Has it never happened to you before?"

"What, someone not liking me?" He snorts. "Actually, it hasn't."

"That's shocking. I mean, it's so hard to imagine that you haven't called anyone a 'twit', or a 'gaffer' or 'Donald Duck' ever. Or maybe all three at once."

He looks at me, his lips hanging slightly open. "Right."

Without another word, he picks up the phone, his back to me. He calls the reception and orders me a taxi.

"Do you have money on you?" he asks gruffly as soon as he hangs up.

"Yeah. . . "

He doesn't say anything else, so I call the elevator.

"Look, I. . ."

"I just apologized to you, Ari!" It bursts out of him. He'd already started walking away, but he turns back to spit a few last angry words at me. "I asked you to just have dinner with me. I asked you. . . Oh, never mind. Huh. It's obvious you can't get out of here fast enough." He grabs my canvas bag from the couch and flings it at me. I catch it instinctively.

The next second he's gone.

As I get into the elevator I hear the shower running in the bathroom; he's gotten into the shower. I just stand there, speechless, as the sound of water hitting the marble tiles reaches my ears a bit too loudly—of course, I realize in a second, the door is open, it can't close since he broke it.

*Time to get out of here.*

Just as the doors of the elevator close with a *ping*, I think I hear a muffled curse coming from the direction of the bathroom. A thud echoes as though he just banged his fist on the wall.

I hung my head, but no more tears come. I'm cried out.

*Well*, is all I think. *So that was that.*

...

"*Pappou*, I need a favor."

About an hour later, as soon as the taxi deposits me in the yellow villa's parking lot, I call grandpa from my car  before I lose my nerve. He answers on the second ring, as he always does.

"Anything for my doll."

I love it when he calls me his doll—*koukla mou*—in Greek. Right now I'm so emotional, even this is enough to start me crying again.

"*Eisai kala, Ari mou?*" he asks if I'm okay. What should I tell him now?

"I'm fine, *pappou*, listen, it's a big favor and I want you to keep it entirely secret from everyone. Don't tell my dad, don't even tell *yiayia*. Promise."

"I promise," he answers, his tone changing to serious.

My grandpa is one of the most ordinary-looking people you'll ever meet. A little balding, not tall but not short either, of medium weight, old corduroy pants and sweater vest. And he's my hero.

He is the bravest and kindest man I've ever met; he's the kind of person I want to become. He and my grandma practically brought me up, since back when I was a baby dad was really busy working two to three jobs all at once.

Grandma, who I'm named after, is my favorite person in the entire world. When I think of her, I think of home. That says it all.

And it's not just the smell of fried bacon and *loukoumades* that I associate with her, or her patient smile as she spent hundreds of hours watching me trying to nail that particular trick shot in our neighborhood's football court. She always had a word of encouragement ready on her lips, and then she'd wipe my scraped knees as though it was no big deal and stick my muddied shorts in the hamper without a word of reproach. And when I came from school crying because the other kids made fun of me for being too tall or too athletic 'for a girl', or—even worse—they bullied me because I had no mom to show up at the PTA meetings, she and grandpa would wipe the tears from my cheeks and make me French fries and ice-cream and take me for a walk down at the pier.

I love them both to pieces.

And now I'm going to break their hearts.

"I need you to book me an appointment with Spiros at the Health Clinic," I tell him, as calmly as I can. "Book it in your name, but he'll know it's for me and what it's about, he won't ask any questions. Can you do that for me, *pappou*? As soon as possible, tomorrow."

"Spiros? Doctor Razatos? Ari, why would. . . ?"

"Please, *pappou*, I'll explain everything tomorrow. You'll come with me, won't you?"

He came with me on all of my first days. Kindergarten, high-school, the first time I met Coach—even though I was old enough by then that I didn't need him to hold my hand, but it made it easier somehow. And now this. I feel my throat close up again.

"Of course I will, *koukla mou*," he answers without hesitation, his voice a familiar, soothing baritone next to my ear.

I send him kisses and hang up.

My vision is blurry from crying, but I get home all right. I sneak upstairs, not wanting anyone to see me crying, grab a snack from the kitchen, and go hide in my room.

Doctor Spiros Razatos is a family friend. (In Greece, pretty much everyone is a family friend, but he's a really close one.)

He's the one doctor I'd trust with something like this, because I've known him practically my entire life: he was a fixture at my grandparent's house when he was in his twenties, just starting out as an MD, fresh out of Med School. I remember him playing hide and seek with me in the *kantounia*, me shrieking with laughter, he all angles and tall as the sky, pushing back his black-rimmed glasses after landing on his face as he rounded a corner too fast.

He's been keeping my secret for over a month now, and even more importantly, he's been keeping his word. I have no idea what he's going to say to me. No matter what he says though, my mind is made up.

Wes' confused, accusing eyes yesterday convinced me that I'm not handling this maturely. In fact, I'm not handling this at all.

And I said I would stop acting like a child.

So there.

...

Early next morning, *pappous* gives a random excuse to my grandma and walks to the pier, where I told him I'd meet him. I pick him up in my car and we head silently for the clinic.

Spiros does neither of the things I imagined he would. He just looks at me with those serious eyes beneath his thick black eyebrows and nods in approval.

"Come on in," he says. "I've got everything ready."

With one final look at my grandpa's tremulously smiling lips, I open the green door to my left, and then I step inside for a CAT scan. A head scan.

"Ari." That's the first thing I hear as I come out, dazed, from the radiology room.

Just that. My name.

But the way he says it.

I already know. There's nothing else he needs to tell me, so I sit down gingerly and he sits next to me, watching me silently.

"How big is it?" I ask, feeling as though I'm floating outside of my body.

He wipes his eyes with his hand and I see that he's holding his glasses with the other—I don't think I've ever seen Spiros without them. He looks suddenly younger, unsure of himself. His dark eyes are so desperate, I can't look him in the face any longer.

"Pretty big," he says, clearing his throat, "the size of a nut."

*What type of nut are we talking here?* That's all I can think of.

# LOSE ME.

Stupid, right?

"You're going to be fine," he adds in a thick voice. "I promise, nothing that's possible for human medicine won't. . . "

"I know," I interrupt him. His panic is breaking my heart. "I knew that's what you would find, it's okay."

I feel weirdly calm. What is there to be afraid of now? Now I know. The ignorance was what was scaring me before. Maybe that's why I'm not nervous anymore.

And now for the hard part. Spiros turns to *pappou*.

"That day, this past August, when Ari fainted at the barbeque. . . you remember?" Spiros asks grandpa, and he simply nods, threading his fingers together. "Well, I told you at the time that it was nothing, and indeed there was no reason for anyone to worry, except when I saw Ari later I. . . I asked her about it."

I'd fainted during the town festival, on the fifteenth of August. That day is a big deal in Corfu—in all of Greece, actually. It's a national holiday and all the shops are closed, so what else is there to do? Eat. (That's almost always the answer in Greece.) Also, invite the entire village to your home to share your food. That's Greek customs and Greek hospitality for you.

Anyway, I'd been having one of my good days that day; no sign of a headache in sight, nothing. And then, sometime in the early afternoon, it happened. Just like that, no warning or anything. I fainted.

Dad told me, after I came to in my room, the windows shut and blessed silence surrounding me, that I had been out of it for about half an hour. Which was quite a big deal, so they'd already called Spiros, who was at a beach down south with his wife.

He did tell me it was nothing, probably the heat or the exhaustion of intensive training, and just told me to rest. I fell asleep almost directly after he left.

About a week later, though, I bumped into him randomly. I was out on the town, running some errands for grandma. He saw me from a street away, I remember, and lifted a hand in greeting. I waited for him to come closer, and as he did his smile faded away.

I have classified that moment in my head as the end.

I know it started long before then; I've had these headaches since June, but that was the exact moment when I knew something was wrong.

"Hey there, Ariad—" Spiros had started saying, but the words died on his lips as he walked over. He looked me over in a glance, head to toe, and he turned pale.

He ran over to me and, with a harshness I had never seen him show before to *anyone*, he grabbed my arm, almost hurting me in his hurry, and drew me aside to the shade of a grocer's tent.

"Have you lost weight?" he frowned.

I simply looked at him. I didn't need to tell him, I knew all my fears and worries were written on my face.

He exhaled loudly and rubbed the bridge of his nose.

Then he cursed. "Tell me." Sweat was glistening at his forehead.

The day wasn't boiling hot yet, although it would be in a few hours, but noticing that little detail, that he was sweating, just sent me over the edge.

I can still remember every moment, as if it was yesterday: I collapsed on the pavement, super-market bags spilling half-open next to my bare legs, and in a second he was crouching next to me, rubbing my back, and telling me it was probably nothing and to tell him, for chrissakes.

"I've fainted before," I told him as soon as I could breathe. "I haven't told anyone."

"How often?" he asked, going all doctor on me.

"Monday," I said. "Friday before that. Then a couple of weeks ago before that."

He swallowed. "Anything else? Nausea? Vomiting? Headaches?"

"Yes," I said. "Yes, once. And yes, all the time."

"Headaches? All the—?" he repeated, looking dazed.

"All. The. Time." I replied.

He placed a thin, long arm around my neck, and touched the top of my head lightly with his fingers.

"Dammit," was all he said.

He helped me pick up the bags and we walked for a bit in silence, down towards the sea, although this wasn't the direction either of us was going.

Then he told me.


## ashby magazine

### THE BIG Q
### *WES SPENCER EDITION*

*excerpt*

**Q:** Weston, let's talk about your newest film, which hits theatres in a few days, August fourth. It's called *Peter*, and it's a psychological thriller about a teenager with a Peter Pan complex, whose little sister disappears and he. . . has to deal with all of that.

**A:** Well, it's mostly a coming-of-age story, a quest of sorts.

**Q:** A quest to find his sister or himself?

**A:** Both, actually.

**Q:** So, as to the young actress who plays your sister. . .

**A:** Candice Marks.

**Q:** How was it working with her? I mean, Candice is quite young?

# LOSE ME.

**A:** She's six. Well, five and a half actually during shooting. Oh, she was just great. Brilliant as an actress too, you wouldn't believe how efficient she was, how concentrated on her work. I just. . . yeah, we became best friends.

**Q:** That's so rare to hear. . . And there are already Oscar rumors circulating! You play the title role, right?

**A:** I do. Well, it's too early to speak of awards yet, I'd rather not go there. . .

**Q:** All right, so we're all very curious about your long-awaited next step in the industry! Will you tell us about this new project of yours? According to some, it will mark your transition to more mature film roles. That's kind of a big step in your career.

**A:** If you put it like that it is.

**Q:** (laughs) So, tell us a little bit of what the plot is about.

**A:** Well, it's supposed to be a modern retelling of a classic, I'm not sure I should say which one at this point. Mostly it's a romantic story, not so much romantic comedy though. I think Tim [Tim Halls] would rather put it as a love story. But that's up to the viewers to decide, really.

**Q:** Oh, I'm sure they'll be delighted to see you on the big screen, no matter what. This is set up to be a big change for you, a great separation from your role as Tristan in the popular sitcom The Water Wars. How are you feeling about that?

**A:** Ah, you know my therapist keeps asking me the same question. . .

**Q:** (laughs) Seriously?

**A:** No, I don't have a therapist. I mean, technically I do, but. . . Anyway, I'm rather glad to be leaving Tristan behind, you know. It was a great part and a real um. . . privilege to work all those years with all of these amazing people, we were a strong team and really close to each other, but I think it's time to move on.

**Q:** It will mark the beginning of your adulthood in the industry.

**A:** I don't know if it will mark anything, except a month or two of filming on an island somewhere.

**Q:** Oh, where? Can you tell us?

**A:** Tim is currently deciding, so even I'm not sure.

**Q:** All right, we'll have to wait and find out. Now, I want to ask you a question concerning your TWW costar, Elle Burke.

**A:** Are you sure you want to go there?

**Q:** Well, your romance with her was a big part of both of your careers, and I think of your lives too, considering that you first got together when you were what? Fifteen?

**A:** Ah, listen, I don't like to talk about personal matters with anyone other than my close friends. . . but yeah, Elle was a big part of that franchise.

**Q:** Our readers will want to know something about your relationship, anything you could tell us.

**A:** Let's just say that TWW being over was a great thing both for her and for me.

**Q:** You'll be costarring again in the new film, right?

**A:** That's what I hear, too.

**Q:** And speaking of best friends, Oliver Sikks will also star in the upcoming film, is that confirmed?

**A:** At this point everything is up in the air still, but I can tell you almost certainly that if Ollie isn't in the final cast I probably won't be either.

**Q:** Wow, that's some seriously cool bromance I'm sensing you two got there.

**A:** Well, some have called it co-dependence and some other stuff, but, yeah, basically he's my best mate. He's the one who keeps me grounded, he's the one to lean on during emergencies. And adventures.

**Q:** Adventures. . . That sounds saucy.

**A:** If you mean saucy like, actual sauce, then yeah. I mean, this one time we went on a cruise with my boat, the L&H, to get away from the photographers and we had absolutely no food on board, I mean nothing. So we decide to cook spaghetti bolognaise. Yeah, that wasn't pretty. Good thing we didn't burn the whole boat down. Just the kitchen. Had to learn how to cook properly after that.

**Q:** Ladies do you hear that? (laughs) The L&H, your yacht, right? It's become almost as famous as you. Is it named after Laurel and Hardy, the famous turn-of-the-century comic duo, correct? I'm not sure many of our readers are familiar with their black and white films. . .

**A:** Well, they should be. They're just a double act, pretty simple stuff, from a technical standpoint—their most active years were between the twenties and the forties, after all—but the execution is flawless. Their films are hilarious, I grew up with them. My boat is named after them, they're my idols. Basically, it's named after me and Ollie, in a way. And she's my other best friend. If I have my those two I don't need anything else.

**Q:** Not a girl or two on board?

**A:** (smiles) Now what kind of a question is that?

**Q:** Time for the big Q. As you know, this interview is going to end up on *the big Q* column, so as it's nearing its end, I have to ask you a pretty big question that most of our readers want answered. Ready?

**A:** As I'll ever be.

**Q:** Only real answers accepted, mind you.

**A:** I'll do my best, ma'am.

**Q:** So, here goes. Have you ever been in love?

**A:** Ouch. Are you sure they wouldn't like to know the answer to something more scandalous like I don't know, booze, or snogging or. . . .

**Q:** That's the question the ninety-five per cent of them wanted answered.

**A:** Tough crowd. Then, no.

**Q:** You haven't?

**A:** Not even remotely. I'm not sure I even can, you know?

**Q:** Oh, when the time comes, you surely will be able to... to...

**A:** I've shocked you, haven't I?

**Q:** Oh, no, I mean, well...

**A:** Listen, before you rush off to put it in the title, like "Hollywood actor claims to have a tin heart" or something, let me clarify what I mean. I don't mean physical attraction or a fun weekend aboard the L&H. I don't even mean holding hands or gazing at the stars. I've sort of done all that, but it never was with the right person. There was always something missing. To me, being in love is to not belong to yourself anymore. And in a good way. To belong to her. To care about her, to forget about yourself, to be able to forgive... Yeah. That's what being 'in love' to me means. And, to find a person I'll feel deserves that kind of devotion... to be honest, from what I've seen of the world, I'm not sure it even exists for me.

**Q:** Wow. That's... wow. Thank you so much, Weston, for being here today.

**A:** Pleasure.

## F I V E

"You didn't even ask about life expectancy."

We're driving back in complete silence, and this is my pathetic attempt to lighten the mood. But *pappous* doesn't even flinch.

"No need," he answers simply. Tears are streaming down my cheeks again. He wipes them off with a gnarled finger. "Don't cry, my beautiful Ariadne. It's all going to be fine."

Is it?

You see, I did check life expectancy on the web, along with my symptoms. And that's why I'm crying.

I can remember word for word what Spiros said to *pappou* and me. A chill runs down my spine.

*"After listening to her symptoms and examining her, I was almost sure in my diagnosis of a brain tumor, but we needed the CAT scan to confirm it. I told Ari that she should come in when she was ready, and that's what she did today"*, Spiros' calm voice still rings in my ears.

*Just hold it together until you get home.*

"Don't let Spiros or anyone rush you with the operation," *pappous* tells me as I drop him off outside the *Matchbox*. "You have a career to launch off."

He winks at me and he's gone.

We don't say anything else. We never needed to, the two of us. It's all been said today, and not one word was necessary.

I continue on to Pelekas.

I know what *pappous* was trying to tell me. It's not that he doesn't care.

Far from it.

But what he wanted to tell me—and Spiros—above all, is how strongly he believes I'm going to be fine. That I'll have a life, a career to get back to.

...

What's left of the week passes before I can even begin to think about what to do with the brain thingy issue. Maybe it's because I don't have any major incident like before, although the headaches persist. I'm beginning to get used to them, I think.

That's a temporary solution to say the least, but it's enough of an excuse to put the entire thing out of my mind.

As for the kisses, well, *they*'re not so easy to put out of my mind.

But I do my best.

I wake up every day at dawn and hit the gym, then cool down in the pool. I dive into the deep end, and do forty, fifty lengths without stopping, relishing the calmness and quiet of the early hours of the morning, my body slicing the smooth water evenly, while the sunrise paints the sky pink. Then Coach and Matt join me and training starts. It's pretty merciless, but I enjoy doing this while I wait for my scenes far more than watching thirty takes of Elle try to get her lines right.

Once or twice Wes comes in to talk with Coach and Matt about the stunts he'll be performing, and we train together. Or not really together, just at the same place. He doesn't look my way, and I don't look his—at least I try. He's wearing headphones, and so I don't even know whether he realizes he's not alone. He certainly doesn't act like he does. I catch a glimpse of sculpted pecks and decide that's it, I'm going to pretend he isn't here. So we just work in silence, focusing on the rhythm of our muscles straining, filling up the space with our quick breaths. Thankfully his schedule is pretty packed, so apart from the pool, he rarely shows up to train.

On Wednesday, Katia calls to proudly announce that she's bought a phone—with her own hard-earned money, moonlighting as a waitress at MacDonald's, but we don't talk about how her parents are idiots—and now we can skype any time, any place we want. Which we do.

If things were even slightly better between Wes and me, maybe I'd have sneaked Katia in on my phone at one of the interior shootings and shown him to her, I'm sure she'd have a stroke.

But as it is, I can barely look at him and my heart constricts.

You wouldn't know it from looking at me that I had gotten such devastating news only a few days ago. I act as though there's nothing going on. I go through the motions of normalcy: wake up, shower, train, work, then come back to cook for my dad and watch a movie with him or hang with Katia. Most nights I just fall asleep on the couch—which is something I never did before—but other than that everything is the same.

# LOSE ME.

If my dad notices any difference he doesn't say anything.

My appetite is almost completely gone, but I don't notice having dropped any more weight, so it's all good.

At least that's what I tell myself. Occasionally a friend from school will message me on Facebook or something, and we'll talk for a while. They're all moving on with their lives, some of them in Athens, others in Europe. And that's when I realize that deep down inside I've begun a countdown. I'm already jealous of them; I'm already picturing my future as a void.

I look at everything in my life with hungry eyes, judging if I'll have time to enjoy it again.

The clock is ticking. But as long as I don't think about it, it's silent.

And that's all that matters right now.

Except on Saturday, at midnight, I get a call that changes everything. Again. The call is innocent enough. It's from Matt, who asks me if I can do a car scene rehearsal early tomorrow. He asks politely, as though I have a choice.

I scream an excited yes and dad runs over to see who is strangling me.

Then Coach comes over and dad, Coach and me spend an hour or two eating pizzas and discussing techniques. Actually *they* discuss techniques well into the morning, after sending me to bed at twelve thirty like a baby.

"You'll need your sleep," they both say, nodding knowingly and, after fighting the urge to bang their foreheads together, I obey, yawning.

So Sunday morning, I wake up at four and head to the villa. Matt meets me at the gate and leads me to the car I'm going to use for the stunt. It won't be filmed today, he explains, he just wants to go over my moves and show the cameraman what we're going to do.

I watched a few films with the actual, period Mr. Darcy in them a couple of days ago and I have to say, there's a lot of fast horse riding in them. I guess we'll be doing the equivalent of that.

I step towards the car, and I stop in my tracks, speechless. She's a sleek yellow Ford Mustang 5.0 V8 G. In other words, yum. I get in and my arms break out in goose bumps just from the excitement of being inside this car, after years spent admiring the Mustang's muscle and engine from afar. She just looks so elegant and brawny at the same time, I can't stop staring at her.

*Just imagine steering her, the feel of that impressive body control. Or how those brilliant brakes will grip the road, after I've poured that week-long bonnet into the Corfu sharp bends at speed. Matt, come on, come on, let's go.*

The ignition turns and I feel a thrill as the vibration runs through my legs. Hearing the engine hum is music to my ears.

Matt drives first, to demonstrate what I'll have to do. The car's performance is beyond imagination: easily zero to sixty mph in less than five seconds. I pay close attention to Matt's technique, and then I take over with him in the passenger seat. We head up over the winding ribbon-like road, until we reach the tiny town on the top of the hill. The engine is smooth as silk, and my foot is itching to floor the gas.

We do the same route a couple of times, and then Matt gets out, so I can do it on my own. As soon as I'm ready, volunteers close off the streets with orange cones and I start practicing taking the swift bends of the road. Matt's phone rings at one point and he walks away, giving me the thumbs up as I execute a difficult spiral.

I see him gesturing in frustration through the windshield. He looks at me, shaking his head. "Everything all right?" I ask as he climbs in.

"No," he answers in a clipped tone. "Crazy kid insists on doing his own stunts."

"Wes?"

He nods. "He's on his way; wants to drive the Mustang."

Oh, for crying out loud. Can't he buy himself a million-dollar toy to amuse himself with?

In two minutes Wes' silver BMW skids to a halt beside the cones. He gets out, leaving the door open, and his long legs take him up the steep path towards us in a few strides.

He raises his hand in a bored gesture. Matt sighs deeply.

"Hand it over," Wes says, lowering his sunglasses on his nose. Matt gets out of the car, I stay in the driver's seat.

"You're not trained for this, Spencer," Matt tells him wearily. "Something goes wrong, and you could get hurt." He sounds tired, as though this isn't the first time he's had to deal with something like this.

"Tell her to get out," Wes goes on as though Matt hadn't even spoken. "That's my seat."

"She's a stunt performer," Matt insists patiently, "she will be safer than you. And *she* hasn't been drinking."

Wes shrugs. "Who's been drinking? Relax, would you? I'm not hammered. Not yet, anyway." He winks at Matt, who frowns even more. I roll my eyes. "She can stay if she wants, I don't care. As long as she's in the other seat."

"I'm sorry, kid," Matt says and it's so funny that he calls him 'kid', because he can't be over twenty-eight himself. Wes is twenty or twenty-one, I think,—although he's acting like he's four right now. "Tim's orders."

"Hold on." Wes puts his phone in his ear, and with his other hand he lifts the driver's door and stands there, waiting for me to get out. I ignore him. Or at least I try.

"Hey, Tim, mate," he says into the phone and walks away from the car. After a few seconds he passes the phone to Matt, who lifts his arms up in surrender. Then he runs a hand through his long hair, messing his ponytail, exasperated.

He shouts something into the phone and then he gives it back to Wes, who flashes him a sarcastic smile full of teeth. "One round," Matt shouts, "just one! And I'll be inside the whole time."

Wes ignores him.

"Slide over," he says to me.

I look at him and he nods to me to do it, so I find myself in the next seat. Before Matt has so much as a chance to get near the car, Wes steps on the gas and we're off.

Next thing I know Matt's kicking the dust in the rearview mirror, and we're leaving the white and orange cones behind.

I know Wes practically told me to never speak to him again, but the way he's pushing the gas and taking the steep curves of the road is so wrong. The Mustang doesn't generally *feel* brutally quick thanks to her kerbweight, but that doesn't mean we're not taking the turns at a rapid speed. The sea is sparkling on either side of the road, light blue under the hot sun, and below us the sharp precipice gapes over the edge of the cliff. The road is really narrow and uneven, and Wes clearly has had no training on a terrain like this. I see that he can easily handle the manual six-speeder gearbox, but the engine groans, breaking my heart, and I know he hasn't had as much experience with this kind of machine—a little is not enough when we're going at this speed. He grabs the e-brake, but it's a fraction of a second too late, and the Mustang spins before it rights itself.

A fraction of a second too late can be horribly too late. Damn it.

"Don't step on your break so much," I try to warn him, but he won't listen. "Give it more gas," I say in a minute, and he does, because this time he could see it was getting out of control, but immediately he rights the wheel, the engine's noise dulling to a smooth murmur, and smirks in my general direction.

"Listen, I know you're into driving the Stang, but this isn't the sma—"

"Yeah!" he screams, elated, as he manages a particularly dangerous twist of the road at the speed of practically, well—light. He's not even heard me. "Sweet, huh?" I don't think he's expecting a reply.

He's better than I thought he would be, but I don't know what he'll do if the unexpected happens.

I look sideways at him, wondering if he lied about being drunk.

He doesn't look it, but you can't always tell. I seriously wonder if we're going to die here, on a narrow country road in the mountains of Corfu, the olive trees spreading down the precipice, silvery green, their branches too brittle to catch us if we fall. Another sharp bend almost swallows us, but at the last minute Wes swerves and we're temporarily safe.

Just temporarily though, because in the next twist of the road there's another car coming towards us from the opposite lane.

"Wes!" I yell at the last minute, although Wes has already seen. But there's precious little he can do at this speed.

The freaking moron of a driver has swerved into our lane, going at a break-neck speed, as he or she took the last bend in a stupid, inexperienced way that threw the car out of the curve, and there's no time for them to react.

Wes curses and turns the wheel hard, trying to dodge the other car. In his panic, the other driver loses control and heads directly for us, running us off the road, and Wes frantically tries to steer the other way, but there's nowhere to go. The turn is tight, tighter than most—if you accelerate or step on the brakes before you've rounded, you'll spin out.

"Don't touch the clutch and let off the gas," I gasp and Wes obeys immediately, only it's too late. We're headed for the cliff and he's turning the wheel wrong. We're already skidding out.

I put my hand over his and turn the wheel with force the other way. Wes quickly removes his hand underneath mine, giving me full control.

Without hesitating for a second, I take off my seat belt and jump to the driver's seat, landing sideways on top of him. I grab the steering wheel with both hands and steer it in the direct opposite direction, while my feet find the brakes. My legs are long enough to reach the pedals over his, as I'm seated at the edge of his seat, in front of him. In his panic, he still has the presence of mind to part his knees to give me some room, but it's not easy to move like that, seated on top of him.

I don't have time to think of that, though, as it all happens with so much speed that I barely have time to doubt if I'll make it. I'm doing the best I can, slamming on the breaks and shifting into third, then immediately second. The car corrects itself, but it's sliding left, towards the precipice. I've practiced driving for stunts in even weirder positions than this, with half my body hanging out of the window, but this isn't a stunt. It's real. We're about to either crash into the trees or dive off the cliff; we're dying.

Dust clouds around us as I hear the sickening screech of the tires seeking purchase on the hot asphalt—the GT 'Stang is a dependable car as only a Ford can be—and press my feet down on the pedals with all my strength, putting the car into neutral and lifting the e-brake. I feel the ABS kick in, and not a moment too soon, because the front left wheel is slipping downwards, off the road and into empty space. The cockpit lurches over thin air.

Wes realizes what I'm doing, and he places his hand over mine, his fingers curling over the e-brake. He pulls with all his strength. My head bangs with force against the steering wheel as all movement stops abruptly. Wes' chest rises and falls beneath me; other than that, he's completely immobile. Seated on his lap, I wonder how we should move in order to get out as fast as possible, but without making the car move any more—we could still find ourselves tumbling over the abyss, head over tail.

Do I smell gas? My head is spinning and black spots are dancing in front of my eyes, as though I'm about to pass out. I grit my teeth. *Not now.* I try to swallow, but my lips are dry.

"You all right?" Wes gasps, still in shock.

"Out," I croak. "We have to get out."

"'Kay," he says. "I've got you."

The gaping hole of the precipice yawns right beneath me. Dazed, I feel Wes slowly and carefully move to get me and himself out, keeping an arm around me, just as the car begins to moan and shift.

"Are you with me?" he asks in my ear and I manage to nod. My head hurts, but not from inside, which is a relief. Something warm and liquid glides down my nose and my mouths fills with the metallic scent of blood. That's not such a great relief. "Almost there."

"Quick," I pant.

He grasps my waist and drags me out the door. We roll on the ground and he places a hand behind my head as I tumble on the road, unable to crouch into a safe position. *Okay, we're out, we're safe. That's good.* What's not so good is that I'm so dizzy, I feel like throwing up. The front wheel of the Mustang is still spinning on thin air, somewhere above my head, and it blurs in and out of my vision as I struggle to remain conscious.

"You need to open your eyes, Ari." I hadn't realized I'd closed them. I open them, although that isn't much of an improvement. My vision is turning black. "No, no. No, this can't be happening," Wes' voice sounds frantic. "I'll just get the triangle, hold on. Can you move?" He fumbles in his pocket for his phone.

I try to get up and a sudden wave of nausea overwhelms me. Everything goes blurry and I brace my hands on the hot cement, raising myself on my elbows as I get sick. Wes moves quickly next to me, and turns me on my side so that I don't choke.

"Oh," he breathes. I feel his hands on my hair—they're shaking. "Dammit."

He tries to wipe my mouth before I push his hand away, and brushes the blood-matted hair out of my face, but there's nothing else he can do. Wisely, he doesn't touch my forehead wound, which must be shallow since it's already stopped bleeding.

"What have I done? What have I done?" His voice, hoarse, repeats over my head.

I press my palm to my forehead and moan. "Are you hurt?"

"Not a scratch," he reassures me. "Ari, I'm sorry, so bloody sorry. Are you in too much pain? What can I do?"

"I just need to be still," I murmur, but it's too much effort to talk.

"Okay."

Then he must find his phone, because the next thing I know he's yelling.

"Lee!" he shouts. "Come on, pick up! Hey, listen. No, we were in an accident. I'm fine but she. . . " his voice catches, "she's hurt badly, man. She leapt in front of me. . . she got hurt instead of me. She's bleeding, she's hurt her head. Not in a second, *now*! Do you hear me? Now!"

...

They take us both to the Health Center and it turns out I have a mild concussion and he has a dislocated finger, plus a few bruised ribs. That's what he meant when I asked if he was hurt and he replied 'not a scratch'. *He should have thought of acting brave and tough before driving off the cones like an irresponsible brat*, I think, too exhausted to call him out on it. Plus, he looks pretty freaked out without me pointing out anything. I'm sure he gets it now.

Now that it's almost too late.

Of course the driver who caused the accident has disappeared. No trace. Did he or she even wait to see if we'd get out alive? Matt called the ambulance, the driver didn't even do that.

Wes waits for me at the door as I leave with Coach, who came to get me as soon as I called him, because the doctors said I can't be alone in the next 48 hours in case something happens.

"Ari?" Wes says my name as soon as I walk out the swinging doors. His eyes, haunted, are searching for mine. He sounds so worried, so unsure of himself that all the anger deflates from me. His shirt is torn at the elbow and bloodied, his hair all messy, his eyes tortured. It breaks my heart just to look at him.

He looks worse than I feel, dark circles around his eyes, his hands hidden in his pockets.

"You the one that hurt my little girl?" Coach asks. I wince as I try to suppress a smile. He knows, fully well, who Wes is.

"Yes, sir," Wes almost snaps to attention.

"Not now," I hiss in Coach's ear, but he ignores me. Wes looks utterly defeated, his shoulders drooping. He looks freaked out. But he's not just in shock. He looks legitimately scared. As tough he's out of his depth.

As though there's something seriously wrong.

"They find alcohol in your blood, actor boy?" Coach asks.

I groan. Wes' eyes lift to meet Coach's squarely. His back straightens. "They did not check, sir," he says quietly.

Coach grunts, sounding almost exactly like grandpa. "Do you get the impression," he tells him calmly, as he takes my elbow, steering me towards his jeep, "that if I wanted to hurt you, the fact that you're a billionaire would stop me?"

"I am so sorr—" Wes begins to say, but flinches as Coach takes a step closer to him.

He brings his face close to Wes', who flinches, but stands his ground. Coach's eyes are flashing in contempt. "Obviously you're not sorry enough, or you wouldn't be talking," Coach says in that low, menacing voice, getting in his face. "We can arrange that, jackass."

I can feel his hand on my elbow trembling. Gosh, I hope he doesn't start yelling—

"You almost *killed* her!" Nope. Too late. Coach's neck is roped with veins, his fists clenching. Wes presses his lips together, turning white. "I don't care what you do with your own life, but when you start being an irresponsible ass and put another person in danger, then a simple 'I'm sorry' just doesn't cut it."

"Coach," I murmur, feeling that my endurance has reached its limit.

I mean, I've had my share of dudes thinking that what I do is no big deal, they can compete or join me any time, without putting theirs and my own life in danger. Usually they're morons I can just ignore and they'll leave me alone. But this time... I don't even think it's worth talking about it. Wes Spencer isn't just any guy. He's someone who's used to being the best at everything, having the best of everything. Even worse, he's used to others thinking that he's the best at everything. Without trying. Without actually deserving it, maybe, sometimes. So, to my thinking, there's no use yelling at him. And right now he looks so pathetic that I don't even want to waste the energy it would take to be mad at him.

He's one of those people who get a free pass through life. It's what he does. He gets what he wants, and who cares about the consequences. I was just an idiot to think otherwise for even a second.

I need to get out of here; every bone in my body is hurting. Coach looks at me and frowns, as though he's just remembered I'm here too. He turns to Wes, grabbing his sleeve.

"You better get your act together as long you're working with Ari. Or you'll be walking on crutches for the rest of your life. If you can walk at all." He turns to me. "Come on, sweetheart." He curses under his breath.

Wes stays there, scowling after us.

Coach and I hang at home and when dad comes back we've decided not to let him know all the details of my accident. I just tell him I got concussed—it's not the first time it's happened to me, anyway.

"Not again," he says. "Okay, just rest, and I'll come check up on you. Feel okay?" I nod, then wince.

His eyes grow worried and his gaze travels all over my body. "You've lost weight, Ars?" he asks suddenly and my heart is gripped with terror.

"Um... it's just this shirt, daddy," I say as calmly as I can. "It's a bit too big."

"Hmm," he says, unconvinced, but he doesn't ask again.

At about eleven thirty that night, I'm almost asleep when I get a text alert. Drowsy with sleep, I grab my cell.

You awake?

It's from an unknown number.

Who r u? I type lazily.

It's Wes, wanted to check if you're ok.

I sit up. *Keep it simple, Ari.*

**Me**: fine u?

63

**Wes**: 'Fine' apart from the concussion, right?

**Me**: I'm ok. used to getting hurt

**Wes**: You're used to getting hurt by me?

**Me**: talking abt training and stunts here

**We**: Oh

**Me**: finger ok?

**Wes**: Better than it deserves to be. Look, sorry I'm keeping you up, you were probably sleeping. I wanted to say again how sorry I am.
**Wes**: Also. . .

**Me**: also?

**Wes**: To thank you for saving my life today.

**Me**: it's fine.

**Wes:** Goodnight.

**Me**: hey wait.

A thought has occurred to me, and now that it's planted itself in my head, I can't shake it off. I have to ask.

**Wes:** What?

**Me**: why didn't you defend yourself to Ben? U could have said that a car was headed straight for us, and u had nowhere to go. Why didn't you?
**Wes:** Because it wouldn't have been the truth. I was as much at fault as that other bloke. More so.

That word he wrote, 'bloke', is so British, it looks weird. He mostly talks in an American accent, in front of the cameras and everyone, except for when he's with Ollie or on the phone with one of his friends. And now with me. Kind of. I feel as if a shift is happening, as though I'm forced to look at him as he is. Not Wes the actor. Wes the person.
And to be frank, it's scaring me like nothing ever has.

# LOSE ME.

**Wes**: You there?

**Me**: yeah. thinking I forgot to give ur book back. I read it

**Wes**: You did!!!!! That's brilliant. What did you think??

**Me**: ok, didn't expect so much enthusiasm. . . yeah, loved it actually
**Me**: got bored only once or 2ce

**Wes**: WHAT

**Me**: Just kidding. I'll bring it tmrow

**Wes**: It's yours.
**Wes**: It has a dedication and everything, didn't you see?

**Me**: I did, it also said to be careful and abt yr grandma n stuff

**Wes**: Yeah, that's true. So please take care of it.

**Me**: isn't it a family heirloom or sth?

**Wes**: It is

**Me**: so?

**Wes**: Consider yourself lucky to have it.

**Me**: k

**Wes**: I'm sorry, Ari. I'm sorry.

**Me**: wht 4?

**Wes**: For so much. For almost killing you in the car today. And for what I said the other day.

**Me**: don't worry abt it

**Wes**: I mean it. Am I forgiven?

**Me**: sure

**Wes**: You know what? I sodding hate this. I hate how you say that, as if it's what you expected anyway, me acting like a complete knobhead. I hate that it's official now, that's who I am.

**Me**: Well, did you think it was ok, what you did?

**Wes**: Getting you killed? No, I didn't bleeding think it was ok.

**Me**: You didn't actually get me killed. But I meant, before. Getting into that car, why did that seem like a good idea?

**Wes**: I just needed a rush. . . To escape, you know? To stop feeling caged, to stop suffocating. I wasn't drunk, but I'd drunk enough to be reckless. Enough to not think about what I was doing.

**Me**: Maybe that's the problem.

**Wes**: Of course it is. I mean in the past I've been actually intoxicated and done things that I'm not proud of. The opposite of proud.

**Me:** oh

**Wes:** I don't want to be that person anymore, the person who has to risk his neck or be pissed out of his mind in order to be able to endure his own life. The person people have to be rescued from. I want to be the one who helps, not the one who needs help all the time. I want to be the person I thought I could be the day you almost. . . the day I first met you.
**Wes:** Why am I telling you all this?

**Me**: . . .

**Wes**: You're killing me here, Phelps

**Me**: What do u want me to say? I don't know why ure telling me either. all this talking of killing is making me sleepy

**Wes**: I'll go. One more thing

**Me**: what

**Wes**: Will you help me?

**Me**: with what?

**Wes**: I want to quit.

# LOSE ME.

The breath catches in my throat. What do I write in reply to that? He wants to quit. So does that mean he *does* have a problem with drinking after all? And how do you 'help' someone quit?

I mean, this was the last thing I expected him to say. What do you do when someone lays bare their darkest secret to you? What do you say?

You never imagine a person who would do something like what he did today, someone who acts so arrogant and entitled. . . you don't expect a person like that to just confess that they have a problem.

But why on earth would he want *me* to help him? He doesn't even know me, not really. Maybe he doesn't have anyone else, although that's hard to believe, with that posse of agents and assistants and fans following him everywhere.

Maybe I'm the first person who has made zero excuses for him. Yeah, that actually sounds more than probable.

It's already been a full minute and I haven't texted him back. But his last text. . . That's not something I want to leave unanswered.

Is he even sincere? He might just be reacting to the scare of the crash, although I can't outright ask him that now, can I? What do I do?

**Me:** What do u need me for?

**Wes**: Don't you know?

**Me:** ?

**Wes**: Ari, you're the only genuinely good person I've met. I get it if you don't want anything to do with me though.

What can I say after that?

**Me**: of course I'll help

**Wes**: You will? You're serious?

**Me**: yeah

**Wes**: Just saying, it's not going to be pretty.
**Wes**: Ok, sweet dreams. I'll call you in an hour to check on you, doctor's orders.

**Me**: no need. Coach and dad are here

**Wes**: You wound me.

**Me**: haha  night, Will Darcy

**Wes**: No, you say: night, dude.

**Me**: night, dude

**Wes**: Night, Phelps.

When he calls me exactly an hour later, we only speak for a moment and don't say anything important. His voice, thick and sexy with sleep, melts like honey in the soft darkness of my room. I shiver down to my toes.

He calls again and again, every hour on the dot, until day breaks.

After we hang up for the last time, as the sun is painting my window pink, I wonder if he put his alarm at exactly one hour from his last call. Six times. Then again, maybe he stayed awake all night, thinking. Like me.

What have I gotten myself into?

## crazy planet

### The Lives and Loves

All of you readers of our celebrity blog out there have been craving a little more gossip about our favorite pirate, Wes Spencer, and his lady loves, so I decided to compile a recap for you. The good, the bad and the crazy.

Below is a list of all the ladies he's ever been connected with (that we know of) and if we were like those people who love gossip we would say that his 'real' number is twice as high. But we're not. ;)

### 1. The First Love - Olivia's Kiss

We all remember the sweet on-screen romance between a fifteen-year-old Wes Spencer and a fourteen-year-old Olivia Kiss in the teen drama *Letting Go* and its tragic conclusion when Wes' character, Morgan, was crushed to death in an earthquake. Turns out the two co-stars had started their own romance about three months before that, if the rumors are to be believed.

### 2. The Tristan years - Rachel Teir

Rachel Teir played Tristan's first love interest in the franchise *The Water Wars*, where Wes Spencer played Tristan, the beloved post-apocalyptic pirate who was fighting for his country's survival by providing the people with water in a quickly drying out planet. Teir and he were rumored to have been in a relationship for the first two years of the show. The tabloids were full of photos of them together, they were being photographed everywhere: at red-carpet events, in little bistros in France, in clubs. The relationship ended abruptly when the next love appeared in Spencer's life and if the evil tongues are to be believed, it ended badly. But again, who really knows?

### 3. The girl next door

We never had a name for Spencer's next love. Rumor has it, she was just a waitress, and little else is known about her. The relationship lasted an intense three months, during which Spencer mentioned his intention to retire. *Shudder*

### 4. The older woman - Darla James

Spencer's notorious affair with an older *and* married (although she was talking divorce already at that point, but still) A-list actress swept through the tabloids like a tornado. He was 'her one chance at happiness' (according to sources) and 'the best she ever had'. (We can believe that one.) Why did she blow it then, by reconnecting with her ex-husband a few months into their relationship? Our pirate never looked back.

### 5. The model - T.J. Roberts

Looking at those two together as they strolled the beach in Santa Monica, one wondered which one was the model, Spencer or Roberts. Definitely one of the hottest pairings we've ever seen, this short summer fling made for a couple of really gorgeous photo spreads.

But that's all that it amounted to in the end. When fall came around, Wes and T.J. went their separate ways. They still remain close friends, or so they insist. They are the same age, by the way, in case you were wondering, both twenty at the time of their romantic liaison.

### 6. Triskat - Elle

Maybe someone will disagree with me when I say that Elle Burke is the one true love of Weston Spencer's life. Well, I don't care.

I've said it before and will say it again, I'm team Triskat

forever, and although Tristan and Kat turned out to be star-crossed lovers on the show, they will be my OTP. So will Spencer and Bourke, whose romance started on the set of *TWW* and bled into real life in the space of two months.

We are still holding out for their happily ever after! (It will happen, people. You read it here first.)

### 7. The other woman - Chris Cley

Yep. The popular indie singer and YouTube sensation was the other woman in the perfect relationship between Elle and Wes. Their affair was brief, but enough to send Burke into a Juliette-style meltdown.

Wes came to his senses after seeing pictures of her pale, tear-streaked face plastered all over the media, and although they haven't confirmed it yet, sources say that they've been together since.

That's it for Wes' serious relationships up to now, leaving out the brief affairs or *things* that lasted for a month or less.

So, tell us what you think. Have we forgotten any of the famous loves of Wes Spencer? And who else's love life would you like to see featured on this blog's popular column 'Lives and Loves'?

Answer in the comments below or write us at crazyplanetblog@crazyplanet.net

**Lissa P. Jones**
**for www.crazyplanet.net**

## S I X

A couple of days later, it's time for the dreaded diving sequence. Tim says he will cram it in the same day as Will's love declaration to Lizzie, the first one, the one she rejects. Which basically means he'll have to be in about three million different places at once, but hey, I wouldn't put it past him. We begin early at dawn and shoot until midday.

I dive and climb and swim and dive again and everything seems to be going smoothly, until at around twelve fifteen Tim leans over the villa's balcony and yells at me over the megaphone to get out of the water.

"What did I do wrong?" I ask as soon as I reach the beach, dripping.

He's standing on the terrace, looking down at me. "For once it's not you," he says, his brow furrowing. He's in a black mood today. Lovely.

"Who then?"

"Our golden boy is off his game. Today of all days. He's asked for you. Come on up," he says curtly, nodding to an assistant to get me a robe.

I climb the fifty steps to the villa, then walk through the spacious living-room to step out on the terrace. You can cut the air with a knife in here. Wes is frowning down at Elle, who's seated in a corner, hiccupping, her face bathed in tears. Everything is white, from the marble floors to the décor and the lawn chairs, white and drenched in light, and I feel so out of place, I start backing up with slow steps, when Wes spots me.

"Hey, Phelps is here!" He raises a hand in greeting, his face lighting up.

He's wearing a white button-down with the sleeves rolled up to his elbows, and his hair falls over his forehead in messy blonde curls. Elle is wearing a tight cocktail dress and pumps, but no heavy makeup. They look so good next to each other, like models, exuding glam and perfection. Then I see Wes wince, bringing a hand to his cover eyes. He thinks nobody is looking at him, because everyone is occupied with Elle, fixing her makeup, telling her not to cry; even Tim is bent over her, talking to her with barely held-together gentleness. Maybe I'm the only one who notices Wes take a deep breath and ball his fists, turning his back to the set. Now that I think of it, it's the first time ever I haven't seen him with a drink in his hand. I remember his promise to quit, but he doesn't look in my direction again.

Either way, there isn't anything for me to do here. I'm thinking of leaving, when I see Ollie in the corner. He flashes me a smile and walks straight up to me, giving me a warm hug.

"Hey, what's up?" he asks me, smiling, and grabs a glass of orange juice. He hands it to me and stands beside me as I sip it slowly. "Drink up," he says. "Looks like we'll be here a long time. They've been shooting the same scene since morning; I haven't even started my own scenes. Wes can't. . . " he pauses, looking for the right word.

"Seems that loverboy over there," Tim says helpfully, coming up behind me, "has some trouble delivering his lines in a *believable* manner." He shoots a glare at Wes, who jogs over.

"Have her sit there," Wes says to Tim calmly, "right behind the camera, where she'll be in my line of vision. It will help, I swear. Didn't I deliver my lines perfectly on the first day? Didn't I?"

"It's not the first day anymore, loverboy." Tim drags me to a chair unceremoniously.

"Make up!" he calls, indicating Elle's wet cheeks.

Wes approaches her slowly.

"I'm sorry Elle, it's not your fault," he says in a soft voice, but I'm sitting right next to her so I hear everything. "It's me, okay? The lines, they're just so intense, I need something to distract me. Someone who's not. . . an actor."

My cheeks burn at his last words and I remember that first day I was introduced to him and he called me 'a gaffer'.

"Okay," he yells, not even bothering to check the script. "I'm ready! Action."

"That's my line," Tim says dryly and in a few seconds the cameras are rolling. I just sit there and Ollie drapes his arm lightly on my shoulders and squeezes.

Wes places his hands tenderly on Elle's arms and turns her a bit to the side. "Perfect," he mouths to the camera crew.

Then, shifting his gaze from Elle's face to mine, he begins to speak. His eyes meet mine squarely and I feel acutely out of place, just sitting here in my bikini and robe, salt water drying all over me.

"I think I'm falling in love with you, Lizzie," Wes says softly to me, and in his voice there's hope and fear and excitement and a tiny trace of tears. His face is transformed. "I. . . I didn't plan it, I actually tried to fight it because your family, they're a little. . . well, you know." He flashes her (me) an irresistible grin, but his eyes are serious and intense. "But it's no use. I'm going mad without you, that's the truth. Please save me; you're the only one who can."

His eyes are pleading and my heart almost breaks because tears are rolling down his cheeks for real. How is he *doing* it?

"How dare you!" Elle snaps, her cheek showing red. Wes' face turns wary and ashamed and disappointed all at once.

He swallows. "E—excuse me?" he says, still not taking his eyes off me.

"Are you serious? You insult me and tell me you're falling in love with me all in one sentence! " Elle bursts out, furious.

"Insult you? I only said the truth. . . " he goes all little-boy on her and it's all I can do not to get up from my chair and hug him, because his eyes are still locked with mine.

"You d—Oh, what's my line?" Elle whines, and Tim yells "cut!"

The silence swells for a moment, as we all wait for the verdict, hardly breathing. Finally, Tim speaks. "Spencer, you bloody genius," he says, "it was perrrrrfect!" He falls on Wes, hugging him, and his voice shakes. "You do this to me every time," he complains, "I despise you, you know. Print," he calls to the general direction of the cameras.

Wes, laughing, pats him on the back. "I know," he says, "I know."

Then he lifts a finger to wipe the tears from his cheeks and his gaze meets mine—for real this time. "Thanks," he mouths to me, no sound coming out, and I nod. He turns away, abruptly, his eyes filling with clouds once more.

For some stupid reason I feel like crying, too.

They finish shooting the rest of the scene within the next hour. It's a huge fight, with both of them throwing accusations and insults to each other (great job, Jane Austen, by the way, I read the pages after Mr. Darcy's first proposal to Elizabeth compulsively; I just couldn't believe a classic novel could be so honest and well-worded at the same time. I loved how Lizzie stood up for herself. I think that was the moment when I decided I was proud to be working on an adaptation of this work.) So now I totally get the sparks thing Wes had tried to tell me on that first day, in Drops. The day he kissed me.

He keeps delivering his lines to me, his eyes focused on mine as though we are the only two people in the room, and everything goes great. I hardly move for about an hour and a half, while they repeat the same thing a million times, and then Tim declares the sequence over. Everyone celebrates and there are snacks all around, but I have to continue with the diving.

...

When I get back to the beach, Coach is there, talking animatedly to Matt. After we talk about my moves for a minute, Tim comes down too, and after a bit more talking, we get into the motorboats and head for the Rubble. Three directors, five crew members and me. The cameras will stay on shore, except for two, which are mounted on rafts.

As soon as we reach the rocks, I start climbing, with all of them watching. Lovely.

I dive in and start climbing back up again while the cameras are being set, trying not to feel so nervous now that I've got an audience. Excitement is coursing through my veins, the adrenaline pumping up.

"Ready, Ari?" Matt yells.

Half an hour later and after the fifteenth time that Tim has yelled "again!" from his little boat, I no longer care who's watching.

I'm tired and cold.

I start swimming back to the rocks, and just float for a bit, trying to work up the energy to start climbing again. Coach has left and Matt is watching me from the boat with a look of disapproval in his eyes. I guess I suck so bad that I have to do it over and over again until I get it right.

"Hey," a smooth voice says to me suddenly, as I lean against the Rubble, panting, before my sixteenth climb.

I somehow missed it, but Ollie has gotten in one of the camera crew rafts, and now he's leaning towards me with a conspiratorial smile.

"You okay there? Don't let Tim bully you."

"I'm fine, I won't," I tell him, smiling back.

"Promise?" he says, grabbing my shoulder with a sun-burned hand.

I swallow. "I've got to do this right," I murmur.

"You're already got it perfect from where I'm standing," he says and slides back onto the raft. "Just don't go past your endurance point, okay? Stay safe."

I nod, looking away from his concerned stare. Gosh, I hope he doesn't tell anyone I almost drowned here the other day. I'm sure that's what he was referring to with that 'past your endurance point' thing. I've seen him surf a couple of times this past week, he's really good. But from just being a surfer to cautioning *me* about water sports safety. . . ouch. I perform two more dives, and, after I come up for air the last time, my head starts aching.

Miraculously, Tim says we're done at exactly the moment when I feel I can't go on anymore, so I get out of the water, trying not to let them see how badly I'm shivering, and cursing my body that has become untrustworthy.

"You look beat," Wes tells me with a frown as I lean my hands on my knees, breathing heavily. I hadn't seen him on the beach, so I look up astonished.

"Thanks, I'm good."

"You say it enough times, you'll make me believe it," he answers gruffly.

Then he opens his arms wide, a fluffy towel stretched in them, and wraps me tightly in it, rubbing my arms vigorously.

"I got it, thanks," I say through chattering teeth, and he lets me go. I stumble in the sand, just as Ollie jumps onshore. Behind him, people are dragging the rafts on the sand.

I head for the changing rooms they have quickly set up in one of the rooms of the villa to put on my clothes. No point in asking for a shower, those are just for the actors. There were a lot of extras today as well, so the pandemonium is complete. I leave as soon as I can, looking for my car, but before I've taken two steps, someone blocks my path; Wes' tall frame is in my way. I lift my eyes to his face. The sun is setting behind him, painting his hair golden. His face is in the shadows, but his eyes sparkle as they search mine.

"Have dinner with me?" he says.

"I have a headache," I reply, and he winces.

"Yeah, I know." He takes a step closer, placing a tentative hand on my arm. His fingers are shaking slightly, his touch burning my skin. "Listen."

He sighs, and when he speaks again his voice is rough.

"It doesn't matter if you don't want to tell me what's going on with you. I don't care at this point, all I want is to spend some time with you away from. . . all this," he engulfs the villa and the crew with one gesture. "Besides, Ollie and Anna were talking about grabbing a bite to eat, maybe we can meet them for drinks afterwards, if that will make you more comfortable."

"Ollie?" I perk up.

His expression darkens. "Yeah, fine. So, what do you say?"

What do I say? How long can I be putting this off without looking weird? I mean, he's actually trying to persuade me. I take a deep breath. "Okay."

I must not be very convincing, because the light goes out of his eyes. I hate it when that happens. Especially if it's because of me.

"Ari," he sighs, "is this about Ollie?"

"What?" I squeak.

"I mean, not that you can't hang with both of us, but you

kinda. . . Would you rather it was just him?" He's looking at his shoes.

"No," I stop him. "That's not. . . that's not even a thing."

He raises boyish eyes to mine. "No?" he asks softly.

"No," I say firmly.

"Good," he nods and turns that heart-stopping smile on me again. "So, meet me outside your house in an hour?"

How can I possibly say no to him? "Okay."

"Okay," he repeats.

He runs his thumb along the line of my jaw and leaves.

...

He shows up at my house just as night is descending.

I haven't planned it too much, because after all this isn't a date, we're trying to be friends, right? Right.

I've put on a gray, long-sleeve jersey dress over a pair of leggings and my combat boots. I let my damp hair hang around my shoulders and try not to notice how much my collarbones are protruding.

He's dressed in fitted black jeans, and a simple tee. He's holding a leather jacket in his left hand, and I hope that the night gets chilly enough that I'm going to see him wearing it. His hair is damp like mine.

I open the front door and see him there, his silhouette filling the entrance, and my breath just stops. Whoa. That's a strong reaction to someone I thought was a douche.

Well, a douche who saved my life. And kissed me. Twice. I want to stop fighting this attraction so badly, it's not even funny.

*Keep it together*, I tell myself as I pop a couple of aspirin into my mouth, grabbing my keys on the way out.

He opens his arms wide, lifting his eyebrows. "It's just me," he says. "That okay?"

I open my mouth to answer and I swear, all that comes out is a sigh. Who *is* this girl that I'm becoming? He just smiles, doesn't say anything. Points for that.

"Car's right over. . ." he starts saying, but I interrupt him.

"No cars tonight. I'll take you to the town. You'll see *my* Corfu, not the tourist version, okay? I mean, do you even know what a *kantouni* is? I bet you don't. There's a whole network of them, so narrow your shoulders won't fit. Sounds good?"

"Oh, gosh," he says, laughing, and grabs my hand.

We walk in silence. He's busy taking in his surroundings, and I'm trying and *not* succeeding to pretend that I'm cool and calm like him. Our hands are linked, fingers lightly touching, and I shiver as his touch sends tingles up my skin.

I take him around the promised *kantounia*, where the night is so thick we can't see our hands in front of our faces, and we stumble in the darkness, giggling. There are no cars allowed in the *kantounia*, since they are too narrow to fit a car—some of them are too narrow to even fit a vespa—and so if you're on foot, you can move freely through them.

Lines of laundry, let out to dry, hang in criss-crosses over our heads, from window to window, that's how close the houses are to one another. A tiny square of night-sky peeps from between their terraces, and we crane our necks to catch a glimpse of the heavens. There's absolute silence down here, nothing but the scent of jasmine and the distant crying of a baby from an apartment overhead.

We've climbed quite a few stairs to get here, practically on the highest point of the town.

"I can't take it anymore, Phelps," Wes says at some point. His voice sounds weirdly choked. "My kingdom for a light."

I inhale deeply, lifting my face to the star-studded sky. "Don't you just love this?" I say. "The quiet, the calmness. Time seems to stop. I can't imagine ever being stressed or scared of anything up here."

"I can't imagine ever breathing again," Wes replies in a barely audible voice. I turn to look at him with sudden concern; I can't see squat, of course, but his breath is coming short, ragged. And I know it's not from climbing all these stairs. He sound absolutely miserable.

"I'm sorry, are you claustrophobic?" I say, starting to walk briskly, so that we'll get out in the open as soon as possible.

His steps follow close behind me, and pretty soon he has to walk sideways, because the road is not wide enough for his shoulders. He's probably having the worst time of his life right now.

"No," he answers, surprising me. A full five minutes has passed since I asked him if he was claustrophobic. "Not really. Just being this close to you, in the darkness. . . I can't. . . It's getting bloody hard not to be my usual self."

Oh. So I might be wrong about him having the worst time of his life. My cheeks are flaming red, and I'm so grateful for the darkness.

"Are there no places that are brightly lit and immensely crowded," he continues, "where you keep bumping into people, and can't catch a moment alone?"

"Of course there are, but they're full of tourists; they're loud and. . ."

"Take me there," he says abruptly, "please."

"Fine, be a tourist." I laugh.

We emerge from the narrow streets and take the main road towards the town square. I lead the way to the church with the tall steeple, next to the clock tower, that reaches all the way to the stars. He's not touching my hand anymore, walking a few paces behind me. Swarms of people are promenading down the cobbled road, window-shopping idly (yes, the tourist shops don't close up until the small hours of the morning) and you have to walk at a slow pace, or you'll walk into someone.

"Well, here it is," I start to say, "coming right up: one order of the most crowded, noisy—Oh!"

My eyes nearly pop out of my head as I spot something incredible happening a few paces away from us. "No way!" I practically yell in my excitement. "Come on." Without thinking about it, I grab Wes' hand, dragging him towards the cluster of people gathered on the cobblestones.

"Hey! What are you—?" he protests, but he's laughing, letting me lead him on. Our steps echo in the narrow streets.

We emerge from the crowd at the east side of Corfu's town square. "There it is," I say, as the philharmonic orchestra comes into view.

We walk even closer, stopping by the crowd that's already gathered to watch them play in the middle of the cobblestone square. There are about fifty musicians seated on chairs, under the bare sky, and the maestro is standing on a small crate, head and shoulders above everyone else, brandishing his baton. A poster says they're performing Tchaikovsky's violin concerto in D major.

We stand there for more than half an hour, mesmerized by the swell of the music, watching the musicians sway with the rhythm of the violins and flutes and cellos and percussions.

There's such an intimate kind of beauty in the act of listening to music being created right in front of your eyes, watching the notes fly off of the performers' fingertips, the night enveloping you like a blanket. Wes stands beside me, silent, focused on the music. I lose track of time.

The music swells between us, filling the air like a fragrance.

Finally I look up and see that Wes' eyes are misty. Mine are too, probably. "You okay?"

He squeezes my hand with both of his, rubbing it absently. My skin has turned ice-cold; the night is getting chillier by the second. "What is this place?" he whispers back. "Where have you brought me?"

I smile at the wonder in his voice. "Corfu is one of the word's most musical places. These events happen in Corfu regularly over the summer, here in the centre of the town, as well as in the Old Fortress, in *Benitses*, *Kassiopi*, *Sidari*, all over Corfu. This is the philharmonic orchestra of Corfu's outdoor concert series. Most of the performers are music students at the Ionian University; some professors and a few professional musicians also volunteer. This is their last performance for the summer season, but I didn't know it was today."

The maestro bows deeply and the crowd bursts into applause. A group of teenagers cheer to our left. Wes puts his fingers in his mouth and lets out a fierce whistle.

"What, that's it?" he asks in a minute, as the crowd begins to disperse and the musicians get up, stretching, to start packing up their instruments.

"We've been here for almost three quarters of an hour," I tell him. "You weren't bored or anything?"

"Are you joking?" he retorts. "I can't remember the last time I felt so. . . " his voice trails off and he smiles in that half-mocking way of his. "Happy, I guess." His eyes travel over my face, warmth shining in their green depths. "Or so hungry," he adds in a second. "Aren't you going to feed me?"

"Well, have you tasted *souvlaki* yet?" I say, wrapping my arms around me.

"I beg your pardon?" he replies.

"Oh no," I groan. "Don't tell me you've been on Greek soil for two weeks now, and you haven't tasted our most famous and popular dish? I mean, *dude*."

He bursts out laughing. I don't think I've ever seen him so happy. He sweeps a hand in front of me.

"Lead the way," he says.

"You're not a vegetarian, are you?"

"Nope."

We sit at a little *taverna* that's bathed in the glow of a nearby streetlight, in the quietest corner of the tourist market. You can't see the sea from this angle, but the day's din is dying out all around us and it's really peaceful here.

Wes doesn't even look at the menu, he just gazes at the tall, colorful buildings that surround the street on either side, and then lifts his head towards the stars that are peeping down at us from the night sky.

"Nice?" I ask.

"Yeah, more than nice. Beautiful." He keeps looking at me in this unnerving way that makes me blush furiously.

We're seated below an ancient arch, the marble gleaming white in the moonlight, an olive tree leaning its gnarled branches on the columns, and Wes probably gives himself a crick in the neck staring at it until our waiter arrives.

I order Greek salad and quite a bunch of *souvlakia*, judging from how many my dad usually needs to eat before he's full—five, in his best days. Then I order two sodas and a plate of French fries.

The waiter asks me if we would like to drink wine, and I say no firmly, thankful that Wes can't understand what we're talking about in Greek.

Then we wait.

"So what are you going to make me eat?" Wes asks. "Frog's tails or something?"

"Frogs don't have tails," I say, thinking back on what Elle told me the other day, while I was trying to eat that chicken and she was eating her water.

"Yeah, because you Greeks have eaten them all," he insists, laughing again, and I conclude that he doesn't remember—maybe he wasn't even listening.

"Stop it!" I swat at his hand. "No, *souvlaki* is very simple. It's like a kebab or an Arabic pita, only fluffier, wrapped around a stick filled with tiny pork chops, tomato, sauce and fries."

"A stick?" he asks. "Made of wood?"

"Well, yeah, but they remove the stick, don't worry."

"And what? That's it?! That's the big-deal-meal you're going treat me to, on the first day I'm out in Greece?"

Suddenly I realize that he really hasn't had time to do any sightseeing or even to go out in Corfu, because he's been working all the time. Literally. And before that, who knows how long it's been since he was able to go out somewhere alone, without hordes of paparazzi and fans and bodyguards to protect him?

I lean back, flabbergasted by my discovery.

"What are you thinking?" he frowns, watching me.

"You work harder than... practically anyone I know," I tell him suddenly.

"Yeah, I do," he answers matter-of-factly, "at least for a month or so, while shooting lasts. You do too, actually, you work both on-screen and off. And today, you'd still be working if I hadn't taken Tim to task."

I look at him strangely. He was the reason Tim stopped yelling at me today? I'm not sure that makes me feel too good. I mean, it's gallant and all that, but I wish he hadn't noticed that I needed to be 'rescued' again.

Suddenly I remember his text from last night: *'I want to be the one who helps, not the one who needs help all the time. I want to be the person I thought I could be the day you almost... the day I first met you.'*

If only he knew... I need rescuing on a much larger scale than he'll even know. Maybe I should enjoy it. Maybe I should take this experience of having a guy notice me and want to take care of me, with me as I go under the knife. Oh God. Under the knife. The whole intensity of my situation hits me like a wave and I shudder, the breath catching in my throat.

He notices immediately and drapes his arm around me. "Are you cold?" he asks. "Should we sit inside?" I shake my head but he frowns some more. "You look as though a gust of wind would blow you over. Have you lost weight since I first met you? What...?"

I look down, embarrassed, and he seems to realize this conversation is making me uncomfortable, because he takes his hand away and leans back in his chair lazily.

"So, anyway, you thought of my work schedule while I was asking about the frog's eyes you're going to make me eat why?"

While he's talking, steering the subject away from dangerous waters, he nonchalantly takes his jacket and drapes is across my shoulders. It smells of new leather and Wes, and I thank him with my eyes, because there's a lump in my throat.

"No reason, just..." I reply, turning to hide my blush in the darkness. "You're not at all who you appear to be. Who you think yourself to be."

"And who do I think myself to be?"

"You told me once that I shouldn't trust people like you, Wes. But you're not like Elle and Anna. You're not even like Tim. You're... you."

He shuts his eyes for a second. "Say it again," he whispers.

"You're you?" I say, feeling a little weird repeating it like that.

"No."

"You told me once..." I try again. What, he didn't hear me?

"That's not it, either," he replies, looking away.

Suddenly I get it. "Wes," I say his name again, my voice going wobbly and shy.

"I love the way my name sounds on your lips," he says.

And then the waiter comes out with the food and our moment is interrupted by the fact that Wes' eyes go round with surprise at the colors of the salad and the size of the *souvlakia*.

"You ordered me four of these?" he asks, terrified.

I am already biting into mine. "Try it."

He does.

And that's it. He's in love. I can tell from the way his eyes slide closed with pleasure and the little moaning sounds he makes as he swallows.

"Stop making sex noises while you eat," I murmur after five long minutes of watching him eat with almost ritualistic concentration.

"Ba bon't bake bex boises," he replies around a mouthful, indignant, and swallows with relish. "That being said, I think this might be better than sex."

We eat and talk and laugh the night away.

He is so full by the time we get up to leave that he claims to have no room for dessert, but that lasts only until we turn the corner and he sees the ice-cream vendor slowly making his way through the crowd.

We each get two flavors and try all four of them. He leans forward and takes a bite of my pistachio and strawberry cream cone and all I can think of is his kiss. Those lips fitted around mine, the feel of his tongue against my teeth, his hands messing my hair, sliding to my waist.

A low moan of pleasure interrupts my thoughts and I turn to see him gazing at the ice cream as though he wants to take it to bed. So I tell him he's weird and to stop it.

We're standing in the middle of the famous cobblestone walk that leads from the ancient *Palati* to the town square; it's called *Liston*. On the right bank, it's lined by rows of tall archways of shops and on the left there are little bistros and cafes, lit up with the yellow lights of lanterns and table candles. Right now the only arch above our heads is the velvet night sky and the branches of bougainvillea rustling in the soft breeze.

Wes is holding my hand while devouring his ice cream and talking about how he hated playing Tristan with his mouth full. "It was hell," he says casually around a huge bite of vanilla and cookies. "I signed when I was young and stupid, and depended upon my agent for my fix, but the minute my six-year contract was up, I was out of there. Two days before, to be precise."

"Your fix?" I ask, a chill running down my spine.

He shoots me a hooded look. "Yeah," he shrugs. "Everyone gets into that stuff, in case you didn't know. I just beat most of them in age."

"You were a kid!" I'm trying to get what he's saying. "And. . . it was your *agent* who made you?"

"Well, he had to," he says in his sarcastic way. "Keeping me up at all hours, kissing up to every producer and talk show, smiling like a lunatic. . . There was no way I'd be able to make money for anyone at that age, all I wanted was to play on my PS3. Not to mention I *had* to date every pimply teenager I worked with, from Olivia to Elle, no matter if they got on my nerves or not, because it was good publicity to be photographed with them. No one can do that sober. Hey. . . "

I hadn't realized it, but tears have started coursing down my cheeks. Wes looks shocked. "Don't. . . " he starts saying, but he doesn't know how to continue. His jaw is working. "Don't be sad. I'm sure I was so annoying, I had it coming," he tries to joke, but his voice is rough.

I can't bear to think of him like that, a little kid, lost, everyone taking advantage of him. I take a gulping breath, and turn my head to the wind, so that it'll will dry my cheeks.

"I mean," I say, trying to make my voice sound upbeat, "how could you *do* that? I loooooved Tristan, he was *endgame!*" I make my voice imitate the sing-song tone of my fangirling classmates; it's not hard, I've had to listen to them gush over him for years and years.

And. . . it works.

Wes looks at me with round eyes, as though for a second he's wondering if I've gone crazy. Then his face breaks into a relieved smile and he sighs, attacking what's left of his ice cream.

"Don't you ever say that name in my presence again," he says majestically. "Now, where will we go next? Do you have any other Greek meat-thingies you want to me to try, 'cause I know I said I'm full, but I think I may be up for it, after all."

"I think we've had enough of the meat-thingies for one night," I tell him firmly.

"Okay," he nods. "Then. . . what to you want to do now?"

"Oh, whatever *you* want, Tristan," I start answering and, before the name is out of my mouth, he attacks me.

"That's it! You're dead, Phelps."

He starts tickling me all over and I scream with laughter, and then he has the brilliant idea to start pasting what's left of his dripping ice cream all over my right cheek. I shriek and run away, but I can hear his shoes slapping the paved stones right at my heels, his breath panting in my ear. He's laughing as he runs, but it's not as if that's slowing him down at all. He's almost caught me, when he stops abruptly. I sense him freeze behind him, and I stop running instinctively.

"What—?"

"Oh," Wes says to someone.

I turn around to find Elle's arms draped all over his torso. When did that happen? Did she fall out of the sky, literally on his lap?

He scowls at me. "What are you doing here?" he asks her. "Where's Ollie and Anna? We were supposed to meet them at the pier." He keeps craning his neck, but she's alone.

"Um, Ollie left, silly," she replies, ignoring me completely. "Anna's in the yacht with the other girls, we're all waiting for you."

'The other girls' must be the ones I remember seeing on Wes' yacht that day he fished me from the sea. They're all blurry forms in my mind, the 'bikini girls', but I've recognize a few of them in the group of girls Elle is always walking around with; she's even brought over two of her friends from LA to 'hang out when she's not shooting'. So she could be talking about anyone, basically.

Wes seems to know which girls she means, though, because his expression turns sour.

"Waiting for me?" He looks uncomfortable and I'm fighting the urge to tap my foot. "Why on earth would they—?"

"Come on!" Elle squeals in his ear. "We've been looking all over for you! Where did you hide? Ollie promised us a movie night, only he had to go somewhere. He said you'd fill in for him, no problem. It's almost starting!"

"Look, Elle," he says, raking a hand through his hair, "I'm kind of in the middle of something here. . . "

"Oh hey there, you!" She pretends she's just noticed me. Wes tugs her away, but she walks over to me, smiling that smile that doesn't quite reach her eyes. "How did the puke girl end up in this part of town? What is she doing here?"

She says it as though no one else has the right to be 'in this part of town' except herself and whoever she approves of. She says it as though the very ground belongs to her. I suppose she's used to thinking that way.

But 'puke girl'? I didn't puke that night at Drops, at least not until I got home. Unless she means the time I almost drowned and then threw up water all over the M&M. . .

"Hey, I know!" She turns to Wes. "She should come too, don't you think? She'd love to meet the girls, they're your friends, too—"

Wes grabs her by the waist and whisks her away.

"What are you doing?" He hisses at her. I think I'm going to leave. "Ari, wait!" He calls to me, but he's still looking at her. "I'm not doing this anymore, you understand? I'm so done. Just go."

She pouts. "You promised, Wes. You know I need you, you know how I get when you leave me alone. . ."

Wes steps away from her, and takes a deep breath. "Elle, we've been over this," he tells her in a low, strangled voice. "I'm not doing this anymore."

"Not doing what?" she asks, lifting up her eyes at him. She raises her voice, looking directly at me. "I'm just telling you, we're all waiting for you. If puke girl here—"

"Did you just say 'puke girl'?" I interrupt, taking two steps forward. I tower over Elle's head, and she starts to look scared. "*Twice*? Who do you think you—?"

"I got this," Wes cuts me off. He looks in my general direction, but he doesn't meet my eyes.

I try to give him a chance before storming away, I mean after all he didn't say we were on a date, and acted like a friend and nothing more the whole time, but still. . . What was all the 'say-my-name-again' deal?

# LOSE ME.

"As I was saying," Elle says to Wes, pretending I didn't speak at all, "if *that*'s your only problem, I'm sure she'll be thrilled to come along." She turns to me, swaying a bit. I stare her down, but pretty soon I realize it's no use. Her eyes have that glazed look in them; she's been drinking. "You know, you should totally join in, we've been talking about which of the cast Wes has fooled around with. You can tell us about how he was with you, or even better, maybe he'll give us a demonstration. . . " She giggles, turns to Wes.

He shuts his eyes for a second, clamping his lips.

"I mean, it won't be the first time Wes has had more than one girl w—"

"Elle, come on now." His voice sounds strange, unfamiliar. "Enough."

She juts out a hip and cocks her head. "Oh? What are you going to do to me?" she purrs.

"Nothing. Ari can kick your butt much better than I ever could." He laughs, nodding towards me.

A snort escapes me and Elle turns towards me, her expression going openly hostile.

"What are *you* laughing at?" she hisses at me. "You need to leave us alone."

"*You* need to stop" Wes hisses.

"Oh, I'm not supposed to talk to her now?" She turns to him. "I've got a few things she'd love to hear. Come on, Amy," she says to me. Doing that pretending-I've-forgotten-your-name thing. "Wanna hang out on Spencer's yacht? All the girls are there already, we've got a few stories to tell you about your boyfriend's girlfriends over the years."

I feel my cheeks burning. Wes just clenches his jaw, saying nothing. I can't believe she called him 'my boyfriend' like that, in front of him. I've never been more mortified in my life. I've had enough. I start walking towards her, flexing my muscles. Her mouth hangs open, and she just stands there, looking ready to barf.

"Just stop," Wes mutters, but it's not clear who he's saying it to.

And then, before I even realize what's going on, he moves quickly and gets in front of Elle, blocking her from my sight, his back to me. He says it again, louder:

"Stop talking, okay? Fine, I'll go, come on." It comes out in a rough voice, through gritted teeth. He grabs her arm again, and they walk away. Her steps falter once or twice, but he keeps walking on, almost dragging her along. They disappear into the night, side by side, Elle's heels clack-clacking on the pavement.

He doesn't even turn to look at me as he leaves. I see his hand, clenched tightly in a fist behind his back, his knuckles white, his muscles rippling.

And that's it.

## texts

**Wes**: You're so dead, Binge.

**Ollie**: what d I do now?

**Wes**: Why did you have to go and set El loose on me?

**Ollie**: didn't set anything, I'm at *Roda*.

**Wes**: WTH is *Roda*?

**Ollie**: It's a wicked beach in the north

**Wes**: Been sightseeing, have we?

**Ollie**: is there any reason why I shouldn't?

**Wes**: Don't know, maybe the fact that you'd said we could meet for drinks tonight?

**Ollie**: Dude I told you, I'm not doing that w you anymore.

**Wes**: It wouldn't be just me. Ari, too. You'd want to have drinks with her, I'd bet. Oh, and according to El, you'd promised her and the 'girls' that you'd spend the night on the L&H, watching movies. . . ? Ring any bells?

**Ollie**: Oh maan.

**Wes**: Yep. So I'm in here now with them.

**Ollie**: nonononono hahaha

**Wes**: Don't laugh, man, you ruined my life.

**Ollie**: LOLOLOLOLOL

**Wes**: They came looking for me Ols. She. . . I was in the middle of something.

**Ollie**: I'm intrigued now, Darce

# LOSE ME.

**Wes**: SOS

**Ollie**: what or may I say, whom, were you doing?

**Wes**: Seriously. Save me.

**Ollie**: soz, man. My bad. My ride is not going anywhere for at least eight hrs. . .

**Wes**: Why?

**Ollie**: cause right now she's on her eleventh vodka

**Wes**: *She?!* Oh, you're definitely dead. Who is she?

**Ollie**: Can't remember her name rn. But she's cute. Kinda. Not yr type.

**Wes**: Get serious for a sec, what do I do now? HELP

**Ollie**: I'm really sorry. I messed up big time.

**Wes**: I thought we had specifically spoken about this, about me and El. I'm not doing this anymore. I won't have her dragging me into her drama, threatening to take pills if I don't do what she says and

**Ollie**: Not again.

**Wes**: Yes, again. Wanted to tell her to eff off, but Ari was there and she has a low enough opinion of me already.
**Wes**: You were supposed to save me.

**Ollie**: I know, I know, I know, sorry sorry sorry. Tell them u need to sleep, they'll leave.

**Wes**: Yeah, right. She kept insinuating that there were ex-girlfriends of mine on the boat. It was disgusting. And now she keeps staring at me. Two of the extras she's invited are staring as well. I hate this.

**Ollie**: u didn't always hate it

**Wes**: Always hated it, just didn't know I did until now. Have any ideas?

**Ollie**: Dunno, just say you want to be alone w one of the girls. That'll empty the boat fast, and get Elle off your back.

**Wes**: I don't want to do that.

**Ollie**: Not like you've never done it before.

**Wes**: I don't want to do it now, though, ok?

**Ollie**: Dude, I know you. Shouldn't be too hard.

**Wes**: Know what? You just shut up, Ollie. Shut up, ok? I mean it.

# S E V E N

I wake up on the floor.

I lift my head off the cool linoleum and gaze dazedly about. The darkness is complete; it must be the middle of the night. A wave of nausea hits me before I've even opened my eyes properly and I make it to the bathroom just in time.

Dad comes rushing when he hears me being sick, but I wave if off as a stomach bug.

Now I'm actively lying to him. Great.

He goes downstairs to help *pappou* and *yiayia* close the shop, his frown still in place. I go back to my room and lay down on my bed, closing my eyes. I feel the tears roll down my cheeks and wipe them angrily away. As I expected, grandpa comes racing up as soon as he hears the news about the 'stomach bug'.

"How is my little *kouklitsa*?" he asks me, calling me a little doll in Greek, but his eyes are sad.

I just stare up at him and begin to cry in dry, wrecking sobs.

He grabs a chair and sits next to my bed. He takes my hand in his calloused ones and we cry together. Neither of us says anything. There's no need.

"*Yiayia* is going to cook you some soup, all right?" he tells me as he leaves, wiping his eyes.

I just nod. I can't speak, I'm so exhausted.

Dad comes up to kiss me goodnight, his eyes scared and his lips grim. That's what I hate most about this whole thing. I decide I'll wait one more day before telling him. I don't have the energy for it right now.

He sits with me and we talk nonsense until my eyelids droop and then he shuts the door softly behind him. Still, I can't fall asleep. I keep thinking of Wes.

And of *her*. Will she even care when it happens?

I'm so pathetic.

At twelve thirty my phone beeps. I pick it up from my nightstand and flick it open lazily, expecting a text from Katia. And. . . it's Wes.

**Wes**: Is there anything I can say to explain my behavior to you today?

I have half a mind to ignore him, but only half. The other half is already typing.

**Me**: Is there? Let's see

**Wes**: Ah, you're mad.
**Wes**: Listen, I just needed to get her away from. . . From you. That's all I could focus on.

**Me**:...

**Wes**: Ari, dammit, I'm so sorry I left you there. It kinda. . . It gutted me to leave you and go with her.

**Me**: then why did u?

**Wes**: I panicked, Ari. Didn't know what to. . . I've never had to deal with someone good coming into the mess of my life. And I blew it.
**Wes**: I just wanted to get her away from you, she. . .She wouldn't have budged until she'd destroyed everything. She was saying all this stupid stuff about me in front of you, I couldn't stand it. She has a history of ruining things for me when I'm into a girl. I mean, back then in Drops, with your drink. . . I knew it was my fault in a way, because of that time on the L&H, when you almost. . . when I was so worried about you. She was there, she saw that. In the past, she's gone to great lengths, even threatening suicide and other messed-up stuff to get me to do what she wants. To keep me close to her.

**Me**: . . .

**Wes**: And then the other day at the shoot we were eating and I just wanted to sit next to you and she said those vile things. I can't even think about what she said, and she can do worse. She'll start telling you things about me that would make you hate me.

**Me**: …

**Wes**: It was bloody stupid to just walk away, I know, but I didn't want her to think I cared about you. She started saying stuff about me and I couldn't stand it. I couldn't let her say anything else. I had to get her out of your face.

**Me**: is that for real?

**Wes**: You don't believe me?

**Me**: having a hard time

**Wes**: You have no reason to trust me, do you? Except the fact that I'm always apologizing, I've got nothing going for me here. I actually think you might hate me.

**Me**: I don't hate u

**Wes**: But?

**Me**: but can I trust u?

**Wes**: Yes.
**Wes**: Yes.
**Wes**: Yes.

**Me**: k

**Wes**: You really mean that?
**Wes**: Just so you know, what she said, about me and all these girls, she was exaggerating, it's not true, not all of it, she

**Me**: Stop. That's none of my business

**Wes**: I want it to be your business.

I don't know what to type in response to that, so I don't write anything. Ten minutes pass. I pick my phone up again.

**Me**: Wes? U there?

**Wes**: Yep.

**Me**: is what u said b4 true?

# LOSE ME.

**Wes**: ?

**Me**: r u

**Wes**: Am I what?

**Me**: r u. . . into me?

**Wes**: Hell, yeah.

**Me**: I thought u said u wanted to be friends.

**Wes**: Yeah, that too.
**Wes**: So, what do you say?

**Me**: k

**Wes**: Would you stop it with that k already

**Me**: I'll try

**Wes**: It's so confusing, you know? What did it mean? Was that 'k, we'll be friends', 'k, I like that you're into me' or 'k, you're a bit of a jerk, and I'll say whatever you want so I can get rid of you'?

I can't help it; I burst out laughing. Overthinking much? Not that I'm not doing the same. Darn it.

**Me**: just ok, we're cool

**Wes**: In that case will you spend some time with me tomorrow?
**Wes**: Please?

**Me**: u don't have to make it up to me.

**Wes**: So no?

**Me**: so I'll think abt it.

**Wes**: Great! Pick u up at 8, your place.

**Me**: 8 in the evening? And I haven't said yes yet

**Wes**: 8 in the morning, Phelps. There are only 24 hours in a day, and not nearly enough.

**Me**: enough 4 what?

**Wes**: You'll see

**Me**: listen, Wes, u're a great guy, but

**Wes**: No.
**Wes**: nonononononononono
**Wes**: I'm leaving before you say anything else.

**Me**: I don't have time 4 a summer. . . thing

**Wes**: Me neither. Besides, it's not summer.

**Me**: Wes, srsly

**Wes**: I know. Look, you'll tell me everything you need to tomorrow. I promise I'll listen to you. I just need to see you, to get to know you. I shouldn't have said that I was into you, I don't want to scare you, so forget it, would you?

**Me**: I'll forget it if that's what u want, but. . . already halfway there, if u must know

**Wes**:. . .
**Wes**:. . .
**Wes**:. . .

**Me**: aren't u gonna say anything?

**Wes**: c u tomorrow.

**Me**: that all?

**Wes**: Have u read page 133 yet?

**Me**: yeah, but I don't remember what it said.

**Wes**: Well, read it again. There's something you need to know in there.

**Me**: fine. Goodnight.

# LOSE ME.

**Wes**: Night, baby. x

*He sent me a kiss* is what I think over and over again until I finally fall asleep.

...

When I wake up the next day, my headache is worse.

I call Wes to tell him not to come and his voice sounds all happy and out-of-breath as he picks up.

"Can't wait to see me, huh?" he says. "I'm outside."

"And I'm sick," I tell him.

"Open your door, would you?" he replies, unabated. "I can't find where to ring."

So I get up in my pajama shorts and spaghetti strap top to buzz him in. I can't even think about how my hair looks. I go to the bathroom to splash some water on my face and I find a note from dad telling me to stay in and that grandpa and grandma will be checking in on me, and also to '*CALL him immediately if I feel WORSE*'. And hugs.

Then I almost pass out again, so I drag myself to my room, hands leaning heavily on the walls as I walk, worried that I'll stumble and fall. I flop back onto the bed, gasping in pain.

And that's the precise moment Wes chooses to walk in the door, calling my name, as though he's been looking for me through the various rooms of our apartment. Perfect.

"What's wrong?" he asks.

"Stomach bug," I whisper, not daring to look up to him. I look—and feel—a mess. No need to see the expression of disgust on his face. "Sorry," I add, trying to sound normal. "You should go."

"Um... could I stay for a sec?" he sounds embarrassed, as though he's worried that I don't want him here. Which is ridiculous, isn't it?

"Sure," I say, turning my head away from the sun streaming from the window. "Grab whatever you want from the kitchen, if you haven't had breakfast."

"Thanks," he replies, but his voice sounds rough. "Wait here," he adds in a moment, placing a hand on my back. He gets up.

A second later I hear the window-shutters bang on the wall and blessed darkness envelopes me like a blanket. Wes moves the ancient ventilator slightly at an angle, so that it will keep me cool but not cold, and starts looking around him with curiosity.

My room is small and plain, its walls painted a light green, old-fashioned windows that overlook the back yard of the building block.

Ever since I finished school, all that's on my desk is my laptop, my phone charger, and a notebook, where I keep a journal—it's not even that, per se. It's just that sometimes I need to write my thoughts down in order to process them. I used to write in it a lot when I was little and missed having a mom; I haven't written anything for ages. I never let anyone touch it.

Other than that, my room is pretty uncluttered. I don't like to have things scattered around; all my clothes are put away in the wooden closet, and there's a small office chair with wheels for my desk—the chair is currently next to my bed, where dad left it last night. There's nothing else in my room right now, except for a tall, gorgeous pirate and the smell of my fear.

Wes steps close to my desk, and starts ruffling through my notebook.

"No, don't touch tha—," I start saying as another pain doubles me in two and cuts my phrase short. He's immediately by my side.

"Ari? Hey. . . " He keeps talking to me until the wave of pain passes. I swallow the nausea following it, and lean weakly back on the pillow.

"Just go," I tell him.

"What can I do?"

His voice is pleading and cracking, and I hate the pain I hear in it, but unless he's a highly-qualified brain surgeon, I don't know what to tell him. Those damned tears start to fall again.

I have no idea what to say. I moan softly, the sound muffled by my pillow and his hands are in my hair, on my neck, supporting me.

"That bad?" he asks tightly. I start to answer, but another stab of pain steals my breath. "Breathe for me," he murmurs. "That's it, you'll be fine in a minute."

He's right. It does pass in a minute.

He stays with me for hours.

At some point grandma comes with soup and freshly baked bread and he greets her politely. She proceeds to stand by my bed, and give him the history of our island in a jumble of Greek and English, the bits she's picked up over the years. I'm sure he doesn't understand most of what she's saying, but he keeps nodding and gazing at her intensely.

Greek people do that, by the way.

They'll stop tourists in the middle of the street and try to give them the ancient historical roots of the place they're standing on, whether they're interested or not. (Usually they are). If you ask a few questions, show a bit of knowledge of the ancient Greek history and philosophy, they'll invite you into their home for lunch. That's just how we are.

Grandma's wearing her apron. Knowing her, she must have just finished cooking and immediately brought the soup up to me, not taking the time even to take her apron off. Her hair is combed in short curls, and her eyes are shining with kindness as she tries to explain to Wes that our island was the home of Homer's Ulysses.

I steal a glance at Wes' face as she's talking animatedly to him. He's towering above her, ridiculously tall and fit next to her short, plump form, but he doesn't look bored. He actually looks interested. Maybe not in what grandma's actually trying to say to him; in her. I don't think he's ever met anyone like her in his entire life.

I try to stop her around the second world war, but Wes shushes me.

The guy actually *shushes* me. I mean, he doesn't even turn to look at me, just gestures at my general direction with his hand, and wheels the chair in front of grandma.

"Please sit down," he tells her and she does, with a long-suffering, I've-been-on-my-feet-all-day sigh.

"Where was I?" she asks him in English.

"Mussolini," he replies immediately. Satisfied that he's following, she continues. How he picked up that name among her torrent of Greek words, I can't even imagine.

Eventually she goes away, leaving me almost dead from embarrassment, but he stays.

For a couple of hours I'm better and we talk, then when I'm worse he takes out his phone and shows me photos of his family and childhood—his actual one, not his Tristan one. He looks so different when he's not on screen, his eyes smiling for real, but still there's a sadness there, an emptiness that tears my heart in two. He talks to me about his one-eared Labrador, Hook, whom he rescued off the streets three years ago and I ask him if he misses him and he winces.

We don't talk about what happened last night, although he tries to open the subject once or twice. I steer him away from it. I don't care right now. All I need is to feel him near me, to savor these moments for as long as I can, with no darkness threatening to interrupt them.

Then I must fall asleep, because the next thing I know it's dusk and soft voices speak over my head. The one is his and the other is dad's. I open my eyes and look at them, chatting like old friends, and declare that I feel much better.

Dad goes out to get groceries, and I get up and head for the bathroom, hoping to make myself look somewhat human.

I'm standing in front of the mirror, trying to drag a comb through my beehive and fighting back tears at the sudden realization that I look *gaunt*, when a sudden wave of dizziness knocks me to my knees. *Ouch.* That's going to hurt tomorrow. A searing pain shoots up my thighs.

"Ari?" Wes yells from the hallway, and I hear his shoes thudding on the floorboards as he runs through the hall. "Ar—"

I turn blindly for the toilet as a violent wave of sickness shakes me and I start retching—there's nothing left in my stomach to come up. Strong hands, *his* hands, grab my back and hold me close, as his voice murmurs soothing nothings in my ear.

Through the spasms of retching I feel his chest heaving against my back, and I wonder if he's panting. His hand is on the back of my neck, sending warmth through my thin top to my chilled skin. Then I feel his fingers on my hair, wiping the cold sweat from my forehead.

"It's o-o. . . " I try to tell him it's ok, but I can't catch my breath.

"Come on." He slides an arm around my shoulders and helps me stand. His height dwarfs the entire bathroom; his rapid heartbeat drums against my clammy cheek.

"I mi-might be sick," I say through clenched teeth.

"You can be sick all over me for all I care," he says fiercely and walks to my room.

He lies on the bed beside me and holds me against his body until the shaking subsides. He glides his hand across my back in a continuous, comforting motion, until I emerge from the blackness, gasping and sweating.

My dad comes in after a while and Wes gets out of my room as dad helps me change the bedclothes and wipe the sweat off my skin, like he used to do when I was five years old and crying for a mommy who would never show up.

"Are you running a temperature?" he asks, worried, but I'm too scared to check.

"I don't feel like I am," I tell him.

He makes me eat something and Wes comes back into the room, looking pale.

"Hey," he smiles at me.

"Hey" I say. "Sorry for before."

He shakes his head and I scoot to the side of the bed in case he wants to lie down next to me again. He chuckles, his laugh low and sexy.

"I'd better not," he says. "It was far too painful before, if you know what I mean?"

Suddenly I do, and I cover my head with my pillow.

I feel his weight on the mattress as he climbs on top of me, his knees sinking into the mattress on either side of my hips. He pries the pillow away. His green eyes are focused on mine.

"You know what you do to me," he says slowly. "That day when you were... that day in the hotel, and I came into the shower to help you... I could barely stand it in there with you, holding you, touching you. It was... I nearly went crazy. And the other day, when you were holding my hand and we were walking in those bloody claustrophobic alleys..."

"Do you mean the *kantounia*?"

"Your whole leg was pressed against me at one point, it was pure torture, I could scarcely breathe."

He's still looking down at me, his eyes never leaving mine. I can't believe what he's saying to me. I remember when I first met him, I kept thinking of how he must be used to just having anything he wants, the moment he wants it; how he looks down on everyone as though they're inferior to him.

I swallow.

"Why are you still here?" I ask him.

"Because you're here," he says simply. "Where else would I be?"

"What about the shoot?"

"I have today off," he explains, raising himself off me. "I had an important date with a kick-ass stunt girl—"

"Which I ruined," I interrupt him.

He looks at me, his gaze intense as fire.

"Except for your pain," he says slowly, "I wouldn't change a thing."

...

He's still there when I wake up the next morning, looking all kinds of gorgeous, his hair a disheveled mop, his eyes tired, as though he fell asleep in my chair. He stretches painfully as he gets up, but he smiles at me like he hasn't seen a more wonderful sight than my serious bed hair.

"Could you give me two days?" I say quietly, after we have both visited the bathroom.

He gets what I'm asking him. He looks at me searchingly, and I know he sees right through me. I know he understands that I'm pushing him away for some reason, he just can't imagine what that might be.

"No." He says it with finality in his voice, an authority I've never heard before. "No," he repeats more fiercely. I hate the naked pain in his voice.

*I don't want you to watch me dying*, I tell him silently.

"Please," I say aloud.

"Ari. . . " he runs a hand through his hair, messing it up even more. "Tell me how I'm supposed to survive two days without you. I can't. . . I'll start being the old Wes again if you're not there."

For a moment I say nothing, savoring his words as they wash over me. And then, out of nowhere, the words come out of my mouth.

"Do you pray?"

"Like what, to God?" he asks, uncertainly.

I nod. Where am I going with this? I have no clue.

"Nope," he answers.

"Do you believe in God?" I ask him.

"I guess I do," he answers, frowning. "I've never really thought about it, actually. But I hear a lot of Greeks are very religious people, so you must. . . "

"No," I tell him. "I'm not like that, I've hardly been inside a church my entire life, but. . . "

"Yes?"

"I somehow feel like I need it right now. I feel like I need you to do it for me."

"Okay," he says simply.

I let out a breath. Won't he ask for an explanation again? But he doesn't. He just lifts a hand to my hair, looking down at my lips, his eyes half-closed. "I just. . . I can't figure you out, you know?" His voice is quiet, as though he's thinking out loud, and he's looking at me like I'm a puzzle he wants to solve. "*I can't make out your character*."

"What?"

"It's an Elizabeth Bennet quote. From Pride and Prejudice," he ducks his head down, smiling ruefully.

"*I am most seriously displeased*," I retort.

Now it's his eyes that fly to my face, surprised. "Excuse me?"

"Sorry, it's the only line I remember. It's from Lady Catherine. . . "

". . . de Bourgh, yeah," he finishes for me. "Hold on, you read the entire novel, and *that's* the only line you remember?"

"Yep," I reply, tucking a strand of hair behind my ear. "She's my favorite character, she's badass, man. I watched all of her scenes twice in the BBC adaptation. At the last scene when she visits that Elizabeth chick and just sits there, looking superior, clutching her cane. . . goals."

He throws his head back and laughs. Moments tickle by and he can't stop, clutching his chest. He falls on the bed, trying to catch his breath, wiping his eyes.

Finally he looks at me, and the laughter dies from his eyes. The breath leaves his body. "Ari." He gets up and comes over to stand next to me. "What's going on in that head of yours?"

*Well, wouldn't we all freaking love to know?* My eyes start stinging again. *You're not going to cry anymore today, Ari.* I grit my teeth. He looks confused as hell. Poor guy.

"So you'll try it?" I persist, not knowing how else to answer him.

"You mean, what you said before. . . ?"

"Yes. Pray for me, will you?"

"I will," he says quietly. His eyes widen, and I see that he's beginning to grasp the implications of what I'm asking him. "What's going. . . ?" his eyes narrow. "You know what, you'll tell me in your own time. Right now, I'd try to bring you the moon if you asked for it."

He laughs in that self-deprecating way of his and lifts a finger to my chin, leaning down to look into my eyes. "I am completely under your spell," he says, in a tone that's half mocking, half serious, his voice husky with desire.

I just stare at him. What do I say in answer to that?

"So, I'll try to pray for you, Ari, if that's what you need," he goes on. "I don't know how, but I'll figure it out." He kisses me lightly on the cheek, presses his eyes shut and leans for a second against me. Then he's gone.

. . .

I sleep in for the rest of the day, but surprisingly I don't get even one phone call by Tim or Matt yelling at me to come back to work. I get about a million calls from Katia though, who sounds, and looks, really worried. I try to reassure her, all the time thinking to myself, *great, another person I'm hurting and lying to.*

This can't go on.

Dad wakes me when he comes back from school, relieved that I look better. "Dad, we need to talk," I tell him, trying to breathe beyond the catch of tears in my throat.

"What is it, honey?" he asks me.

I take a deep breath and tell him.

"No," he says immediately.

Then he starts crying.

96

My heart is in pieces.

After another nap—I'm like a freaking 90-year-old, I swear—I wake up to find him still sitting beside me, his mouth set, his eyes full of fear and pain.

He has a thin stubble on his chin, his brown hair, matching mine in shade exactly, messy and wild. "How are you feeling?" he asks me, wary.

"Like always," I answer. "Rested, fine. Don't start with the questions, okay?"

"What are you going to do?" he asks, nodding.

I sigh as I get up. "I'm going to wait until the last moment," I say, looking at him squarely in the eye.

"Yes, but, honey, is that wise?" he says. "I mean, this operation might save your life, isn't that what the doctor said? What if you get worse? What if the operation shows that the. . . " he struggles to pronounce the word, "what if it shows the tumor was not malignant after all?"

I swallow.

Is this real? Is it happening?

It is. It is.

"What if the operation kills me?" I whisper, and he nods, sobs wracking his body as he lowers his face to his hands.

## truth or dare

Ok, Binge, you won this round of 'truth or dare' fair and square.

First of all, I would like to go over EXACTLY what happened, so that future generations can see how you TRICKED and MANIPULATED me into this.

OK.

(You also said that you want it written on actual paper, so that you can blackmail me. I say fine, I lost fair and square. We'll see what happens in the next round. I also say you're an idiot, but I say that ten times a day, so what.)

Here's what happened:

We're shooting a bromance scene between Will and Binge, and we're almost done when you, as always bored out of your tiny mind, get it into your stupid head to dare me to scratch my head and cry like Stan Laurel when the cameras started rolling.

In front of Tim and everyone. You dare me to start crying and scratching my head. Okay. So, naturally, I say no. You get that evil smile on your face and tell me that I'll hate the penalty, I still say no. I'd have done it though, if I knew what losing would mean.

Then we drive to a surfing beach in Lefkimi and on the way you announce me the penalty. I'm to shoot a remake of a Laurel and Hardy bit, with <u>you</u> no less, and upload it to YouTube. You also said I get to pick up to ten sketches, write them down, and you'll decide which one  we'll recreate. Well, how bloody generous of you.

Don't think there won't be retaliation; cause there will. Oh, and since you stupidly decided that we're in this together, although it was my penalty, and you could have walked away, but you didn't, I'll make you suffer as much as possible.

Right. So here is a list of potential—mind you, <u>potential</u>—**Laurel and Hardy** sketches that I would be considering to recreate with you.

Just remember the rules.

You can choose ONE of them, and you'll have to participate. Also, I have two vetoes. That's TWO.

Oh, and about uploading it on YouTube like you said, yeah. Dream on.

So, here is my list, and in case you didn't notice, this is a leaf torn out of a bleeding notebook, it's hand-written and I don't have digital back-up. So, for Pete's sake, DON'T LOSE IT.

1. **Pardon Us** - the scene where the boys are taken to jail and Stan's lose tooth keeps buzzing as he talks to the officer. I'd be Stan, of course. Naturally. (Not that you're fat or anything, still, your name is Ollie after all. . . Hmm, maybe I'll start calling you Babe, like people used to call Oliver Hardy. Just a thought.)

2. **The Finishing Touch** - the scene where Ollie puts ten nails in his mouth in order to start nailing them to a wall, and then Stan steps on his foot and he swallows them all. (Real nails included in the actual performance, I insist. Babe. Dude.)

3. **Our wife** - the whole abduction scene, climbing from the window with a tiny suitcase and trying to jam the buxom lady into a tiny Volkswagen, it's not that long. (And Anna plays the wife, in a fat suit.)

4. **Berth Marks** - now I admit, that sketch is pure gold. Good old stand-up. Pure, grab-your-stomach can't-breathe tears-streaming-down-your-face laughing. I'd love to do this. Climbing in and out of two tiny train berths, wearing pajamas. Now that's art.

5. **Another Nice Mess** - the piano scene. Nuff said. (You'll provide the piano.)

# LOSE ME.

6. **You're Darn Tootin'** - now this we should handle with care. We wouldn't want a photo of us both inside a massive bloke's pants, walking in step, tipping off our hats (like the boys do in the last scene of that film) circulating the media, would we? It's their most famous pic to date. It won't be ours, though. It won't. (One can only hope.) Well, anyway, this is one of my picks. That's right. I play dirty.

7. **County Hospital** - all of it. You as Babe with a cast on your leg and me as Stan, trying to drive you home while I'm doped up on anesthetic, well. . . need I say more, good sir?

8. **Beau Hunks** - yep. My favorite. I'd be willing to let you butcher it, just as long as I can feast my eyes on the sight of you sighing over the photograph of a devil-woman, and then enrolling yourself to the desert soldiers. (There's no way I'm touching your boots though to clean them, as Oliver does in the film, not from a mile away. Let's be realistic here.)

Ok, so that's it. Get crackin'.


P.S. I'm never playing truth or dare with you again, I swear. I mean, Babe. You're one evil dude.

P.P.S. hahaha 'Babe' hahahahahahahahahaha

P.P.P.S. I'm going to make you watch my entire golden collector's edition of the works of Laurel & Hardy right after Ari is done shooting her underwater sequence. Oh, and she's invited too. (hope she wants to hang out with us sorry lot.)

Cheers, 'Babe'.

Signed
WESTON SPENCER




# E I G H T

I go back to work a day later, feeling almost normal.

Almost being the key word here.

I spend practically the entire day with Coach at his home gym and he tries his best to get me back in shape—as in, he tortures me for eight hours straight. He keeps stealing these weird glances at me, as though he's wondering how a simple stomach bug could leave me so worn out.

Anyway, we do our best, and by the end of the day I tell him I feel a bit more energized. The truth is I feel tired and sick and scared.

"Glad to hear it," Coach says with a look that tells me he isn't buying it, and we take it to the pool.

...

The next morning I'm one of the first in the yellow villa, but Tim's assistant immediately whisks me off to a beach somewhere in the south.

"This is what you've got to do," he says, and gestures for Matt to take over.

I'm already dressed in the white bikini that looks like Elle's, and warmed up, but as I stand there, listening to Matt explain to me what I will have to do, I feel a frown coming on my face. The beach around us is deserted, and it's a little chilly today, but the sun is shining in the sky, peeking between the clouds. I hate this in-between weather, but that's not why I've got that sinking feeling in my stomach. I wrap my arms around my waist.

"You've got this," Matt tells me with confidence. "You've got this."

*Do I?*

I turn to gaze out into the sea. Crew members have already installed a huge, and I do mean *huge*, plastic tube in the water, supported by a frame of metallic beams, invisible from the surface. All I can see is a light, rubber structure—right now, only the top half of it is visible above the surface, rising about five feet in the air and forming a round shape like a half-ellipse. It's bright orange and scary and there are divers and waterbikes with divers bobbing on the waves beside it. The scene is surreal.

Or maybe *scary* would be a better word.

The camera crew is already heading out to the water and it suddenly hits me that within minutes I'll be in there, too, performing. Being filmed.

Yes, definitely scary.

Coach and I have trained endlessly for this sequence, of course, but this is the first time I'll be working with this equipment. And they'll be filming me, too.

I can't even begin to think how much equipment like that may have cost. The mere sight of it is intimidating. I mean, I've done flyboard stuff before—it was *the* single most exciting stunt thing of my life, by the way; it's a combination of flying and surfing, as well as skateboarding, in a way. I can't wait to try it with all this equipment. But this. . . this is going to be a legit massive-scale underwater sequence with no more than three to four cuts, and it's freaking intimidating.

Matt sees me freaking out and puts a hand on my shoulder. He is seriously the coolest dude I've ever met. Calmness is exuding his every move, he doesn't even look nervous. "I'll guide you through it."

Here we go.

# LOSE ME.

Today is Fake Dolphin Day.

Or, actually, rubber dolphins. I'll be filmed swimming with them out in the sea, and they're going to add the real dolphins digitally in post-production. Tim stressed the importance of this stunt, it's one of the most expensive shoots we are going to do, he said. Great, I replied.

I've never done anything like this before, and it's making me nervous. I get into the water to start practicing before the camera crew is all set up, and Matt strips his shirt off and joins me, giving directions as I go.

I have to perform a ridiculously well-calculated sort of circular dive from the top of the plastic tube and then swim along with the dolphins, matching their slow, rhythmic movements. There will also be a few underwater close-up shots, but we'll do them at the pool on a different day.

Tim has given a day off to the cast, seeing as they are more than half-way done, and he *really, really* wanted to try this today. He tells me not to think about the cold or the possibility that it might rain, and I tell him I won't.

It's the long dive and the synchronized swimming that worries me.

Matt does it over with me a couple of times and then I'm on my own. He shouts corrections and then pronounces himself satisfied and me ready.

I'm shaking with nerves.

I get out of the water to rest for five minutes before we begin the take. As I approach the beach, a strange sight greets me.

There is a literal crowd watching us. Most prominent, in the middle, is Wes' tall form, and he's holding a tablet in front of him, somberly filming my every move.

He's wearing boardshorts and a light blue linen shirt, which accentuates his tan and makes his green eyes pop. Almost the entire cast and crew are gathered next to him. Wait, weren't they given a day off? And yet, here they all are, waiting to watch the stunt sequence. Wes starts running towards me.

Okay, so this stunt is an even bigger deal than I thought. Even Tim looks a little red-cheeked and nervous, which is so unlike him. And he did say it was the most expensive shot.

Well, everyone being here and watching me is making it that much easier. Whatever, I just have to focus on my performance.

"Hey," Wes' voice says softly in my ear.

"Hey."

"How are you feeling?" His eyes are searching mine.

"Nervous."

I haven't seen him since the day I was sick. His hair is getting too long, curling at the nape of his neck, and he looks worried, sort of uncomfortable. Elle approaches him in a minute, and he stiffens.

"Hey, babe, come on," she says. He ignores her.

"You okay?" he asks me again.

What to answer to that? "What did you tell Tim to let me off the hook for the last two days?" I ask instead.

He bends his head down, hiding a smile. "You'll never know," he says after a pause.

"O-kay," I reply and get up to go. Tim is frowning at his watch.

Wes blocks my way abruptly, taking my arm, and his touch sends shivers up and down my spine.

"What?" I whisper.

"Nothing, just . . . take care out there, will you? I can't . . . I've reached my capacity of watching you get hurt. Promise me you'll put yourself first, and not a stupid stunt."

"That's not the way it works," I reply softly and he presses his eyes shut.

"I'm serious, Ari," he says. "If anything goes wrong, I'm going in and pulling you out, no matter what."

"Great." I look up at him, half-smiling, half-frowning. "That doesn't add to my stress level. Nor will it ruin the shot." I try to lighten his mood by joking, but it's not working.

"Sod the shot," he says.

I laugh. "You don't need to keep saving me, you know," I tell him. "I'm not that girl."

"No, I know." He's shaking his head. "'Sides, it's the other way round. *You* are the one who saves *me*."

He slides his hand down my arm, once, and then I'm running to the water.

"All right, children, we'll try to get it all in a couple of takes," Tim yells over the speaker. "Three, max. So don't screw it up for me. After that the light will change."

Did I hear him correctly?

Matt nods at me to dive. A tall, dark figure waves at me next to him, and immediately I feel safer. Coach is here.

I dive in and come face to face with the lens of an underwater camera. A plastic dolphin is waved in front of my face and I pretend to play with it. I touch its mouth carefully and try to hug it, while not making it obvious that I'm holding my breath. Then, just as the air in my lungs is running out, the cameraman gives me the thumbs up, and I turn my back on him and swim towards the base of the tube. I grab on, just as Matt instructed me to do—at this point I'm practically bursting for air—and push my strength into the whole rubber structure, so that when I let go, my body will burst through the surface, propelled with force into the air in a—hopefully—graceful arc.

I pull it way down until I almost reach the bottom of the sea, more than six meters deep.

Then, when I can push no more, I let go.

I am thrown upwards with such force that my breath slams into my throat. I try to relax my muscles, my mind wandering to the texts Wes sent me the other day.

# LOSE ME.

*Can I trust you?*
*Yes.*
*Yes.*
*Yes.*

With a gasp, I shoot to the surface. My body arcs gracefully over the water, and I throw my head back, as Matt told me to do. I turn slightly, while I'm in the air, gathering my body to dive in again, head first. It feels terrifyingly like flying. It's awesome. Once back in the water, the world slams to a stop. I lift my head above the surface, slowing my movements, and start a slow freestyle alongside the rubber dolphins.

Somewhere behind me the camera crew rafts are following me closely, but I pretend they don't exist. I swim rhythmically, synchronizing my movements to those of the dolphins, slicing the water evenly—there are divers holding their nylon strings, making them move as naturally as they would if they were real.

"Cut!" Tim yells from the shore and I can already hear the excitement in his voice.

I lift my head from the water and the sound of heavy applause fills my ears. Out on the beach the crowd is clapping. Wes lifts his arms in the air, hands in fists, and whistles long and loud.

Tears prickle the backs of my eyelids.

I'm never going to that operation table, I vow inwardly. I don't want to miss even a second of this. Of living.

"Bloody brilliant," Tim yells, and Matt leans down from the boat and grabs my shoulder, giving me an encouraging squeeze.

I turn to look at him and he's smiling, beaming really, as he nods his approval. "Good job, Ari. That was excellent."

I have to do it many times again, and none of them is as flawless as the first time, but that's okay. They take as many shots of the stunt as they need to—way more than three, of course—and then we're done.

Immediately as I step onto the beach, Wes' arms envelope me in a warm hug, saltwater and all. "That was really hot," he whispers into my hair, "for a twit." He lowers his eyes to mine and my throat gets dry when I see the naked desire in them.

*If only he knew what a coward I am.*

And that's when I realize it: I can't do this anymore. I asked him not to contact me for the past two days, and he's completely respected that. But now he's here and I can't put it off any longer. I'm lying to him, I'm pretending to be something that I'm not, and it's not fair to him, no matter who he is. It's not right. It has to end now.

I've made this huge mess and it's up to me to fix it.

I'm not yet fully convinced that Wes is that serious about me; all these endearments and stuff, I don't know if that's just flirting. I don't want to put more meaning into his actions than I should, but it is clear he is beginning to care for me. And I for him. And that's so not okay. I have to stop this thing between us before it becomes stronger.

His arms are rubbing mine quickly, trying to warm me up; so many people surround us, talking and laughing, but he doesn't stir an inch away from me. I'm not even looking at him, but still he stays.

Dammit, how do I tell him that I have an expiration date on my back? It wouldn't be fair to drag him into it, it wouldn't.

*This is it, Ari. For once, you'll have to be brave.*

All I do is push him gently away, but he senses the movement immediately and his hands freeze on my arms.

"Ari? What is it?"

"Let go."

Just like that, he steps away from me, no questions asked. People I've never met swarm in to fake-congratulate me, I guess mainly because Wes is there, watching me from the side, tight-lipped and frowning.

Then, out of nowhere, Anna is there, looking at me with regretful eyes.

"That was cool, girl," she says and then her face turns serious. "For the record, Ari, I wish I had handled things better."

I am completely thrown. *She does? "*You could have apologized."

"Would you have listened?" she asks me, surprised.

"Of course. We're all human, we make mistakes."

"Wow," she says. "I never thought. . . Okay, listen. I'm really, really sorry for what we did. I have been from the start. I hope you will give me another chance."

"Anna. . . " I start, but she interrupts me.

"That's not who I really am," she says, her eyes looking honestly at mine. "There aren't many decent people around, and I know you're one. That's why I wanted to get to know you. That day on the yacht when you had that accident. . . I don't think many girls would have been as brave as you—you didn't even look scared. I know if it had been me, I'd be panicking my ass off."

Suddenly, I laugh. It's impossible not to, the way she speaks, all her words coming out in a tumble, as though she doesn't bother to put them in order, just says what she thinks. Maybe my first impression of her was right, after all.

"I was freaking out," I tell her.

"Well, so was I," she answers. "And Ollie and Wes. Especially Wes. After you left, he went downstairs and we didn't see him until the next afternoon."

I look away at this, not knowing what to say.

She puts an arm on my shoulder.

"I want to try to be friends," she tells me, "if you can forgive me. I didn't even want to do it, but Elle. . . she has a way of making people do what she wants, you know? I'm weak like that, but I'll try to keep away from that kind of toxic people in the future."

"It's okay, she's your friend, I get it," I reply, wondering at the vehemence in her words. "And yes, I'd like to get to know you better. One mistake doesn't define who you are."

She flashes a brilliant smile at me, looping her arm through mine, as she had done that first day on board the M&M.

"I've been dying to get to know you better. Someone has been talking my ear off." She smiles, nodding towards Wes' tall form behind us. "Oops, better watch out," she goes on, indicating Elle's approaching form with her eyes. "Toxic waste incoming. And... yep. She's going straight for Wes."

"We're just friends," I answer, blushing.

"*He* is clearly not," she retorts, as Elle reaches him, a few paces away from us, and starts chattering in his ear.

A few minutes later I head for the trailer to get changed into dry clothes—this wet suit is making me so cold I can barely stand it. Tim said I should normally wear a diver's suit for this kind of stunt, but a bikini would be sexier in the movie, so that's what we'd have to 'go for'.

I saw him checking out my rake-thin arms and my ribcage that's showing through my skin nowadays, as he said the word 'sexy' and waited for him to fire me. He didn't. Probably he was hoping that my current un-sexiness wouldn't be noticed from this angle.

"Hey, Phelps!" a voice stops me as I reach the street. It's Wes. He runs toward me, kicking up sand with every step. "Where are you going?"

"I just need to change," I reply, feeling suddenly self-conscious about my almost naked body in front of him.

His body tenses and he runs his eyes all over me, as though he's thinking the exact same thing. He sighs deeply. "You're mad at me," he pronounces.

"It's not..." I begin to say. *I can't do this*, I think frantically.

"You're shivering. Go, I'll wait here."

He's in his car, at the exact spot, when I return. He's parked on the curb and the engine is running.

As I come out in jeans and a light sweater, still shaking from the cold, he looks up at me. His expression turns wary as he sees the determination in my eyes, and I quickly look away. "Gosh, your lips are blue," he says, opening the door. "Come on in."

He turns the heat at full blast, but I don't get in. I close my eyes, thinking of that hot air hitting my chilled skin. Thinking of his knee next to mine... *No, I'm not getting in*.

"Ari," he says softly, his hands still on his lap, not making a move to grab the door for me. Leaving it up to me.

"Don't you have to work?"

"It's a Lizzie-Will scene. I'll have to say my lines to Elle," he says, wincing. "I'd love it if you were there, Ari, I sort of... need you to be Elizabeth, so I can be a proper Darcy." He flashes me a smile. "I bet Tim will let you say one or two of Catherine de Bourgh's lines, if I ask him nicely. You don't mind coming along, do you?"

"I'm sure that's not true," I tell him. "You're an actor. And I hate to admit it, but you actually don't suck."

He looks down, hiding a smile. "Ah, you caught me," he murmurs.

"I'll just be honest then, and say that I'd like you to be there?" His voice tilts in the end of the sentence, as though it's a question.

"Wes... what I said the other day, that I don't have time for a summer... " I don't know how to continue.

The smile fades from his face in a second. He turns his head away as he grips the steering wheel with one hand. His knuckles turn white. Then he makes a laughing, scoffing sound.

"Man, it's true isn't it? You don't want anything to do with me," he says quietly. "You really don't. I tried to get past your defenses, because I thought you were scared to trust me—not that I blame you—but it's not that at all, is it? You simply don't want this."

I can't deny what he's saying to me, because then he'll ask me why, but I won't admit it either.

So I just stand there, suspended by my own fear, trapped inside all this truth I can't tell him. I don't realize it until he does, but tears start rolling down my face.

He takes a sharp breath and opens the door. He gets out and stands in front of me. I don't move, frozen on the spot.

"I'm sorry I yelled, it wasn't at you. I was disappointed in myself for blowing it." Placing a finger under my chin, he turns my head towards him and wipes my cheeks dry. Fresh tears fall and his lips go white. "Don't... don't be hurting." he says softly, "I can't deal with it." I look down; the look on his face is killing me. "You said you were halfway into... you said... " he whispers in a small, hurt voice. "Was that a lie? Was it... was it because I'm Wes Spencer?"

Oh, no.

I can't do this.

I turn around and run blindly into the street as he yells my name, his voice catching like a wounded animal's. I don't know if he's following me or not; all I know is that his voice fades as I run and run, the asphalt thudding beneath my sneakers, until I bump into someone.

"Whoa!" a pair of arms grab me to stop me from falling, and Ollie's worried eyes meet mine. "Ari? What's wrong?" he asks, his brows meeting in concern. "Did Wes—?"

"Ollie," I say, trying to catch my breath. "I'm so sorry, I just left, I... I hurt him."

"It's okay," he says calmly, studying my face, "there's never been anyone to tell him no. He hasn't ever had to work for people's affection or approval. It's good for his ego, right?" He smiles.

But of course it's not. It's got nothing to do with his 'ego'. He's been nothing but considerate and sweet to me, especially this past week. No wonder he's so confused by my behavior.

The memory of how he looked is tearing me apart. And maybe it's doing the same to him.

"Please," I tell Ollie.

"I'll take care of it," he answers. "But I can't leave you like this. Tell me what's wrong."

I don't know if it's because of the initial attraction I had for him, which by the way has now completely faded away, or the weird familiarity I feel when I am with him, but I suddenly know I can trust him. "You can tell me anything," he says again, locking his blue gaze to mine. I believe him. For the first time in days, I feel safe.

In the distance, Wes' car takes off with a furious spin, disappearing in a cloud of dust and a sickening screech of tires.

I inhale sharply.

"Let's go somewhere we can talk," Ollie says, his eyes on me.

We sit in one of the cafes at *Liston*.

Ollie frowns at me, and proceeds to order enough food to feed the entire cast of *First Sentences*.

His eyes are watching me, waiting, and I suddenly realize what I'm about to do.

You know you've had it happen to you. Suddenly, a literal stranger, a cashier or a taxi driver, starts telling you their life story. Their wife left them, their kid crashed their car, they need money for their mom's hospice care. And you wonder, wow, this person must be really desperate to talk if they started spewing out their darkest struggles to a stranger.

Well, if you've ever wondered what kind of person would do that, look no further. That's me right now.

Poised to tell everything I've been scared to even *think* about to this dude who, sure, he isn't a total stranger, but he isn't much more. The thing is, if I tell him, if I let the words out of my mouth, then there's no going back. Even supposing I can trust him not to tell Wes or anyone else, he'll still know. Which means it will be real.

It will be out there.

"I. . . I have a problem," I say, lamely.

"Anything I can do to help?" he says immediately. I smile. How long has it been since I last smiled?

"No," I reply. "Thanks. It's. . . it's personal. But what I mean is, I can't deal with a. . . a boy in the middle of it."

"Why?" he asks. "Listen, I know Wes is not the easiest guy to. . . to deal with, but he's decent. He's a good guy. And I haven't met a more loyal person in my life. If you've got his respect, then he's in it for life."

"Wow."

"Yeah," he nods. "He's been my best friend ever since I can remember. I have had some issues of my own with an alcoholic mother and an absent dad, and he has had his share of stuff too, but he's always put everything aside for me. Always, from the first moment."

"He has—" I hesitate. "He's been pretty amazing to me too."

"Yeah," he replies, as though he'd expected nothing less. That is so different from the original impression I had of Wes, I'm shocked by how wrong I got him. "But this. . . I've never seen him like this," Ollie continues. "He's done a one-eighty. He was even telling me he wants to believe in God. He's not drinking, he's staying in at nights. . . I'd almost say that he's a different person."

"Well, don't look at me. All I've done is hurt him. And I'm going to hurt him even worse, if what you're saying is true."

"Look," he says suddenly, sitting up, bringing his face close to mine. "Normally, I would destroy you." It sounds like a joke, but it isn't. He's dead serious.

"Normally?" I lift my eyebrows.

"No one hurts him," he replies simply. "Not on my watch. And he looks out for me as well. We're Laurel and Hardy, after all."

"But this isn't 'normally'?"

"It's not."

He's trying to tell me something, but he can't get it out. He looks like he's struggling with himself. Well, that makes two of us.

"Will you come to the beach party tonight?" he asks suddenly.

I already know about this, Anna told me. She practically begged me to come, to give her another chance. But with the situation with Wes being what it is, I don't think I can do it.

Also, speaking of 'tonight', it will be tonight in practically half an hour. Twilight is already enveloping us in a warm blue light, lanterns beginning to glow orange all around us, in the bistros.

"Who will be there?" I ask him.

"I will," he answers simply. "I'd like to talk some more. I just found you, after all. I want to get to know you."

He just found me? What is that supposed to mean?

"If you text me that Wes won't be there, I'll come," I tell him.

"He won't," he says. "He's worried he'll be tempted to drink." He watches me for a minute. "How did you do that, by the way?"

"Do what?"

"I've been trying to get him to quit for years. I thought. . . I said it would take a miracle to save him. He wasn't headed for a good place." He's staring at me again. "It looks as though it *did* take a miracle," he says finally.

...

The party starts at ten, and it's going to be at the beach, which means it will be cold, so I wear a long sweater over denim shorts and soft ankle boots.

I tell my dad that I won't stay for more than two hours, tops, and he kisses the top of my head.

"Have fun," he whispers, his voice rough.

"Thanks," I say. "I'll try."

I'm more intrigued at what Ollie said than anything. And I really hope Anna proves her honesty this time, because I would so hate to have been wrong in her for the second time.

"I really, really hate you right now," Katia tells me as I call her from the car. "Going on a beach cocktails party with Tristan and Kat. . . . while I'm stuck serving obese ladies with bad manners all night. Not fair."

Before I can reply, my phone blinks on and off, and there's a call waiting. The name on the screen makes my breath catch.

*Spiros*

I'm so shocked at seeing his name like that on my phone, that I swerve to the left by accident, and right the wheel just in time to avoid oncoming traffic.

"Hey, Katia," I'm trying to sound normal, but my heart is thundering in my ears. "I'm almost there, I'll call you as soon as I'm back home."

"You better," she laughs. "Love you."

I end her call as well as Spiro's and turn my phone off.

*Breathe*, I remind myself.

The private beach that leads to Club Med is lit up with dozens of torches, their flickering flames reflected across the inky surface of the sea. Sweltering waves crash on the beach, their rhythmic sound mingling with the buzz and laughter of high-pitched voices, which carries all the way to the street. The smell of roasted meat and alcohol greets me as I approach a group of giggling girls with bare feet and Anna greets me with a hug. Electro music bleats from the speakers, and there's barely room to stand, it's so crowded. Everyone is here, actors, crew members, extras, people who were just passing by.

There's security everywhere, of course, but no paparazzi or cameras anywhere, and it feels like an informal party between friends.

Half an hour passes and I'm feeling pretty chill, actually. There's no sign of Wes or a headache and I'm almost surprised to find that I'm laughing and joking around with Anna like a normal person. She's so down-to-earth and funny, it's difficult not to like her immediately. I feel like I've known her for ever, although we don't talk about anything hugely important.

No sign of Elle either.

I begin to breathe a bit more easily.

I notice Ollie craning his neck and searching for me four minutes later. I see him spot me, and the next second his tall form starts approaching, making his way easily around the crowd. He grabs a cup and sits with us on a log on the other side of Anna, water lapping at our feet.

"Dirt, nice," he grumbles. "Wasn't there a place where we could have a civilized party?" He winks at me, but he seems a bit preoccupied.

A guitar is strumming to our left, and two or three guys are trying to remember the lyrics to a popular song about drinking twelve shots in a row.

Ollie's lips are smiling, but his eyes are sad.

"What's up?" Anna asks him.

"Wes," he says curtly.

"What now?" Anna asks and my head snaps up.

"He's not here, is he?" I ask.

Ollie takes a swig out of his plastic cup and nods. "Smashed. He's been—Ari, no, hey," he interrupts what he was saying and grabs my hand. "I know what you're thinking, and it's wrong. If he's drinking, it's no one's fault but his, okay? No one else's responsibility."

"But, Ollie, I. . . "

"Look at you two, one big happy family," a voice interrupts me out of nowhere. "Aw hashtag *cute!*"

It's Elle. A girl is standing next to her, looking down at us with sneering eyes—I think she plays one of Elle's sisters in the film. Or is it one of Ollie's sisters? Yes, she must be Caroline Bingley. Man that book is heavy on sisters.

With one abrupt movement, Ollie gets up, his cup rolling at his feet, forgotten.

"You need to go. Now." He takes her elbow and starts tugging her away from us, but she doesn't budge.

The 'Caroline' girl starts talking. "Why are we on a beach, Oliver?" she purrs to Ollie, inching close to him. "Don't they have any roof gardens in this place? I mean, a beach party? What is this, high school?"

Ollie sighs and rubs his fingers over his eyes. "It's called 'having fun'," he tells her tiredly. He puts his arm lightly on my elbow and starts tugging me away. "Welcome to the country that invented it. Let's go, Ari," he says to me in a lower voice.

She shrugs, following us. "Elle says it's third world, the way they—" she stops, pretending she's only just noticed me. "Oh, I'm so sorry, am I interrupting something? Were you and your sister talking about anything important?" she tells him, her eyes on me.

As though she's suddenly realized something, they go huge. She brings her hand to her mouth. "Oops, does she even know that yet? How is that even possible?" She turns to me. "Gosh, this is beyond funny! Don't you read Young People magazine, honey?"

"Shut up!" Ollie shouts at her, his eyes spitting fire, and everyone around us goes quiet, staring.

"What?" I'm suddenly feeling light-headed. A weight is pressing on my chest and I have a hard time breathing. "What did you say?" I ask again, hating the trembling in my voice. Maybe I didn't hear her right.

"You're one of Christina Taylor's brats aren't you?" she asks me, sitting down beside me. "We all know that that's the only reason why you're here. She arranged it for you, right? You're her dirty little secret!"

Laughter erupts somewhere behind me, but it feels like I'm underwater and the noise is coming to me from a distance. The shapes of people blur together and the beach dips to one side. I feel Anna's hands on my back and she's yelling at them to stop. Ollie looks about to murder them both.

But they don't look bothered in the least. Actually, I think they're enjoying this.

"Ooops, did we spill the beans?" Elle twinkles. "Well, better hear it now, right? I mean, it doesn't look like anyone was going to tell you. But, yeah, you'll find your picture next to his all over the internet soon enough, comparing your noses—" she pauses to snicker, "for sibling likenesses and what not."

"Ollie, is it true?" I ask in a low, foreign voice.

I'm waiting for him to deny it, to tell me it's all lies, but he doesn't. He doesn't.

Oh my gosh, I was. . . I was *attracted* to him. I told him—He is Christina's son? *Hers?*

So he was in on it from the first. And what about Wes? That first day in his yacht, did he know. . . ?

I can't even think about it.

"Look at me Ari, I'm so sorry, I didn't even know myself until. . . " Ollie is lifting my chin, trying to capture my eyes frantically, but I turn away from him and start running. "No, not that way!" I hear him yell, then he curses and lowers his voice. "Dammit, I can't go with her, we can't be seen together. Anna, can you get Wes?"

Everything is getting blurry at the edges. I run smack into something hard, and stop, looking around in a daze.

"Awww." Elle gets in my face. "Look at that shocked face! Know what would be perfect right now? "

A flash snaps before my eyes, blinding me, and then more laughter and more pictures. I hear their phones clicking away, snapping pictures of my misery like a sinister soundtrack to my horror and I am up and running away before I realize it.

*'Don't go that way.'* So that's what he meant.

I escape from the flashes, running harder into the darkness, away from the laughter, away from the lies. Away from the truth. *No,* I think. *No no no no.*

Couldn't this have waited until I was dead?

I just found you, Ollie said to me only this afternoon.

No no no no no.

I run along the shoreline until the catch in my throat closes up and I can't draw breath. When my legs give way, I flop down at the edge of the water, gasping for breath, the world around me going fuzzy.

*Air,* I think, *I can't breathe. Air.*

My lungs begin to hurt and I open my mouth but nothing comes in.

I'm drowning on dry land.


tumblr.


page 133

"In vain have I struggled. It will not do. My feelings will not be repressed. You must allow me to tell you how ardently I admire and love you."

#ari

Originally posted by: @spencerstumblr

Notes

|

|

|

**@wesspencerforpresident** reblogged **PAGE 133**
from **@spencerstumblr** and added: You guys, he's added a
tag #ari at the bottom of his post do you know who/what that is
does ANYONE know please I'm DYING here anyone know
anything pls pls pls who is that ari thing I have NO CHILL

## N I N E

I've never felt like this before. I panic, clawing at the sand, looking
for something solid to hold on to, but it feels like I'm falling endlessly.
My heart is beating wildly and darkness dances at the edge of my vision.
I can't catch my breath, no matter how many gulps of air I take in. This
is how I get before I pass out. Lovely.

Water splashes at my calves and its coldness takes me by surprise.
When did I get in so deep? A wave crashes next to my cheek, and it
almost covers my head, the salty taste of the sea reaching my lips. Cold
sweat breaks on my forehead. *What is happening?* I try to breathe once
more, but my throat has closed up. Just as I'm about to give up, I hear
steps splashing through the shallow water. A voice calls my name in the
darkness and in a second Wes is there, kneeling next to me. He grabs
me and pulls me out of the water, dragging me onto the rocky beach.

"I can't breathe," I try to tell him, but nothing comes out of my
mouth. Everything starts going black.

"Ari?" His voice is tense. "Look at me." I'm sinking deeper and
deeper into the darkness. "Sweetheart, you're. . . " His voice is coming
to me as though from a great distance. "Come on, Ari. Ari!" He swears
as he turns me around, so that we're face to face, and he cups my face in
his hands. "Hey, hey, come here."

The next minute I'm tasting the bitter taste of alcohol on his lips as
they circle mine. He gives me his breath until I get enough air in my
lungs and then I push him away and gasp, trying to get my breathing
under control.

"Can you look at me, love?" he still sounds freaked out. I turn my
eyes to his. "That's it," he says, keeping his hands at his sides, but ready
to grab me if I fall. "That's it. Better now, yeah?"

Then I remember.

A sob breaks out of me.

He's next to me immediately, crushing me to him, kissing my hair, rubbing my back. "You had a panic attack," he tells me calmly.

"What. . . what the hell happened to me?" I murmur. "I don't even. . . I've never felt like that before."

I feel his breath on my hair as he chuckles, leaning his chin on the top of my head. "Well, join the club. I've been having them since I was six. I used to pass out all the time because of them, but you learn to handle it. Although I've never had one as brutal as this."

A hiccup of a sob escapes me and he tightens his hold around me. "No, don't, it's over now," he says. "You're okay, you're fine. Let it all out, Ari."

"I'll never stop falling," I whisper against his shirt.

He gasps as though he's in pain. "I've got you. I'll be here always, I swear."

"But I won't," I murmur.

He draws a shuddering breath and then his lips crush mine again. This time it's a real kiss though, and I abandon myself to it as is my life's depending on it.

I can feel my bones melting as he runs his hands around my back and then cups my neck between warm palms.

The time he kissed me in Drops, aggressively, almost violently, doesn't count. And that day on the surf boards he was Darcy. But this kiss is all mine.

Wes moans softly as my hands travel to his tapered waist and I feel every delicious inch of muscle beneath his damp T-shirt. He presses closer to me, deepening the kiss. His lips are on mine, and he's teasing my tongue with his until I'm sure I'll go crazy, and then he lifts me to him carefully, turning his head so that our mouths fit perfectly.

A slow burning sensation begins from the pit of my stomach and sends electricity bolts to my limbs. I raise myself on my knees and Wes imitates the movement exactly, pressing me against his chest, folding his arms around me. His hands start sliding to my waist, and I lift mine to the nape of his neck, playing with the wisps of hair, teasing it, curling it around my fingers. A low moan escapes him, and he sinks against me. He turns his head the other way, exploring my lips, and I stop breathing. Only now it's a different kind of not breathing.

Our knees sink in the sand, our bodies parallel to each other, until we are a tangle of limbs and panting breaths and shut eyelids. I remember what he'd told me the other day in my room, about how it was 'torture' for him when we were walking so close in the *kantounia*. We're even closer now. It doesn't get much closer than that. He lifts his leg, curling it around me, and drawing me to him, until I'm totally encircled by his body.

My limbs melt, they become honey, electricity, fire.

Finally, we part and stare at each other, not daring to move. His eyes keep studying me in the darkness, glowing like a pair of coals. His lips are swollen.

"I want you to know something," he starts saying, his gaze sober, clear, although I did taste alcohol on his tongue. "That night at Drops, the girl I snogged after I kissed you." He looks away. "I was picturing it was you the whole time. I'm sorry. . . I couldn't help myself." He draws a shuddering breath.

"It's okay," I say.

"I'm not drunk," he says suddenly. "I mean, I was. But I'm not anymore. As soon as Ollie said he'd lost you I started running, not thinking. I'm sorry I broke my promise to you."

"I broke mine to you too. I promised to help you and I left you." I hung my head in shame, but he takes my chin in his hand and makes me look at him as he shakes his head firmly. He lifts a strand of hair away from my burning cheek, his eyes not once leaving mine.

"Can you stand, baby?" he asks me in a minute. "I won't let you fall." I nod and he helps me up, one arm around my waist. Then he starts brushing the sand off my wet clothes, catching me as I almost fall on wobbly legs. "Come with me?"

I hate the uncertainly in his voice as he asks me that. I hate knowing that I put it there.

"Anywhere," I tell him and the sun comes up in his eyes.

...

My mom, or 'she' as I call her, is Christina Taylor, the famous Hollywood actress of big screen hits such as *Princess of Mesopotamia* and *What You Should know about Women*, as well as the most recent hit *Rebecca's Side*, which is based on a novel, *Rebecca*, retold in Rebecca's perspective. She has received many accolades for this role—the protagonist, which belongs to a ghost, how appropriate—and people keep writing about her that she's 'a Hitchcockian heroine', whatever *that* means. It also won her an Academy Award. Anyway, yeah, that's my mommy.

Only I've never seen her.

Apparently she had a summer 'thing' with my dad in Athens many years ago, when she was there for a brief holiday, and she got pregnant with me. My dad had had no idea about her pregnancy until he received me, about a year later, all bundled up and handed over to him by an assistant in the airport. Lovely, right? Christina wrote and told him he could do whatever he wanted with me.

My dad was a twenty-year-old university student with no money, and no plans to settle down for years to come. He'd thought she was a sweet, gorgeous tourist, and had been waiting for her to call ever since she'd gone back to America. What he got, instead of a call, was me. In a bundle. (And the realization that *she* had been a really good actress and nothing more, but anyway.) He took the bundle and then took a look at me and he was a goner. At least, that's how the story goes.

He raised me on his own.

He got us a small apartment in the city while he finished school and then we came back to Corfu. Grandma and grandpa lived nearby and so were able to help while he was at work, but he refused to let anyone else do the parenting but him. Dad wanted my childhood to be perfect, he wanted me to miss nothing. Except my mom, of course—that couldn't be helped.

We both wrote her thousands of letters throughout the years. Actually *I* did the writing, he just never told me no when I asked him if I could add kisses and hugs from him. I don't think she even read them. They probably ended up in a bin somewhere in the office of the assistant of her assistant.

That time when I caught a really bad case of pneumonia and almost died, my dad lost his job because of all the hours he had to put in at the hospital, but she never gave a sign that she even heard his frantic pleas for help.

Growing up, I decided I would never ever ask for anything from her.

Two years ago, when she sent me Coach, along with a note—a *note!*—telling me that she'd been told this was what I wanted to do with my life and that she wanted to do something for my future, I couldn't pass up the opportunity. She only ever contacted me once more, to tell me she got me a part in a new film. And that was it.

I don't think she will even care when I die.

...

I tell all of this to Wes, brushing over the worst parts and, of course, leaving the last part—about me dying—entirely out.

I watch as his face turns pale with anger, but he doesn't interrupt me.

He has taken me to the L&H. Man, is this thing larger than a house. He gives me dry clothes to wear—*his* clothes—and as I put them on he laughs at how big they are on me. I envelope myself in his scent and we sit in this massive living room slash restaurant. The yacht's chef—*chef*—has prepared us a 'light snack' which is in fact the equivalent of a four-course meal in a five star restaurant. Wes keeps talking about the 'meat-thingy *souvlaki*' we had the other night, and threatening to ask the chef to scrap everything and make us two of those.

But then he asks me if I want to talk about *her* and I do.

"I'm so sorry," he says when I finish, his eyes clouding. "That bitch wouldn't deserve you if she lived to be a hundred. She lost out on the most amazing person. You've missed nothing. You know that, right?"

"Okay," I say quietly.

"I'm serious, Ari. She's the one that missed out on the most amazing, gorgeous human being. . . " His phrase trails off as he turns to pass a hand over my hair. "Stupid cow," he spits under his breath.

I burst out laughing.

"What? It's true." Then his eyes soften. "How are you feeling?"

"Freaked out."

He nods. "Don't think about her, she doesn't deserve it. You have a new brother, though. Ollie is the greatest guy. I am so jealous of you being related to him." He sweeps his gorgeous eyes all over me.

"Although," he adds as his lips curl around a smile, "if I was too, I wouldn't be able to do this."

His head comes down and he fits his lips to mine, kissing my breath away.

"So it's good," he smiles into my mouth.

"It's just. . . a lot to take in," I tell him.

"I know. He only found out about a week ago, you know. By bloody *email* she told him. Can you believe her?"

"Really?" I ask, taken aback.

"Yeah," he says. "He was pretty cut up about it. Took me hours to put him back together. And then he began worrying that you would hate him too once he told you."

"He really did?"

"He kept watching you for days. Drove me bloody mad."

I love how he goes all British on me when he's feeling some strong emotion. I can tell just by how British his talk gets. At the shoot, he talks to Tim in this sexy accent that melts my freaking *bones*. Then, as soon as the cameras start rolling, he goes into drawling, thick American mode. Talk about an on and off switch.

"About Ollie, I need some time," I say and he nods.

"I already texted him not to come here. He knows you do. All he wants is for you to give him a chance, to realize he's there for you. I mean he was so excited, he—well, I'll let him tell you himself." He smiles. "I was murderously jealous of him for a while," he adds softly, to himself.

"I sort of wish this had all happened in a normal way? But I guess that wasn't possible, with all of you being in the industry and everything."

We fall silent for a while, listening to the sound of the waves gently lapping against the boat's hull. Wes' long fingers are absently playing with my sleeve, which belongs to a light blue and black striped sweater of his. The sleeve is slightly longer than my arm, so that only the tips of my fingers are visible.

I shiver at the slightest brush of his fingers and he lifts his eyes to mine.

"The part that bothers me most about. . . *her*, the part that makes me not be able to breathe—" I stop to swallow and a muscle in his jaw jumps.

"Yes?" he prompts.

"You know she arranged for me to be in this film, right?"

"I didn't," he replies, his eyebrows meeting. "But now that you told me I'm starting to think that I owe her a huge debt."

"Well, anyway, she felt she had to do this for me, I don't know exactly why, since she's never. . . " my voice trails and he grips my hand, squeezing it in his. "So I was wondering if you knew about her and me. And if that was the reason you. . . "

"No," he stops me. "No. Is that what's been bothering you? No." He frowns, looking at our joined hands, and brings them on top of his knee, drawing me closer. "That day I jumped after you in the water; that was the first time I saw you. I mean, I'd seen you before, but this was the first time I looked at you, properly."

I look down in embarrassment, remembering that awful day, but his voice goes on, bringing it vividly to life.

"I see it every night," he says. "It's there before me, every time I close my eyes. I don't think I'll ever get over it."

He swallows hard, his jaw clenching.

"You were sinking, your hair floating around you like a mermaid's. I kept you in my sight, as I swam towards you, scared that you'd get dragged further by the current and I'd lose you. You looked so small and lost, and still you were turning away from me, trying to tell me not to bother. I reached you, took your face in my hands to drag you up, and that's when I saw it. Your eyes, they were so scared, so desperate, but there was still fight in them. And I knew right then that if I couldn't save you, if. . . I let go, I would have lost something infinitely precious."

He smiles. The city lights from the window are playing with the highlights in his hair.

"And then," he says, half-laughing, "when I was trying to call an ambulance on the yacht, and you said. . . I wonder how I didn't go crazy that day. You asked me if *I* was hurt." He stops and presses his lips together. "I had never met anyone like you. No one had ever made me care so much. I didn't know then what it was about you that had touched me so—so profoundly. I sensed it that moment when you asked if I was hurt. So brave, and compassionate, so. . . you. I was a lost man after that moment."

I stare at him. His lips, his eyes, his hair. His fingers.

"You said I was stupid."

"I believe the word was twit," he replies, his eyes fixed on mine. It sounds like a caress on his lips right now. "Lost cause, like I said."

I laugh and his entire face lights up.

"So, no," he says. "It had nothing to do with Christina. I didn't even know then. It had everything to do with you. And the fact that you turned my world upside down."

I'm afraid to ask him what that means—*if* it means anything. I'm afraid that he'll tell me it does and I'm afraid that he'll tell me it doesn't. I'm so sick of being afraid. "I'm just so scared," it comes out in a whisper before I have time to hold it back.

"Why?" he frowns.

"That's the scariest part," I reply. "I have no idea."

"I'd take it all away if I could," he answers quietly.

I study him for a second. "You're a good person," I say impulsively. "You care about others." I don't know why that needs to be stated right now; maybe I need to hear it. I, more than he.

He's shaking his head even before I finish talking. "Wrong again," he says. "I didn't care about anyone but myself—not before you. But saving someone's life. . . it's this immense thing, you know? Of course you know. How could I be the same afterwards? It changed me, I think.

Or maybe not." He shrugs, but I can see from his expression that he's been thinking about things a lot. "Anyway, your first impression of me was the right one. "

"Would you. . . ?" I hesitate.

"Anything," he replies quickly.

"Can I stay with you tonight?" I ask him, shyly, looking away from him.

"Look at me," he says, waiting until I do. "Ari, I have never wanted anything as much as I want you. I've wanted you since that first day." He sighs. "When you showed up for our first date, and yes, it *was* a date, in those leggings, I thought you'd take one look at me and know what I was thinking. Those damn legs. . . seeing you run and dive and swim all day for weeks. . . It's been killing me, Phelps."

I smile up at him, feeling my cheeks grow warm. "Then I'd better not tell you how badly I've wanted to do this." I trace my fingers over his bicep and he shudders, sighing in pleasure

His eyebrows meet suddenly. "Gosh, have you ever even. . . ?"

"Even what?" I ask, defensive.

"Had a boyfriend before?"

"Nothing serious, no."

"Well, now you do," he says, leaning in to kiss me breathlessly on the lips. My spine melts as he tips my chin up with his thumb, and places his other hand lightly on my hipbone. He sighs against my lips, the breath leaving his body with a whoosh. *I did that to him. He can't breathe because of me.*

I press myself against him, tasting him once more, leaning into his hard chest, letting him support my weight. Nothing exists beyond this room, this sea, this moment. I shove my misgivings to the back of my mind.

I won't hurt him, I can't do it.

He takes his lips away from mine for a second, lifting his eyes to look into my face. His hair is a golden mess, and he can't stop touching me; his hands are everywhere at once: across my collarbone, down my arms, on my shoulders.

He only says one word: "Please?" His voice is a rasp.

I nod. "I just need to make a call first," I tell him, and step outside, straightening my shirt. He doesn't let go of my hand until I disentangle my fingers from his.

The cool air hits me as I step on deck, and I cross my arms over my chest. *This is it. Stop overthinking it, okay?*

I call my dad real quick, just to say I won't come home. He doesn't ask, but I tell him that there's something I've got to do before it's too late. He's silent for a bit, and I wait for him to realize what I'm talking about. In a minute he does, and he sobs as though his heart is breaking. Which it is.

"Be safe," he tells me and it's not even awkward.

It's not even funny.

...

Wes takes me downstairs to the yacht's cinema.

Yep. It has a freaking cinema. It has a library too, of course, but we don't stay in there for long.

He puts on an episode of *That 70's Show*.

"Good choice," I murmur.

"Oh, I didn't choose it, it was just in there. Do you hate it?" Wes asks. He's sitting back lazily.

"I don't watch it, but Katia does; she binge-watches it every time she feels sad. She says it's the only thing that can make her laugh on the days her mom goes mental on her." He just nods. I've told him all about Katia already. "Do you know these guys?" I ask him about the actors.

"I've worked with him and him and her," he replies while lazily kissing my neck. He hasn't glanced at the screen once. "Just introduced to the others."

"Wow."

"Mmmhm," he murmurs absently.

"Dude, seriously?"

It's not easy to think right now, because his hands are doing something to my neck, tangled among my hair, and his tongue is doing things in my. . .

He comes up for air, his eyes sparkling.

"Yeah. *Dude.*" What? Oh, right. I called him 'dude' again. Stupid brain that stops to function whenever he touches me. "I'm glad that knowing them impresses you far more than meeting me ever did."

His is voice low and sexy, and his eyes are devouring me. My heart starts beating wildly at the raw desire I see in them, but before I can say anything, he takes me in his arms and lifts me onto his lap.

"Let's see if I can impress you another way," he whispers huskily into my cheek and right then my phone beeps.

I look at it quickly before I turn it off, but I see it's Katia. "I have to take this, I'll be just a sec," I tell him and get up. He moves away to give me some privacy, but all I want is to end the call quickly so I can be near him again.

"Hey, Kat."

"So? How did it go?" she asks me with her mouth full. Oh, so it's going to be that kind of a conversation. I know how lonely she is and how hard a time she's been having. Clutching my phone close to my ear, so that Wes won't hear what she's saying, I walk towards a small window that's almost at sea level.

"Okay," I answer, resting my palm on the cool glass. The window is open and a slight breeze lifts my hair from my face and I touch the spot Wes had just been kissing at the nape of my neck.

"You're such a liar," she answers, swallowing. I hear her fork clinking on porcelain. I bet she's eating noodles drenched in tomato sauce, her favorite. "It was more than okay. . . I can hear it in your voice. Wayyyy more."

I laugh, letting myself enjoy the sound. It's so quiet outside.

"Well," I start, but that's all I get to say before she interrupts me.

"Hey, I almost forgot, Spiros called me earlier, he said he couldn't get you on your phone. Do you know what he wanted? Is. . . is your grandma okay?"

I hear the concern in her voice, but I can't answer her. I concentrate on breathing. Suddenly the M&M seems too small, the walls closing in on me, the deck confining me in this tiny space, water all around. The peace is gone.

"Ari?" Katia sounds freaked now. Perfect. "You. . . you would tell me if something was wrong with her, wouldn't you?"

"It—it's fine," I croak out. "She's great, she probably wants him to prescribe her medication or something. Listen, Katia, I'm not home. . . I won't be back till tomorrow."

She squeals and I hold the phone away from my ear, but then her voice turns serious.

"Are you ready?" is all she asks.

"Nothing's going to happen," I reassure her, but deep down, I wish for once she wasn't so direct.

"Uh huh," she replies, unconvinced. "Well, if there's one person in the whole world who knows what she's doing, that's you. I trust you completely. Don't do anything I wouldn't do."

We laugh and hang up.

I don't tell her she's wrong.

If there's one person in the whole world who doesn't know what she's doing. . . *that*'s me.

I go back in. Wes is sitting on one of the plush cinema seats, typing on his phone. I sit next to him quietly, and right away he asks me what's wrong.

"I wasted five minutes of my time with you," I answer, "that's what's wrong."

He lifts an eyebrow, but when he sees I won't tell him anything else he lets it go, and presses the pause button. The screen lights up.

"Tell me when to stop," he whispers, burying his head against my neck, and trailing his fingers down the side of my body.

Are you kidding me? I *never* will.

The next second he's cupping my head, lifting it to his lips, and fitting his mouth on mine. I'll never get used to this heat coursing through my veins at his touch. I'm shaking all over, wanting to press even closer, to climb into him.

My hair gets tangled in his hands and I can feel my lips swell from his kisses, but I'm too busy exploring the contours of his back muscles to notice. Then he slides his hand underneath my oversized sweater and I almost flinch. I wasn't expecting his hand to feel so hot against my bare skin. A shiver travels from my spine down to my toes, and I part my lips from his, taking a deep breath.

He lifts cautious eyes to mine. "All right?"

"Yeah," I gasp, breathless.

And then his hand slides lower down my arm to find my bare skin. It's as though an electric shock runs through me, white hot heat spreading through my body. I've never felt like this; it's a heady, swoony feeling, but I can't enjoy it, because suddenly the enormity of what's happening hits me at full force. Just for a split second, I falter. He freezes immediately, not daring even to breathe.

I leap away from him, freaked out at what we're about to do.

What am I doing? He thinks this is it. He thinks he's got a girlfriend. He thinks we could have fun together. He hasn't signed up for tears and hospitals and sickness and pain. He hasn't signed up for death.

*Death.* Oh God. I put my head in my hands, as I stumble.

"Ari?" Wes calls my name, worried. He still doesn't dare move.

I turn to leave, breaking into a run. Wow, I'm getting really good at this.

"No!" he shouts and rushes after me, grabbing me from behind, fitting his body to mine. He holds me there for a moment and leans against me, repeating over and over again: "I'm sorry, I'm sorry, I'm sorry, don't leave, baby, don't go."

"I need some air," I croak.

"Of course," he says with a sigh, and releases me. "Just please, don't—I'm so sorry," he whispers, his voice coming out rough.

I turn to face him.

It's time I stopped being the most pathetic coward in the world.

"You did nothing wrong," I tell him, looking into his haunted eyes. "It's all me. You. . . you are perfect."

He tightens his grasp on my hand, still without saying anything, and leads me up a winding staircase to the top deck.

The air hits me with refreshing coolness and I try to breathe past the tightness in my throat.

I'm sick, I try out the phrase in my head. No.

I'm dying.

Also wrong way of breaking the news to the guy I was making out with a minute ago.

I won't be around much longer.

This won't work either.

So we just stand there, holding hands beneath the stars, and watch the lights of the night clubs of Corfu pulsate in the distance.

"I don't think I've ever been happy before tonight," Wes whispers against my cheek.

My arms get covered in goose bumps. How is he not mad at me?

"Me either," I say and he squeezes his arms around me.

In about ten minutes my eyelids start drooping with exhaustion. Wes laughs and takes me inside.

We're going to sleep in separate rooms, he says. I try to apologize for being weird again, but he doesn't look mad. He just kisses me on the nose and proclaims that we have all the time in the world to be 'naughty all we want' later. I think he senses that I'm not ready, which is true, even if what he said about 'having all the time in the world' is not.

A painful spasm wakes me up with a vengeance at about four in the morning.

I sit there, holding my aching head in the darkness, biting my lip so that I won't scream out in pain. I've taken painkillers, nothing works. This is new—the anger. Suddenly I'm so mad I could smash something. Mad at the pain for interrupting my life, mad at the deadlines I won't be able to meet. I'm so tired of being inside my head; inside this stupid, sick, broken head. I fall back on the mattress, closing my eyes, waiting for the wave of pain and dizziness to abate a little bit, but it doesn't. And I can't stand it anymore. I get up and I run blindly for the hall.

I stumble and fall to the floor with a thud that must wake Wes up, because his door is next to mine. I pick myself up again, but Wes has already opened his door. A thin ray of yellow light slices the small carpeted corridor between us.

"Wes." It comes out in a trembling, small voice.

He comes quietly and kneels beside me. He's barefoot, in his boxer shorts, his hair sticking up in all directions, his cheeks red with sleep. "Baby," he gasps.

He takes me in his arms and I lean my head on his chest. His hands come around me like wings.

"I need you," I whisper. "I need you. Just. . . be with me."

"I'm here, baby," he says, "I'll be what you need."

He starts kissing me, kneeling right there in the tiny yacht hallway, his back against the wood-paneled wall. He runs his hands all over my body and then holds me as I shake against his lips, wetting our kiss with my tears.

"Shhh," he murmurs, starting to sound scared. "Don't cry, sweetheart. Don't cry." He starts to shake too, a sob catching in his voice. "Tell me what's wrong," he begs me. "I'll fix it for you."

"You can't fix *me*," I say against his mouth.

His kiss deepens and he crushes my head between his hands, trying to tell me without words that he is enough to fix me.

But he isn't. He isn't.

We kiss until I'm too tired to cry anymore. Then we go into Wes' room—and I was right, it *was* the one he took me to that first day, it was *his* bed I got all wet—and he wraps himself around me.

"Go to sleep, Ari," he whispers next to me. "I'm here. Whatever it is, it can't hurt you now."

And it must be true, because I sleep peacefully until morning. When I wake up, my headache is completely gone.

At least for now.

But 'at least for now' is enough.

The next morning, we get up with half an hour to spare and head for the second deck. We just sit down by the pool and gaze out to the sparkling water. The sky looks like rain, but not for a couple of hours yet at least.

Wes grabs one of his sweaters and drapes it across my shoulders—it has the Tottenham logo on the chest—while two ladies set every imaginable breakfast dish on the table. There's tons of tea, too (of course).

"Hungry?" Wes says and I reply that I'm not, so he picks up a piece of fruit and brings it towards my closed lips. I laugh and push his hand away, but he presses it until I open my mouth and gulp it down. I laugh so much I almost choke and Wes' lips are smiling, too, but his eyes look determined and a little scared.

I chew and swallow, and by the time I've eaten the piece of fruit, I don't feel like laughing anymore. Wes looks out to the sea. He doesn't ask me anything about last night, but I feel like I need to give him some sort of explanation.

"Listen, about last night," I start, and he stills, watching me.

"What about last night?"

*'What about last night' indeed.* "I'm sorry," is all that comes out.

He shakes his head. "I wouldn't change anything," he says, the same thing he told me the other day, when I was sick and he was taking care of me. "Except for your pain."

"Wes, you. . . " Up goes the eyebrow. "You're an amazing person," I finish lamely. *And you don't deserve this.*

"Thought you knew that already," he teases. He smiles at me his crooked, shy smile that I've only seen once before. "Although yesterday I was perfect. Just saying."

"That too," I answer, and with a sharp intake of breath he pulls me to him and kisses me long and hard, our breakfast forgotten.

...

He has to shoot some indoor party scenes today, and I leave him reluctantly, because I have to go home to change. On the way I call Katia, just as the rain starts slashing at my windshield.

"I have bad news," I tell her as she picks up.

"What?" she asks. Her voice is sounding sort of choked up and I immediately ask her what's wrong. "I. . . I don't think I can do this," she tells me. "I'm not smart enough."

"Katia, stop talking nonsense," I tell her furiously. "Did anyone. . . Did your mom come over for a visit?"

"Yep," she says quietly and I know she's crying.

"Oh, Katia."

"No, it was fine. . . Except she started me on a diet. And said I don't study hard enough. She's right, I probably don't."

I step on the gas angrily. "*What!*" I shout into the phone. "Are you serious? I'll kick her ass to—" Her parents make me so mad. Why can't they see how amazing she is? She's always not studying enough, not beautiful enough, not something enough for them. I've seen her grow up doubting herself and it breaks my heart. Every time.

"It's okay," Katia says, "it's fine, she's right."

"She. Is. *Not*." I say so furiously that she laughs. But it sounds hollow.

"So, what did you want to tell me? What's your bad news? Is. . . is it something about last night?" I can't tell her now, of course. I'm not sure I'd have the guts anyway, so there goes that. "Ari? Did you. . . you know, with the hot pirate?"

I laugh out loud, but it starts sounding fake even to me, so I stop.

"I don't know what to do," I tell her. "Not about last night, nothing happened. But remember that you told me to make him fall in love with me a little? Well I think *I*'m falling in love with *him*."

She's silent for a minute. "Isn't that a good thing? Or does he not like you back?"

"No, it is. He does."

"That's cool." She doesn't sound as excited as before. "Then why are you crying, Ari?"

I wipe my cheeks but fresh tears wet them immediately.

"Because one of us is going to have to leave soon," I tell her. And it's not the one she thinks.

I spend the rest of the day with Coach, who takes one look at my pale cheeks and asks me what's wrong.

Nothing, I tell him.

You're lying to me, he answers.

Well, I say.

And we go back to doing triceps pushdowns.

texts

**Wes:** What's up, Teddy?

**Theo:** Same. You?

**Wes:** I'm actually doing good.

**Theo:** Good for you.

**Wes:** How's your brother? Is he any better?

**Theo:** No change. Still waiting for him to wake up
**Theo:** but it's not happening.

# LOSE ME.

**Wes:** Don't know what to say, man. I'm sorry.

**Theo:** No one knows what to say. They keep expecting me to say/do something. Don't effing know what.

**Wes:** Tense atmosphere?

**Theo:** Lava is less tense.

**Wes:** Hey, look, do you want to come over here? I'll done with the shoot in a few days, and I'm thinking of creating something.

**Theo:** Something crazy?

**Wes:** Of course. But maybe something good, too.

**Theo:** Tell me.

**Wes:** Have no idea yet, but I think I want to write something. A script.

**Theo:** Not my thing, man.

**Wes:** And I want to make it into a short film or films.

**Theo:** Ha. You did say crazy.

**Wes:** I did, so what do you say? Creative outlet and all that?

**Theo:** Parents won't let me out of their sight. Won't let me breathe either.

**Wes:** I can make a call.

**Theo:** Since when?

**Wes:** What do you mean?

**Theo:** Since when do you care about parents and making calls and stuff?

**Wes:** Since never, but I do care about you. I want you to breathe. You with me?

**Theo:** . . .

**Wes:** Teddy?

**Theo:** I wish it was me, you know? Then no one would care.

**Wes:** Don't bloody say that.

**Theo:** Why not? Everyone else keeps saying it.

**Wes:** Stop it, Teddy, or I swear I'm hopping on a plane and coming over.

**Theo:** Send me your encyclopedia when you write it. But include a synopsis because I don't freaking read.

**Wes:** Will do. If I ever actually write anything. Stay safe until then, ok?
**Wes:** Teddy? Promise me.
**Wes:** Still here.

**Theo:** I hope you enjoy waiting.


## T E N

Christina Taylor arrives in Athens that very afternoon, a swarm of paparazzi in her wake.

I'm back home, cooking dinner, when her face appears on the television, in the evening news. The next second I hear dad's shoes slapping the stairs and he runs up from the basement he has converted to a gym, flushed and sweaty.

His eyes are hooded, as they are most of these days, but he doesn't look as shaken up as I thought he would.

I grab a Young People Magazine from the bathroom and show him the article in a gossip column, the one that was calling her a 'mother or a monster'.

"Yep," he says, "that must be it. That must be the reason."

A second later, my phone rings.

"Are you home?" Ollie asks me tightly.

"Yeah," I tell him.

"Don't move. I'm coming over."

I make coffee—the strong, Greek kind—and wait. He runs up the stairs after I buzz him in, and we sit together in the kitchen, all three of us, sipping from tiny cups.

"I'm so sorry, sir," Ollie says to my father, his blue eyes sad and honest. "I'm sorry I didn't tell you and Ari sooner. . . I was really freaked out."

"Well, Christina seems to have that effect on people," dad replies dryly, glancing at me.

I shrug. Ollie grabs my hand in his and squeezes it. I think that's the moment when I begin to trust him. He *gets* it, without me even having to explain it.

"Listen, Oliver," my dad says in his most stern P.E. teacher voice.

"It's Ollie," Ollie says.

Dad smiles and his voice softens a bit. "Listen, Ollie." He leans forward in his chair until his nose is mere inches from Ollie's face. "I don't want that woman coming near Ari. Not even a hundred feet."

"That makes two of us, sir," Ollie tells him, not breaking eye contact.

"I'm 'sir' at school, you know," my dad lifts an eyebrow. "Plus, I could very well be your dad."

"That would be fun," Ollie says, sitting back, and I get up to start serving the *pastitsio* I made.

"What would be?" I ask him from the kitchen.

"To have a dad for a change," he tells me as soon as I walk back with a plate in each hand. My dad's eyes cloud over.

"You already have one, kid, for as long as you want," he tells him and stretches an arm to hug his neck—that thing men do instead of a hug.

Then they both get up to help set the table and we eat until we feel sleepy. Ollie can't stop saying how he loves the food I've cooked and at first I think he's trying to compliment me, but after refilling his plate for the third time I laugh and promise to give him the recipe.

After that we watch TV, half-asleep on the sofa, but it's still early, so I tell them we have to do something productive until it's time for sleep.

No one feels like going out, so we end up playing charades of black-and-white Greek films from the sixties and seventies. Ollie knows nothing about these films of course, but still he makes a genuine effort to guess what we mean. His every guess is so far off the mark that dad and I end up on the floor, crying with laughter.

We order pizza around midnight, because all the laughing has made my dad and Ollie hungry, and then Ollie heads for the guest room. I put clean sheets on the bed and he smiles at me, his eyes crinkling at the corners.

"You're so lucky," he whispers.

"I know," I whisper back. And I do know. Tumor and all, I am one of the luckiest people alive.

None of us talk about why Ollie is staying the night. I feel so warm and protected that it makes my heart ache. I know that if they could fight my sickness for me, they would do that too.

Wes calls me just as I get into bed.

"How are you?" he asks.

"Ollie is here," I tell him.

"I know," he says. "That's why I haven't called you every five minutes. I thought you two needed some alone time."

"Thanks."

"That's what I'm here for," he replies easily. "Listen, about Christina. She's already been taken care of, okay? She won't bother you. I don't think she even knows where we are exactly, the location has been kept secret so far, and there haven't been any photographers, that I know of."

"Do you know what she came for?"

"Yeah, I know what she came for. The fish in the sea know what she came for, not that she's shy about telling. She came to have the paparazzi snap a picture of her having brunch with you, that's it."

"Oh. Wow," I say.

It's not her fault that she doesn't know about what's going on with me, but I'm guessing at this point that even if she did, she might not care.

"I can't deal with this, baby," Wes whispers in a choked voice in my ear. "I can't stand it when you hurt."

"It hurts much less when I talk with you."

"Listen, I need you to do me a favor," he says after a minute's silence.

"What?"

"I can't sleep. Thinking of you in that tiny bedroom, all alone, and that. . . " he hesitates. "And that some kind of sadness may wake you up in the middle of the night, hurting."

I know he's referring to the night we spent in the yacht. "I'm fine," I tell him, remembering it with embarrassment.

"Please promise me that if that happens you'll wake Ollie up," he goes on. "He. . . he's the kind of guy that probably won't sleep anyway, thinking about you, about things. You can tell him anything. He's the best mate you could ever have."

"Okay."

"Promise me."

"All right, I promise," I say, smiling and then my smile abruptly fades as he speaks again.

"That's my girl. Maybe. . . who knows, maybe you can tell him all the things you can't tell me. Maybe you can trust *him*."

Ouch.

Then again, I deserved that. I can't ignore the hurt in his voice and it tears me apart.

"I trust you, Wes," I whisper into the phone and I hear a sharp intake of breath on the other side.

"It's fine," he replies in a minute, "I said I wouldn't press you and I won't. It's enough for me that you're here, talking to me, that's all that matters. I won't risk losing you again." Then his voice turns gruff. "Only, I'm thinking, some day maybe things will catch up with you and you'll need either to trust me or to run."

I swallow.

"That day, when and if it comes, I hope you'll be able to trust me."

"Wes, I—"

I can't say it. I can't. No matter how hard I try, the words just won't come out. What's the point?

"Tell me," he prompts, his voice warm, familiar. "Tell me."

"Shooting is almost done," I say. Great, use the film as an excuse. Gosh, I'm such a chicken. "Soon you'll have to go back."

There's silence for a bit, as though he didn't understand me. Then, he erupts.

"Are you seri—? What are you talking about? Is that what this is about? Is that what you've been thinking all this time? That I'll take off and just forget all about you?"

"I thought," I whisper, feeling the tears threaten again. "I thought. . ."

He speaks again, putting me out of my misery, his voice full of understanding. But there's pain in it, too.

"Ari, you should have talked to me about it, before assuming I'd leave you the minute I. . . " he falters. "Have you not listened to one thing I ever said to you?"

"I'm sorry."

"Dammit, stop apologizing to me." His voice gets softer. "It's okay, I'm here."

"Still?"

"Always."

"Okay, Snape." I say lamely.

He laughs. "You're it for me, Ari," he breathes into my ear.

...

Christina calls Ollie as we're having breakfast the next morning. Well, breakfast in most Greek households is black coffee in a tiny cup, which you sip as you run around the house putting on socks and yelling at your brother to grab the car keys. Which is what I'm doing, when her face appears on his phone and, as I'm standing next to him, she sees me as well.

"Oh, look at you," she croons to me, casually, as though this isn't the first time she's seen me in like, ever. "You're pretty as a picture. So skinny, wow look at those arms! Good job, Ari. Oh, you have my eyes, lashes that go on for days! You know, you can make that dark gray eye-color really pop if you try to learn the basics of makeup."

I just stare, cup of steaming coffee in hand, trying to wrap my mind around what's happening right now.

She goes on and on about how gorgeously skinny I am. As the moments pass and she keeps talking about it, I feel even more scared and ashamed of how I look. I clear my throat.

Ollie just stands there, looking numb.

Someone should try to say something sensible here.

"I wanted to thank you for getting me this part." My voice sounds weird. Formal. I am talking to a complete stranger, after all. She looks confused. "This stunt role? I would never have gotten a break like that if it wasn't for you. So thank you for that."

She's still looking at me as though she has no idea what I'm talking about. I send Ollie a desperate look. He wakes up suddenly and grabs the phone, taking her out of my line of vision. He asks her what she wants in a resigned voice.

"I was thinking of catching a flight to the island," she says, pronouncing the word 'island' dreamily, as though she's talking about the Caribbean, "sometime this afternoon, perhaps, and then Ariadne and I could go shopping. How does that sound, Ari, honey?"

Ollie turns to me with one eyebrow raised. We have to go to the villa right now, but I'll have some free time in the evening. "What do you want to do?" he mouths.

And that's when I realize it: I feel nothing.

I've heard her say my name twice now and still no emotion. She's a stranger, after all. I don't hate her, I realize; she's simply irrelevant.

I just want to spend these days with my family. These last days perhaps, these difficult days. Yes, that's what I want. I shake my head. "Tell her maybe some other time," I whisper to him, "and thank her again from me."

Before he can turn the speaker off, she's talking again.

"Oh, now I remember. You were talking about that little movie Oliver is in, right? I had nothing to do with it, Ari, honey. My publicist thought it might be a good chance to throw you two together, since the story was bound to come up in the tabloids sooner or later..." She pauses for a second, just enough for me to realize that the 'story' is me. "I thought it was smart. Paints me in a good light, don't you think?" she giggles.

And that's when Ollie loses it.

## emails

To: Wes Spencer < therealwes@wesspencer.com >
Fr: Pan <ajpan@gmail.com >
Subject: Hamlet

Hey Wes, man, how are you?

Long time no see. I hear you're in Crete or some such lame-o place. My condolences, dude, hope you'll be done shooting soon.

Everyone here is talking Oscars and wedding bells for you—I'm assuming only the first one is true. Please don't tell me the second is as well, I won't be able to sleep at night.

As for that little project you were talking of, dude, I'm all in!

Freaking Hamlet in a post-apocalyptic London?!

Did you come up with the idea by yourself? It's brilliant, Spence, and you know I don't use that word for anyone but myself, ever.

Tell me when you plan to start and I'm *there*, classes be damned. I'll make a deal with the profs at school here, no problem, I have them wrapped around my little finger. So, let me know.

Cheers, English boy. And keep those hands to yourself. No one would want to live in a world populated by Weston-Burke brats.

–Pan.

To: Pan <ajpan@gmail.com >
Fr: Wes Spencer < therealwes@wesspencer.com >
Re: Hamlet

Pan, you conceited, brilliant bastard! How are you?

First year in college, right? You a professor yet? Ok, first of all, stop calling me an English boy. It's 'sir' to you. You might be a seventeen-year-old genius, but I'm Weston Spencer, not to mention a good four years older than you.

Anyway, I'll probably be nominated, yeah. But as for the rest of the rumors, dude, don't even joke about that. Burke is insane. I mean, she's made my life hell in the past, but now there's this girl here, I'm falling hard for her, man. I can't. . . I can't control it. And don't start laughing. I'm in deep trouble and El is at every corner, watching her, looking for a chance to put her down. My girl can kick her butt anytime, but for me...It's just hard to watch someone you care about being treated that way, you know? I bet you don't. I'm telling you, the next time El fake-threatens to kill herself I'm letting her do it.

Right. On my little Hamlet idea. Do you really think it's good? And more importantly, do you think it's doable? I mean, I'll be on my own, you understand? I'll be directing and starring too, if all goes well.

You in? I'll need a score and a couple of songs and an Official Soundtrack thingy. . . Can you mix, too? I know nothing about this music stuff, do you think you've got this? I mean, no offence, but your ego is bigger than your career, at present at least. Well, as long as it isn't bigger than your talent. I'm sure it's not—nothing is.

I'm in Corfu, a smaller island than Crete. It's so beautiful here, you'd lose your head. I can't wait to get my girl over to New York for you to meet her, you'll be blown away, I swear. You've never met anyone like her.

Ok, got to go, talk to you soon, Beethoven.

W.

To: Wes Spencer < therealwes@wesspencer.com >
Fr: Pan <ajpan@gmail.com >
Re:Re: Hamlet

No offense taken. I mean, sure, there's not much that's bigger than my talent, but my ego for one is not.

And yeah, we've got this. Relax. Enjoy your Greek island and make a fool of yourself with the anti-Burke you've got there. I'll meet her all right, but don't expect her to look so charming once you're away from the moonlights and beaches and stars. Believe me, it's happened to me enough.

They're not so cute anymore once they've gotten their claws into you. At least that's my experience. I'll be in rehearsals every day during the next two months, so you'll have to come to me, ok? Oh, and one more thing. Don't call me Beethoven. Pretty soon you'll have to call Beethoven by *my* name.

–Pan.

**To: Pan <ajpan@gmail.com >**
**Fr: Wes Spencer < therealwes@wesspencer.com >**
**Re:Re:Re: Hamlet**
Dude, I'm laughing so hard, tea legit came out of my nose.

I have the unsettling feeling I'm going to regret working with you. Oh, what the hell, at least it will be worth it, having it on my resume that I've worked with the next Beethoven.

As for my girl, well. You'll see. That's all I have to say on that. ;)
W.

**To: Wes Spencer < therealwes@wesspencer.com >**
**Fr: Pan <ajpan@gmail.com >**
**Re:Re:Re:Re: Hamlet**
Emojis? Seriously? What has 'your girl' done to you, dude? I mean, you never were chill to begin with, everyone knows that, but come on. You'll be an Academy Award winner soon, don't set the bar so low.

**To: Pan <ajpan@gmail.com >**
**Fr: Wes Spencer < therealwes@wesspencer.com >**
**Re:Re:Re:Re:Re: Hamlet**
Hahahaha. I have more chill than you, anyway. Go study something, kid.

# E L E V E N

Ollie gets up so quickly his chair falls back with a thud.

"Stop talking," he yells at Christina. "Just stop. *Now.*" He walks from the room and takes the phone with him, talking over her voice. I hear my bedroom door shut with a bang. He comes back five minutes later.

"She says bye," he says cheerfully.

I turn to the window and take a last sip from my coffee. Suddenly going out of the house doesn't seem such a good idea. "And now, how about what she really said?" I ask him.

He sighs. "It wasn't pretty." He carefully sits down next to me. "Let's see. She started popping pills and yelled for her assistant to alert the paparazzi to take pictures of her leaving the Athens airport at least. Then she. . . "

"What?"

"Nothing," he shakes his head with a sad smile. "Just. . . You're perfect okay? She's a bitch."

"She said something about my nose, didn't she?" It should have been funny. It isn't.

He looks down at me, frowning. "She said. . . well, she said something, doesn't matter what, and I got so mad I hung up on her. Wes warned me about this," he mutters. "He said to keep her claws off his girl, or he'd kill me."

"He what?"

"Oh yeah, he said," he imitates Wes' British accent; he's got even the tone of his voice spot on. "He said, Ols, I swear I'll kill that bitch if she goes near Ari. You promise you'll take care of her, innit?"

"Okay, now I know you're lying. He does *not* say 'innit', I've never heard him say it!"

"He *so* does," Ollie insists. "He's just careful not to let his inner Brit show when he's with you, because you said something to him about Austen being an English nobody or something—"

"I did not!" I say, laughing. "Well, hold on, I may have, but that was before I read her book, it. . . it actually didn't suck at all."

"Anyway, he's scared to. . . to be too English in front of you."

By this time I'm laughing so hard I nearly drop my cup. I try to interrupt him, but it comes out like hiccups. Ollie snorts coffee into his nose, he's laughing so hard.

I slap him on the back until he can catch his breath.

Yeah. My family is all I need right now.

We get into Ollie's car. A light drizzle has started to fall outside the window, stray drops gliding down to the sill.

"Did you. . . ?" I start, then hesitate. I suddenly feel shy around him. "Thank you for what you did, what you said to her."

"No prob," he smiles.

"Did you know about me that day in Drops, when you—when you took me home?" I ask, forcing the words out. Something he said today made me realize that he may have known.

He nods slowly, looking straight ahead to the damp road. A trickle of traffic is gathering in front of us, cars stopping for the red lights.

"I'd rather not remember it," he replies. "But in a way it was also one of the best days of my life. I'd found out I had a sister only a few hours ago, you know. I was so freaked out I wasn't planning on coming to the club at all, I just ran away until I was lost and Wes had to come get me. I didn't tell him the specifics there and then, that happened much later, but he talked me into coming to the club, to forget myself, he said. I thought he wanted to see you, but I did too, so I came along."

He pauses for a second. "I didn't take my eyes off you for a second that night, hoping you wouldn't notice me stalking you. Wes knew there was some major Christina drama going on, but I hadn't told him anything else yet."

I try to take it all in. "How old are you?"

"Twenty-two, same as Wes. Why?"

"Oh." I realize something.

"What?" His eyes cloud over with worry. He's keeping an eye on the road, but his attention is on me. "What is it? Your face fell."

"Nothing, it's just I had a thought. I've always assumed that she couldn't go on with her career with a baby, that's why she didn't want to—to keep me. But. . . she already had one, didn't she? Did she have a husband too? When she was with my dad, did she have—?"

"Hey hey hey," Ollie lifts a hand off the wheel and puts his arm around my shoulders, drawing me to him. "No, she didn't have a husband," he murmurs above my head. "And she didn't have me either. I was raised exclusively by nannies until I was fourteen."

"Then what?"

"Then I fired them," he answers with a smile.

"So. It's just me she didn't want," I conclude.

He swallows hard. "Look at me." His eyes are filled with kindness and pain. The rain keeps puttering outside the window, and I draw the sleeves of my cardigan lower, to cover my chilled fingers.

The weather's changing; it's officially fall.

"I want you," Ollie says, gripping the wheel. "I knew I was the luckiest guy alive when I found out you were my sister."

I shiver and he turns on the air-conditioning. "You know, I'm used to being alone my entire life; well, not alone alone. Just sibling-less. And now you. . . I can't believe it."

A stupid tear glides down my cheek. Seeing it, he steps on the breaks and leans sideways to kiss my cheek lightly. His stubble stings. For a second I think it might feel awkward, but it doesn't. It feels safe. Familiar. As if I've knowing him all my life. "Crap, I can't believe I'm crying again," I sniffle.

He chuckles. "I hear girls do that a lot. Actually, I don't mind."

"Hey, who you calling a girl?"

"Ah, I thought making you mad might help," he says. He's right. The tears have stopped.

After ten minutes, his phone vibrates. We're almost there. He stops at a red light and reads the text.

"Okay, Wes is losing it. He won't be at the shoot with us today, but he's really bugging me about seeing you. Do you feel like going over to *Kanoni* after?"

"We'll see," I answer, wiping my nose. I'd hate for him to see me like this.

"No worries, I'll tell him we need some brother-sister time. But," he swallows and his eyes turn intense. "For future reference, I don't think that there is anyone you'd rather trust to see you at your lowest point than him. And believe me, that's not how he's usually with. . . with people who aren't me. That's the Wes he is with you."

I don't really know what to reply to that and if he says anything more I'll start feeling guilty again, so I just nod silently.

After the shoot we meet up again, and I introduce Ollie to Coach, who looks him up and down, like he's seizing him up. As soon as the awkwardness is over, we head to the *Matchbox*. Grandma showers him with kisses and pies and grandpa meets my eyes with deep, unmasked pain in his.

"Look at our little doll, all happy," he says in Greek, as he kisses my forehead, pulling me in for a tight hug.

Ollie's face breaks out in a huge smile as he watches us. "I'll have to start taking classes in Greek, if I'm going to hang around you guys," he tells my grandparents.

"You would do that?" I ask him in a whisper. My eyes begin to mist again. He nods as though it's the most natural thing in the world. He nods, in a what-else-would-I-do way. I turn my head away.

Right then the tiny door bursts open and Wes' tall form fills the doorway. "Sorry," he says, his eyes searching for mine. "I couldn't wait."

Ollie just looks at him, letting out an exasperated sigh. "Dude."

Wes nods to my grandparents, his gaze darting to my red-brimmed eye, but he doesn't walk towards me, waiting to see if it's okay that he's here. I feel my chest constrict. All of these wonderful, amazing people, each one more precious to me than the next, their focus entirely on me, and I'm hurting them all.

I turn to smile at Wes, and he comes in. "Hey," he slides a hand around my waist.

"Hey yourself. I've got an idea. Are you free?"

"As a bird." He has a wary look on his face, as though he wants to ask me what's wrong, but he'd rather I tell him on my own.

"What are you planning?" *pappous* asks me in Greek, noticing the tension between us, so I tell him. His eyes sparkle mischievously. "Do you need me to come along?" He's been asking me that since I was five and arranging a play date with Katia. The answer is usually no, and he *so* knows it, but he loves to pretend he didn't have any idea he'd be in the way.

"I'm going to ask if anyone wants to play soccer," I tell him, and grandma bursts out laughing.

"That's the way to a man's heart," she says.

*Pappous* looks at Wes' skinny jeans and pinstripe fitted Oxford shirt and shakes his head. "This one looks like he belongs in a magazine. You're never gonna get him to get dirty," he says.

"He's a good guy."

"Do you like him, *Ari mou*?" he asks me in the same tone. I nod. "He'll never deserve you," grandpa says. Then he walks over to Wes—Wes is more than a head taller than him, still he looks absolutely terrified—and grabs him in a breath-stopping hug. It actually looks as though he's hurting him.

But Wes' hands come up slowly around my granddad's back, and he hugs him back just as tight.

"*Na tin agapas,*" he whispers into Wes' ear—'love her always'.

"Yes, sir," Wes gasps, all somber and serious as though he understands exactly what my granddad told him. And somehow, I think he does.

"Okay," I say, wiping my wet eyes discreetly. Grandma looks at me. Her eyes are red too. "You guys play soccer?"

There's five of us when we get to the field.

Coach and dad have joined us too, and then it turns out Matt is crazy about soccer as well, so I call him and he says in this calm, quiet voice of his that he'd be really excited if he could join us.

As soon as we've all changed into sweats and shorts, we meet up in a soccer field in the centre of town, big lights illuminating the rapidly falling dusk all around us. Wes pulls me aside.

"Why do we need all those other people?" he asks me sullenly. He looks gorgeous in a pair of dark gray sweats and a black tee that accentuates the green of his eyes.

"It's going to be a bonding experience," I tell him.

"So I'll to have to wait an eternity to find out what *this* is all about," he says softly, running a finger down my damp cheek.

I try to shrug it off, but he puts his hands on my shoulders and forces me to look at him.

"Ari," he whispers hoarsely.

"Some of it is joy," I tell him. "Pure joy."

He nods. "I'm so glad to hear it. And the rest?"

"The rest has to be there, or I wouldn't be able to recognize the joy," I say.

He crushes me to his chest, lifting me off my feet, and kisses me, shutting his eyes tightly. "What have you done to me?" he whispers in my ear so quietly that I almost think I imagined it. But I didn't. My breath catches.

He lowers me to the ground and I see the way he's smiling down at me.

*You're it for me,* his words from the other night haunt me and for the first time I'm certain he actually means it. Is it possible he's falling for me as hard as I'm falling for him? But. . . he's Wes Spencer. And I'm no Elle or Chris or TJ. I have my dad's nose, for crying out loud!

Wes leaves me and heads for the guys who are huddling up on the other side of the field, but he changes his mind and turns around. He runs back to me to cup my cheeks in his hands, kissing me hungrily.

And that's when I realize it.

I may not be any of these girls, or anything *like* them, but right now I'm the girl he wants. That's it.

And I can't even let myself enjoy it.

"Okay, kids," Coach yells and we part, panting. "Let's play ball."

# LOSE ME.

I team up with Dad and Matt. Coach insists that whichever team gets him will have a huge advantage and it will be unfair to the others, and Ollie tells him that's he's a bit up himself, to which Coach replies that he—Ollie—is an okay kid, after all.

And so we start.

Matt calls referee—we're not playing properly, because our numbers are too weird, but who cares. The other team kicks off. I steal the ball from Ollie and then feint to the right, easily scoring the first goal. Wes tries for their team, but dad—he's our goalie—blocks him.

"Too bad you lost to a girl," I yell at Wes from across the field and he runs over and tackles me to the ground. He's being careful, but he's also being an overgrown mass of limbs. It's okay, I can take him.

Ollie jumps in and lands on top of us, and we fall in a sweaty mess on the damp grass, all tangled up.

"Hey, cut it out," my dad calls and I can hear it in his voice that he's worried I might get hurt or sick. But he's wrong this time.

I could exactly echo Wes' words from the other day.

"I've never been happy before today," I tell him as he grabs my hand and hauls me to my feet. He leans in to lift a twig off my ponytail and twirls his fingers around the little hairs that have escaped at the nape of my neck.

"God sure answered my prayers the other day," he says, leaving me flabbergasted. Say what?

The next second he's running back towards Matt again. "Bring it on!" he yells and the match resumes, so I don't have time to ask him what he meant.

"Pass me the ball," I call to Matt.

I start to jog across the field, keeping the ball in line with my feet and Ollie steals it from me, but not for long. I score a second goal. Coach lifts a fist in the air, as though it was for his team.

"That's my little girl," he says. "Damn, I'm good."

Dad scoffs. "Excuse me. *I* was teaching her how to kick when she was in diapers. You weren't even out of high school yet."

"Diapers, huh?" Wes lifts an eyebrow and I kick him in the shin.

"I don't know if someone did a good job on teaching this one how to kick," Matt says, "or a really lousy one teaching the rest of us."

Ollie looks him in the eye. "This means war."

We agree that whenever someone scores a goal the other team will drop a hundred push-ups and vice versa. "Easy there," Coach says, "what happens if *we* score a goal?"

"That's not going to happen," I tell him. "And just for what you said, you'll have to drop *three* hundred our next goal."

Which comes after two minutes. We only end up having to do the hundred push-ups once because they score one goal. I'm the first to complete them, as expected. Yeah! Still got it. Coach looks sheepish.

Ollie times me as I do the hundred push-ups. When I finish he and Wes start whistling like they're in a freaking boxing match.

"All right, Ari!" Ollie screams.

"That's *my* girl, 'Babe'," Wes tells him, and he, Ollie, jams his knee into his stomach, sending him sprawling on the grass. In a second Wes is on his feet again and Ollie punches him in the back, yelling at him to stop calling him that.

My team, of course, destroys them.

When night falls we go to sit at the dark, deserted beach, cooling off in the sand and drinking beers. It's dark all around, and there's a chill in the air, but the quiet is welcome after the craziness on set. Wes picks up a bottle casually and takes a small swig. I slide my hand into his, hoping he can't tell I'm shaking a little bit, and take the bottle from him.

"I'm good," he tells me, his voice calm.

"Okay," I say, giving it back to him quickly.

"But you should probably hold on to that," he adds. "Thank you."

My cheeks turn red, but I don't have much time to feel embarrassed, because next thing I know, he's picking me up in his arms and running into the sea with me, sweats and all, threatening to throw me in the water.

"Don't you dare!" I squeal.

His hands tighten around me.

"I've got you," he says, laughing. He lowers his head, and his lips come down to meet mine.

...

The next days pass in a blur of training, shooting and Wes.

I'm happy. That's all that matters, right? *Right?*

Everything goes well and the time passes along smoothly, with no accidents or bad surprises. I almost forget myself. No headaches, no pain. I have no appetite, but I don't even notice. Sometimes I wake up in the middle of the night, covered in a cold sweat, but there's almost always a text from Wes waiting on my phone, at all hours, telling me he's thinking about me, or a stupid joke he made up, or what he's planned for us to do tomorrow. And I'm distracted from my fear.

I don't try to believe that everything is going to be fine. I don't even try to tell myself lies. I try not to think of anything other than this moment. And it works. It works so well it's almost a miracle. It works so well it turns out to be a curse.

## phone call

"*Hello, Weston, Andy here.*"

"Whatever you're calling for, the answer is no."

"*Well, that's not a very nice way to talk to your manager now, is it? Is shooting going all right?"*

"I'm not doing it."

*"You're not doing what?"*

"Whatever it is you called to get me to do."

*"Look, Weston, we've been talking about the promotional plan for your newest film, and Hugh and I, we both think that the time is perfect for a photo op between you and Elle Burke in that picturesque island, very romantic. Perfect for you two, the tabloids will love it!"*

"Did you tell Hugh I said I'm done?"

*"Pardon?"*

"I said I was done being photographed with Elle, and I mean it. I don't know if she's got a hand in this or not, but I made it perfectly clear both to you and my agent, that I will cut all ties with Elle after walking away from the Wars."

*"Elle Burke is your co-star and as such—"*

"Elle Burke bought and threatened and blackmailed her way into this movie, and if I'd known she would be in the film before I signed, I wouldn't be here right now. I mean it. I respect Tim and I'm grateful for everything we're doing right now, but make no mistake, I'm done with the Wars."

*"Weston, come on, you know this goes with the territory. The media has covered your story with Elle since day one, since you were kids, we've been over this."*

"No, they've covered the fake story, the one you fabricated, and made us play out. It wasn't enough that we were kid actors, we should act that we were a couple in real life, too. Well, I'm not doing it any more."

*"It will be just a spread in a few magazines, a few blogs, and that's it. Just to get the word out."*

"Are you even listening to me? There will be no photos, nothing featuring me with Elle. She can lie to the media by herself, if she wants to."

*"Weston, listen. . . "*

"No, you listen. I know you're doing your job, Andy, and you're pretty good at it, but this is as far as it goes. Things will be different from now on, and if you want to stick around I'm all for it. But we'll be doing things my way. No relationship tabloids, no more lies. I'm done with that. There is. . . There are real people in my life, people I care deeply about, and I'd sooner quit my career than see them hurt by the media."

*"Quit your—Whoa, okay, come on now, you know we'll never do anything you aren't comfortable with, no need to start talking about quitting."*

"Sorry if I gave you a heart attack. But I mean every word."

*"Just think about it, will you just—?"*

"Every. Word."

*"I'll call you again in a few—"*

"I'll still feel the same, I can promise you."

*"As in, you'll still feel that you won't let me do my job?"*

"Do your job, Andy, do it. Get me photo ops, interviews, anything you like. I'm just putting my foot down about one thing: it will have to be me. Me as myself. Take it or leave it."

*"What you? You don't exist without our team. We made you who you are, Weston. It takes years and hard work and real smarts to create an image people will fall for, I thought you knew that. I'm not putting you or your talent down, of course I'm not. But do you realize that what we've built over the years, what you've built, the image of Wes Spencer, the star, the actor. . . It could all come crashing down with one wrong choice? One ill-prepared plan is all it takes. One flop and you're done."*

"Maybe I don't want the image of Wes Spencer, the star. Maybe I want to be Wes Spencer, the person. Or, as someone put it. . . 'an amazing guy'. What do you think about that?"

*"Are you on something?"*

"What?"

*"Drugs. Are you high? You can tell me, you know that. No big deal, I'll call later."*

"No, Andy, I've never been saner in my whole life. Let me know if what we spoke about today is going to be a problem, and if I need to find another manager. I have to go now. Cheers."

# T W E L V E

On Tuesday morning I have to do the Rubble sequence again, because they've rewritten some parts of the script. I think, *are you kidding me?* But I say, of course, fine, no problem.

It's one of my last sequences. Maybe next to last. The crew is leaving on Friday, and only the stunt team and a few cameras will remain in Corfu for about two weeks.

And then, basically, it's done.

A team of stunt actors has already arrived, and they will be joining Wes and me for a couple of surfing scenes, but that's not why they're here. They're here so that they can train with Matt. They'll stay on with the second unit for the remaining shots, after the actors are done. Wes told me that Tim had planned to have them as a backup if I turned out not to be equal to the task of performing almost every stunt in the film—a rather daunting task, to be honest.

"Of course, you kicked that task's butt," Wes said matter-of-factly. "So he didn't have to call them until the end. What *was* necessary, though, was for me and Matt to yell at Tim for giving you a hard time in the beginning. What?"

I was looking at him in shock. "You yelled at—? Why?"

He shrugged. "Because you're bloody brilliant. Even I could see that from day one, and I'm a pig-headed cock, you'll agree. "

I opened my mouth to protest, but he didn't give me a chance to.

"'Sides, it's all good, he said, "I always yell at Tim at least twice a week."

Then he kissed me silly.

...

So, here we are. Tuesday, the Rubble. It's really simple, this scene I'm shooting today.

"I want a kiddy dive," Tim tells me.

"You want a what?"

"Dive from the Rubble again," Matt quickly explains, as he sees the look of dismay on my face, "feet first. Not professional diving, just have fun with it. Grab your knees, cross your ankles, let your hair fly."

I get it now, so I nod.

"Right," Tim says. "Then swim sloppily to the shore."

"Okay," I say.

I'm not sure what a 'sloppy swim' exactly is, but okay.

The headache starts as soon as I get into the water. It's not serious, except for the fact that it brings me down to reality with a crash. I try to ignore the dull, throbbing pain as I swim towards the rocks, but it grows to an unbearable level by the time I've finished my first dive.

"That was too good to be realistic," Matt tells me when I surface, his face close to mine, as he leans down from the orange raft. "Loosen up a little, take a jump, and then let go."

I nail it by the third time.

"Yes!" Tim yells over the megaphone from his own boat, "that's it, that's the way I want it. Do it again."

By the ninth take my head is splitting. That's nothing new, of course, and somewhere in the past weeks I've learned to work with it. I've learned to grit my teeth and focus and make myself stronger than the pain and the fear.

So I 'swim sloppily' towards the shore.

I swim back and forth for a dozen yards until they have all the mid shots and close ups they need, and then Tim wants the panning shots before the light changes.

"How soon are you going to be done?" Wes strides over to me as soon as I get to the beach. "You look a bit pale."

"I do not!" I reply, pretending to be offended, but then I take a look at his face and stop joking.

He looks scared.

"I don't think they'll want many takes," I tell him calmly. "I'll be fine."

He nods and lets me go, but not before pressing a kiss to my temple.

Then, as I get in the water again I notice him climbing into the raft that has the two cameras in it. I suppose he wants to watch the action better than he could from the shore, but something in the fierce way his eyes are fixed on me tells me that's not the reason.

The rest of the cast that came out here today are relaxing on the beach, having soft drinks and sandwiches, chatting and waiting for the sun to peek from behind the clouds so they can tan, since this is one of the hottest days we've had yet.

And Wes is with the crew, his back straight, his muscles poised, following me to the Rubble as though he's afraid something bad is going to happen.

As though he's scared to let me out of his sight.

I did that to him.

They row me to the Ruble, because I won't have to be filmed swimming there, only back. Then the boat takes off, stopping somewhere in the distance, leaving me alone in the green-blue water. I take a deep breath. A sudden tingly sensation goes up and down my spine, but after a minute or two it's gone and I try not to think about it.

"Let's go!" Tim yells.

I climb slowly up the rock, like a random tourist would, not an athlete, and then I dive. As my body splashes into the water, I feel the cold in my ribcage first. I don't know if it's because I've lost weight, or because the weather is cooling, but I start shaking badly. The familiar tingly sensation overwhelms me suddenly, and everything goes black for a second. I immediately feel better, though, and I swim to the surface, gasping for air. I take one or two calming breaths.

"One more," Tim says and I start climbing again, feeling a weird shortness of breath. *I've got this*, I tell myself. *Only one more and then I'm done. Only one.*

I dive again, and this time I know it, it was perfect.

Tim doesn't say anything to me, so I start my sloppy swim, as we had discussed. I kick and lift my arm for the first stroke, and suddenly the building tingles become a crippling force that knocks the air right out of my lungs. My body doubles in pain, my muscles locked in a spasm.

I start to sink. I try to kick my legs, but they won't obey me.

Crap. Not again.

Of course, this time there's an entire beach of people watching me, but still I'd rather finish this shot like a pro and not like a cripple being carried out in an ambulance.

I open my mouth to breathe and water comes in, choking me.

# LOSE ME.

Cripple it is.

The spasm lets out a little and I kick wildly to the surface. I feel my body heavy though, lethargic, and my vision is turning black at the ages. I open my lips to yell for help, but I go under for a second time. I push my body to the surface with a huge effort that leaves me heaving for oxygen as I resurface once more.

I hear Wes roaring my name in the distance and the furious splashing of his strokes towards me. I struggle to keep my chin above water, tipping my head back, but it is a losing battle, and I hear Wes curse heavily, almost five meters away, as I choke on a mouthful of salty water.

"Hurry," I whisper, trying to spit the water out. I gurgle instead, and more comes in.

I can't feel my limbs.

I try to push myself upwards again, with tremendous effort, but all I manage is to lift my eyes over the surface for an agonizing second. I'm exhausted. Is it time to give up? I can't lift myself further up and I submerge again, all sound drowning out around me. I kick my legs weakly but it's no use. I'm suffocating, my lungs filling with sea.

Just then the pain fades to a bearable extent and I spring to the surface with one last kick, taking in a deep gulp of air. I flip so that I'm on my back, and float on the surface, trying to fill my lungs with oxygen, coughing out the water I'd swallowed.

I try to swim slowly, testing my strength. Was this it? Is it over? Did I panic for no reason? The questions run through my head frantically, my heart beating like crazy, but I try to even out my breathing and pretend all is normal.

Then suddenly Wes is there, in the water, next to me. His hands grab my waist and he pulls me up against to him. I can barely stay afloat and I'm trembling like a fish, but I keep edging my body away from his, so that he won't see how badly I'm shaking.

"We have to stop meeting like this, Tristan," I joke.

He doesn't even smile.

"What's wrong?" he asks me, grabbing my hand. "It looked like you were in trouble. Are you okay?"

"Hey, I'm fine," I answer him, turning to swim towards the rock again. "A little embarrassed, but fine. Go back and tell them I'll do it again."

He doesn't move.

He's in his clothes, a blue polo shirt that looks black now that it's soaked with water, and dark jeans. He's kicking his legs, just floating, not making a move to swim back, watching me. The water around us is perfectly still and my stomach tightens at what almost happened.

"Really, Wes. It's all good," I insist. "Please go back before the whole crew gets over here, I've got it now. Something. . . something went wrong before as I landed." I propel myself backwards, putting more distance between us, but still he doesn't leave.

"You're lying." He looks me in the eye. Swallows hard.

"You. . . you've gone all white." He lunges for me, but not in time.

This time it gets ugly.

My vision goes black abruptly and I feel water in my mouth, choking me.

Next thing I know, Wes is yelling in my ear to wake up. He sounds weird, as though his voice is coming out of his throat with difficulty, hoarse. He has one arm in front of me, keeping my head above water, and with the other he cups my neck, trying to support me so I can breathe.

I can't move. I can hardly breathe. Everything keeps fading, reappearing, going dark again.

"Ari?" his familiar voice says in my ear, but it sounds wobbly and uncertain. Dizzily, I wonder why. "Look at me, open your eyes!" He props my head on the hard muscle of his shoulder.

*Why did he have to do that?* I try to lift my head on my own, and nothing happens.

He shakes me and water runs violently out of my mouth and nose. I gag and choke and gasp, trying desperately to breathe.

"Easy," he says, holding me firmly, as he starts treading water again. He grabs the back of my knees to lift me out of the water, curling his legs around mine to help me stay afloat. "What's wrong, baby, is it another cramp? Save your energy, I'll drag you, yeah? Just breathe— hey, hey, you're sinking. . . Ari? *Ari!*"

He catches me before I go under again and I feel my body go limp against him. Although I'm conscious still—barely—I can't do a thing to pull myself up.

"Ari? Talk to me, dammit!" He's yelling now, practically screaming. Still, his voice is fading. He lifts my head and I feel it flop back. Everything goes black, and his frantic voice is the only thing left. "Fight, Ari, baby, come on! No no no. Oh God no. No no no no."

I'm losing him. His voice comes from far off and everything goes fuzzy. He's crying now, sobbing as he holds me, shaking worse than me. He supports my back from underneath so that I float as he cups my chin and begins breathing into my mouth. I feel the air entering me but my lungs can't move.

Someone grabs my legs and Wes lifts his head from mine to yell at Matt to keep me steady, and then his lips meet mine again, filling my mouth with his warm breath, but my lungs are still burning.

"Come *on!*" he screams. "Someone help me," he yells over my head, the cry mingling with the tears in his voice. "Step on it, faster! She's not breathing, she's dying on me!" He gives me his breath again and again, until he's gasping next to me. I don't know how much time passes as I'm lying there in the cold water, forgetting how to breathe, fading away.

Other hands grab me abruptly and I'm hoisted out of the water—it's the medics, probably. This is so stupid, I'm dying here and my brain still keeps processing every little detail around me. Wes' panicked eyes fill my blurry vision. "Stay with me, baby," he whispers brokenly. "Please. Please."

I try to move my hand to hold his, but I'm trapped inside this spasm, barely able to breathe. I'm so cold everywhere.

My chest constricts painfully. I feel more compressions and more water comes out of my mouth, but no air. Then Wes' warm hands on my neck. "I can't find her pulse."

His hand is shoved away and more expert fingers press my throat. Then a mask is covering my mouth and some of the tension in my lungs escapes. I try to lift a badly shaking hand to the mask, and Wes' hand covers mine.

"Come back," he croaks out in a hoarse, silent voice.

"Call my dad," I try to say, but I can't form the words. "I'm sorry," I want to tell him, but that's impossible too.

The last thing I hear is Wes' frenzied heartbeat next to my ear as he carries me, panting, to the shore. And all the same time he's talking. Talking without stopping to take a breath in, talking in a continuous string of words, as though his very existence depends on it. But he's not talking to me. He sounds so desperate, so broken, as though it actually hurts him to form the words. At first I think he's swearing, but he's not. He's pleading. He's praying.

The words he's saying remind me vaguely of something else he said to me a few days ago. '*God sure answered my prayers,*' he had said. I didn't get to ask him what that meant. Now I may never know.

"Oh God, oh God, oh God, help." That's all he says. Over and over again.

And then I'm gone.

...

In the ambulance, I keep fading in and out of consciousness. The paramedics are hovering above me, and I know Wes is always there. I can feel him near, even though my eyes can't stay open long enough to see him properly.

Then I'm wheeled into the hospital on a stretcher, his hand never leaving mine, and I drift off into the darkness without knowing whether I'll ever come back again.

Sometime in the afternoon I wake up and I'm able to breathe. Well, I've got an oxygen mask on, but still.

Dad is here. He's watching my face and as I open my eyes, he gets up and walks over. I'm in a hospital bed, bare, white walls all around. Dad's familiar face is smiling down at me, his eyes sad, frantic. He's wearing his P.E. sweats—I guess they pulled him out of class to come to my deathbed.

Well.

Let's not be overly dramatic.

"Dad," I croak. "Is this it?"

His eyes are red, but he smiles at me.

"You need to have the operation," he tells me, straight to the point. His left hand is smoothing the hair away from my damp forehead, veins popping out, as though he'd been clenching his fist.

"When?" I ask with a small intake of breath.

"Yesterday. It's. . . " he chokes for a minute and he turns away from me, shielding his eyes with his hand. "It's grown quite a lot."

"I guessed so," I tell him.

I'm surprisingly calm right now. Maybe because I'd rather have anything other than the pain and the drowning.

"Your boy is out there, crying his eyes out," he tells me after a while. "What should I do with him?" I turn questioning eyes to him. "Yeah, he knows," he adds quietly.

"Is he mad?" I ask and dad shrugs.

"He's soaking wet," he answers. "They brought him dry clothes, but he's turned zombie on us. Oh, and Ollie is out there too, he drove all the way from *Roda* in two seconds to get here."

"Can I talk to Wes first?"

Dad gets up and in a second Wes walks in.

He's not dripping wet, but his clothes have that damped, soaked look as though they've started to dry on him. His shirt is clinging to his skin, contouring the outline of his ribbed stomach. His arms are hanging at his sides as his eyes look me up and down.

He sniffles and a choked sound comes through his nose as though he's been crying for hours. He looks scared, his shoulders drooping, his steps faltering.

"You should get into dry clothes." That's the first thing I tell him. Somehow it suddenly seems so lame to start apologizing.

He nods and peels off his wet shirt right there, in front of me. His back muscles ripple as he raises his arms over his head, tossing the wet tee aside, and bending his head to put on the dry one. His jeans are clinging to his legs like second skin, and they're slung so low I can see the V at his hips. I start to cry and he scrambles half-naked next to me and wipes my tears.

"No, baby," he whispers, his voice barely audible.

"You're so gorgeous." I sniffle. There's no way I'd act so pathetic if I wasn't on so many meds. I think.

But he doesn't even smile. "I'm yours."

He gets up again to put on a dry shirt and a pair of jeans and then he sits down on my bed, grabbing both my hands in his and running his thumb over the tubes sticking out of my skin.

"I'm sorry, Wes," I tell him. "I'm so sorry for not telling you, I. . . "

"There's one thing you need to know," he begins, ignoring my attempts to apologize. His eyes are burning into mine, intense, focused. "Day one of the shoot, that day when I kissed you on the water. I meant it. It wasn't for the cameras. That was an excuse to do something that. . . I felt I would die if I didn't kiss you again. After that night in Drops, Ari, I—" he swallows and tugs at his wet hair. "I couldn't eat, I couldn't sleep. I was already thinking of you way too much, but after that you were *all* I could think about."

"Me too," I whisper. "I wish I had left you alone, though. I wish you didn't have to live through all this."

"I wish I was the one who was sick." It bursts out of him with vehemence.

"No, don't say that. Don't even think. . . Don't wish it. . . "

"I'm sorry, it's okay, it's okay," he says. "Don't cry, love, I shouldn't have said that." He inhales sharply. "I should have known something was wrong. That first day when you kept fainting on me, you were in so much pain, I could tell, oh baby. . . I should have insisted on calling an ambulance then."

He wipes his nose clumsily, with the back of his hand, like a three-year-old.

"I should have forced you," he continues in a broken voice. "Only I was so. . . so *bleeding* intimidated by you and your brave attitude and your independence. For the first time in my life, I was fighting all this sudden, intense emotion around a girl and—and it was freaking me out. I'd never felt that way before. I pretended to be cool, but inside I was shaking all over. For an entire day. I had saved a life. Someone almost died in my arms."

"I hated you for saving me," I say slowly. He shakes his head, not looking at me. I'm only now realizing this. "The fact that you had to, you know? It made it all feel real. I couldn't run away from it any more. Although I did my best."

He sits back, shuddering. Our shoulders touch.

"All this time," he says, "all this time, you've been fighting for your life. That's why you were so sad, isn't it? That's why you didn't want to go on a date with me? You knew. . . Oh God. . . "

"I didn't do a very good job of fighting for my life, did I?" I say it calmly, feeling the needles prick my skin.

Wes lowers his head between his knees, as though he wants to shut my words out. His breath is coming rapidly. "I got to you in time," he says, repeating it, trying to calm himself. "I got to you in time. You're safe, you're here. That's all that matters. For a moment there I didn't think I—" His voice breaks.

"You saved me again," I whisper through dry lips and Wes grabs a cup of water from the nightstand and brings it over. He cups my neck and lifts me, helping me drink as though I'm a baby. His eyebrows meet in concentration and I wonder what he's thinking.

"My private jet lands in half an hour," he says after a moment of silence, glancing at his watch.

"Your what? In what?" I ask, trying to get up, and he slides his thumb over my collarbone, where a tube is logged onto my skin.

"Shh," he says, his voice the sound of naked pain, "It's okay. It's gonna be okay."

"What. . . what's gonna be okay?"

"Your dad and grandad and this, um, this 'Spiri' dude have been talking all day over your head. I finally had enough of them mulling over plane tickets and planning to contact the clinic in Athens on

Monday." He makes an impatient gesture. "I finally barged in there and yelled at them to get a grip and that I'm taking you to New York."

He says it quietly, as though it was the simplest solution and I want to protest but I can't and he knows it, because I have run out of time. *We* have run out of time.

"They finally made the calls they had to and they've arranged the details for tomorrow with the hospital over there. I had to call in a few favors, and your dad tried to be a bit stuck up about it, but finally he gave in."

"Wes, you. . . you called in favors? What did you do?" I ask him, dread clamping up my throat.

He leans over me and places his hands on either side of my face. I feel my tears sliding onto his palms—it seems I haven't stopped crying since this morning.

"You know it had to be done," he says, green eyes glowing into mine. "I'm just glad I was here to speed things up a bit."

"It's just so soon," I mutter, as the pain cramps up my legs.

He looks at me. We both know it's not so soon. In fact, it's so late. It's too late almost.

"Everything is going to be fine, you'll see," Wes says, pressing his lips to my temple. "Meet me for *souvlaki* after the operation?" I try to smile.

"Wes. . . "

"Yes, baby?"

"They say. . . The statistics say I might be brain damaged afterwards, even if I. . . survive," I whisper. "It might be cancer, there's a big chance. I'll need chemo, and—"

He bends closer, taking me in his arms, tubes and all, and I feel him shudder at the word 'survive'.

"Don't be scared," he says into my hair. "I'll be there right next to you, I won't let you out of my sight. I'll do anything you need, I'll help you walk and feed you soup if that's all you can eat, I'm not going anywhere."

I'm crying by the end. How original.

"Don't cry, baby, don't, there's nothing to cry about," he says.

"Are you for real?" I ask him and he nods, kissing the space between my eyes.

The room is beginning to spin again, the throb of pain around my head tightening ominously. Not again. I'm exhausted beyond words.

"You're still on about—" he starts saying, but stops abruptly and starts calling my name instead. "Ari? Ari!" I hear his voice urgent and frightened. He's shaking me, but I can't respond. The darkness swallows me again.

...

I wake up in the plane. It's only dad and three paramedics in here.

"He didn't want to leave you," dad tells me, holding my hair after I wake up with an intense wave of nausea that almost chokes me until I throw up.

"Thanks," I gasp. "I don't want him seeing me like this."

Dad sits tight-lipped next to me and tries to make up tacky jokes to take my mind off the pain. "This time tomorrow you'll be all better," he tells me at one point.

Well, that's one way of putting it.

...

Next thing I know, we're in New York.

Well, sort of.

Wes meets us at the hospital after the long flight, his eyes red rimmed with lack of sleep, his clothes crumpled, but he flashes a brilliant smile down at me, and that makes me forget the pain for a second. Dad says I went into cardiac arrest during the flight and they had trouble stabilizing me, but I don't remember anything.

The hospital is called Memorial, of all things.

It's vast, from what I understand, but I'm not interested in sightseeing right now, my body rigid with pain, my brain fuzzy with medication. Wes runs silently along the stretcher and exchanges a glance with my dad.

"Thank you," dad tells him.

Wes just nods, out of breath. He grabs dad's shoulder to support him as he falters, and they run next to my gurney until we get to the operation room. Then the nurses ask them politely to step back.

Dad kisses my forehead and wets my cheeks with his tears.

"I'll see you in a few hours," he tells me and I nod.

This is happening. Okay. *This is not the day I...*

"Hey," Wes' warm voice envelopes me like a hug. His eyes frantic but no longer scared, dart left and right, as his jaw works. *There's no time,* I think in a panic. *No damn time.*

"Phelps," he says, his eyes filling with tenderness. "Ari." Just my name, rolling like a caress off his tongue. Even now, just the sound of his voice is enough to send sparks all over my skin.

"I couldn't even say your name, did you know that? I thought for sure, anyone would guess how I felt if I so much as pronounced it." Tears are running freely down his cheeks now, his voice thick with them, but he doesn't even bother to wipe them away. "You're the best thing that's ever happened to me. Remember what I said to you that first time, yeah? This is real."

He presses his mouth to mine hurriedly, thirstily, his tears mingling with mine. I drink him in, tasting my own sadness on his lips and I don't ever want to let go.

"Wes, I need to say—" I begin, but he cuts me off, deepening our kiss.

"Don't you dare say goodbye," he says against my lips.

Then he grabs me, lifting me bodily from the gurney from the waist up, and pulls me to his chest in a bone crushing hug. His whole body is shaking. My nose fills with his scent, my fingers aching to bury themselves in his hair.

"I'll be here when you wake up," he whispers, his voice husky with intensity, as his cheek brushes against mine. "I'll be right here, okay? I'm waiting for you. That's a promise."

There's no time for more, I'm being wheeled in.

"Don't you keep me waiting, Ari!" he shouts as the doors shut him out, in the pristine white corridor, away from my sight. "I love you," he adds more quietly—or I think he does.

His voice just about reaches me before the anesthetic kicks in.

# PART TWO

MEMORIAL

MEMORIAL

MEMORIAL

# Ari's Journal

## *Day Three*

Is it ironic that everything around me is stark white? Clean surfaces, bare walls, marble floors, stiff curtains, beeping machines, pristine windowsills. This is the world I've woken up to.

I'd like to think it's a symbol of the second chance I've been given, the clean slate that will be my life once I'm fully recovered, but the truth is much more brutal and simple than that: this is a hospital. People here die or live, they get better or worse, they come and they go. And now I'm one of those people.

The verdict is that I'll be fine.

Not all tumors are cancer, the doctor explained to dad. I was drifting in and out of sleep, but I heard enough. This one would have crushed my brain as it grew—it was lodged near the vital bits of my head, which is why I almost died, but once they'd completely removed it and done a biopsy on it, it proved to be 'benign'. Which is an obnoxious way to say 'not cancer'. Anyway, I'll need no chemo, no further observation, nothing. I'm not sick anymore.

In fact, I'll be as healthy as ever, once I recover and get out of this place.

So, long story short, I'll live. The tumor is out, my brain works just fine, no cancer in sight. Good news, right? Not good, the best.

I've been assigned 'nurse Jamie'. He's a twenty-nine year-old dude with purple hair and steel toe Crocs, which is nice, but what isn't so nice is how nosy the guy is. He started by asking me all these weird shrink-y questions about how I'm feeling and stuff and then he said he found an old, mostly empty, journal in my things and that it would do my head good to start writing in it.

I asked him if he'd read anything and he said of course, he read everything. How did I expect him to pass the time while he was watching me sleep the anesthetic out of my system?

I told him he didn't have to watch me sleep, for Pete's sake!

He said gently that yes he did, because some kind of big-shot movie star was breathing down his neck the whole time. At this I clamped up and he smiled smugly and left, his shoes squeaking on the polished floor.

So here we are.

Everyone is gone now, dad and Ollie both, since they hadn't slept for three days straight. But now that I'm awake and 'pretty much fine' to quote Jamie, he sent them all to bed—they're staying at a hotel in the next block.

Wes left, too.

They didn't allow anyone who wasn't family in to see me, and dad said he stayed in the lobby until I woke up and responded, and then he had to fly to London to enroll in this prestigious college for actors or something. He left me a note, which I still haven't opened.

Great.

I've written fifteen lines and I'm exhausted. This is day three after waking up.


I took a nap.

Another one, I should add. Then Jamie woke me up to force some foul-tasting soup down my throat, and I tried to eat it, honestly I did, but it tasted like dirt. So he brought me chocolate.

I tried it and almost threw up, it tasted so bad.

"What's wrong with your food in this country?" I asked him as soon as the retching stopped.

He looked down at me with something like sympathy in his light blue eyes. "You have no appetite, honey," he said. "It's not your fault. But, let me tell you, that scrawny look is *so* two thousand and twelve."

"I do not look. . . " He lifted a dark eyebrow. "Oh," I said and he nodded.

"You'll be fine," he said and took my tray out.

After he left I turned on the TV, but was so bored by it that I turned it off again after a few minutes and opened this journal instead.

Ok. Let's see what we have here: I can't move, I'm too weak, so I'm not allowed to get up and walk, because apparently I tried it yesterday and I was so dizzy they had to carry me back inside my room. I feel so weak it's making me cranky and my head starts swimming whenever I move. Not to mention everything hurts like hell.

Oh, and I have no hair.

Like not even one. They shaved it all off before the operation. No way am I letting Wes see me like this. So it's


## Day Four

Now I really hate Jamie. The idiot was right. Not that I honestly think he's an idiot. (Jamie if you're reading this PUT IT DOWN! It's none of your business, you sneaky, purple toy of a nurse.)

And no, I don't really hate you. Nobody can give a sponge bath like you.

Anyway, he was right. Turns out it *is* therapeutic to write things down. I *may* have suddenly fallen asleep in the middle of writing, but I woke up feeling much better all of a sudden. I even managed to keep down a bit of mashed potatoes that tasted like shoe.

Ollie and I walked all over the hospital hallways, and Jamie said that tomorrow I might be allowed to <u>maybe</u> go out. That would be nice.

The doctors reassured dad that I'm completely fine, and so he's thinking of going home and back to work in three days, if all goes well.

Wes has been ringing my phone non-stop since the day before yesterday, so finally today I turned it off. I'm not ready for this, yet, and that's what I told Ollie to tell him, when Wes switched tactics and started bombarding him and dad instead.

I asked them to tell him to give me some time and that I'm fine.

He hasn't called either of them for three hours, so that's progress.

The hospital is settling down for the night. Dad and Ollie have left, so I'm all alone again. My room is a deluxe suite, spacious and full of light during daytime, and I'm the only occupant of it. I hate to think what it's costing Wes, but Ollie said he'll take care of it.

I feel a bit more comfortable letting him pay for it, since he's my brother and all, although that's new too.

All right, we have a problem.

I just woke up sweating from a nightmare. I was crying too, which was fun. The thing is, it wasn't exactly a nightmare. It was more of a memory. At the end it had a bad twist, but the rest of it was as real as when it happened.

And that's what makes it more painful than anything.

An hour later, I'm still crying. I can't stop.

So, here's the thing. I haven't told Ollie or my dad, because I know they'll try to make me change my mind, but with every passing minute one thing is becoming more obvious: I can't do this, I can't call him.

Wes. I can't call him. I haven't spoken to him since before I was lifted onto the plane. I haven't even called him to thank him.

But I can't do it. I can't talk to him.

I don't know if anyone who has ever gone through something like this felt the same. There's no one I can talk to. All I know is this:

I'm not the same person who was wheeled into that operation room. I'm someone else. I am the survivor of a sickness that almost claimed my life. I am someone who almost died and lived to tell about it. I am someone who is fighting for her life.

That's who I am now.

I'm not the athlete, the stunt girl, the. . . I'm not the person he met. I'm someone else. A survivor.

I don't know how to be anything else, and right now, I don't have to.

I just hope he understands.

And waits.

Okay, it's two hours later, and I've decided to write my nightmare down. I'll write it the way I remember it, and I know I will re-live it, but maybe I'll get it out of my system. I haven't stopped thinking about it, and it's made my head hurt and I had a panic attack, because my stupid brain thought that a headache automatically meant it was sick again.

Jamie was <u>not</u> happy about it. He said, do what you have to do, but stop freaking out on me, I've got an entire wing to take care of.

Those were his exact words.

Stop freaking out. Easier said than done. Weird, isn't it, how I never was afraid of doing a stunt, and this sickness, *this* is what's crippling me with fear. After it's passed.

Anyway, he said to do what I have to do. This is what I have to do.

WARNING TO FUTURE ME: don't read this, Ari, it's highly triggering! Listen to me, don't read it again. You promised yourself before writing it, you'd only think about it once while you wrote it to get it out of your system and NEVER AGAIN. It's freaky and crazy. Like you, right now.

All right, here it is:

It started out as a very real memory, as I said. Gosh, it felt so good to lose myself in the happiness of our last week in Corfu. Before it turned into a horror story, that is.

Wes had come to pick me up from the pool where I was doing laps with Coach.

I remember that day. It was three days before the end. I remember lifting my head as I was climbing out of the water, my eyes meeting his, his golden head illuminated by the sun setting behind him in a pink sky.

"Hey," he said, coming over to crouch by the poolside. He removed his sunglasses with a blinding smile.

"Hey," I answered back, completely intimidated by his very presence. "Done for today?"

"I'm all yours," he answered me with a wink, bracing one hand against the blue tiles and reaching out the other to lift me from the water. He insisted that I not change out of my swimming suit. "You. . . you've kinda whet my appetite for a swim," he said, looking at his shoes, all pretend shyness.

"Wes. . . " I fake-whined. "I've been in the water all day."

"So yes?"

Next thing I knew (in the dream), we were diving into the dark waters of Paxi.

In reality, he'd taken me to the L&H, and we'd sailed all the way to the southern part of Corfu, and from there to the tiny island of Paxi. As the sun came down, we'd thrown anchor in the middle of the sea, struggling to see the coast in the gathering darkness.

I remember standing on the hull and looking down to the inky waters, tugging at the long sleeves of my sweater. Wes had already stripped down to his swimming trunks, but now he looked down to my shorts and saw that my legs were covered in goose bumps.

The heat of the day had fled with the dwindling light and the air was cooling rapidly.

"I didn't think. . . " Wes had said, frowning. "Maybe it's too chilly for a swim. Wouldn't want you to catch cold on me."

I shivered at the way he said 'on me', and turned around so that he wouldn't notice. I quickly shrugged off my clothes, before the cold would penetrate my skin.

"Last one in is a total twit!" I yelled and dove.

The water was warmer than the air, as my body slid into its depths. We surfaced next to each other in deep water. The sky was so dark by now I could hardly see in front of me. But before I had time to search for him, Wes was there, his hands cupping my neck, his thighs wrapped around me, supporting me so I was raised half-way above the water, his lips on mine.

"Who's a total twit now," he'd whispered huskily into my wet neck.

DON'T CRY, ARI. DON'T YOU DARE CRY.

I remember every little detail of that day, but I won't write it all here, I can't, it's too painful. Let's just say that when we finally made it to shore we were both breathless and exhausted.

There was a cave opening in about a hundred meters, so we swam over and got out of the water. The darkness was so thick inside, I couldn't even see where to place my foot.

"Wait, I got this," Wes said, keeping a hand on my back.

He had brought a little waterproof torch in the pocket of his trunks, and he turned it on. The light bounced off the surface of the water, reflected on the shiny walls of the cave. Wes apologized for not having a towel, and pressed up close to me, rubbing my arms, pretending to warm them.

Only pretending, of course, because we were both panting, our breaths echoing in the coolness of the cave. We weren't cold anymore—how could we be? My entire body was on fire, I bet his was too.

We sat at the edge of the water, the waves rushing in and out under our toes, cooling our hot skin. Wes started throwing pebbles in, and I tried to judge by sound how many splashes they made. There was no one around for miles. The water was inky black by now, the stars a blanket overhead, beyond the opening of the cave, and although our eyes had adjusted to the dark enough so that we could discern each other's silhouettes, we couldn't see a thing beyond our noses.

"You know, I don't think I've ever been to a more peaceful, beautiful place," he said, gazing at the water. "How many times have you been here?"

"To Paxi? I don't know. Nearly every summer, I suppose. This cave? Never."

"*What?*" His voice was squeaky. He couldn't believe I'd never been there before.

"It's only accessible by boat, you twit," I replied. "And I'm not exactly a billionaire, you know."

"Ouch. I taught you that word, didn't I? Serves me right." He was silent for a bit. "I can almost imagine you here as a kid," he spoke in a dreamy voice, his eyes on my face. "Growing up like a mermaid in this perpetual summer, brown as a nut from the sun."

"Who you calling a nut?" I said.

"I wish I knew you then," he went on. "I wish I had grown up here with you, with your dad and *pappou* and *yiayia* and the sunshine. . . I wish—" his voice caught and I wrapped my arm around his shoulders.

"I wish that too," I said softly, and he pressed his lips to my temple so hard it almost hurt. "On the other hand," I went on in a second, "if I had watched you grow up, being an ass to girls in first grade, or pimply in middle school. . . . grabbing your first cigarette behind the toilets, along with your first kiss. . . maybe I wouldn't have thought you were so cool anymore."

He burst out laughing and the cave around us filled with the sound. When he stopped laughing, he bent his head to mine, so that I could see the earnestness shining in his eyes.

"There would have been no other girls if you had been around from the beginning," he said in a whisper, lifting a strand of wet hair and tucking it behind my ear. "And I wouldn't have been an ass to you, I swear. Not you."

A moment later, in reality, as soon as he saw my teeth chattering from the cold, he bodily picked me up and ran into the water. I swatted his arms away and we raced each other back to the yacht. I let him win this time.

We dropped anchor in the marina of *Lefkimi*, while we showered and changed, and we went to a little *taverna* to eat, before returning to town again.

In my dream however, things ended differently.

In my dream, directly after we'd suddenly found ourselves on the yacht, he'd said some more deliciously dirty things—which I'd never heard him say in real life, and if I had, frankly I would have thought them ridiculous. Well, in the dream somehow they worked. Boy did they work.

Anyway, moving on. After we were done with that whole weird (but hot) thing, we dove in.

Only, as soon as we were in the water, I started sinking again, my body suspended in pain. It was just like that last day by the Rubble. I was drowning right next to him.

I went under and Wes dove after me, but I sank deeper and deeper into the inky water. I kept trying to kick towards the surface, towards Wes' frantic eyes, but a force was dragging me downwards. I couldn't breathe, my lungs were burning. And Wes, refusing to let go of my hand, was dying along with me.

The last thing I saw (in the dream) were his green eyes, open and lifeless, a bubble of water escaping his lips and his fingers clasped white around mine.

Then I woke up.

### Day Five

I called Katia very early this morning. I tried to give her a brief description of what has been happening all month between me and Wes, and she was really cool and understanding, although I could hear it in her voice she was a bit hurt, too.

"I'm so sorry for not telling you," I whispered into the phone. "I felt so guilty all this time."

"It's okay," she replied. "I'm just mad that you had to go through all this alone, that I couldn't be there for you. . . " Her voice trailed off into silence. Outside the window all was dark and calm, no sign of the dawn just yet. My head felt dull, as though it was filled with cotton.

"I was stupid enough not to tell anyone until pretty much the last moment," I told her. I hadn't turned the camera on, I still wasn't ready for her to see me like this. "But I wasn't alone. I had grandpa and dad and. . . Wes." My voice broke.

"Oh, Ari," Katia said, and her voice sounded hoarse. "Was it. . . good with him? Before everything happened?"

Ha. Was it good? How to even begin to. . .

"He saved my life," I said simply. "Twice. Have I told you that? That's how we met. And that's how we parted, in the end."

"Ari, you sound sad. Really sad. As though you're wishing he hadn't," she said. Waited. "Do you?"

"Of course not. "

How does she do it? How does she find the exact thing to say that will pierce me like the knife? She just gets it. Every freaking time.

"Okay, sometimes I wish it hadn't been him," I admitted, feeling ashamed. "I keep waiting for the other shoe to drop. I mean, sure the tumor was benign and everything, but all I can think about is when it will start getting big again, and try to kill me."

"It's too soon to have gotten over your fear," she told me eventually. "After all you. . . you must have been scared all this time, maybe not even realizing how much you were dreading that something bad would happen." I scoffed, but she kept talking. "Give yourself time."

"You're my therapist, you know that?" I said and she chuckled. "Will I always be this scared from now on?" I murmured into the phone.

She didn't answer.

"I'm so embarrassed about what I did to Wes," I went on, aching at the familiar way his name rolled off my tongue. "Embarrassed and scared. I. . . I haven't even spoken to him since. He's had enough drama for a lifetime. Saving lives, rushing to hospitals. I don't know what I was thinking, bringing him into this. I just. . . I want him out of this."

"Does he—" Katia stopped to clear her throat. "Do you think he'll be hurt by you not calling him?" she asked, and because it was her, I didn't mind the question. If it had come from anyone else, I would bristle. But now all I could feel was emptiness.

"Well, we knew each other all of three weeks," I said. "That's so little. So soon. . . We weren't in a relationship or anything. And who can be sure, after everything, that it would go much beyond that, anyway?"

"It didn't sound like a three-week thing," Katia replied.

"He won't mind. He's Weston Spencer."

"Do you really believe that?"

I didn't know what to say to that. Do I believe that he won't care? Of course I don't.

It's night-time again, but for once I'm not sleepy. Now that's what I call an improvement. I've been thinking all day about turning my phone on and calling Wes, but then I would always remember something stupid I did to him and I'd change my mind.

Or something stupid I did to my dad, like lying to him all summer. Or to grandpa and grandma. Or how irresponsible I was, swimming and diving and surfing and driving around while at any given time the bomb in my head might go off.

I've realized that I was in denial this whole time—textbook denial—and had sort of persuaded myself that as long as I pretended everything was all right, and threw myself into doing stunts, then nothing bad would happen.

Still, that's no excuse.

I could have put so many people in danger.

Not counting traumatizing everyone who watched me nearly die a couple of times.

And Wes. Gosh, I couldn't face him.

I owe him an apology. And an explanation. I owe him so much.

Plus, I owe him my life. How am I walking away from that? *Am* I walking away from it? It seems so easy, now that there's already an ocean between us, to just let go. Not to pick up the phone, not to call, not to talk to him. To let time and space flow between us, until. . . Until what? Until I'm better? Until I'm my old self again? Until I'm no longer ashamed and scared and weak?

Who knows how long that will take, though. . . Wouldn't it be more fair to him to let him go?

Dammit, I can't believe I'm even thinking about it. It might have just been three weeks—only *one* of which we actually spent together—but. . . that was the most important week of my life. I faced death with this guy by my side. I already miss him so much it hurts.

But when I even think about picking up the phone, I'm paralyzed. It takes me back to how I was. And I can't face that. Not now. Not yet. Whether I like it or not, he's part of what happened to me. *He's* in it. He's in the memories, in the pain. And I can't get rid of them. They're like the second tumor that the doctors didn't remove.

Aaaargh, I'm going crazy here.

I'll just stop thinking about it for a second, I'm already getting a headache, Jamie won't be happy with me.

Let's write about what happened today instead. It's not like I've got to do anything else, anyway.

I spent the day with Ollie.

His face looked pale and drawn, and he didn't talk much (at first). We watched TV for about an hour, chancing upon Anna's vampire show. Ollie insisted all the girls love it and I hated it, but it had some sick stunts, so I focused on how the hell they did those.

I put the TV on mute as a blonde teenaged vampire was getting ready to drink from her human dad's neck—only he wasn't human, as we'd seen in the last scene, he was a werewolf, whose blood would kill her once she ate him. Deep. I turned to him.

"Okay, what's up with you?" I asked him. "You're brooding."

"I'm not," he replied, looking straight ahead.

"You could give that vampire Count a run for his money," I retorted and he said 'pfft'. "So, spill. What's wrong?"

"I don't know. It's depressing in here. Wanna go out?" He got up and paced around my bed. "Although for that you probably should get dressed."

Was that a dig to how I'd gotten used to stay in my pj's all day? Fine, I'd show him.

"Just give me a sec," I said. "Meet you out back?"

So he got out and I got out of my pajamas and into my sweats and a light blue beanie he bought me yesterday, stealing a glance at the mirror. I almost had a heart attack.

The only thing I recognized were my eyes. Or, to be more specific, the *color* of my eyes. It was exactly the same as always.

As for the rest, it belonged to a stranger.

A bare head, all angles and bones, cheekbones pronounced, huge eyes staring back at me in terror. I mean, not just fear. I look terrified. My lips look too wide for my face, and ready to cry. And scared, of course. Everything on me looks scared.

Get a grip, I told myself.

Then I noticed how red and puffed up my eyelids looked from last night's crying spree and, disgusted with myself, I pulled the beanie as low as I could over my forehead. Good. Now at least I looked angry and scared, instead of just scared.

Much better.

As soon as I walked through the sliding doors of the hospital, Ollie strode to me across the wide, park-like area, and pushed up the rim of my hat so that it wouldn't cover my forehead entirely.

"Where are your gloves?" he asked me.

By the way, it's cold here, wearing-gloves cold. We're not in Corfu anymore. Home seems so far away, like a dream I once had.

"I'm not a grandma, that's where they are," I replied, snorting. "So now are you going to tell me what's wrong?"

"How are you feeling?" he asked, instead of answering. "And before you lie again, let me tell you that you look like crap."

"Thanks!" I kicked him in the shin.

"I mean, you look as though you're *feeling* like crap."

"I am," I shrugged.

We started walking towards this massive green area, our shoes sinking in the soft grass. A fountain was splashing along to our left and a few birds were crowing overhead in the gray-blue sky. Wooden benches were scattered around, and a few patients were walking slowly along, some of them dragging drips or wearing medical masks. It felt pretty peaceful—as long as you forget

161

this is a freaking hospital.

"Aren't you happy?" Ollie stopped in his tracks and turned to me. I gaped, taken aback. He sounded. . . kinda mad. "I mean, you're alive, you're fine, you'll be released in five days, at most. What's there to cry about?"

"You think I'm ungrateful." I realized.

"No, no, no, I don't." The frustration left his face as quickly as it had come. He pulled me in for a hug, and I think I may have tensed at first a little, not being used to it, but soon enough I leaned against him, letting his warmth envelope me. "I was just so so scared, you have no idea. You—you nearly died on us, Ari. I don't think I'll ever get over that. And every time I look at you since, you're a miracle. Alive and breathing. A miracle on two feet."

I laughed, but his eyes were serious.

"I know," I told him.

"So what is it? Your dad, he's been worried out of his mind about you, he's convinced there's something wrong with your head. But I spoke to the doctors, I spoke to everyone in this place, and they all agree, you're pretty damn fine. Why don't you feel it?"

"I'm. . . I'm. . . " I couldn't get enough air in my lungs to speak.

"What?" Ollie asked more gently. We sat down on a  bench overlooking the street. I swallowed, playing with the cord of his jacket.

I opened my mouth and, without warning, everything poured out of me, so quickly, in a flood of words that barely made sense.

"I'm *scared!*" I almost yelled it, springing to my feet. Ollie turned to me, a look of surprise in his eyes. "I'm so tired of being scared all the time, of expecting something horrible to happen at any moment. When I stub my foot and pain shoots up my leg, when my head starts aching even a tiny little bit, when they put food in front of me and I can't eat it. . . and every other little thing, every damned thing that I used to take for granted. . . the first thing that comes to mind immediately is, is this it? Am I sick again? Does this mean I'm still dying? If I paid too little attention before, I should pay more now, right? Only, it's driving me crazy!"

I sat back down, exhausted by my outburst, and Ollie stayed silent for a couple of minutes. The silence began to weigh heavily between us, and from the corner of my eye I could see his jaw working. He sighed and stretched his long legs in front of him, burying his hand in his hair.

Then he cursed.

We ate in the hospital's restaurant—that is *he* ate and I pushed the food around on my plate, but for once he didn't force me to eat. He smiled and made jokes and it was a bit forced, still we both made a good effort at pretending to enjoy ourselves.

It was raining again in the afternoon, so we stayed in my room playing cards.

"Listen, you. . . you know you don't *have* to stay here, right?" I said and he laughed. "I mean," I added quickly, in case he thought I didn't want him there, "I've known you for what, like ten minutes? We hardly know each other. I hardly know you. And now you suddenly have to sit in my hospital room—"

"What do you want to know?" he interrupted me.

"Huh?"

"I get it. I need to be here right now, for you, but I do realize that you hardly know me," he said. "So get to know me. What do you want to know?"

"Oh." His blue eyes were fixed on mine intently. I turned aside, trying to hide my red cheeks. "What do you like? What do you hate? What do you dream of?"

"All right, slow down, Sherlock. Why don't we play twenty questions?"

"Sarcasm," I answered. "Nice."

He laughed, leaning back on the pillows, and then turned around to rearrange them, throwing one that was bothering him to me.

"Hey!" I shouted. "Sarcasm I appreciate, violence not so much."

We were both in sweats and he was lying on my bed, me on the little bedside armchair, the food tray between us as a card table.

"You call *that* violence," he laughed, "you should have been on the set of my first movie."

"Why?" I asked, intrigued. "What was it about?"

"Ninjas," he answered. "The 'Boy Hero' anime that was made into a kid's flick? Ever heard of it? I was the voice of Mex. . . and then I *was* Mex."

I'm ashamed to say I immediately sat up and looked at him with new-found respect. But not really ashamed, because that's my *brother* we're talking about here. Internally I was like YAS.

"You were. . . You—?" I started, but he lifted an eyebrow and I stopped quickly. "Sorry, it's just I used to watch this all the time. My friend Katia and I, we used to shut ourselves in my room all Sunday morning, pausing every sequence and trying to replicate it. Well, actually I tried the stunts and she calculated the integer spin and the momentum of the orbital something, I can't even remember the words, trying to prove whether your moves were possible or not, from a scientific standpoint."

"She sounds like a delightful person."

"Oh, she is. Wait till you meet her, she's a physicist," I said and he pretended to shiver with horror at the word 'physicist'. "You'll love her. You have to, because I love her."

"I'm scared now."

"I'm telling you she's the best, okay? You'll see."

"Can't wait. Okay, care to make this interesting?" he asked, kicking off his shoes and crossing his striped-socks-clad feet at the ankles.

"Always."

"I'll answer one question for every bite you take," he deadpanned, lifting a plate with a PB&J sandwich, which he had been trying to make me swallow since lunch.

"You play dirty."

"All right, I'll sweeten the deal," he said. "For every five questions you ask, and for every five bites you take, you can do as many crunches as you can, up to fifty."

I froze. I hadn't exercised since the operation. *Can I still do crunches?* My stupid brain thought. I told it to shut up.

Ollie was still smiling up at me, but suddenly he looked uncertain.

"Can I do pushups too?" I asked, narrowing my eyes.

"Anything you want, except maybe for somersaults. We'll have to wait until it stops raining for that."

"Cool," I said. "Okay let me think. . . Oh, I know. Favorite song."

"That's your first question?" he asked, pushing the plate towards me and picking up the cards in his long fingers, straightening them perfectly before he put them back in the box. His face looks completely focused.

"It's the most important one," I replied, watching him. "After your favorite car, but I'm scared to ask that one. A little OCD, are we?"

"Okay," he said. "There is no *little* OCD, either you have it or you don't. And it's way more complicated than just fixing a pack of ca—" He stops himself. "One question at a time, okay? One question and one bite, before I answer."

"All right, dad." I bit into the fluffy bread. It tasted like mud, but I managed to swallow the entire bite.

"Guns 'n' Roses, November Rain. And Alfa Romeo Spider, although you cheated."

"Oooh," I said, trying not to show how hard it was to swallow down the mouthful of PB&dust, "that might be a problem."

"Song or vehicle?"

"Both."

"Ah, don't you know? There's no getting rid of me, I'm family," he replied easily. "I mean, I've got a sister who cheats at twenty questions, but I'm not complaining. At least not out loud." He winked at me. "Next question."

I felt a slight shiver as the word 'family' came out of his mouth. "I wasn't trying to cheat, it's just the questions keep popping in my head. . . Oh, I've got another one. What age did you get your first role?"

"Eight."

"Name of your dad."

"You didn't take a bite."

"Fine. I'll take the freaking bite. What's his name?"

"John Kovack."

"What?! *James Bond?*"

"Is that your next question?"

"I didn't know your dad was freaking James Bond. . . I didn't know the most eligible bachelor of Hollywood had ever been married."

"Yes, he was married briefly to Christina, and by briefly I mean for about two months. I see him every second Christmas at Vegas. Okay, two more questions and then you can do your crunches."

"Every second—? That's. . . that's cool."

"Well, cooler than most dads in the business," he shrugged. "Still it sucks as far normal families go. . . But who am I to talk about normal families? I've no idea what the words even mean." He laughed and got up gingerly, stretching. "I'll be back in a sec."

And he simply walked into the little bathroom closet right inside the hospital room. I stifled a giggle. I think that's when I realized he was feeling so at ease with me, truly at home. Because we *are* each other's home.

And then it happened.

His phone beeped.

I know I shouldn't have looked, but it was sitting *right there* on the nightstand. At spitting distance. I just glanced over, and for a second the text message blinked on the screen.

The name on top.

Aaargh.

It was Wes, of course.

The text read:

**Hey, 'Babe'. Ha. So, how is she today?**

Then the screen faded to black. My heart started beating like crazy and I took a deep breath.

Okay, first of all *Babe*? WTH? And the 'she' could be anyone right? Right. Anyone, could be anyone. I tried to breathe calmly, looked out the window. Then the phone blinked again. Some demon made me look—yeah, like I could resist.

**She feeling any better?**

The screen went dark in a second.

Inside the bathroom the faucet ran. *Come on, Ollie. Hurry back, it's gonna blink again.* And then it did.

**Give me something, I'm dying here, Ols. Come on.**

Right then the door opened. I couldn't speak, couldn't breathe, just sat there not moving a muscle.

"Next question, girlfriends," I asked, hardly knowing what I said. Ollie looked at me strangely, because my voice sounded a bit too loud, but he plopped himself on my bed with a thud and sighed dramatically.

"Oh, you don't want to go there, that's just not something a dude talks about with his little sister."

He picked up his phone. "Did this thing beep, like, ten times while I was in there? Sheesh. . . " He flicked through the three texts, then flung his phone away carelessly, murmuring, "idiot!"

"Do you know," he turned to me, "what it means when a guy you've known since you were six suddenly starts to call you 'Babe'?"

"Babe?" I repeated in a choked voice.

I could almost hear Wes' voice in my head, retorting some really lame response to Ollie. I missed him so much it hurt to breathe.

"Yep. Babe," Ollie said. "There was some comic actor in the nineteen thirties, you know, vintage black and white flicks, not much sound apart from a piano played in a frenzy, and a few white-letter frames thrown about to give you a sense of the plot. . . It doesn't get any more vintage than that, right? And this dude is fat. Not obese, but chubby in a cute, funny way, doing stand up comedy, getting into scrapes with his friend who was thin as a rail. It was a big deal back then for someone to be chubby, I suppose—people didn't have much to eat usually. Anyway, they're called '*Laurel and Hardy*'."

"Oh I know them, we have them in Greece, too," I said, my thoughts momentarily distracted. "There's a poster of them in Chandler and Joey's room, in Friends."

Ollie laughed. "Yep, them."

"Oh. *Oh!* The L&H," I realized. "That's where that comes from?"

"Exactly!" Ollie said, snapping his fingers. "Wes loves these two dudes. So, he got it into his huge head that I'm the fat guy, cause his name was Oliver Hardy—or Ollie. Turns out people started to call him 'Babe', cause with his chubby face, always laughing like that, he looked like a baby. So he's calling me that now. As in 'Babe'."

"Sounds normal to me," I murmured, hardly knowing what to say.

"He started it after our latest round of 'truth or dare'. He lost, of course. It's such a stupid thing, but we've been doing it since we were kids, daring each other to do lame stuff in front of the cameras to pass the time. How should I know that this one would turn into the weirdest . . . "

Suddenly he frowned, realizing he'd been talking about *him* all this time. He winced.

"Ah, sorry," he said and I shrugged, trying not to let him see how much it hurt. "I. . .Sorry, I shouldn't...Wes said you guys haven't talked—"

I held my breath. This was it. Wes had totally told him we hadn't spoken since before the operation, and who knows what else? How Ollie hadn't asked me about it until now, I don't know.

"I. . . um," I said intelligently.

"You know what?" he interrupted me. "None of my business." He lifted his hands in the air. "I'm here for you right now. What was your question again?"

He grabbed a handful of chips from my plate and shoved them into his mouth. And that was that. Subject dropped.

I stared at him as he was sprawled there on my bed, chewing noisily, in that way people do and piss you off, but when they're your brother or your dad you're used to it, and you don't even hear it anymore. That's when I realized it: I loved him.

I love him. That's it. That's how it happened. (I'm glad I've written this down for future reference, by the way. That was the exact moment. The moment I knew. Because he understood. That's all it took.)

"So. Girlfriends. Spill," I told him as casually as I could. "I didn't swallow that nasty bite for nothing. And without anybody having to yell at me to do it."

"I never yell. All right, have it your way. Girlfriends. . . let me see. None. Girls. . . about a million."

"Oh, so you're *that* guy."

"One more question, smartass."

"I think we are nearing dangerous waters of TMI, as in too much information, so let's talk about something else. Hm. . . .Oh, yep. I've got it. Happiness."

"I beg your pardon?"

"Happiness. What does happiness mean for you?"

Ollie was silent for a moment, thinking. "I don't suppose you're expecting a real answer right now, are you?" He fake yawned.

"Do you expect me to keep all of these bites down?"

"Crap," he said. "Okay. Happiness. I'll need a sec here."

It took him almost five minutes to answer. Then,

"Cruising on the L&H with just Wes, no girls, only the sea and us. Skyping with my dad when he's on his plane, on his way to or from a set. Oreos. Lying on my bed, headphones in, eyes closed, listening to really tacky nineties music. *Grand Theft Auto V*. Surfing in a beach in Sydney where the curls get as tall as twenty feet, maybe higher. Watching your dad and you playing charades. The day I called you sis for the first time."

"Oreos?" I said.

"Drop me five," he replied.

I did twenty-five push ups. But then he had to literally pick me off the floor and call a nurse because I couldn't catch my breath. Thankfully Jamie was off duty—that's something, at least.

And then, like the grandma that I've become, I slept for nine hours straight. Woke up in the freaking middle of the night, and couldn't sleep anymore.

Now it's six thirty in the morning and I've been writing for an hour. My wrist hurts, but I'm wide awake. I'll try to get some more sleep anyway. If Jamie comes in here in three hours and finds me still up, there will be hell to pay.

### *Update*

Apparently I did fall asleep. Something woke me at about eight seven; a cool hand on my forehead.

"Dad?" I squinted up at him.

"Go back to sleep," he said. "Just wanted you to know I'm back. Your brother fell asleep on the couch outside your room, I'm taking him back to the hotel. You ok?"

"Yeah," I said. "Wait, can I talk to him for a sec before you go?"

There was something I wanted to ask him before I'd fallen asleep like a freaking baby.

"What?" Ollie asked as he came in, frowning, his eyes all blurry with sleep.

"You never got to tell me what's wrong with you." I said. "I did, but not you."

"Ari. . . " he sighed, rubbing his eyes. "I'm still asleep here."

"I won't go back to sleep unless you tell me. Or I'll have terrible nightmares, I always do when there's something unresolved in my mind."

He looked at me sheepishly for a second, and then I groaned, because I finally got it. His eyes were telling me that my nightmares would be even worse if he told me. Which could only mean one thing. Wes.

"Tell me," I said, sitting up.

"You already know." His voice was resigned.

"Is he. . . is he struggling with—is he drinking again?" I whispered.

"Bingo," he said and yawned. "Do me a favor," he went on, placing a hand on my shoulder. "Please get it through your thick head that it isn't your fault and go back to sleep, ok? I know what you're thinking, and I want to tell you, what you're thinking? Don't think it."

"Ok," I said in a small voice.

"Ari?" he stopped at the door.

"What?"

"I'm—I'm glad you're okay. Really glad." He smiled. "For a few days it looked like. . .I'd found you too late. I'm incredibly happy it wasn't true."

I just stared at him, dumb. "When will *I* start feeling happy about it?" I said finally in a voice I hardly recognized as my own.

He was next to me in two long strides, hugging me so fiercely my breath caught.

"Soon enough, I hope," he said against my bald head. "You have your whole life ahead of you. This will just fade to a bad memory, nothing more, you'll see."

Then he said goodnight and left.

And I picked this thing up to write until I felt sleepy. Which I don't, not in the least. I feel tired, but not sleepy.

I feel guilty.

I feel scared.

He said it's not my fault but. . . Oh, it is. It is. Wes, I'm so sorry. So so so so sorry.

That's it. I'm calling him tomorrow.


### Day Six

I'm going to write this down right now, just after I woke up, in case I forget it. I mean, I'm pretty sure it's branded in my memory forever—not to be too dramatic or anything—but it's the details that count, right?

## LOSE ME.

So the memory came so vivid it was almost real, right at that point where sleep meets wakefulness, and I don't think that kind of lucidity comes too often. It's eleven to nine now so, considering Ollie and dad went to bed about three hours ago, I have hours until they show up.

All right, let's do this. (Jamie, I hate you.)

This memory is from the day I was sick and Wes came to my house and stayed with me practically all day. The day that he said 'he wouldn't change anything, except for the pain.'

I was lying on my side, on top of the bedspread, between bouts of pain and nausea. Wes was on the bed beside me, his body parallel to mine. He had his head propped up on his hand, his elbow next to my nose.

"How come you don't have a boyfriend?" he asked me out of the blue.

The tone of his voice was conversational, as though he just wanted to make small talk. Or maybe to distract me from feeling lousy. It worked, anyway.

"I don't know," I said. "All my friends are in Athens or Europe, in college or university, studying. I kinda. . . skipped that step."

"Well, in the industry," he said, "kids don't study. They don't have to. They don't even read actually, no one does except for me, but. . . that's another story. Anyway, I plan on attending a college interview in a few weeks. *If* they even consider my application. I mean, it's one of the most prestigious schools for dramatic and visual arts in the world."

I almost scoffed at the thought of any school not accepting him.

"Sounds cool," I said. "Good for you. There's no doubt you'll get in, though, right? If *you* don't get into the best school there is, then who will?"

"You really think I can do it?" he asked me, his face lightening up, and I said of course he could. "You've been lucky with your choices in life," he said quietly and I shuddered.

"More than you know," I replied in the same tone. "Speaking of boyfriends, how come *you* don't have one?"

I blushed as soon as I realized what I'd said, but he didn't laugh at me. I've been speaking English with my dad since I was a kid, but it's not my mother tongue, after all. Wes had never once corrected me, though, even when I knew I made mistakes or slip-ups.

"Girlfriend, you mean?" he asked. "I don't. . . I don't do girlfriends. Relationships in general. I did once or maybe twice, but I don't go there anymore. Is that bad?" he added with a smile.

"On the contrary," I said. "It's good."

"That's what I think too."

I turned slowly on my back so as not to invoke any unpleasant dizziness, and he moved to give me space. I had the impression what we were talking about wasn't as simple as boyfriends and relationships, that there was an underlying tension to his words, but my head was too fuzzy to untangle the thread.

"How are you feeling?" he asked.

I just shrugged. I hated the fact that I was sick, and that he was here, seeing it.

We stayed silent for a few minutes, lying there, next to each other. His body's warmth was spreading to my skin, the golden hairs of his arm brushing mine.

Just as I was beginning to relax (and maybe nod off a bit), he sat up suddenly, jostling me, and I opened my eyes to see him leaning over me with a freaked expression on his face, as though a horrifying thought had just occurred to him.

"Listen, promise me you'll never read anything about me," he said. "Promise me you'll never watch an interview, never look at a blog or an article or a. . . a gossip column."

There was such vehemence in his voice; he said the word 'gossip' as though it was a swear word. His green eyes were burning into mine with an intensity I'd never seen before.

"O. . . kay," I said slowly. "It's a bit too late actually, 'cause I have read Young People magazine already, and I've watched that interview on TV, where you talked about THE WATER WARS, not to mention. . . " I started counting on my fingers.

"No." He grabbed my arm. "No. Forget it. All of it. Please, please."

He was serious. I'd been joking, but there was nothing amused about his expression.

"All right," I said, in my best 'calm down, dude' voice. "All right, I will."

He nodded, thanking me silently.

"Are you afraid I might. . . I might say things, spread—?" I started asking, but he stopped me with an impatient gesture.

"It's the exact opposite," he said. "I can't, I. . . " he swallowed. "I can't be scared every single day that you might read or see something that will make you think differently about me."

"That won't happen so easily," I tried to interrupt him, but he didn't even hear me.

"What Elle did the other day, when she talked about those girls. . . she couldn't be able to cause so much damage if I wasn't. . . who I am, you know? Even as we speak, who knows what she or anybody else for that matter will be saying to the press, feeding them stories that are made-up, or even partially true, and then, ugh. . . " he was out of breath.

"Hey. Hey hey hey." I raised myself to my knees and took his chin in my hand. I turned him to look at me, his eyes wild and scared. "Wes."

He gasped aloud, his breath coming uneven. "They control my life," he whispered, his eyes wide. "I can't—I go crazy even thinking of it, I just want to feel numb. I just want to forget this prison I'm in."

"Look at me," I said and he did.

I still had my hand on his jaw and before I could drop it, he placed his fingers on top of mine, suspending me there.

"No one controls your life but you. This is just a way to make a living, it's your job, that's all." I was speaking slowly and calmly and he was drinking my words in, his hands squeezing mine. "Okay? No one can control or even affect you without your permission. You are who you are, Wes Spencer, and you don't need anyone's permission for that. You're that kid who survived being the water pirate since you were practically a baby, and you went through rehab and grew up alone and built a career for yourself all on your own. And now you're going to college, and choosing the films you'll work in, not to mention rescuing stupid stunt girls from drowning next to your yacht, because that's who you are. And there's no way in hell that could change. Unless you let it."

"Ari. . . " he sounded lost. He smoothed down my hair, which was probably sticking up every which way. "What if I let it?"

"You won't," I told him. "You won't."

He smiled but I could tell he didn't believe me. And, truth be told, why should he? Sure, he didn't know it yet, but I was the one who had let everything else except myself take control of my life, and not him.

"How did you get so wise?" he said and his hand slowly traveled down my arm to my waist as we kneeled there on my bed, face to face, but the next second my dad was yelling from downstairs that he was home and asking if I was feeling any better, and he got up faster than lighting and pretended to be interested in the view of my window, on the other side of the room.

Then that little incident of me being sick in the bathroom and then having to lie through my teeth to him and my dad interrupted our conversation for good.

Oh, and I didn't call him.

You knew I wouldn't, didn't you, diary? I couldn't.

Not after remembering that. How he opened his soul for me to look into, and all I did was lie to him. And then lied again.

And then almost died.

How do I start? What do I say? 'Sorry for lying'? 'Sorry for letting you spend an entire day with me when I was sick, but not trusting you enough to tell you what was really the matter'? There's so much to apologize for. . . I haven't even  apologized to myself for everything I did to myself—the danger I put myself in, the hours, the days of pain. I freaking had to remind myself not to die every day, for crying out loud.

That sounded really cheesy, didn't it?

Well, welcome to the new me. Cheesy. And chicken. Most of all chicken.

Haven't even turned my phone on.


### Day Seven

Ollie went back home.

I'll be released tomorrow. I'm up to a hundred crunches and fifty pushups.

Sweet.

Still no phone, which means no Wes. Whenever I think of him, I just. . . can't.

## Day Ten

Still here.

Two days ago I woke up in the middle of a night with a sky-high fever—I don't remember it, dad told me afterwards—talking in unintelligible gibberish, among which could be discerned that I wanted someone to make the pain stop and let me die.

I'm so proud of myself.

Turns out the incision they had to dig inside the back of my head suffered a mild infection (doctor's lingo, not mine). I suppose I'm lucky it was 'mild'. I hate to think in what state dad would have found me in if the infection was huge. Probably would be out of my mind by now.

Anyway, not to be ungrateful or anything, but I spent the next three days including today, dozing on and off, antibiotics trickling into my veins, my fever flying off the charts.

I'm better now, but this means no leaving, no crunches, no Greece for at least ten more days.

What can you do?

Right now is the first time since day six that I'm feeling somehow normal. My fever isn't completely gone and my head is throbbing, but I don't feel like screaming in pain anymore, so that's a plus.

Ok, so now you know that I'm alive, dear diary, I think we can both go to sleep.

## Day Eleven

Jamie came into my room today to take my temperature and check my medication. Then he flops onto the bed next to me, folding his white-scrubs-clad legs beneath him, and told me in a serious tone that he wanted to talk to me.

"I write in my journal every day," I told him, "what else do you want from me?"

"I want you to see a therapist," he replied coolly.

I'm not proud of what I did next, but I kicked him off the bed. Not that he fell, of course. He just slid to the edge and then immediately sat back again, making himself at home against half of my pillow.

Then he squeezed my almost nonexistent bicep and tsk-tsked.

"Haven't you any gyms down in Cyprus?" he asked me.

"It's Greece, as you know very well," I told him, annoyed. "And I'm an athlete, which you also know. What are you—are you leading a second secret life as a boxer? Your muscles feel hard like stone."

"Don't let the hair fool you, baby," he said. "I run three marathons every year."

"Cool," I said, impressed.

I could see it now. He's built slight and wiry—with enough muscle, this is the perfect sport for him. And his movements are always synchronized and graceful, plus he doesn't ever look tired despite being on his feet all day.

"I couldn't even manage a hundred pushups the other day," I mused.

"Which brings us to what I was saying. I think you should see someone," he turned serious again.

"Like my coach?" I asked innocently.

"Like a therapist," he repeated, as though he was talking to a kid. "Like someone who could help you with all this feeling-sorry-for-myself, being-in-denial, can't-come-to terms-with-the-new-reality issues you've got running all over the place." He made an eloquent gesture with his hands, but I was too seething angry by then to find it cute.

"What did you say?" I sat up. "I. Do not. Have. Issues."

He sighed. "Ari, honey. Like hell you don't. You've been crying every day since you woke up."

"Well, isn't that to be expected for someone who has been through so much trauma. . . ?" I started saying, but my voice sounded unsure even to me.

He nodded. "It is," he said. "But tell me this. When was the last time you laughed?"

I considered telling him he's an idiot, but I didn't.

"When did you celebrate your recovery, the excellent, *miraculous* news that there is *nothing wrong* with you? You were almost *dead* one minute and the next you're *completely* healthy. Do you know how many people are given this chance? About. . . zero point one in a million. And you're one of them. Have you even talked to your grandpa? He's been calling your dad every *three* hours. Your grandma too, that other girl who is a scientist, and your boyfriend—"

"Would you just." I had to stop to take a deep breath. "Would you stop bombarding me with all of these questions, it's none of your business, okay? Where do you come off yelling at me? You don't even know me!"

Somewhere in the middle of his italics-riddled speech, I'd sprung from the bed, and was now pacing around it, furious.

He got up calmly and came up to me. We are almost the same height, so his eyes were on the same level as mine, looking at me directly in a way that made me really uncomfortable. But for some reason I couldn't look away.

He gently took my hands in his.

"I know what's happened to you," he told me. "I've seen it so many times. You didn't want to face the fact that you might be dying before, but now it's finally real. You *were* dying. You almost did. And you're so scared of that whole idea you'll do anything to push it away from your mind."

He cupped my cheek with his hand and I felt the coolness of the ring he's wearing on his middle finger against my bare skin.

"You'll end up running away from everyone and everything that was in your life before, and try to erase the fear along with the people who love you and stood by you at the worst time of your life. The people who are worth keeping in your life. But they will keep reminding you of what *almost* happened, just by being there. If you don't deal with it, you won't be able to get close to them ever again. You'll push them out of your life to survive."

I wasn't crying by the end.

I was mad.

I swatted his hand away and turned my back on him.

"Get out," I said in a low voice.

He chuckled.

"You hate me, don't you?" he said. "You would really kill me if you could right now. Well, my job is to keep you alive, and that's not what you are right now, not by any consideration. Think about what I said, will you, Goldie?"

I spun around so quickly I got dizzy and wobbled on my feet. He didn't make a move to steady me, just stood there looking at me like he felt sorry for me, a sad smile on his face.

"WHAT did you call me?" I asked as soon as the room stopped spinning.

"I don't know, you tell me," he smirked. "At the very least it will take your mind off of planning my murder."

So I thought about it and I finally figured it out.

Goldie.

As in gold.

As in shiny.

As in my bald head is shiny under the fluorescent hospital lights.

You're dead, Jamie.

### Day Thirteen

Not much happened yesterday. I slept. I ate. I told dad to go back to Greece about a trillion times and he said, and I quote, 'no way, dude,' for about a billion point nine of them. The rest of the time he was dozing next to me—he's spent a few sleepless nights worrying about my fever, but even that's almost gone now, so it's all good.

Plus I spoke to *pappous* and *yiayia*. In your face, Jamie.

*Pappous* sounded calm enough, but his voice was shaky so I know he was crying, but from happiness (I hope). Grandma whooped. She actually whooped at me.

Then she asked me if she could send me some Greek homemade pie via courier mail. I said no, but I'd be eating it soon enough in person. A shudder ran through me at the thought of being back. More fear than excitement. More trauma than healing.

Which brought Jamie's words from the other day back in a rush.

174

# LOSE ME.

I told her I'd be seeing her soon, hopefully, and she told me to take my time and get my strength back.

A couple of hours later I was outside, trying to walk around the grounds with a little bit of dignity and stamina, but sweating and panting like a dog instead, when dad met me, coming out of the side entrance in a brisk pace. In his hand he was holding his phone carefully, which meant there was probably somebody on the line.

"I think," he said as he reached me, "this is for you."

It was Katia. I mean, not just her voice. It was Katia, in all her crazy-hair glory, her lips huge as she was leaning down towards the screen, her delicate eyebrows frowning in disapproval.

"Put it down!" she was yelling at my dad. "I'm getting vertigo."

I sprawled myself on the nearest bench, fighting to catch my breath.

"Take it, Goldie," dad said, extending his hand.

"Good," I told him, "I'm glad this nickname is catching on."

"Revenge time," Katia said, as soon as I was holding her steady in front of my face.

"What?" I gasped, still panting.

"All these years of listening to you make fun of my hair, its frizziness, its curliness, its. . . "

"I did NOT make fun of your hair. Ever," I protested, but she was going on, not even listening.

"Now," she said. "Let's see it. Take off your hat."

I spent the rest of the day with her. We weren't necessarily talking all the time, just hanging. "I want to come see you," she said sullenly just before she hung up, because grandma here had to go to sleep.

"I'm fine," I told her. "There's nothing to see here. I'll see you at Christmas, when you'll already be looking down your nose at us mere mortals who aren't studying to be the next Einsteins and I'll have an inch of hair."

But today something different popped up. And I mean that literally.

I woke up to Katia's voice screaming at me from Jamie's laptop. He knocked on my door and came in to place her—I mean his laptop, with her face squinting from the screen—there, next to my bed, and rushed out without a word.

"What?" I asked groggily.

"You. Have. To. See. This."

It took me a minute to realize Katia was talking from the laptop's screen. There was a monitor next to her, and she pointed her phone to it so I could see.

She was on YouTube.

"Isn't this your brother?" she said.

"What?" I leaned down closer, trying to shake the sleep from my eyes.

She had clicked on a seven-minute video titled '**How to finish a Boat**'.

The channel's underneath read **GreyRibbon** and it had a bit over eight hundred subscribers. The first comments were:

'Actual friendship goals.'

'funniest thing on the internet, lmao'

'I started laughing, but then HE came on and now I'm swoooooooooning.'

'This video is life.'

And so on and so on. Okay, moving on.

I pressed play, curious to see what Katia was talking about. And she was right, it was Ollie. The first frame was of him. Only he wasn't alone.

Wes was there too, his golden head filling the screen in a close-up shot, as he positioned the camera to film himself and Ollie putting the finishing touches to a small yacht, which was docked in harbor. Ollie kept calling him 'Stan'.

The water looked familiarly light and green. I recognized the place at once. Paxi. Tears stung at my eyes but still I watched with fascination. Before long, I was laughing.

They weren't speaking much, except for grunts and small phrases like 'come on' and 'are you a complete knobhead? You have to do it *this* way' and stuff like that. They were both wearing plaid shirts and builder jeans with thick sturdy boots, their hair plastered on their sweaty brows, as though they'd been hard at work all day.

They should have looked seriously uncool, but it somehow worked for their advantage. They both looked so hot (well, I'm basically talking about the person who <u>isn't</u> my brother here, but you get the point.)

It was basically stand up comedy. They kept stepping on each others' foots and falling off the boat into the water with ridiculously sloppy back flips. At one point Ollie put about ten nails in his mouth, wanting to save himself a second trip to the tool-box. Then he walked carefully to the top deck, looking to nail a pair of boards on the wall.

But Wes had left a hole on the floor, and Ollie's foot went right through it. He fell to the deck below, swallowing every one of the nails.

I roared with laughter at the expression on his face, and Katia was crying right next to me on the screen, hiccupping as she tried to breathe through the laughter. The boys 'finished' off their work by springing a huge leak in the bottom of the boat, as they threw a humongous champagne bottle on it to christen it, and the boat started slowly sinking. By the end, my stomach hurt from laughing.

I can't describe it, you had to be there.

The credits at the end said: *Wes Spencer as Stan Laurel and Oliver Sikks. . . as himself.'* The script was written by Wes, too.

As soon as it ended, Katia tapped on replay without even asking me. We watched it five times.

"It's gone viral within less than twelve hours," she yelled at me from Jamie's laptop as soon as we could breathe again. "You do realize it's for you, right?"

# LOSE ME.

I didn't know you could go from laughing to utter horror in a split second. I felt the blood drain from my face.

"What?" I croaked.

"Yeah, look here," she pointed. "GreyRibbon? The name of the channel, that's the color for brain tumor awareness."

"C-could be anything," I said.

"And the description," she went on, tapping the page down button. I squinted at the screen, even though I knew I'd regret reading it.

"Crap," I said as soon as I did.


## Day Fourteen

I'm feeling much better today, fever-wise. Otherwise, I'm feeling like dirt. There have been two more videos since yesterday. Seriously, how fast are these boys uploading them?

And what are they doing still in Corfu? Shooting wrapped more than a week ago.

The first video has about five hundred thousand comments now. On the very top (stop looking at them Ari, stop reading them. Yeah, like that's going to happen) a single comment from the channel 'GreyRibbon' has gotten nearly a thousand likes.

And this is what it is:

*"I am most seriously displeased."*

It's a Lady Catherine de Bourgh quote, one of her last ones in the book. I don't even know why people are liking it, surely no one gets the reference but me. It's put there for me. He put it there for me.

And then there's the descriptions.

I wish I'd listened to my brain and not read it. It was really short and simple.

*"For Ph. Hope it makes you laugh."*

Ph as in Phelps.

The second video is titled '**How to pick up a girl**' and it's Ollie, Wes and Anna (Anna?!) in a fat suit. (Only Anna is in the suit). It's even more hilarious than the first. They are on the M&M now, and both Ollie and Wes try to flirt with her in the wood-paneled narrow gallery Wes had carried me in that first day. She picks Wes. Duh.

Then she and Wes are on his bed, having a wild (and hilarious) make out session, while on the pier Ollie is struggling with a tower of her suitcases, wrestling with their ridiculous weight, and trying to manage them all at once, until of course, her (Anna's) delicate little lingerie thingies end up strewn across the street, a couple of her pink set of expensive brand handbags sinking in the water.

The skit ends with Wes discovering one of Anna's tiny panties and going bananas over her sex-appeal. It zooms out (pretty romantic) on her chubby hand in his, Wes brushing the hair from her face tenderly and telling the audience in a heavy American accent that he loves himself a 'real woman'.

That one has already reached a million views.

In the description they've added a disclaimer, stating that this is 'a poor attempt at a remake of Laurel and Hardy's movie '*Our Wife*' and a link on where to find more info about it. Under that it just says:

"*Wish we were there, with you.*"

There was a similar disclaimer on the previous video, explaining it was a remake of the film *The Finishing Touch*.

The third one is '**How to sleep with other people**'. It says it's supposed to be a remake of a Laurel and Hardy film called *Berth Marks* in the opening titles—I didn't read the description at first. It's Ollie and Wes in a tiny cabin inside a ferry, trying to sleep in bunk beds, Ollie on the bottom one, Wes on the top, his tousled hair touching the ceiling.

They fight over the blankets, even though they are nowhere near each other, but still somehow they manage it, they fall on top of each other, they dismember the mattress, feathers flying in a white cloud around them. Then Ollie starts listening to his ipod too loudly and Wes tries to hit him, but he misses and falls down from his bed. And so on and so on. Finally a booming voice on the speaker announces that they've reached their destination and to please start disembarking. Ollie and Wes, of course, don't make it in time, and end up having to stay on board until the ship's next destination. They decide to try and get some sleep until then.

There's virtually no plot, and it's like two minutes in total. But the expressions on their faces. . . priceless. I was shaking with laughter by the end.

Finally I scrolled down to the description.

It was lengthier this time, but as soon as I started reading I knew what it was. I shut the laptop down with an abrupt snap of the screen, and moved my leg out of the way, letting it drop on the comforter as though it had burned me.

"*. . .to her utter amazement, she saw Mr. Darcy walk into the room. In an hurried manner he immediately began an enquiry after her health,*"

That was all I read, but I didn't need to continue to know what it was. I recognized it at once.

It's the beginning of page 133. The scene of Darcy's first proposal to Elizabeth. The scene Wes and I had filmed in the beginning, when he'd kissed me and I believed him.

When he'd told me it was no lie.

He must have copy pasted the whole page on YouTube.

Katia had logged off skype by now. I reopened the laptop to see whether I had damaged the screen in my haste, and everything looked okay. I placed it carefully on the chair next to my bed for Jamie to find when he next came in, and I covered my face with the blanket, pretending I was asleep.

Pretending the tears weren't coming.

# LOSE ME.

The next morning, dad came in and flung the covers away from my face. I had officially been under there for approximately twenty hours.

"Enough," he said and he sat down next to me. "You look awful," he added.

I sniffled.

"Are there. . . ?" I started asking, but I had to stop and clear my throat. "Are there more?"

"Videos?" he made a 'pffft' noise with his mouth. "Two new ones since yesterday."

"How are they *making* them so fast?"

"It's their job, Ari," he said, but I knew what he was thinking. It isn't their job. Both of them have really busy schedules as soon as they left Corfu, and that means they left other things, important things, to do this for me.

"I can't, dad," I said.

"I know," he replied. "I can see that you can't. . . go on like before. But I'm your father, Ari. I nearly lost you once. I can't lose you again, not now that the danger is finally over. So tell me what you want to do and we'll do it, okay? Anything you want. Don't think of anything else, or any*one* else but yourself for once."

We sat there in silence for a few minutes.

He was staring out the window, and I was thinking. Real hard.

"Daddy?" I said in a small voice. "I need to go to sleep for a few more hours. And then I won't be a baby any more. Promise."

"I never said you were a baby," dad said, smiling, and grabbed my waist, hoisting me onto his lap as though I was five years old. He sighed and I saw that his eyelids were red and wet. "*Koritsaki mou*," he whispered against my ear, rocking me gently back and forth. 'My little girl.' "What would I have done if I'd lost you?"

His chest shook with a sob, but the next second he was calm again. "You've been through much more than anyone should have to go through in an entire lifetime. You can sleep if you want to. You can take all the time in the world. Just get well again, that's all I want."

He was swinging me back and forth across the chair easily—too easily. He didn't have to struggle at all in order to shift my weight. Suddenly I saw how thin I was. I saw myself through his eyes: my unfamiliar, bald head, that unrecognizable face that stares back at me in the mirror every day, the pronounced lines across my collar-bone, the blue veins popping out in my wrists, my forehead, my neck, and my heart constricted.

I think that was the moment, right there.

The moment I realized I wanted to get well.

I *want* to get well.

Badly.

More than anything else.

And so, that's what I'm going to do.

After I finish writing this, I'm going to bury myself in the covers and sleep for as long as I need. I told Jamie too, so he won't bother me until I get up and open the door myself. He started to say something, but I told him he was only allowed to wake me up for my medication and meals, like any normal nurse is expected to do.

He nodded and turned his face away, but I saw that his eyes had darkened.

"I was the first to tell you," he said. "You do whatever you gotta do." And he left.

Now I'm alone. They're both gone (dad and Jamie) and I'm finishing up today's pathetic diary entry.

I'm not sure sleeping is going to solve anything, though. Actually, scratch that. It's not going to solve anything, I know it.

I just . . . I just need to not be thinking for a bit, you know?

### Day Sixteen

Here's the thing.

The thing I've been ignoring all this time, the elephant in the room. (Well, besides me. We did me yesterday.)

So, the thing.

Ollie and Wes did this amazing thing with those videos. They must be working their asses off non-stop . . . Can you even write and film a short video in five days? Let alone edit it. Let alone edit so many of them.

Anyway, the point is, they did it. They uploaded these videos, maybe not especially for me, but they did dedicate them to me. *He* dedicated them to me. It's plastered all over the internet by now, that he's the one who created the channel and produced the films. He's trending on twitter, as well as the name of the channel #greyribbon, and there's about a hundred blog articles about him. (Katia told me as soon as I woke up. I hung up on her. She called again, to tell me that YouTube was already filling up with 'obnoxious reaction videos to *his* videos' that kept getting on her nerves. I told her she was getting on my nerves, and she said, Ari, you know what I'm trying to say here. I said yeah, I know, and then she had to go out.)

So, anyway, the question is: if he did this thing for me, this beyond amazing, beyond all imagination, this huge thing for me . . . If he broke the internet for me, and I still can't call him . . . Then when I be able to?

When will I feel I can?

It's two hours later.

I've just been pacing up and down my room like a caged animal, and I've only just sat down because my head is splitting and I'm getting light-headed from all the movement.

I don't know what happened. *How* it happened. I was so careful. I did everything I could to avoid something like this.

Man, I can't even—

Okay, Jamie just walked in and ordered me to bed. So, I'll just have to vent on this page. He took his phone back, too.

I decided to call Ollie.

That's where it all started.

Isn't that what big brothers are for? To help you decide whether you're actually insane or not? I was going to talk to him about the videos and ask him about Wes maybe. . . Or maybe try to figure out why the hell I still can't muster up the nerve to freaking call him.

Sorry for that. But I told you I'd be venting.

So, anyway, genius that I am, I asked Jamie for his phone, because I still haven't turned mine on. Dad isn't here. Anyway, I was sure that I was safe, calling from an unknown number. Even if they're still together in Corfu, and Wes happens to see the number flashing on Ollie's screen, he won't know it's me, right?

Wrong.

This is how it went: I dialed the number, and waited as it beeped in my ear. Then, a voice answered. Only it wasn't Ollie's voice. It was a familiar, smooth, cocky drawl. Just the sound of that bored baritone was like a slap. It brought a rush of memories: waves swelling, lips meeting, warm skin touching.

"Hello?"

I just stood there, frozen, trapped in the sudden onslaught of emotion that overwhelmed me at the sound of Wes' voice. I'd always thought that when I heard him again it would be on my terms. That I'd have had time to prepare myself, somehow. But this. . . this was out of the blue.

"Hello?" He said again.

You would think he'd repeat it impatiently, as though someone was wasting his time. I'd seen him do it countless times when talking on the phone to his assistant or someone else who annoyed him. But his voice didn't sound like that on this second 'hello'.

It sounded as though he was sitting up, lowering his voice, putting his guard up.

As though he was preparing himself for something hard.

"That you, Ar—?"

And that's when I finally woke up and ended the call.

I remember just sitting down and staring at the phone in my hand, as if it was a bomb that had suddenly gone off and destroyed the entire planet.

And then.

The stupid phone beeped. A text.

**Say something.**

I stared at it, horrified. I wanted to throw the phone in the bushes. Honestly, that was my first reaction. My only reaction. To run away, to leave. *I'm not ready for this*, I kept thinking. *I'm not ready for this. What do I say? What do I say? Sorry? Not yet? Wait? I can't stop thinking about you? I need time? I'm not myself? I can't deal with things?*

What?

Then it beeped again.

**Say something.**

There was a typo or something, I think it actually said 'say somthing'. That's how I knew he didn't just resend the text, he'd typed it again. And his fingers may have been shaking, because he'd never once texted me anything with a typo in it.

I can't remember how I got back up to my room, but an hour later Jamie found me pacing about, about to faint. I can't even remember whether I deleted the texts or not. He'll think I'm crazy. Jamie, I mean.

Wes doesn't think I'm crazy, probably. He must hate me now.

*I* hate me.

### Day Seventeen

Trying to forget everything else, just focus on getting out of here. Calling *pappou* and *yiayia*, Katia, every day, although I still don't feel like opening up to them, trying to eat, trying to coax myself back into a normal existence.

Why is this so hard?

Is it supposed to be this hard?

### Day Twenty

Freedom! (sort of)

Today I'm out of here! Yippeeeeee

Exchanged emails and stuff with Jamie (already have his number memorized). I don't know how I'll be able to leave him behind. They might as well ask me to leave a leg or an arm here, it might hurt less.

He brought me a bunch of colorful scarves for my head and sat with me for twenty minutes, trying them on with me. They looked better on him, actually. I cried when I hugged him goodbye, and these weren't tears I need to be ashamed of.

This guy I've leaned on when I was walking out of death towards life... (I don't care how overly dramatic this sounds). It feels like I'm leaving here with my heart ripped in two.

Also, I can't walk more than a hundred steps without having to sit down to catch my breath, or I'll feel like throwing up and dying, but that's cool, doctors say, it's normal.

# LOSE ME.

Cool my ass.
Anyway, Freedom.
yay


## Day Fifty Two

This is going to be the last entry in this journal. After I finish writing this bit, I'm planning on locking the notebook up and putting it somewhere out of sight. It does not help when something reminds me of that period of time in my life, which already has started drifting away from me, fading into memory. Into the past.

I'm getting better.

First of all, physically—two days ago was the first time Coach said he was satisfied with my performance. He said I was almost as good as I'd been before the summer. I told him he was a pain in the butt and he slapped my back so hard I almost toppled over. That, coming from him, was the biggest compliment ever—the back-slapping, I mean. Not everyone stays upright after it, trust me.

I've put on tons of weight; almost all of my curves are back. Until Spiros is satisfied with my appearance, I have free pass to every pie and sweet thing grandma can cook—and she cooks a lot these days. She and grandpa can't stop smiling.

I've started smiling a bit myself.

I plan on doing much more of it, and closing this journal is part of that process. After a week in Corfu I went back to New York. I stayed in Jamie's place and he took me to a hockey game. Then I went to his therapist. (He made me).

That's not an experience I plan on repeating, EVER.

Not that there was anything wrong with the lady, but sitting on a couch in complete silence and being asked about my feelings is not what I'd call having a good time.

Anyway, she said that within five days we 'did wonders'—in therapy lingo.

I wouldn't call what we managed to do 'wonders', but ok. She says I should be incredibly proud of myself, so I'll write down all I've done since I last wrote here in a quick list, before I lose my nerve.


1. I turned my phone on.

I told my dad to delete all calls and messages before giving it to me, so that I wouldn't be tempted to read them. Then I texted Wes. It was long and complicated and weird, but I didn't wait for him to reply. I turned it off immediately, and went out to buy a new one.

I'm not proud of it, but this is what the text was:

**Hi, Wes. I want to thank you for everything you did for me. I'm so sorry I haven't spoken to you in ages, but I want you to know that I'm thinking about you and I haven't forgotten you. It's just, with everything that's happened to me lately, I can't. . . bring myself to remember the happy time we spent together. It reminds me of how much pain I was in, and of how much I hurt you and everyone involved. I want to put that behind me now. Please understand.**

I read it to Katia first.

She said, "Eighty-six the crap about thinking about him and haven't forgotten him, and add that you don't want to speak or hear from him ever again."

Appalled, I stammered that that would be rude.

She replied, "What do you think closure is, exactly?"

"What closure? Kat, I'm not even sure I. . . "

"Do you want him or not?" she interrupted me, in a no-nonsense tone. "It's as simple as that, Ari. If he's human at all, he'll be mad as hell at you right now, I know I would, if you'd given me the silent treatment after all that. . . after all that you guys went through together." She stopped to clear her throat. I had a hard time meeting her eyes. "But he seems to be still waiting for you. For something, at least. He did that YouTube thing, didn't he?"

I nodded, mutely. We were on skype again. I stared at her chocolate brown eyes, my mind gone blank.

"Well?" she said, finally.

"Well what?"

"What do you want, Ari?"

"I want to stop being afraid all the time," I whispered, finally admitting the truth. "I. . . I'm scared of everything, even moving. My brain is not working properly. And I don't mean the operation-kind properly. I mean the other things that make you feel."

Jamie's therapist would do a happy dance.

But Katia didn't.

"What do you mean 'everything'?" she asked, scrunching up her eyebrows. "What are you really scared of, Ari?"

It took a moment to get the word out, but she waited, looking at me intently. "Dying," I said, finally. "Dying on him a second time. Dying on me. . . And before you say anything smart, I know it's not rational, okay? I just can't help it."

She pursed her lips. She's been pursing her lips at me since we were six. You'd think I'd have gotten used to it by now.

"Yeah, like I'm even capable of saying something smart right now," she said. It was almost midnight. We'd been talking for the better part of the day. "I'm so sorry, Ari," Katia continued. "We'll work on that, I promise. You won't always be this way, it's just because of everything you went through... maybe you need time? But if you don't feel you can be in a relationship right now, I think you at least owe him the truth," she said dryly. "Tell him you're not planning on getting back together anytime soon. It's not fair to drag him along, even if he might be the hottest specimen of a human being currently alive on the planet."

I stole a glance at her face. She wasn't smiling.

"Okay."

I edited the text like she said, right there in front of her, before sending it.

"Did you send it?" she asked. I was hurrying to turn off the phone quickly, before I could hear the beep of his answering text. *If* he answered, after I'd ignored him all this time. And that was a big if.

"Yep," I said in a minute.

"Good," Katia said. "Now grow some balls and call him."

I almost dropped the phone.

But, yeah, she was right. After all is said and done, I don't want to be the kind of person who shuts a person off my life with a text message. So that brings us to

2. I spoke to Wes.

For real this time.

His and Ollie's YouTube channel, GreyRibbon, had come near to crashing the whole site a few weeks back. It went viral within the first two days, and people are still blogging about it, or sharing memes or whatever it is they do with something that's suddenly become popular. As for me, I remembered my promise to Wes—for what it's worth now—and I didn't watch or read anything they wrote about him.

I've learned all of the videos by heart at this point, after having watched them so many times. Some days they're the only thing that can make me smile. There are five of them in total.

Ollie and Wes stopped making them the week after I was released from hospital, but their popularity kept going up daily. The channel was ads free— it still is, and of all the things people could talk about, it's this that they can't wrap their minds around. They can't believe that these two Hollywood actors did this for no profit. For the fun of it.

For me.

Anyway, Wes was gone from Corfu by the time I got here. Ollie was waiting for me, though, but he was perfect. He didn't pressure me to call Wes or anything. So I didn't. I don't know, maybe I was thinking this would all go away if I ignored it.

But, right there, in my tiny room, with Katia watching me severely from my desktop monitor, I realized how stupid that was. So I ran downstairs to get my dad's phone, and I called Wes.

It rang about five times, and just when I was going to hang up, relieved, his voice suddenly burst into my ear, warm and familiar.

My knees literally went weak and I sank down on my butt on the floor.

Katia was making impatient gestures from her perch on my desk, but I could no longer see her. Maybe it was better this way, just him and me.

One last time.

"Hey." He said it quietly. No point in pretending he didn't know who was calling, I guess, since he'd recognized my dad's number.

"Hey," I replied, clearing my throat—*that* must have made me sound pathetic, if the 'hey' hadn't done it. "Did you. . . did you get my text?"

"Uh huh," he said, and I could almost see his eyes turning bored and cold, like his voice. "Listen, did you need something? I'm in the middle of something here. . . "

I don't know if I was expecting us to continue where we had left off (minus the dying, of course), because I knew that he'd be wondering why I didn't want to talk. At least that. But I don't think I'd expected the distance in his manner. That woke me up fast.

I jumped to my feet and started pacing around my room.

"I just—I wanted to say thank you again, in person I mean. So, yeah, thank you for everything you did for me. I really. . . "

"You're welcome," he said tightly, not letting me finish. He sounded guarded, as though he wanted to cut through the unimportant stuff, waiting for something.

"I wanted to make this call, just to tell you that I'm fine, and that I'm getting better every day. Sorry for not letting you know how I was doing sooner."

Wow, who knew I could be this lame on the phone?

He did that half-hearted laugh. "Oh, listen, if that's all you wanted to say, don't worry about it," he said in an easy, cool tone, that was entirely foreign to me. It almost sounded like he'd switched to another person. Then,

"I get it," he added in a lower voice.

Those three words sliced me in two. He 'got' it. He got what? What did he think I was talking about? How could *he* get it if I didn't?

Maybe my silence was enough to give him the message that I didn't want to see him any more. Maybe that's what he 'got'. And I didn't know how to make him un-get it.

"Wes. . . " I started saying, but then I stopped. I didn't know what to say. Telling him I was too scared to be with him, to be anything, pretty much too scared to even *exist*, was way too lame to say over the phone. So I stayed silent, tasting the sound of his name on my lips. Missing it.

"Still not turned your phone on, huh?" he said. "I guess you've a good reason not to." He gave a self-deprecating snort. "Or maybe you deleted everything I. . . everything that was on there. Figures. I never thought that someone like you—Well, you did say it was a fling, right?"

My throat was dry. I wanted to say that that's not fair, but he'd gotten everything else correctly. How could he know me so well? He's guessed everything! Or maybe there wasn't much to guess. Who knows what texts or voicemails he left me? I'll never know, for one. But, coming from a guy who made freaking YouTube videos for me and dedicated me entire pages from a

Jane Austen novel, well. . . Anything he had to say must have been significant. It sent a message loud and clear that I didn't read or listen to any of it.

There was silence forever. Then,

"Ah, listen, I'm really glad you're okay," Wes' voice said in my ear—his real voice this time, gentle and familiar. "Have a wonderful life, all right? You deserve it."

That sounded like goodbye. No, more like a blow-off. I wasn't ready for that yet. There was so much to say. . . And no words to say it with.

I'd let the silence stand too long between us.

I'd let it grow into a wall.

And with a guy like Wes. . . it was a miracle to get through his walls once.

"Wait," I said, just as he was starting to say 'I've got to go' and stuff. "Just wait."

He waited.

I swallowed.

'Say something.' The words from his text were swirling in my mind, torturing me, making the breath catch in my throat.

He waited for me to speak, but I couldn't. "I'm not the one who gave up," he said softly. Or maybe I'd imagined the 'softly' part, because then abruptly his voice sounded harsh again. "I'm not the one who stopped waiting, who—"

"I'm sorry for everything," I interrupted him. "You don't know how sorry I am."

"Sorry for what? Sorry you ever met me?" I could taste the hurt in his voice.

And I couldn't make it go away. Two hurt people can't heal each other. This was us, right now. Caught in a riptide of pain. Each causing pain to themselves, to the other. I was trying to tell him what I wanted, without knowing myself. And in the process, getting really confused about what *he* wanted. Not that he wasn't justified to not want all this drama any more. *I* didn't want all this for him. What a mess, dammit.

So, what to say in answer to his question? The truth. "I'm sorry I let things go too far."

Now, I know I shouldn't have said that. It was an opening I should never have given him. But I wanted to say something. Katia said to have a clean cut. A closure. Well, that was the closest I could get. I wanted to erase the past. But of course no one can do that. No one can grant forgiveness in the blink of an eye.

And that's definitely not what Wes did: he laughed.

I told you I shouldn't have said that last bit.

He started laughing, that non-laugh dudes do to show they don't even care. They don't even. His laughter, a hard, cruel sound penetrated my ear and my heart.

"What too far, Ari?" He said, in that easy, dismissive way of his that I knew so well from before he'd become my Wes. Now he was a stranger again. "Come on, I got to know you for, what? All of ten days?"

The way he was talking took me was back to that night in Drops, when I was talking to the rudest, most entitled and obnoxious British dude on the planet.

Of course, what he said was true, technically. But the thing is, it hadn't felt too soon and too stupid while it was happening—this thing, this *connection* between us. It had been real. It *was* real. Wasn't it? He was making it sound like a joke.

"It was just a kiss, no worries."

*Just a kiss'*. Our kiss, the kiss he gave me. *My* kiss. He called it 'just a kiss.'

"I get it," he said, "you're over this. It's fine. Nothing that hasn't happened to me before. Now I really have to go. Take care, okay?"

A soft click as he ended the call, and then nothing.

'Closure', isn't that what Katia said?

Turns out I was handed closure on a plate. And then some.

He hates me. No, he doesn't hate me. Not even that. He doesn't even care enough to be angry.

I'm so tired of writing, of thinking about this. It's all such a horrible mess. My head, my heart, my life.

But for what it's worth, there you have it, I suppose. Closure. Heart-ripping, soul-shattering, brain-destroying closure.

Jamie would be so proud. (Not.)

### 3. I apologized.

I hadn't officially apologized to all the people who love me and to whom I lied to for so long, due to the fact that I was an idiot and a coward and, well, selfish.

I don't mind admitting these things about myself now. I've realized them and I'm trying to come to terms with it.

This is me.

Hopefully I will be a better me in the future. But so far this is the me that's survived. I have to acknowledge that, too.

I apologized to dad first, then grandpa and grandma. Then Katia, then Ben. All of them forgave me at once, except Katia, who made me work for it for a couple of days and then she burst out crying, and I mean *crying*, in loud, ugly sobs and asked me how could I leave her like that?

I told her I hadn't left her and she said she wanted to hit me and I said ok, when you're home for the holidays you can try, but I warn you I'll be at least ten pounds heavier by then.

### 4. I called Christina

Ollie gave me her personal number, which she answered after the first thirteen tries. When I told him afterwards, he said  that I'd been extremely lucky.

# LOSE ME.

We didn't talk about anything too deep, but still we talked. It went something like this.

"Hi, it's Ari." She didn't say anything, so I thought I should add: "You know, from Greece? I thought we should talk?"

"Oh hello, honey, how are you? Have you decided then?"

"I beg your pardon?" I was sure she hadn't realized who I was.

"Are you coming down to L.A.?"

Her breathy, confident voice brought it all back. Of course. My nose. (I'd pressured Ollie to tell me what else she'd told him that day she called to talk to me, back in September. The thing that had gotten him so mad at her—he'd resisted telling me for weeks, but finally he'd caved. Turns out, she wanted me to go get a nose job at her plastic surgeon in L.A. Yup.)

Suddenly it all seemed so hilarious. Deep inside of me there was no hurt, no resentment, no betrayal. Maybe a bit of pity for this woman who *had* missing, who had missed the whole point. Of herself, of life, of me.

"Not exactly," I laughed. "Just wanted to see if you're interested in. . . keeping in touch or something? And I wanted to thank you for the opportunity to work in that film, it was huge."

"Sure, sweetheart, I'm really glad I could do this little thing for you," she replied in a breezy tone. "I've talked to Ben about getting you an agent, too, he says you're quite good at this. And it's not an overall bad starting point, if you want to be in films in a couple of years." (I'm guessing she meant to be in films as an actor. I couldn't very well expect her to think of my job as a 'real career' now, can I?) "I'd love to get to know you better, Ari. Oliver tells me you're an incredible person, and of course you are. How could you not be, right?"

Her laughter pealed in my ear.

"I don't expect anything from you," I told her. "But recently something happened to me and I feel as though I've grown up suddenly in the past few weeks. In view of that, I'd like us not to be complete strangers."

I don't know what she got from that, but what she said was:

"Oh, we all have to come to terms with how this world of ours runs, honey, sooner or later. I know exactly what you're talking about and of course I'd love for you to call me any time. Any time, really. And you know you're welcome to come down here regardless of It pretty much whether I'll be here or not, okay?"

The rest went pretty much like this.

I wasn't expecting anything more, really. I wanted to do this for me and yes, I'm proud that I did it. Time will tell about the rest.

## 5. Let's do this!

My 'career' has suddenly taken off.

Coach said that after being invited to not one but *two* auditions by Matthew Lee himself, I can stop putting the quote marks on the word career, but it all feels surreal to me right now. Matt also wants to train me himself at some point, he said 'I'd be a valuable addition to his team.' Say what?

In a month or so I'm flying to London for the first of these auditions—I may even fly to Seattle for a few days to train with Matt. It's a futuristic, sci-fi flick, something like that. I'm already training for it. Cool stuff.

<u>6. And now the truth</u>
Let's see what happens when I try to write it down.

The truth is. . . I'm still scared. I still haven't gotten over it. I still wake up in the morning and I'm not sure if it's before or after. I'm hoping this journal will help me deal with that, but I'm afraid this fear runs deeper and that it'll follow me my entire life.

At least now there will be a life for it to ruin.

Not that it will ruin my life. I won't let it.

Okay, almost to the end.

(Jamie, this whole journal thing is your fault, from start to finish. Already thinking of ways to make you pay.)

Speaking of Jamie, I have a tiny bit of hair right now. My head looks almost identical to Coach's, except for the color of my skin. I've bought and been gifted about a million wigs however, so yeah.

The day after I arrived in Corfu, a courier brought a package to my house. Inside I found a wig styled in a straight, shiny bob with bangs. The color was blonde, really yellow, almost gold.

As I took it out of the flat envelope, a note fell out.

It just read: "to Goldie, with love. -Jamie"

Yep. He went there.

I love that dude, I miss him so badly.

Then I went online and ordered a purple wig, just for him. I put it on and showed it to him on skype and he laughed so hard he fell from his chair.

<u>6. The note</u>
The last item on this list, and then it closes. We're done. Da-duuum.

I'm talking, of course, about The Note. The note Wes left me in the hospital, the one he wrote to me as soon as I woke up, but they wouldn't let him see me, so he never gave it to me in person. (He left it with dad). I finally found the guts to read it the last day before I left the hospital.

I'll copy it right here and then try not to think about it EVERY. SINGLE. DAY.

There are aspects to it that I didn't understand when I first read it, and I still haven't. There are some things that he wrote that break my heart just to think about. And then there's his handwriting and his name signed elegantly at the bottom, and it's a bit crumpled at the edges as though he wrote it somewhere on a chair.

I imagine him as I last saw him, his eyes red with lack of sleep, his hair a bit too long, his eyes as green as the clear surface of the sea when the sun's rays hit it at noon. His lips are set, but his hand is reaching out to touch my shoulder, my face, to somehow comfort me, although he's freaked out as well, but he doesn't want to let me see.

# LOSE ME.

Then he leans down to kiss me. . .
And then my memories of him end. I'm the one who ends them.

———

It's over, Ari. Over.

The pain, the fear, the suffering. I'm so happy. . . no, happy doesn't begin to cover it. I have you back. Words fail.

There is so much to be thankful for, so much to say to you, I'll try to be patient and wait for you to be well enough to talk to me. But until that moment, I want you to have something of mine close to you, so that I can feel I've not left you alone.

(Please excuse my terrible writing and the run-on sentences. I haven't slept at all—how could I? Plus, I've had about seven minor heart attacks, because my heart kept missing a beat every time someone came out of the operation room.)

OK. One.

You've been through so much, Ari. I can't even. . . my mind stops when I try to think of what you've been going through all these months, and especially these past few days. I know your journey towards recuperation is just starting now, so I wanted to ask you to be kind to yourself.

I know you, Ari. I know how you detest to show any kind of weakness, how hard you are on yourself and how much you expect of yourself. But this is different.

You'll be scared, it's only normal. *I* am scared out of my mind, and I'm not even the one who was sick.

So take it slow. Give yourself time to grieve and to be scared and to feel the pain you refused to feel for all these months, because you had to be brave for the rest of us. You'll be as good as before, better even. I promise you. But you have to take your time. All right?

All those unpleasant, scary feelings might resurface and you might have a hard time of it for a while. I just want you to know that I'll be there, day or night, whenever you need me. Just one phone call away. Talk to me. Or don't talk, just let me sit next to you in silence. I want to be there for you. I've. . . I've never been there for anyone in my life. No one ever needed me, and no one ever felt they could depend on me.

But this is it. You're it.

I'm here. I'm here. I'm not going anywhere.

All right, next page. One last thing, and the rest I'll tell you in person.

Something weird happened. A miracle, an impossibility, I don't even know what to call it. I'll just lay the facts before you and let you be the judge.

I'm not sure whether you've been told about this yet, and maybe your dad won't even mention it, but. . . you died Ari. Not almost, you did.

This is what happened:

I was in the waiting room, biting my nails almost to the bone, and suddenly I had the urge to pray. Now I haven't yet told you about this, but do you remember that you asked me to pray, back in Corfu?

Well, I did.

I started by saying the few standard words I was taught as a kid, which I'm not sure I even remembered right, but then something happened. In my hotel room I found a book. One of these black, Gideon copies that are printed in three languages—you see them in every hotel room, at least I do, that it gets to the point where I don't even notice them anymore. But this time I did. I didn't immediately make the connection between the 'praying' you'd asked and the plain black book.

I opened it and leafed through it randomly, wondering when you'd speak to me again. You'd asked for two days and already I was feeling the darkness descending on me. And you weren't there to chase it away with your smile and your sass, like you'd done from the first moment I met you. I knew I couldn't stay away from it long. I was already reaching for the bottle.

And that's when I came across it. The thing I'm trying to tell you; that's when I read it.

I found that page by chance, I don't even know why my eyes strayed to that particular phrase, of all the millions of words in that thick book.

It was there, in the right-hand corner on one of the last pages, in this really small print. It read:

*'I loved you at your darkest.'*

And that's when it hit me. It had been a person I'd been praying to. Not just an idea, a thought, an infinite void. A person with feelings, with a capacity to love. I read the whole damn chapter that day, I didn't lift my head from that book until morning.

By then I could feel something happening inside me. I could feel myself changing. Being transformed.

I still didn't know why on earth you wanted me to pray for you, I had no idea then what you were going through, no idea how close I was to losing you. But I knew that that string of words put together had messed with my head. No, not my head. My heart.

So, back to the present, or rather a few hours ago.

I'm sitting here, trying to keep myself sane while you're fighting for your life in the next room. And I'm fighting with you. Only I'm not alone. It's me and Him. He's doing the fighting, I'm doing the praying.

# LOSE ME.

If He loved me at my darkest, and someone must have, because believe me, my darkest was very dark indeed and many people have said I had no business surviving it. . . But if He loved me during that, then He sure was the right person to talk to right now.

So I prayed like I breathed.

Suddenly I felt the urge to start begging for your life. 'Save her,' that was all I said, pacing on the floor—I couldn't sit still. Over and over again. And then some more after that.

In a few minutes that particular agony faded to a dull throb in my heart, and I just sat back down to wait. After an eon, the doctor came out.

What he said. . . it still makes me start to shake.

Ari, you'd died. You'd flatlined on them at some point during the operation, gone into cardiac arrest. I got up, out of my mind with worry, I hardly knew what I did. "When?" I yelled. Everyone in the waiting room turned to look at me, I didn't even care. "When did that happen?"

Your dad looked like he was about to puke. One of the doctors told me the time. It was right at that moment when I said "save her". Do you believe me? I swear *I* wouldn't believe me. But it's true. I was there, it happened.

What do I do now? How do I live, after what happened? I can't continue to live the same way as before, that's for sure. But how to change? I don't know what to make of it, but I'm sure we can figure it out together.

I want to change, Ari. I want to turn my life around. For you and for that. . . for the person who saved you that day.

I know I'm still not who I want to be, no matter how much I've read or how much I've thought, and I know it's going to take work and dedication. . . I'm not sure I know how to become who I want to become, but I'm starting. Right now. I don't even know if I'm strong enough to do it by myself—I'm not like you.

But I want to be someone who deserves you. I want to be the guy you made me want to be that day I grabbed you from the water. I don't want to be the guy who crashed the car with you in it. I want to be as far away as possible from that guy I was the first time I met you when I made that stupid gaffer comment. Would you forgive me for that, by the way? There's so much I want to ask your forgiveness for.

I'm not the 'amazing person' you said I was that morning on the L&H, we both know that, but I'm not the same guy I was that day. I'm not the same guy I was this morning. The guy who walked beside you on the way to that operating room isn't the guy I am right now.

And I know that people, least of all me, don't change so fast, so I'm not saying I've changed. Not yet. I will, though. I'm someone else now. Someone who has something good growing inside of him. Someone with a future.

I can't wait, Ari. I can't wait to see you, to talk to you, to. . . just be with you again. Are you laughing at me as you're reading this? I bet you are. I bet you're thinking that I'm hopeless. Well, I don't care. When I'm with you I'm absolutely invincible. And now that I have you back. . . Just try and stop me.

Hurry and wake up so we can laugh at me together, yeah?

Your *dude*.
-Wes

And this, my dear Jamie, is the end of this journal. It did all it could do, although I don't think that's exactly what you had in mind when you suggested I start it.

I leave you with a puzzle. Even you wouldn't be able to figure this one out—me and him, I mean.

P.S. I opened my phone one last time before I'll have to lock it away with this journal. I might as well write down here what I found.

He hadn't answered with a text.

He'd called me, then left voice mail when he found it was off.

I hadn't expected to hear his voice again, so soon after our last phone call (it was about a week later, I think, and my heart was still scraped raw from that). I sank to the bed, blown away by the force of the feelings that assaulted me. I had to remind myself a couple of times that this was before we'd talked, before the irreversible words that had passed between us.

"Ari." He just said my name at first, then paused. "What's happened to you? Did you read the note I left you? I guess not. I guess this is it. Well, you need to do what you need to do, I understand. Don't survive. Live. That's all there is now for you. Just. . . just do this one last thing for me, okay? Don't look back, Ari. I'll—I'll try to do the same. This is goodbye if you want it to be. And as for not contacting you again. . . well, maybe you shouldn't contact me either, yeah? I don't think, um. . . there would be no point, you see, opening up old wounds."

His voice sounded hoarse by now. And mad.

"What else is there to say? Don't ever thank me again, please. I can't stand it. Goodbye, Ari."

It was only after I'd listened to it a couple of times that I realized: he'd just left me that message, when I called him. He'd just asked me not to contact him. Maybe that's why he ended up being so cruel to me a few minutes later, when I'd called him as per Katia's advice. I mean, he'd written in his note, a month ago, that he wanted to change, but wanting to change isn't the same as actually changing. It's merely a step in the right direction. And if things don't go right after that. . . maybe you abandon the effort.

I'm the 'thing' that went wrong. Or maybe I'm giving too much credit to myself. One human being can't change just because of or for the sake of another. And if they did, how real would that be? Anyway, I'm getting in over my head here.

The thing is that this voice mail had sounded more like the old Wes, at the beginning at least, and that sliced me right through. Of course the more I listened to it, the more I realized how strained his voice sounded, how stilted. As though he was barely keeping it together.

But I guess, by the end of our one and only phone call, he really hated my guts. Even now, writing it, I've lost count of the things we've done to each other. What a mess.

After listening to the voice mail, I cried like a baby, stifling the sound into my pillow. I cried ugly, tearing sobs until morning, and then I got up and went out to meet Coach at the gym.

Now it's midnight again.

And, as this journal is coming to an end, and with it, the whole "hospital" chapter of my life as well (hopefully), here is what I keep thinking about: fake dolphins.

Fake dolphins.

When the movie, our movie, First Sentences, is released, people will see a gorgeous underwater scene, with Elle (although it will be my body) swimming smoothly between two sleek dolphins, and then jumping through the air to land in a pool of foam between them. Probably an upbeat, summery music will be playing in the background.

But the reality of creating that scene on camera was nothing like that.

It was all an illusion, a magic trick, a lie.

Wes' entire world is like that. The paparazzi, the agents, the fans, the Christinas. I mean, we all had to sign elaborate contracts that stated we wouldn't even disclose the location of the shoot for six months. And an army of assistants, bodyguards, drivers and various other people kept following Wes like a cloud of bees wherever he went. Let's face it, I've never lived like that. How do you know where reality ends and the fake dolphins begin? Maybe he deluded himself into believing that there was something between us that never was. Maybe I did too. We both did.

Sometimes I wake up in the night, sweating, in the grip of a panic attack, but I know how to handle them now. I slow my own breathing and visualize a calm scene, like the therapist taught me. But I always, always, remember that first time it happened to me, and how Wes was there, holding me together.

It would be so easy to slip back into being that girl. That girl who needed him, who kept a part of herself secret from him and from anyone, just so that she could stay alive (and sane).

But I'm not her any more.

I'm someone who can't stay away from the truth any longer. I'm someone who is still fighting for her life. Even though people can't see, there's a battle inside of me.

And this one I'll have to win alone.

Well, at least let's say I'll have to fight it alone. Besides, Wes is no longer an option. I'd better delete him from my brain, like he asked me to.

Now how to delete the fear. That's the real issue.

———

I'm locking this thing up. No point in remembering anything else except that I'm alive. That's all that matters, right?

# PART THREE

Sweet Prince

Sweet Prince

Sweet Prince

# T H I R T E E N

The first thing I hear as I walk in through the elegant, steel doors of the London Academy of Creative and Dramatic Art, is yelling.

Now that's what I call a promising beginning.

I cringe as the harsh sound of angry voices meets my ears. I was expecting a lot of things, but not this: I was expecting red velvet theatre seats and polished hardwood floors, and a large, echoey room. I wasn't expecting this cacophony of voices, followed by an uncomfortable silence, as everyone hears me open the door. The voices subside to muttering, and the cluster of students I can see up ahead stop talking and turn towards me.

The stage is even bigger than I had imagined, and a sudden nervousness grips me. *You can do this*, I tell myself, as more than fifteen people crane their necks to look at me, measuring me up.

I walk on, head bent, duffel bag slung over my shoulder, trying to look professional. And then the whispering starts. Voices asking questions, mingling with the remnants of the angry yells, which haven't yet completely subsided at the other side of the room.

Welcome to adulthood.

...

My plane landed at Heathrow airport just a few hours ago, and I emerged into a chilly English afternoon with just a few hours to spare until my audition.

The sky was overcast, so I draped one of Jamie's scarves more securely around my throat, blowing on my freezing fingers to warm them. *Perfect weather for a brand new start*, I told myself wryly.

I got in a cab, giving the driver a slip of paper with the address on. He drove me to Camden, to the little room I've rented, but all I had time to do was leave my luggage and take a quick shower. Then I got out again and hopped on a bus, as the evening gently enveloped the wet streets in an icy blue December night.

It took me about twenty minutes to get to my destination. Finding my way around was surprisingly easy, considering I've never set foot in London before, but the GPS on my phone made everything simpler. I just sat back and gazed out the window as we passed King's Cross, Regent's Park and then finally, the impressive, looming silhouette of the British Library.

In another life—or, rather, three months ago—this would have been the perfect opportunity to call Katia or text her, but before coming here I'd told myself that I would do this by myself. Stand on my own two feet and all that.

# LOSE ME.

Jamie's words to me when I was in hospital, about pushing everyone out of my life in order to get over my fears, kept bugging me, but I pushed them firmly aside.

*This isn't about that,* I kept telling myself. *I'm just doing things on my own, that's all.* About time.

And speaking of doing things on my own, I can still remember my conversation with Christina from about two months ago, when she offered me a personal assistant, an agent and a driver (among other things).

I told her it was too soon for all that, and that I was just taking the next step, for now, and she'd replied:

"It's okay, honey, when you're serious about your career, give me a call."

I didn't get mad at her—well, no more than expected. But she started me thinking.

How serious *was* I about my career?

Matt had called me two days before. I called him back, and accepted his offer of a job in England, trying not to overthink things or doubt myself.

After that, everything happened so fast, it's almost a blur. Only last week, I flew to Seattle with Coach for twenty-four hours, for an intensive training session, although Matt wasn't there himself. But it was awesome, we did everything.

And I do mean everything.

Which brings us to now.

...

I walk into one of those fancy schools you only read about in glossy art magazines or hear mentioned as the school where some award winning actor got their start. From the outside, the Academy just looks like a normal building, squeezed between red and brown London brick-walled houses. But as soon as I walk in, awe mixed with dread grabs me.

The space is large. Carpeted floors, high ceilings, bright lights, no-nonsense. I think it would be a bit less intimidating if it was avant-garde and pretentious. I ride the elevator to the fifth floor and enter one of the many stage rooms of the school, and that's when I first hear the yelling. It's obvious that the audition has started, and if I may take a wild guess, I'll say it's not going very well.

The theatre is a big room, filled with soft, yellow lighting, and, apart from the yelling, there's a general hush, as if there's a play going on. On the other end of the room, there's a wide wooden stage with small steps leading up to it from the sides.

Rows and rows of bench-like seats reach all the way to the front, their backs to me, but they look really comfortable and modern, as they're covered in black leather cushions. The theatre room is rounded back here, looking like the hull of a ship, and rows of seats run across the walls as well, in two separate balconies.

Matt has assured me that this production is going to be nothing like First Sentences, which is fine by me. I want to start with something on a smaller scale, until I can feel sure of myself again. This shoot will be for a short film or films, which will be produced by a collaboration between students of different art schools. The Academy is one of these schools, and, having the biggest stage, it's where the shoot will take place. The students will be the actors, the screenwriters, the directors, everything. They only needed a couple of stunt actors, and our pay will come out of their own pockets. The students', that is. Which is either strange or alarming, but Matt said it's okay, they're all rich kids. That's literally all he told me.

And then we'd spent hours talking about the stunts I'll be expected to do and having extended skype sessions about them, until Coach was satisfied I could do them pretty decently. That's how it usually works, I'm only told my own part of the job. The rest is on a need-to-know basis.

I walk down the aisle, a wooden floorboard crunching under my shoes. I shudder as cold seeps through my five layers of clothing—although I'm dressed warmly, this piercing cold is a long way from winter in Corfu. I think it might have started to snow out there as I was coming in.

The yelling intensifies, then stops.

A voice speaks calmly in a low baritone for a second, and everyone seems to relax. As I quietly head for the backstage door, Matt walks out in front of the stage. The theatre is dimly lit, only half of its lights on, but as he comes closer I can see that he looks exactly like he did four months ago, when I first met him, and I'm suddenly thrown. The mere sight of him almost transports me back to the set of First Sentences.

I shake the feeling off with an effort, as I walk down to meet him. "Hey."

He just nods to me and frowns heavily, his long legs swallowing the distance between us.

He looks mad. *Why is Matt angry?* If I had any time to think, I would be freaking out right now. Or rather, the Ari of a few months ago, who had just come out of the hospital, would be. This Ari, with her first paycheck already in the bank, and about to start a new job away from home, is an altogether different person.

At least I hope she is.

Matt places a hand lightly on my back and leads me wordlessly to a corner. The first three rows, right in front of the stage, are full of students.

"Are you ready?" Matt asks, looking into my eyes.

I nod.

"We got started kind of early," he says calmly. "So you haven't had time to practice on this particular stage, but the equipment is exactly like the stuff you used in Seattle, so it won't be a problem. Oh, one more thing. The filming will actually take place on this very stage, so be as precise as you can with your movements, that's what they're looking for."

He's leaning towards me, his back turned towards the stage. Behind him, two tall guys around my age take their seats in the front row, where a white table has been placed in the wide aisle between the seats and the stage.

"Are. . . are they doing the casting?" I ask, eyeing them incredulously.

"Yep," Matt says, giving no further explanation.

I was hoping for a bit more information; all I know is that the plot of the film is something Shakespeare. That's as far as my knowledge goes. Oh, and the title of course. *Sweet Prince.*

"Is everyone except me a student?" I ask.

"Yes, but not all of them are Academy students," Matt replies, helping me change out of my coat as the remaining lights begin to go out one by one, plunging the auditorium into darkness. He opens the backstage door. Immediately, my ears fill with noise.

A group of students are talking excitedly and nervously, most of them in whispers, waiting for their turn.

"They've come from schools all over the world, apparently," Matt says. "This collab project is going to be different. . . there's someone involved which makes it an exception. A special someone."

The way he says 'special' makes me think spoiled, rich kids. Nice.

"Gear in there?" He points at my bag.

"Yeah."

"Come on."

From what I can see from the wings, the stage is a miracle. It's easily as big as the top floor of my flat in Corfu, and it must be about half as wide as the soccer field at the town centre. There's a jungle of hidden lights, microphones and wiring hovering way above the auditioning actors' heads. A scaffolding frame, loaded with more lights and scenery, is turning the ceiling into a sci-fi star-studded galaxy sky. One by one the students take the stage and recite poetry.

At some point, even I can recognize the lines.

'To be or not to be. . .'

Ah. Hamlet. Of course. British people love Hamlet. A sudden thought passes like a flash through my brain: how Wes loved reading. How he loves reading—I try to think of him mostly in past tense, but that doesn't mean he isn't currently somewhere in the world, creating art, being brilliant. And the irony of it, me standing right here, in a place full of actors, in his homeland.

Okay, dangerous territory, let's steer away from it. *Focus on the students standing all around you, waiting for their turn.*

Some of them are wearing really cool body suits, mostly made of black leather, closely fitted and body shaping, like uniforms. They look like some kind of alien creatures. Nobody is paying attention to me, they are all reciting lines or biting their nails nervously, so I change quickly into my leotard and leggings, slipping into the uniform they sent me. Then I start my warming up routine. I'm in the middle of my breathing exercises and stretching, when I hear a small, unsure voice next to me, whispering in my ear:

"You look like you know what you're doing?"

I turn to find a heart-shaped face framed with blonde curls and rosy cheeks, looking up to me with a terrified expression. She looks about fifteen, and she's so small her head barely reaches my shoulder.

"You don't go here, do you?" she adds, taking an appreciative look at my wig—I still wear them—which happens to be an orange close-cropped bob that pops against my all black latex outfit. I wanted to be myself in the audition, at least, and then they can put whatever hair they want on me.

A week ago, Matt had told me that the audition was just a technicality, since it was up to him to pick the stunt performers, but just now he'd sounded really concerned. I didn't ask him what was going on, he seemed to be in a hurry, but my stomach starts cramping up. Deep breaths. *You've got this.* I've done this particular routine about a million times this past month alone. It's almost gotten boring. Almost.

"I'm Rosie," the girl says. "First semester." Her accent is so cool, it feels like she may have come straight out of one of those Pride and Prejudice films I watched for First Sentences.

"Ari," I reply, "stunt girl." Her china blue eyes go round with surprise.

"What are you auditioning for?" I ask her, as I approach the bar and stretch. Outside, the audience bursts into friendly, comfortable laughter as one of the dudes that was reading Hamlet's lines tried one of the most precarious stunts—which I will be performing in a minute—and fell on his face.

Then a sharp voice yells something and the laughter is cut short. Rosie turns scarlet.

"I'm not an actor," she says, looking horrified, and that's when I notice her apron. It reaches to her knees, ending in pink frills, and it's got all kinds of needles and scraps of fabric strapped to it, as well as two huge pockets filled with buttons and zippers. She's also got a tape slung around her shoulders.

"Costumes." I smile, remembering that stick lady from First Sentences.

She nods with enthusiasm. "Do you like them?" she gestures to a tall, thin girl wearing one of the alien costumes.

"Well. . . " I start. "They're gorgeous, actually, but not. . . "

"Not what?" Her eyes go huge in panic.

Okay, that was a mistake. "Not very medieval," I say as calmly as I can, and drop to the ground for a few push-ups.

She laughs, clapping her hands.

"Well, thank goodness for that," she says as she takes in my questioning look. "Haven't you read the script? It's Hamlet set in a post-apocalyptic universe, on the last day of the earth. Didn't you kno—didn't you realize? Yeah, it's not exactly a school project, like other Academy

Short Films, it has a producer and everything, proper directors from Hollywood and mad stuff like that, that's why everyone is so crazy to get a part in it. There's even a conductor from a New York college. The writer, this actor, he's going here, and he decided to film it in a really artistic way, like a film but taking place on a theatre stage, as though it was the actual play... I think it's quite brilliant, really, as ideas go. You'll see."

Post-apocalyptic... Last day of the earth... I see.

"So it's not actually Hamlet." Just checking.

"But it is," she insists. "That's the brilliance of it. They recite only the original play's words, see? The guy who is playing Hamlet, he's just a stand-in so that he can interact with the actors who are auditioning. The actual actor who will play Hamlet, he's over there... "

She starts pointing, but I interrupt her. Let's not allow the anxiety levels rise to 'post-apocalyptic' levels, shall we?

"Right," I say, swallowing down a clot of nerves. "I think I'm next."

*I'll kill you, Matt.* Dude never said anything about post-apocalyptic, I've never worked on a post-apocalyptic set before. Will there be a green screen? Will I have to wear special gear?

*Will I...?*

There's a teeny tiny bit of a possibility that I might be out of my depth.

In about five seconds my name is called.

I walk out into the blinding yellow lights. Way in the distance, the 'casting directors' or whatever look tiny in their seats. There's four people sitting there, but I can only see the outline of their silhouettes against the bright spotlight's beam, and I have to look away quickly, because my eyes hurt.

"Ready when you are," someone says in a really obnoxious voice, like I'm in X Factor.

The stage manager, an intern, walks on stage. Behind him is a guy who's wearing a utility belt. They hook my waist with the wire, testing that everything is okay. The intern pats me on the shoulder and he's gone. I turn to look sideways at the DJ, a lanky guy with torn jeans and a black tee that says Death on it in letters dripping with blood. He winks at me and presses play.

This is it. *Go.*

As I'm lifted in the air, I reach out my hands to grab a bar that hopefully will be where I expect it to be, and cold metal meets my skin. Matt was right, so far the distances seem to work pretty much the way they did in Seattle.

I bring my knees up and balance on the beam for a second, a few steps below the lights—it feels like a million degrees up here—and then I let myself fly. I tuck my feet in, legs straight like an arrow, and spread my hands out like a bird. I don't land, though, the string allows me to float around the stage for a bit, until it's time for me to push myself to the centre and slightly to the right of the stage. I flip over, coming full circle, and the movement propels me to land on a prop that looks like a rock and I hope it's sturdy because it's about ten meters from the ground and I wouldn't like to discover it can't support my weight too late.

I land on it lightly and turn the cord sideways on my waist.

I am going to dive for the ground, and it can't be in my way. The music settles into a low, rhythmic beat that's really simple, but has an infinite quality of sadness to it. This is the turning point. I take a deep breath and bring in my arms to hug my legs to my chest. I bend my body down low, and jump off. I do three quick somersaults in the air before the ground is staring me in the face, at spitting distance, and then the cord tightens around me, suspending me in the air and giving me just enough time to straighten my body so that I land on one knee, my leg bent at a perfect ninety degrees angle. I look up as though at the lens of a camera and the music fades to a stop.

The blinding lights go off one by one and a lone ray of light remains, focused on my head like a spotlight, as I get to my feet and face the judges, blinking at the harsh light. I try to discern their faces, still blinded by the glare of the stage lights. And that's when it happens.

I stumble.

I almost fall flat on my face, that's how bad I stumble. I have to press my palms on the wooden floor to find my balance and stand up again. I'm shaking so badly, my teeth might be chattering. This can't be happening.

One of the four figures motions to me impatiently to approach, and I walk on trembling legs to the front of the stage and just stand there, shaking. The one who motioned to me is a lean guy in a pristine white Oxford shirt, collar sticking up almost to his ears, black hair falling over his widow's peak, combed to perfection. He's Asian. There's an intelligent, keen look in his eyes as he looks me up and down quickly, and then he just looks away, bored. He looks pretty young and pretty arrogant, but the others seem to have let him be in charge for some weird reason.

He opens his mouth and tells me something, and although I recognize his voice as the obnoxious one that told me 'ready when you are' right before I started, I don't hear what he says.

I run my eyes over the other two guys, a tall, muscular one with a tan and striking eyes, and Matt. And then there's the last one.

He's sitting in his chair, back straight, looking slightly away from me. The first thing I notice about him is that he has a buzz cut. Maybe that's why I didn't recognize him immediately. He looks tougher and younger at the same time. His cheekbones and jaw are more pronounced now that there are no blonde curls flopping over his ears, making his eyes look huge and haunted. There's a steely look of determination in them that chills me to my bones. His face is all angles. He's wearing a light gray sweater with a V-neck that ends right below his Adam's apple, and his long fingers are clasped lightly in front of him.

He has a glass of clear water in front of him and a notepad, as they all do, but he's immobile, touching neither. His eyes are glued to a spot right above my right ear and he looks bored out of his mind.

He turns to his left, where Matt is seated, and suddenly his voice fills the room.

"Two days. Tops," he says to him and Matt just nods with a pained look on his face. "Then she's gone."

"Can't we just. . . " the muscled guy starts saying, and he sounds more amused than anything, but he's cut off abruptly.

"No. we can't. Who's next?" he asks, expecting the others to look at the list, because he doesn't move a muscle.

I stand there, frozen, hardly breathing. Straight-haired guy curses softly under his breath and nudges the immobile form next to him, then bends his head low to meet Matt's gaze across his tall form. He nods in my direction, and Matt gets up with his long, measured stride to walk up the steps to the stage. He reaches me and takes my arm.

"I'm sorry," he whispers in my ear softly and begins to lead me away. His voice barely registers. "Come on," he nudges me. I hadn't realized I wasn't moving. "You did perfect."

Oh yes, the audition.

Did I finish it? I must have. I don't remember even getting here. Did I take a cab? Someone is dragging me by the waist and I try to put one foot in front of the other, but Matt has to almost lift me off my feet, because my body won't obey me.

Someone calls the name of the next person who will audition.

My head snaps around of its own accord to look at the desk again. My brain is numb, my body is frozen.

*No.* No, I'm hallucinating, it can't be.

This can't be happening. Anything but this. It's not him, it's not. It's not possible.

"Get a move on," an angry voice hisses at Matt and me—*his* voice.

Wes' voice. He's the guy with the buzz cut, the V-neck and the glass of water. He's the casting director. He's here, in London, in the school I'm supposed to work.

He's the actor Rosie was talking about.

He's the 'special person' that changed everything.

The Academy was the 'prestigious school' he was hoping to get into, the one he was telling me about when we were together in Corfu, in another lifetime.

"We haven't got all day." That familiar British accent sends a sharp pain ripping through my chest. It wakes me up with a vengeance. Then he finally lifts a hand and picks up his glass, downing a huge gulp. The water reflects the white glow of the lights as it sloshes around. "Any Ophelias back there?"

The other 'casting directors' muffle their laughter. Matt presses my arm, urging me on.

"I'm so damn sorry, Ari," he repeats. "I had no idea."

## proposal

To: Pan <ajpan@gmail.com>, Vanderau <theodore@tdv.com>
Fr: Wes Spencer <therealwes@wesspencer.com>
Subject: Proposal
*Sent 3:45 am 10/12/. . .*

Sweet Prince (working title)

Time: Post-apocalyptic, 200-250 years in the future, maybe a bit more, no less. Last day on earth.
Place: London
Scenery: a theatre stage
Plotline: Hamlet
Length: anything from ten to twenty minutes (short film)

Twist: Hamlet discovers his uncle's betrayal in the middle of the last World War on earth. War has started the domino effect on destruction: waking volcanoes, acid waste rain and fun stuff like that—special effects, Teddy, CGI, that's where you come in. Hopefully.
His dad isn't a ghost, he's data protocol.
His mum is the reigning force, state secretary or something, and she's the one who starts the war.
Ophelia is a soldier. She and Hamlet fall in love during the war, but she catches an airborne virus of the 'mad sickness' that travels along the lines of the army, a mutation the opposite side has developed in their labs as chemical warfare. He almost gets sick too, hovers between madness and sanity, like the bard's Hamlet does, but never leans too far in one direction or another. That's it.

Moral: None. As man destroys man in the bard's original work, here we also have man destroying nature and the planet that used to be his home. The end.

I've already written about three quarters of the final script (which I'm attaching), so send me your thoughts, but I'm not sure I'll take them into account. Teddy, please try to have some thoughts, anything, I know you generally prefer not to use your brain if you don't absolutely have to. Well, you actually have to now. This is your chance. Pan. . . Mate, try not to have too many thoughts, all right? I'm just a mere mortal.
If all goes well I'll be sending you the final draft by the fifteenth of November.

Cheers, Wes.

# FOURTEEN

"I didn't—I thought you two were... talking," Matt says, looking uncomfortable and wary. "I had no idea things were like this."

"Yeah," I just reply. "They are."

It's a couple of hours later and I have only just found my voice.

"You. . . " He has to stop to clear his voice. "You don't want to quit, do you?"

We're eating burgers. It's past midnight, but he wouldn't let me go home. I think he's scared of leaving me alone.

I swallow. The bite tastes like dust and it takes me back to the first few days at the hospital.

"Does he—? Wait, was that what all the yelling was about? Was that. . . was that him?" suddenly the table begins to sway in front of me. "Does he want me to quit?"

It was his voice yelling when I came in, I realize that now. My brain must have refused to register that it was him, and of course I'd never heard him yell before, so there's that. Was he yelling because he found out I was coming here?

Matt shakes his head. "No."

"Then I won't."

"He did yell," he says after a few seconds of silence. "I had no idea he felt that way. I'd never have invited you here if I did; I just thought you two were. . . well, that you both knew. I can't believe I got you into this mess. After all you went through, you don't need to deal with this."

"Hey, it's fine." I'm trying to make myself sound breezy—not sure how that's working out. Matt looks serious as always, but his eyes are searching mine anxiously, and that definitely isn't how I wanted to start this new job with my director. "I wouldn't miss this for the world."

He nods and gestures towards my half-eaten food in a fatherly way, getting up to pay. "Eat up."

He insists on driving me home afterwards. I get into his Alfa Romeo and gratefully lift my frozen fingers towards the air conditioning vent.

"Oh and one more thing," he says as he turns on the ignition.

"What?" I close my eyes in dread and exhaustion.

"He. . . um. . . "

Matt never stammers. Never. I turn to look at him in horror.

"What." I whisper it this time, freaked out.

"Wes is also the leading actor," he says in one breath. "He plays Hamlet. But that doesn't mean you'll have to interact with him," he finishes lamely.

"Of course not," I say past a lump in my throat.

He has to wake me up when we finally reach my hotel, because the jet lag has finally kicked in. I get out of the car groggily and thank him. I may have not been the best company during the past half hour, but at least I haven't been thinking.

And that can only be a good thing.

The next morning, shooting begins right away. Wes gathers all the actors and explains how there will be minimum rehearsals, so everyone has to be 'at the top of their game'.

Matt and I spend the greatest part of the morning in a rehearsal room with the stage manager, poring over a scale model of the set we'll be using, going over every single detail.

When we return to the main stage room, there are three cameras set in front of the stage, and Wes is talking animatedly to the camera crew and the protagonists. Behind him, the two other guys are going over production details.

Finally, Wes climbs on the stage and gets everyone's attention.

"This isn't amateur theatre," he simply says to the twenty-something pairs of eyes that are glued to his. "If you haven't memorized your lines yet, and I don't see why you shouldn't have, open your scripts right now and get to work." People start looking confused, because they've had their scripts for about twenty-four hours, and he's expecting them to know their lines by heart already. *Oh, great, he's gone and turned into freaking Tim.* I wonder whether I should be scared or amused.

Wes fixes his audience with a steely gaze. "Now, let's see. Who here can act?"

Scared it is.

After that, things go on much as I expected them to. We all work hard. From day one there are  struggles and mistakes and many many more takes of the same scenes than there really should be. But there's a feeling of optimism in the air that makes us all want to work even harder, be better, in spite of all our inexperience. We're all learning, and that unites us more than the hard work and the need to succeed. There's a kind of magic in trying something that has never been done before; something  that makes us all work like a team, as one person. I've never worked with such talented, humble, dedicated people before.

Wes stays out of my way and I stay out of his. I work out during the day at a gym in Camden, five minutes from my room, and then I take the bus to Chenies Street and walk down to Gower.

I work hard, train even harder, and talk to Rosie a little bit while we wait in the wings. When I get home at night, past midnight, I'm too exhausted to even call home.

If I had the time to stop and think, it would all seem unreal to me. Seeing him again, being again in the same room and not exchanging one single word. . . the way his cold eyes looked just a hair away from my face, as if he hated the sight of me so much, he couldn't even be bothered to look at me. It's worse than if we'd been perfect strangers, and he was just the guy who had compared me to a gaffer, like he did back in Corfu. But thankfully I'm so busy, I don't have the time to think about it.

I'll fall apart when I get back home, I tell myself every day. But when I get back I'm so exhausted I pass out as soon as my head hits the pillow.

And that's how it goes for the first few days.

...

Three days later, it's the last day of the year.

Shooting is well under way, and it demands much more grueling, hard work than First Sentences ever did, but I'm enjoying every second of it. All the waiting around could be getting on my nerves, but whenever I'm not warming up I'm hanging out with Rosie, handing her costumes and stuff, and so time flies. Wes hasn't been present during my stunt sequences—I'm doing Ophelia's stunts as a soldier, and there's a lot of shooting at things and being shot at by other things and flying about the stage hanging upside down from things involved. He might be somewhere in the back of the dark theatre watching, but I highly doubt it.

The two days Wes gave me are already over, and I'm in no way done, in fact I've barely started. We'll see if he throws me out, after all. But for now, everything is put on hold: there will be no shoot this evening.

Tonight it's New Year's Eve.

It's Christmas break, so the school is empty anyway, except for the students that are participating in Sweet Prince and the director slash producer dudes. And me, of course. We've all been invited to the Royal Albert Hall for a fundraiser charity concert. I'm not sure exactly what the cause is, because I wasn't paying attention; all I know is that it's a super posh event. Yeah, I say 'posh' now.

Since I've been hanging out with Rosie I've been picking up all sorts of English expressions like 'cheers' and 'sodding idiot' and cool stuff like that. She mostly does the talking, as her fingers work on the sewing machine with superhuman speed, and I do the listening. It works.

Anyway, it's Rosie who tells me about the invitation.

"I'm not going," I say, snorting. Yeah, it wasn't even necessary to say that out loud. Like it was ever a possibility that I'd. . .

I freeze. Rosie's eyes are full of tears. We're sitting on the fire escape, taking a small break as they wrap up the shoot on the stage behind us.

"Rosie. . . What is it?"

"Do you even know where we're going?" she asks me, her lips trembling.

"The Royal Albert Hall?" I say, tentatively and she shakes her head.

"We're invited to one of James Pan's concerts. Do you know how rare that is? To get an invite to one of those, I mean. The guy is going to be a bigger deal than blimmin' Beethoven, that's what they say at least. When he was seventeen he got into the most prestigious art college, up in New York. His performances are packed tighter than a Rolling Stones performance; newspapers have dubbed him 'the rock star of classical music'."

"Wow." That's all I can say for a moment. I haven't known her long, but she's told me a lot about herself these couple of days, and I know that she's a grounded, down-to-earth person. She wouldn't exaggerate, at least not that much. And she was definitely the last person I'd expect to start fangirling over a tall, rake-thin teen with a slouch and a permanent scowl on his face.

"That. . . black-haired guy who was at the auditions?"

She smiles. "Isn't he the most gorgeous guy you've ever seen? He's half Chinese, actually, on his mother's side, you know Lin Jiang, the famous pianist?" I just look at her. Name doesn't ring a bell. She sighs. "Gosh, don't you read anything? Anyway, if you're into this stuff," she says, "she's like world famous. But Pan is even more so. Everyone knows him. He plays the cello, the violin, the guitar, the piano. . . I don't think there's an instrument he's not good at. He's a prodigy. He's well on his way to becoming a conductor, and he's only eighteen. Can you imagine? I mean, that school of his has all sorts of music geniuses and professors, and he's gotten ahead of all of them."

"Okay," I say slowly. "So he invited us. It's an honor, I get it. But it's all right if I don't go, right? Nobody would miss me."

She looks down, hiding her expression from me. Her cheeks have gone flaming red.

Everyone else is gone, and we're backstage, cleaning up the costumes and threads and buttons that are randomly strewn about. It's warm in here, but I'm starting to get chilled from having sweated during the shooting. I need a shower badly.

"Everyone fancies him," Rosie says, her voice going quiet. "The girls, I mean. He's just so fit and tall and. . . And those brown eyes. . . Just imagine how they'd look if he smiled."

"Not that he ever would," I mutter under my breath.

"I know he would never look at me, but. . . " Rosie's eyes are pleading.

The idea of someone being infatuated with that arrogant kid is kind of ridiculous to me, but I can't deny I know exactly how she feels. I steal a glance at my watch. There go my plans to skype the new year in with my dad, Katia, grandma and grandpa and everyone else who would be gathered by now in our little apartment in Corfu. At another time zone. Their new year will start hours before mine.

"All right," I tell her and immediately her face lights up. "But I need you to do something for me as well."

"Anything," she says immediately.

"What ha—?" I start saying something out loud, which wasn't meant to be said out loud, and stop myself in time.

"Huh?"

I take a deep breath. "Okay, if I'm to come to this. . . thing, I need to not be left alone before then. Could you do that? Cause if I start. . . getting inside my head, I'll bail." She frowns, but doesn't ask me anything. "But I need a shower first, so fancy a Tube ride to my place?"

She's smiling so hard at me her cheeks must hurt.

"I've got a better idea."

*What have I ever done to deserve people like you and Ollie and Jamie in my life?* That was what I almost asked her out loud.

Her 'better idea' is to take me to her home. She just shows me to the bathroom and gives me fresh towels as though it's the most natural thing in the world for me to take a shower in her house, with her mom and dad and little brothers downstairs.

I start to protest, but she lifts her eyebrows and says that we only have an hour at most and that's pushing it, because Pan hates it when people are late to his concerts. Then, before I have time to open my mouth and reply, she proceeds to announce that she'll start letting out one of her dresses for me to wear and to hurry up, come on.

"Wait, you'll let out a dress?" I ask her, looking around her pink, vintage room, confused.

She looks up at me and laughs. I tower half a head above her and it suddenly dawns on me that I wouldn't have anything to wear to a concert like that even if we had stopped at my place, which would have been a half hour detour at least.

"It doesn't take a genius of Pan's level to figure out you don't have anything to wear," she replies. "I do, but it will need some serious stitching if it's to come anywhere close to your knees."

"Sh-shoes?" I stammer, feeling like a little kid in front of the teacher.

She looks at my feet.

"Seven, seven and a half?" she says to herself. "Same as mum."

At least I have a decent wig with me, the one with the long, wavy brown hair that most resembles my natural hair before the operation. I wore it to work. That's something at least, I think, and then Rosie comes at me with a lip gloss.

And that's the last thing I remember.

An hour and five minutes later, we're standing in the foyer of the Royal Albert Hall. The place is packed with performers, producers, sponsors, reporters and celebrities, all making their way past the photographers' flashes up the wide, red-carpeted staircase, the sounds of musical instruments being strung drifting from upstairs.

I catch a glimpse of Wes' buzz cut at some point—I still haven't gotten used to seeing him with it. My first—idiotic—thought on seeing him at the audition was, *he's gone and cropped that glorious golden mane of his.* But now I see that the buzz cut makes him look more like a man than a wild boy. He's wearing a tux and his cheeks are clean-shaven. He looks a bit thinner, and a bit more tan than he was in Corfu. He smiles at the reporters, but the smile is more of a grimace, never reaching his eyes. His jaw looks sharp, clenched. *Dammit, Ari, look away*.

Soon enough, I find myself seated at a row of velvet seats in a huge auditorium. This is a majestic place.   There are painted cherubs overhead, framing the enormous chandeliers that are bathing us in warm light. The walls are decorated with huge wreaths of holly and mistletoe and on the stage there are sparkling red and black candles giving a modern, kind of funky touch to the austere structure of the building.

On the stage, the orchestra is settling down. As the audience quiets down among the sound of rustling sheet music and tuning instruments, I notice something remarkable: every single instrument is played by a teenager. They all look serious and focused, their instruments lifted gently in their elegant arms, their hair swept back, their black shoes tapping along to the rhythm, but the oldest among them can't be older than eighteen. Rosie presses a program into my hand and I see that they are high school seniors from a private music school from America, but I don't get to read its name, because next to me Rosie lets out a deep sigh, and hangs limply on to my arm, as though she's about to faint.

I turn to ask her what's wrong, but she's not even looking at me. Her eyes are glued to the stage, where the conductor is walking up the three little stairs to the podium. It's him. The black-haired, obnoxious kid. Pan. He turns around and flashes a glorious smile at the audience, then he takes a deep bow.

The audience bursts in applause.

And we haven't even heard anything yet. Rosie clutches at my hand like a drowning person, and after a moment of absolute silence, the music begins.

I always feel, when I listen to music, that there should be more words in the human vocabulary. For example, the words that could describe the sound that comes out of this stage, starting slowly and building up like a hum of energy and feeling, like the rush of cool water that flows to a waterfall. . . they haven't been invented yet.

From the first notes, chills start traveling up  my spine. Music always does that to me, but there is something incredibly gorgeous and poignant about this particular piece. It's really simple in the beginning. It just starts with the flutes, and the rest of the instruments join in one by one, in a simple but powerful tune. Before I realize it, the music has built up to this complicated melody, filled with every imaginable sound in the universe. My eyes tear up as I feel the powerful music tug at my heartstrings.

Maybe this Pan dude has the right to be as obnoxious as he likes. I mean. . . if he created this. . .

"Okay, answer me this," I lean down and whisper in Rosie's ear. "The guy seems to be some kind of orchestra conductor rock star. . . why the hell was he a 'casting director' at my audition?"

"He's best friends with Spencer," she whispers back without looking at me, her eyes round as though she's in a trance. "He's creating a score for Sweet Prince and co-directing or something. And the other guy, the one who was sitting second row, third from the end?"

She's talking about the muscled, laughing guy from the audition.

"Yep."

"Ever hear of the name Vanderau?"

Now my eyes are as huge as hers. And of course, I get it. His face looked slightly familiar, but Wes took all my attention, so I was a bit distracted, you could say.

"No," I mumble in a low voice, hardly able to believe it. "He's not. . ."

"Theodore 'Teddy' Vanderau. Our producer," Rosie nods.

Even I am familiar with this name. The guy is the heir to an empire. It's hard to watch the news or open a magazine without reading anything about the Vanderaus. They are one of the wealthiest, oldest and most prestigious Upper East Side families of New York. They control a big part of the worldwide news agencies and own hotels, shipping companies and charity organizations all over the world. This 'Teddy' guy, his face is on every magazine and newspaper; he's the heir of the empire. Everyone keeps waiting for him to crack under the pressure. But so far, he's been studying at Yale and getting a drug addiction quietly, if what they're printing is to be believed—which it usually is not. Oh, and sleeping with anything that moves.

"He is our producer?" Now my eyes are huge. "What do these boys think they are doing? This is only a school project, most of the actors are students."

"I think they're trying to prove something," Rosie shrugs.

"What?"

"Themselves," she replies. "I think they're brilliant. All of them."

"Well, yeah, you could say that," I admit. They may be a pack of crazy boys, but they sure are brilliant.

"And I think we're the luckiest two people in the world," she finishes, squeezing my hand.

They play nonstop for three quarters of an hour, alternating between popular Christmas songs, a few classics like Vivaldi's Winter and Beethoven's Fifth Symphony, and a few new pieces, that the program says have been composed by students and teachers of the school. The sound they are creating is so amazing it knocks the wind right out of me, sometimes with a raw punch of emotion, sometimes with a slow shimmer of feelings.

The final piece they perform is a badass modern arrangement that no one's ever heard before. It must be a big deal, because right before it starts, people start whispering to each other and craning their necks towards the conductor's podium. I glance at the program as the final minor chords of the violins swell in the air and I read the composer's name: Adam James Yi Peng Pan. Next to me, Rosie is having an orgasm.

As is the rest of the audience, apparently.

The percussions explode and the entire building seems to shudder with the weight of the music. My seat feels like it's on fire.

Everyone is on their feet, clapping their hands raw even before the final notes. Pan turns around and bows once more and after five full minutes of applause he settles the orchestra down for a final number.

They start playing that bringing-in-the-New-Year thingy that I can never pronounce, the 'auld' something, and a hush comes over the room, everyone turning to the person seated next to them, misty-eyed and smiling.

And then I see it.

Gosh, this is harder than I thought it would be.

I can't even remind myself to not think about things anymore. I let the sadness wash over me, and my heart breaks all over again.

"What's up?" Rosie asks as she sees the tears pouring down my cheeks. "Ari? What are you looking at?"

She follows my gaze to the front row, where Wes is seated.

"Stanley Laurel," I answer to Rosie and a smile trembles on my lips, as a flash of his smiling face in the 'How to Pick Up a Girl' video passes in front of my eyes.

A few rows of seats in front of us, Wes is seated next to the Vanderau dude. I saw him take his seat, and have been trying to look away since the beginning of the concert. But now I can't.

Wes turns to his right, where a girl with straight brown hair is seated, and kisses her deeply on the lips. The way he moves, so calm and deliberate, is so different from the drunken way he was sucking face with that actress that day in Drops, that I wonder why my mind is immediately transported to the memory of that day. But it is. And this hurts even more.

He turns back to face the stage and once more the side view of his cheek is all I can see. The girl isn't someone I've seen before. I can't tell if she's a celebrity or not, and I'm not sure I would want to know, if she was. She's wearing a light blue dress with a plunging neckline, her earrings sparking in the candlelight, and she leans into his shoulder in a familiar way that suggests they may have been dating for a bit.

I close my eyes for a second and he appears in front of me as he was that night in Corfu when we listened to the philharmonic, his hair flying in the wind, his hand gripping mine, his eyes filling with moisture as the music enveloped us like a cloud.

"Do you need to go to the loo? They'll be done in five minutes," Rosie whispers to me. I hadn't realized I'd gotten up.

"I . . . I need some air."

She follows me outside and calls a cab, telling me that I'm to spend the night at her house.

"First night of the new year," she says. "No way are you spending it alone. We'll put on pajamas and empty my dad's bottle of Chardonnay. What do you say? Does that sound like a good way to bring in the new year?"

I just nod, too tired to speak. We get into the cab, rubbing our hands together to warm them up. The cold is biting.

And that's when I realize it.

What I wanted, what I needed so badly a few months ago, has already happened: Wes Spencer is now officially out of my life.


### texts

**Ollie:** how r things, Hamlet?

**Wes:** Bad

**Ollie:** always in character. That's my boy. s all good then?

**Wes:** S all bad

**Ollie:** cant we have an adult conversation 4 onc?

**Wes:** Did you know Ari would be here?

**Ollie:** Ari? *My* Ari? Why wld she be there?

**Wes:** Stunts

**Ollie:** what?

**Wes:** Stunts, she's doing the stunts. She's the stunt girl Matt hired.

**Ollie:** this is serious, stop fooling around.

**Wes:** She's here, I'm telling you.

**Ollie:** no. no no no no no nooooooooooooo

**Wes:** yep.

**Ollie:** ffffffffffffffffffffffffff

**Wes:** She didn't know this is where she was coming. My film, I mean.

**Ollie:** I didn't either. Damn. Are u sure?

**Wes:** What? You're asking me if I'm sure she's here?

**Wes:** I haven't seen her in a while, but, yeah, I'm pretty damn sure it's her.

**Wes:** Skinny, orange wig, falls over her own feet when she walks?

**Ollie:** . . .

**Wes:** Ring a bell? We're talking about the same girl here, right?

**Ollie:** Stop it, Wes, come on. Ok. It's gonna be fine.

**Wes:** Guess again.

**Ollie:** I'm so sorry, dude. How are you doing, srsly?

**Wes:** Srsly?

**Ollie:** Wes come on man

**Wes:** I'm in hell. Seriously.

**Wes:** If you tell her a word of what I've told you today, I'll kill you. Srsly

**Ollie:** Listen, if there's anything I can do, if u need

**Wes:** Shut up

**Ollie:** anything, just call and I'll fly over.

**Wes:** I know. Stay put and keep your big mouth shut.

**Ollie:** that's funny, how u don't trust me.

**Wes:** Hell. I'm in hell.

**Ollie:** I'm so sorry

**Wes:** Yeah.

# F I F T E E N

We go back to work the day after New Year's. Everyone is excited, not bugged at all about missing the holidays; after all we chose to be here. Rosie and a few other girls boil tea and bring chocolate-chip cookies in a red tin box to make the atmosphere a bit festive, and everyone stuffs their faces with the tiny confections ravenously, although there are catered snacks offered to us every day at the end of shooting.

Wes directs calmly and with authority, without adding more stress to the shoot, even though he's also playing Hamlet. He has to wear a shiny leather uniform that contours his body and just about stops the heart of every female within a one mile radius near him—me included. He's put on even more muscle and he looks practically enormous with the leather sculpted to his body, his cropped hair glowing golden amid all the blackness of the costumes, the gray platforms and the glaring green screens.

I can't get over how different his face looks: leaner than before, its contours sculpted and sharp, but his eyes, his skin, his lips. . . He's the same. My heart skips a beat every time I glance at him.

*Get a grip.*

He recites his lines in a thundering voice and the camera gets about a million close-ups of his handsome face, painted in make-up so that it looks all battered, dry and cut up from the battle. He doesn't falter once, and his immaculate performance prods everyone else to do their best. He never touches a drop of alcohol, or anything that isn't sparkling water for that matter, and he doesn't smile even remotely.

# LOSE ME.

The millionaire heir is nowhere to be seen, but Pan sits quietly on a seat at the back of the empty theater, watching everything with an unpleasant smirk on his face, and Rosie is almost flustered out of her mind.

By the end of the day, Wes, still in full make-up and costume, sits down beside him and they talk for about five minutes, then they gather us and tell us we did everything wrong. We reshoot a few scenes and I patiently wait for my turn in the freezing wings, trying to warm up as well as I can, until I have to go be 'drowning Ophelia' inside a square, transparent tub of water they have towed on the stage, by dunking my blonde-wigged head again and again in the tepid water.

I have to hold my breath underwater for eons, and when I come up for air my makeup invariably needs retouching, so we have to take a two-minute break before I'm dunked in again.

So that's fun.

...

The next day is a big battle sequence shoot. Wes will be in the stunt as well, although he'll be filmed alone, in different frames than me. A few other guys will take part as well, students, and before I have the time to ask whether that's a good idea, Matt takes me aside and tells me to 'keep an eye on them so that they don't get themselves killed'. Before I have time to say anything in reply, they're bringing in the fog machines and he goes to talk to the stage crew, his eyebrows furrowed.

Rosie and the other artists have taken today off, because no makeup will be needed, it will be mostly far away shots and action sequences that will be digitally enhanced later. I understand this is where the Vanderau heir comes in, apparently he's some kind of computer wizard.

Well.

He won't do the flying and falling off of trees with weapons in our hands for us, that's for sure.

About two hours later, the stage lighting has been tested and reworked to within an inch of its life and three students and I have been positioned near the ceiling of the stage, perched atop props camouflaged to resemble burnt trees. The cameras are rolling.

"Here we go," Wes says to the fog machine operator, and, with a 'whoosh', he turns it on, filling the air with a white cloud of vapor.

I gather my limbs together to jump like I did in my audition, only now I'm holding what looks like heavy war machinery in both hands, so it's a bit more tricky.

The camera is focused on me and the other guys will be in the background, if they manage to float on their cords at all and don't sink from the scaffoldig like stones to the floor.

"Action," Wes yells.

A shiver of pride runs down my spine as I hear the confidence in his voice. Just four months ago he was this conceited British boy who needed Tim to keep him in line, and now every eye in the room is glued on him, waiting for instructions. He's a director, a writer. . . and a complete stranger. His eyes glide over me as though he doesn't even notice me. And that's how it should be. Why would he notice me? I've relinquished any right to his attention.

If only I hadn't. . . No. Focus. Okay, here goes.

It's a disaster.

We have to do it again. Then again.

Wes remains calm and patient through it all, giving us directions like a pro.

We do it three more times.

"Okay, we're getting there people," Wes says. "One more take, then a five minute break. Ready? Action!"

There's that swooshing sound again as the fog machine starts working once more, but this time it sounds a bit weird, different. I open my mouth to ask if we should check it, and then all hell breaks loose. Shards of glass are bombarding me from all sides, and I drop the weapon prop to protect my face with my hands. Suddenly my cord snaps and I'm falling to the ground, but not as fast as I would if I was free falling—so it didn't break after all.

I'm being lowered down from the scaffolding so fast that I land hard, my knees hitting the wooden floor with a snap.

All of this happens with unbelievable speed, just a blur past my failing vision, because I have a bigger problem right now than bruised knees.

I can't breathe.

I choke and gag, desperately thinking that I have to raise my head above this suffocating mass of white smoke, but there's nowhere to breathe clean air in. Everything around me is snow-white and turning a thick, gray color, as my vision starts closing in on me.

Wes is screaming from somewhere to my left: "Get the window! Now! Smash it in, do it!" but I don't feel any air entering my lungs.

Someone grabs me and drags me to the back of the room. Strong hands help me to lean out the window, and I take deep gulps of air, coughing and trying to steady myself in spite of  the dizziness and nausea.

As soon as I can breathe again, I turn around to look at the rest of the room. It's covered in filth. Mick, one of the stage guys, a sturdy dude with a kind face and round glasses, is holding me upright. I grab the windowsill and try to will my legs to support me.

"What. . . What. . . ?" What happened, is what I'm trying to say, but all that comes out is a croak.

"Bloody fog machine broke," Mick replies in a hoarse voice. "Clear out, everyone, give her space! Can you breathe?"

I nod, taking another gulp of air, and I bend my head down over my knees, feeling giddy. In a second the faintness passes. Okay, so these weren't shards of glass, although they pretty much felt as painful.

The dense streaks of smoke have begun to drift to the floor all around the room, settling on the seats like snow, small specks floating to my nose and mouth and causing me to choke again. Mick secures his hold on my shoulder.

"I've got you," he says, "take your time."

The window is broken, and as I gulp in clean air I'm careful not to touch the sharp edges of the glass. Outside a siren is wailing in the distance and freezing air blows in, lifting the dust and debris and twirling it around our clothes and hair. Talk about a post apocalyptic setting!

"Everyone accounted for? Ambulance is on its way," someone yells.

Ambulance is on its way.

Ambulance is on its way.

*Ambulance. . .*

Just these words.

All these months of struggling and overcoming and making progress. . . And all it takes is five words. Five words that catch me off guard. Five words that ruin me.

*Ambulance is on its way.*

Just five words that take me back to the horror of that day in Corfu, they drown me in memory. The darkness drags me under without warning. I lose the ground beneath my feet.

When the room comes back into focus, I'm sitting on the floor hugging my knees. There's someone here, in front of me, and they must have been talking to me for a few seconds, but I can't concentrate on their face or their words.

"Hey."

*Ambulance. Ambulance. Ambulance.* That's all I can hear, that's all I can think. That last day in Corfu. The helicopter ride. Dad and Wes running alongside my gurney in New York. Ambulance. Seeing my bald head for the first time in the mirror.

"Ari, Ari. Come on. . . "

Jamie looking at me with a sad look in his eyes. I'm sick now. I'm not an athlete any longer; I'm an invalid. I'm convalescing. Can't eat, can't walk, can't run. No. *No no no.*

"Open your eyes!" a sharp voice snaps me back to reality.

I open my eyes to find Wes' green stare fixed on my face. His hair is white with remnants of the fog, his face pale next to his black shirt. His fingers are clutching my knee, shaking me.

"Look at me," he practically yells. "There's nothing wrong with you, Ari. Nothing, do you understand?"

I'm looking at him, frozen.

"I need you to nod."

I bend my head, barely.

*"It's the size of a nut."*

*"You need to have the operation." "When?" "Yesterday."*

*"I'm so sorry, baby."*

I try to take a breath, but my lungs are filled with smoke and sadness to capacity; there's no room for air.

Suddenly I'm wrapped in his arms so fiercely it hurts, my nose pressed against his chest, his stubble tickling my neck. He folds me into him until I can't breathe, although it's not like I was doing much of that either way.

"Don't be scared." His lips move next to my ear, almost touching my skin. "This is nothing like the last time, okay? You're perfectly fine now, only everyone has to be checked, it's obligatory. Just routine, nothing more. You know it was just an accident, you feel fine, you're perfect. It's not like what happened before, don't even think about it. It's not worth it, it's over. Over. That dark part of your life is gone for good."

He keeps talking to me like that until it's time to go.

Then he gets up slowly, taking me with him, lacing my arm with his so that I don't fall behind, and starts walking towards the exit. I freeze.

"No." I shake my head.

He raises an eyebrow and all I can think about is how I've missed this, I've missed being in his arms and I've missed his scent and his green gaze and I've missed his voice in my ear so bad it hurts me physically.

"I can't. . . I can't get in that thing," I say instead.

He hesitates a bit, then just nods.

He doesn't say another word as he leads the way to the parking lot below the building, where his car is parked. Absently, I remember how much he loved driving himself everywhere in Corfu, insisting on having his own car around, when all the rest of the actors had drivers. This one is an edgy, red Aston Martin, but I don't even have the energy to be excited about that.

He watches me silently as I get in the passenger seat, then gets in himself and drives us to the hospital.

We meet up with the rest of the guys there, but Wes doesn't leave. He's right there when they take all four of us for X-rays and then to a doctor's office to listen to our lungs. He waits patiently in one of the white chairs, then gets up to bring us steaming tea in plastic cups, his clothes trailing white pieces of solidified fog behind him as he walks.

He makes a few phone calls, and then he wraps me in his coat, telling everyone that we'll continue where we left off tomorrow and to go home and rest.

He drives me back in silence.

He doesn't ask me for directions; he seems to know where I live. I'm too exhausted and freaked out to protest or ask him, so I lean back in the leather seat—at least I won't soak this one, I think wryly—and try to pretend that as soon as I hop into a scorching-hot shower I'll be fine.

As we turn the corner into my street, it starts raining. Tiny drops of water hit the windshield in a steady rhythm, and quickly turn into rivulets, sliding down the glass. The rain falls heavier by the minute.

Wes turns on the windshield wipers and their rhythmic swish reminds me of home. Suddenly I have to concentrate all my energy on fighting back tears. In a minute, we'll be there. I have to thank him, at least.

"Thank you." I clear my voice, hoping that saying it out loud will break the waves of sadness that are pulling me under. "You didn't have to do that. . . "

He interrupts me, waving a hand in the air. "Don't mention it."

I look out of the window. It's raining heavily now, big, fat raindrops bouncing off the grainy surface of the street.

*'My job is to keep you alive, and that's not what you are right now, not by any consideration.'*

*Dammit, Jamie, get out of my head.*

"You with me?" Wes' voice startles me.

He steals a glance at me sideways, and I feel so stupid sitting here beside him. Am I trying to hurt myself further? Why do I keep doing this to myself? Work be hanged, I'm out of here as soon as I take a shower.

Wes rests his hand on the e-brake and I see that his sleeve is filthy with smog.

"That looks nice." The words pop out of my mouth before I have time to filter.

He lets out a low laugh. "Ta."

We're here. He brings the car to a gentle stop alongside the curb, but doesn't turn to look at me, so I open the door and swing my leg out.

"I was scared too," he says quietly. "Still am."

Leg is back in. I don't know where to look. "Did. . . did you get hit by the smoke too?" I muster up the courage to glance at him.

His eyes meet mine full on. For the first time, I notice the stubble on his chin; it makes him look sort of rugged and absolutely mouth-watering. His lips are trembling slightly.

"Scared about you," he says. "Scared out of my mind."

I take a deep breath.

"But, Ari." He turns his body sideways so that he's fully facing me. Water is beating down on the glass, its sound deafening in the sudden stillness. "We can't let fear, no matter how justified or real, rule our lives. You can't let it steal your courage, your passion for life."

I hang my head. "You of all people know what a coward I am," I murmur.

"I of all people know how brave you've been," he answers immediately.

"I. . . I should go." I start taking off his coat, but he puts a hand on my arm to stop me. I shudder, a jolt of electricity passing though me at his touch, even through all the layers of clothing.

"It's pouring," he says. "You can bring it back tomorrow, yeah?"

I run like a scared kid out of the door and into the street. I put my key blindly in, and shut the door behind me, shaking as though I'm being chased.

...

I take a shower and change into dry clothes, and then I decide to eat something. On my way to the kitchen, I pass the front door and notice Wes' coat laid out on a chair to dry. And that's when I make the decision. The decision to be a coward no longer.

I pick up my phone and punch in his number before I can think about it too much.

He answers on the second ring.

"It's me," I say, running a hand through my short, wet hair. "I'm sorry for the way I ran away and I'm sorry for the way I've behaved to you. . . " I need to take a breath, but if I stop now, I'll never get the words out. "I never got to say I'm sorry, that's how much of a coward I am."

He doesn't interrupt me, just waits until I stop panting, in case I have anything more to say. Then he sighs loudly.

"You don't need to apologize to anyone. You survived, you're alive and you're here and I'm. . . I'm so bloody proud of you for it."

I'm lost for words. "I'd like to talk," I say, before I can lose my nerve. "Just once. There's some things I need to tell you before I can close this chapter. . . "

I can't believe I just admitted to him I'm not over him. He probably knows already, though, given the way I become all tongue-tied whenever he's around.

"I'm not sure there's anything to talk about," he replies and I'm angry at myself for feeling disappointed. This is practically the same thing he told me two months ago. What was I expecting? "But, as I told you, if you want to talk, I'm always here. Right now, if that's what you need."

Oh, I see. Is this the 'we can still be friends' thing people talk about? Cause if so, it sucks scissors.

"Right now?" I laugh nervously.

"Yeah. I'm. . . I'm close."

Wait, he's close? What does that mean? I run over and look out the window. The Aston Martin is still there, on the curb. I hurry to put on my shoes, then dash down the stairs and open the front door. The rain slashes at me, soaking my jeans and sweater within seconds. I run across the street and reach for the passenger door, but he beats me to it.

He gets out of the car as soon as he sees me, his door snapping closed behind him, and walks around to the front. He doesn't cross the sidewalk, though, and neither do I. We just stand there in the rain, neither of us saying a word, water seeping into our clothes, just a few paces of wet road between us.

"Your hair," he says.

Rivulets of water are running down his chin and he has to squint to see past the droplets that are landing on his sandy eyebrows.

"Beautiful," it sounds as though he says—not possible, I know. And then his eyes meet mine. There's so much pain in there that my heart breaks all over again. "Phelps," he shouts over the sound of the rain.

"What did you want to tell me?"

I take a deep breath.

"About what you did for me. . . I wanted to thank you. Stan."

It takes a second for my words to register, and then his lips stretch in the hugest smile. He lowers his eyes, as though he's embarrassed.

"Hey, you watched them!" It's hard to hear him over the racket of the rain. "Did you like. . . ?"

"I laughed for hours," I reply as loudly as I can. "The nurse had to come in and check up on me."

"Mission accomplished," he just says.

The smile is gone as quickly as it appeared. He looks down for a second. The rain keeps pelting on him, accentuating every muscle on his torso beneath his soaked shirt. He's clenching his right arm, making a fist.

"*At least* you watched them," he shouts back at me, his voice harsh and bitterness.

*Stop being a wuss*, I say to myself. I've said it a hundred times this past week alone.

"I didn't think you'd still. . . I hoped you would forget before long," I say and immediately regret it.

He turns away, his face going pale as he kicks the front wheel with his shoe. I flinch. "You really didn't hear a word I ever said," he yells, spitting raindrops. "You were afraid it wouldn't work between us, right?" Physical pain assaults me at his words, but I know I provoked him. He's livid, shouting into the cold night, all his frustration pouring out. I let him. "Well, you're nothing to me now. And I'm nothing to you. Is that what you wanted? You decided for me without even talking to me. How is that fair? How is that. . . ?" He turns his back to me and I lift a hand to wipe the rainwater from my eyes. It's shaking. "You were scared to tell me what was wrong with you," Wes's head yells to me, "then you were still scared after everything was okay. I don't get it, Ari. Maybe I was the problem, and not your sickness."

He lifts a hand to grab the nape of his neck, and I watch his back muscles clench beneath his wet, clinging shirt. Well, at least we're talking about it, one part of me thinks, while the rest of me is screaming: not like this, no, God, not like this.

"You're so wrong," I shout at him. "You're the reason I'm alive."

He gives a half-laugh at this, but his lips aren't smiling. "I am in a way," he says quietly and I struggle to hear him. "Now I'm the one who's drowning."

The breath is knocked out of me. Did he say what I think he did? I'm shaking all over. Water drips from his nose, his chin. His hair has turned dark with it. I swallow a few raindrops that have landed on my lips.

"I. . . I need you to forgive me."

"You need to forgive yourself," he replies. Okay, what the hell does that mean?

"Do you hate me?"

"Haven't decided."

This I didn't expect. I take a step back as though he's slapped me. He turns to face me once more. His face is white in the gathering darkness, his mouth a hard line.

"Get inside, Ari," he says, hanging his head as though he's exhausted. His eyes are obscured by darkness, I can't read his expression.

He opens the door to the driver's seat. *It's on the wrong side*, I think absently. Of course, England. "You'll need another shower."

In a moment, his rear wheels spin on the gravel as he peels away from the curb and I'm left alone, staring after his disappearing taillights.

The skies open up overhead, bathing the world into a non-descript dark color of gray and loss.

## Art FM

*Transcript excerpt of interview with Weston Spencer, aired live on 11/10/. . .)*

[. . .]**"Weston, talk to me a little bit about these YouTube videos. They were, they *are* I should say, a good month later, an internet sensation. Let me read you a few of the statistics here, okay? For everyone who has just tuned in right now, you are listening to Art FM. This is your host, Mark Adam, and I'm here today with none other than Academy Award nominee and Hollywood heartthrob, Wes Spencer."**

"Come on, cut it out. Don't. . . don't say that."

**"Don't say what? We're live, we have to give these people something."**

"All right. I can see it, fifteen years from now. . . This thing is going to follow me forever, isn't it?"

**\*Laughs\* "Yep. Pretty much. I can't think why it shouldn't, since you're one of the most successful and youngest at, let's see, twenty two, right? Yeah, one of the youngest nominees ever. . . okay, okay, I'm stopping now. So. Let me read a bit of what the press is saying about your short films that started coming out at the beginning of last month, and were posted one each day for four days**

straight?"

"Five."

"Oh, wow, five. So this is a first time phenomenon. Someone like you, a Hollywood actor, a celebrity, posting entertainment content for free on a social media website."

"Except for music."

"That's right. So what we have here is, let me see: hitting one million views in less than half an hour. That's. . . that's viral, all right. As of today, a total of ten million subscribers to the YouTube channel."

"GreyRibbon."

"GreyRibbon, which if I'm not mistaken is a reference to lung ca. . . ?"

"Brain tumor."

"Right. So, may I ask, what inspired this? Was it—was it someone close to you or. . . ? "

"If we're talking artistic inspiration, then I'll tell you that I grew up watching classic, golden-era comedy. I was watching Monty Python and Chaplin when I was twelve, and I discovered Laurel and Hardy when I was seventeen. I've watched every single movie the made, studied them to the teeniest detail. It's the golden era of film for a reason. So, yeah, I've been into hardcore comedy for years, I just didn't expect it to come to me so soon and so. . . naturally, I guess. But, on the other hand, if we're talking inspiration as in, what made me want to do this, it was a friend. We did it for a friend."

"Okay. Let me say, that's the *sweetest* thing anyone's *ever* done for a friend."

"No no, nothing like that. . . This person who was at one time really close to me, was going through something pretty serious. And they were very important person to me. Actually, it was because of this person that I've started to write and direct. It was always my dream, but this friend made me realize that I didn't have to spend the rest of my life making other people rich, to put it bluntly. I could start something on my own. You don't forget the person who did that for you, do you? The first person to believe in you. Anyway, they were away at the time and I wanted to do something for them, that's all. I ended up doing it for myself as well."

**"I'm guessing we won't even know the gender of this 'friend'. Does he or she even know about this? I mean, it would be hard not to see the videos as they were the most shared YouTube videos for a period of. . . let me see. . . a fortnight. That's amazing."**

"Hey, don't look at me like that, I only posted the stupid things, me and my friend Ollie actually, he was a big part of everything; writing the script and starring and producing. He and Anna Dell, who starred in 'How to Pick Up a Girl'. Yeah, that's all I did. I didn't even announce it anywhere. Beats me how everyone found them two seconds after they were up. It was never meant to be such a big deal."

**"Never meant—Have you *seen* what you've done to the rest of the media? You broke the internet. But still, the million dollar (literally) question is this: Why free? Why YouTube? Why social media? People are saying there aren't even ads on there. Is that for real?"**

"These videos, they saved my sanity. During a really tough period in my life, I needed something to do, to somehow help, to stop feeling so useless. You know how it is, right? I would have gone crazy or catatonic or started smashing things if it hadn't been for creating these videos. You don't. . . You don't sell something you created out of pure desperation."

**"That intense, huh?"**

"The ten days I spent in rehab after that were nothing compared to how therapeutic this whole process was."

**\*Loud laughter\* "Yeah, like anyone can whip up a few short films in a couple of days with the acting talent of a Wes Spencer. I mean, you had James Pan do your music theme, correct?"**

"Correct. Look, I don't know about the talent, but one thing I will tell you. Even if things had gone in a different way, personally I mean. . . I still wouldn't regret a second of those nights we spent, Ollie and me, working like possessed over the scripts and props and lighting. It was the most fun I've had in my entire life. We barely slept or ate for two weeks. I know I had a fever when we were done, but it was totally worth it."

**"Another question is: Why comedy?"**

"I'm sure you're expecting a deep answer to that, but it's not. The answer is: for laughs." **\*Laughter\*** "No, I mean it. That was the whole point. We needed to laugh."

**"You know, this interview isn't going the way I planned at all. It's a delight having you in the studio, as always, Mr. Spencer—"**

"So I'm mister now? And 'a delight'? Who talks like that on a live radio show, mate?"

**\*Laughter\* "Hey, don't tell me how to do my job. Ladies and gentlemen, you're listening to Art FM with a *delightful* insight into. . . "**[. . .]

## S I X T E E N

Three more days of filming pass by without incident, and without so much as a word from Wes. At least he's not frowning every time he has to look over to where I'm standing. He even gives me a glimmer of a half-smile once, and I live the rest of the day on it.

I'm over at Rosie's almost every night. It gets to the point where I'm wondering whether I should check out of my room, but I don't actually do it.

Tuesday night, I'm in her little brother's room—and by 'little' I mean that he's seventeen and towering a head and a half over me. We're playing videogames in his room, cross-legged on the floor, and I happen to be yelling "owned!" at the exact moment that Rosie bursts into the room, whipping the headphones from my ears.

"Why," she thunders, "aren't you dressed?"

Liam, her brother, presses pause with a muffled cry, and I turn to look at her in surprise.

"Cause. . . cause Liam doesn't mind," I answer. I'm in sweats, as is he, but Rosie is dressed in a saucy little number, her legs stuffed into a pair of red stilettos. "Are you going out?"

She grabs my hand and pulls me up from the floor. She's really strong for such a small person. "*We* are going out. You haven't forgotten, have you?"

"Oh, Zozie!" Liam whines. "Leave her alone, we're just—"

"Didn't you agree we'd go with. . . with the others?" Rosie turns on wounded, little-girl eyes on me and I sigh, giving up. "Pub crawl."

"What on earth is a pub crawl supposed to be?" I ask, as Liam lets out a guffaw.

"It's what normal people do for fun. Which probably means those posh blokes have never done it in their lives, right?" He laughs. "The Genius will be there," he adds softly and Rosie punches him in the neck. "Ow! What'd I say? Do you have claws instead of human fingers? What *is* that?" He's checking a scratch, trying to turn around and look at the back of his neck.

He's right. Rosie is wearing fake red nails and everything. Her face is all made up and shiny, and a tiny bit of her boobs is showing.

"All right," I say, giving up.

Her dad drives us. He's silent on the way, having been robbed of speech as soon as he saw his daughter's dress, but I know he's not really mad at her; just concerned.

Rosie doesn't have a curfew, but I don't think she's ever been out past one, and that's pushing it. She's only ever had two boyfriends, both from school, and her boyfriends' parents had been friends with her parents for ages. She's what you'd call a good girl.

I'm sensing tonight is some kind of a turning point for her; she's trying to be someone different, she's experimenting, getting out of her comfort zone. The only reason I came along is because I know how important this is to her.

It's snowing heavily. We pass lit up streets lined up with cozy, decorated shops and fogged-up pub windows. Oxford Street looks like something out of a fairytale.

I feel like a kid, being driven to a party by my friend's dad. I miss my own dad. Christmas school vacation has just started in Greece; he must be lonely. But of course he'll have a million things to do, helping grandpa with the shop, playing soccer with his buddies. Besides, I'll be back in a few days.

I miss Katia too. We used to chat almost every night, but neither one of us has time for it these days, it seems. Besides, I need to do this alone, wasn't that the thought? Well, I'm not really alone, not since Rosie's family sort of adopted me, but I could be, if I wanted to. Of course, if I was by myself right now, I'd probably be eating crappy take away food, or, let's be honest, not eating at all. Freaking out about Wes. About my panic attack the other day. About everything.

Finally, we're there.

The first pub in the 'pub crawl'—more new words—is a cozy, black building with fogged up windows, tucked away in a street corner in a street behind the Liverpool University. Rosie's dad starts to ask us to call him when we need a lift back, but Rosie shuts the door on him and grabs my hand, running across the street to the pub.

# LOSE ME.

By the time we get in, our coats are crusted with snowflakes. We shake the snow off our hair as a blast of noise assaults us and a damp, human warmth envelopes us, almost choking us. The inside of the pub is bathed in a soft, bluish light, and it takes a moment for our eyes to adjust to the semi-darkness. Soon enough the cooped-up feeling passes and a tall guy waves at us at the back of the room. It's Theo Vanderau. Rosie walks over to him excitedly, and only I can tell how nervous she is. He says hi to Rosie and me, and grabs us a couple of drinks, which we start sipping while trying to talk loudly enough so that we can hear ourselves speak.

Almost all of the crew is here—except for Pan. Rosie cranes her neck looking for him, and as soon as she realizes he's not here, her face falls. I don't see Wes anywhere either, but that can only be a good thing. I watch Rosie's face fall as she searches every face for Pan's and my heart constricts. I slide an arm around her waist and she leans against me for protection. I can guess that she suddenly feels exposed and uncomfortable in her dress, so I step in front of her, trying to protect her with my body.

"So, Liam," I blurt out, trying to take her mind off of Pan's absence, "um. . . has he got a girlfriend or something?"

"Why? Are you interested?" she asks immediately and we burst out laughing, but it's forced.

We talk and pretend to laugh for about twenty minutes and then we have to go to the bathroom. There's a line, of course. She finishes first so I tell her to go back in and I'll follow. When I come out, a few minutes after, my heart stops.

There's a guy on her.

And I do mean *on* her. He's standing way too close to her for comfort, and he's got that glazed look in his eye. As I scramble to reach her, I can already see his hairy arm slithering around her waist and his hands splaying across her breasts. She's trying to push him away, but she looks too terrified to make any real effort to escape.

"Rosie!"

I push and shove people away to get to her, but she's too damn far away and I won't be in time. The man presses his lips on hers and she makes a gagging motion. I don't think she's faking it, she looks like she's about to pass out. Then suddenly, everything comes to a screeching halt.

In a split second, a tall form slides in between them, and the next minute the man is lifted off of Rosie, as someone starts punching him in the face.

It's Theo.

I stop dead on my tracks. Theo is beating the crap out of the guy in slow motion, his knuckles turning red as the blood starts flowing freely from the man's nose. Meanwhile Theo looks cool as a cucumber, barely breaking a sweat; his face is concentrated but otherwise impassive as he keeps throwing the punches with calculated precision.

"Stop it," the man slurs, trying to dodge Theo's hits, his left foot inching towards Theo's kneecap. "Not my fault this tramp was wearing. . . "

He doesn't have time to say anything else. My fist collides with his teeth and he flies backwards, legs in the air. He lands with a thud on the floor. Theo's lips spread in a huge smile and he gives me a thumbs up before bending down to kick the guy one last time.

As soon as she's released, Rosie collapses in a heap on the floor and I run and put my arms around her, holding her up as she sobs uncontrollably.

The man picks himself up and limps towards the door, as a couple of men in black approach us menacingly. Theo walks over, ignoring them.

"Is she okay?" he asks, frowning slightly.

"She needs to get home," I say and he nods.

"You can take my car, driver is out front," he says.

I get up, but Rosie sags against me, and Theo quickly bends down and picks her up in his arms, starting for the door.

I want to run after them so badly, but I glance around me and stop. There's broken glass everywhere. People have taken a step back from us and a few members of the staff are just standing there, staring at us pointedly. I'm guessing they can't ask us to leave, because of who Theo is, but they don't look very happy either.

"Crap," I whisper. "Just go on," I call to Theo, "I'll settle here and take a cab."

"You sure?"

"Yeah, thanks." I'm sorry, but this guy is nothing like the drug-snorting frat boy the tabloids paint him to be. He's well-trained, plus he's full of confidence and doesn't mind carrying a half-drunk girl out of a club. . . I can't remember the last guy I met who wasn't obsessed with how he'd look if he did something and people saw.

*You should just give room to people to surprise you,* I tell myself and turn around to almost collide with someone's chest. I raise my eyes and meet a pair of brilliant, green ones.

Wes is here. He's looking down at me with a desperate expression on his face, and his lips move as though he wants to ask me why the hell does disaster follow me around everywhere I go? But he doesn't say anything.

*When did he get here? Why didn't I see him? Why am I not prepared for this?*

I drop my gaze, feeling hot embarrassment burn my cheeks. As I look down, something catches my eye: his fingers are wrapped around another person's hand. A girl's hand. The brunette whom he kissed at the concert is draped all around his arm, gently trying to drag him away from me.

"Leave it," he tells me quietly, untangling his hand from hers to reach his pocket. "I'll take care of it."

"Okay," I croak out.

# LOSE ME.

I escape to the bathroom to wash my hands again, then I quickly make my way out, trying to keep my eyes on the floor the whole time.

The freezing air hits me with a force that steals my breath. The snowfall has slowed to a powdery sprinkle. The street is quiet and white, everything around me impossibly still. The pavement is deserted.

A car passes in the distance, slowly making its way across the soft sheet of snow. Its wheels make that sloshing sound, as though the ice hasn't yet solidified on the gravel.

I sit down on the edge of the curb, barely feeling the snow seep into the seat of my jeans. I take a few gulps of air, thinking that I should have put on my jacket first, but I couldn't stay another minute in that suffocating little room. I left it behind. *Good job, Ari, running away again.* Well, sometimes you have to cut your losses.

Just as I'm about to give in and go back inside, there are suddenly footsteps crunching in the snow behind me. Next thing I know, someone's crouching on the street next to me. Black buckle boots, white with ice at the edges, come into my line of vision. I don't even have to look up to know who it is. I recognize his scent, the very sound of his breathing.

My jacket falls on my shoulders gently and I push my arms through the armholes gratefully.

"You okay?" Wes asks, bending over me. "Did you get hit?"

"Nah," I answer, still staring straight ahead. "Besides, I didn't do anything, it was all Theo."

"You'll freeze your butt off," he says.

I shrug.

"That's mature." The next minute he's stepped off the pavement and is folding his long legs to sit next to me. "What's this?" He points to my hand.

I'm holding a piece of paper. It feels frail as my numb fingers clutch it, protecting it from the wind. I took it out of my pocket a second ago. I've sort of gotten used to carrying it around, I guess, without thinking about it too much. It's still folded, but that's only because—luckily—I didn't get to open it before he walked over.

I know what's written on the paper by heart, but I like to glance over it every now and then, just as a reminder.

I pretend he never spoke. "You should go back inside to. . . "

"Heather," he supplies helpfully.

"Heather," I repeat. "Are you kidding me in there?"

"What?" A hint of defensiveness creeps into his voice.

"Is this how you guys have fun? I mean, you kept looking for a 'pub' back in Corfu. . . Yeah, not impressed."

"We can't all go out for sou-laki every night, you know." He eyes me, a mocking grin starting to form across his mouth. "Like you do in Corfu."

"Not that going to that posh club in Corfu was much fun either," I say and immediately I'm embarrassed. We went together to that 'posh

233

club' in Corfu; that's where he kissed me for the first time.

Wes' expression doesn't change. *He remembers, silly. He's just pretending he doesn't.*

"Did you just say 'posh'?" he murmurs.

*Quick, subject change.* The cold is seeping into my skin, but I feel my cheeks flaming.

"It's just, I was wondering what was up with this thing that you missed so much."

He shifts his weight. It's a slight movement, but it means his body is turned away from me. Isn't it amazing how much a person can say without even speaking? But he speaks, too. He sounds bored, dismissive.

"Oh, I didn't really want to go to a pub. I just kept saying it because I enjoyed watching you scowl at me. Whenever you were there, your face took on such a disapproving. . . almost disgusted look when I so much as spoke. It was hilarious."

There's the old Wes we all know and love. Okay, I need to get out of here.

"You called me a gaffer," I say, lifting my feet out of a puddle.

"I did, didn't I?" He laughs, a low, private sound. For the first time I turn to look at him. He may have just arrived as Rosie and I were going to the bathroom, but his cheeks are flushed and I'm not sure it's from the cold. Has he been drinking?

A snowflake lands on my nose, and I don't even feel it. I sniffle; I used to love the way your nose gets wet when it's cold, like a dog's. Will I now forever associate the sight of snow with this horrible, horrible night? Gosh, I don't even have the energy to get up.

I shudder and furrow deeper into my leather jacket. I should have brought something even warmer with me. Wes is wearing a tweed long coat with a turned up collar and although it's not buttoned up he doesn't look cold.

"Hey, you're shaking," he says suddenly. "Are you still cold?" He lets out a low laugh. "Maybe you're scared of me. Or is it yourself you're scared of?" His voice is dripping with sarcasm. "Can't trust yourself around me, huh?"

All right, this is it. I get up.

"What you said the other day. . . " I swallow past dry lips. "Wes, if you hate me, then tell me so and I'll leave."

He's on his feet before I finish. "I care about you," he says in a cold, bored voice that belies his words. "I can't stand to see you hurt, or in danger. Maybe that will never change. But, Ari. . . " he shuts his eyes tightly. "You—you broke me."

I'm robbed of speech. I open my mouth, then close it.

"Your silence. . . It broke me." He turns around in a violent movement and punches a tree full on with his naked fist. "You didn't even tell me what I did." His voice has dropped into an intense, angry whisper, that terrifies me. "What did I do wrong? Where did I fu—mess up?"

He's not looking at me, but I raise my eyebrows. Did he just try not to swear?

"Yeah," he laughs bitterly. "I gave that up too. Swearing, among other things. I figured, if I'm asking God for favors, I might as well try to live decent. Ironic, isn't it? I reckon it won't last much longer."

At the word 'favors' I begin to shake. What favors? His note from the hospital flashes before my eyes, and I sway on my feet.

"I, um. . ." I clear my throat and try again. I can't feel my fingers and my vision is blurred by tears, but I'm going to do this.

*'Say something.'*

I'm doing this.

"Here." I extend my hand to him, shoving the piece of paper at him. "You didn't do anything, Wes, not even close. This is my reason. I wrote it down so that I won't forget when I—when I start missing. . ."

My voice is all choked up, but I don't need to say anything else. Wes has already snatched the paper from my fingers and he's walking away in long steps, his back to me, as he opens it.

He starts reading. I can tell the exact moment he reads the first sentence, because he stops mid stride; his back goes rigid. A string of curses escapes him. So much for not swearing.

He turns back, breaking into a run as he approaches me, furious, his eyes spitting fire. He stops half an inch from my face.

"I asked you," he whispers in a shaking voice, "I *begged* you not to read them."

"It's not what you think," I tell him quickly. "This has got nothing to do with the tabloids. And, for the record, I didn't read or watch one single thing after you asked me not to. This one was posted the week you came to Corfu."

He doesn't reply. He just stands right there next to me, spreads out the paper and reads.

And reads.

It takes him forever.

A full minute later, he's still standing there frozen, immobile, staring at the piece of cheap printer paper in his hand, snowflakes landing on his hair, his cheeks, his fingers.

Silence descends between us, heavy and thick.

"Did you write this? Why would. . . ?" I look at my shoes and he sighs. "I don't get it. What does it mean?" he asks in a changed tone. "Are you sick again?"

"No, no, I'm not," I say quickly. "That's not what this is. The thing is. . ."

He's looking at me with such intensity that I can't look away. His whole body is tense, air coming out of his nostrils as if he's out of breath. I can't think when he's staring at me this way, like there's an entire universe hanging upon my answer.

"The thing is. . ."

*Gosh, what is the thing? What was I going to say?* He didn't get it from just that piece of paper, he didn't understand, of course he didn't. I've just written four lines on there. I'll have to tell him. I'll have to use actual words.

"I have this huge fear." I swallow, trying to keep my voice steady. "Well, not fear exactly... it's more than that. It's this crippling, debilitating thought: what if it starts happening again?"

"Why—" his voice cracks and he has to stop. "Why didn't you tell me?"

I stare at him; he's shaking.

"I just wanted to leave you alone. After what I did to you... I couldn't die on you again," I whisper. "I couldn't let you go through that a second time, don't you understand?"

If anyone had told me two months ago that I would miss therapy, I'd have punched them in the face. Now, however, I'd give anything to be talking to quiet little whats-her-face, instead of laying my inner demons out in the open to the one guy I swore would never know.

And it turns out there was a reason for that.

His eyes turn cold and hard. "No, I don't understand. I don't get it. Your reason is a 'what if'? That's it? All these months of wondering why you suddenly hate me, what I did, and you... you're just worried about something that will never happen."

I stagger back, as though he slapped me. The accusation in his voice stings worse than that.

"I'm not worried about something that *might* happen," I say in a low voice, to myself. "I'm scared about something that *did* happen. I was scared that—"

"Dammit, Ari!"

Something falls on the paper, startling me. At first I think it's just another snowflake, but it's not.

It's a fat tear that starts to dilute once it's come in contact with the paper. Another one follows it down Wes' cheek. His long finger wipes it away, smearing the ink, before another one follows it.

"I'd never have... If you'd just told me that you—I wouldn't... Dammit."

He turns his head away and presses the back of his hand to his lips. Then, in one swift movement, he tears the paper up in tiny pieces, letting them scatter from his fingers to the ground.

"For heaven's sake," he whispers brokenly, "are you still hurting about this? You went through hell, but it's over now. Just let it go. That girl you describe in there, she's not you. It's so stupid, it's like you wanted an excuse... You know what? Sod this."

He turns around and walks back into the pub without a single glance back.

...

I take a cab home and call Rosie on the way to check up on her.

"What's wrong?" she asks me immediately.

"That's my line," I tell her, letting out a sound that was supposed to be a laugh. We both reassure each other that we're fine, although I hope that it's more true in her case than in mine. Then we say goodnight.

About an hour later, I've just gotten into bed, when my phone blinks. It's Wes. I let it ring a couple of times, deliberating what to do. Finally, I give in and I answer it.

"Hi, love," he says.

He's drunk.

"Wes, what do you want?"

He's not even listening. His voice sounds high-pitched and weird, like it belongs to a stranger.

"You've. . . you been my Rosencrantz," he says.

"Your what? Listen, Wes, don't drink any more, just get some coffee, all right?"

"That sklull hath a tongue in it," he replies.

Oh, he's quoting Hamlet now. Or trying to. Great.

I'm starting to hang up when I hear a loud noise as though his phone is hitting the floor. I call his name a couple of times, but all I can hear is static and music in the background. He must still be at the club. *How is Heather letting him drunk call me? Maybe she's left. Who cares?*

Mad at him, I turn off my phone and bury myself under the covers.

The room is perfectly still and quiet, and all I can hear is my own heart beating like a drum. I grab the covers and drag them over my head, creating a warm cocoon that I can crawl in, sleep and forget. I close my eyes.

Five minutes later I'm at the door, dressed, and pulling on my gloves as I call Wes again and again. He doesn't answer. I get into a cab and give the address of the pub. I secure a thick scarf around my neck— I'm sleepy and freezing in nothing but my pajama top, a pair of jeans and a jacket—and settle down in the back seat to wait nervously.

The fairy lights on the trees blur past my window, and I try to close my eyes, but I can't fall back asleep.

I finally allow myself to think of the paper Wes tore up.

Sometime after I locked up my journal, I'd decided I needed something tangible, as a reminder. Something I would be able to look at whenever I missed Wes so much it hurt. So I'd printed out an online post from a blog called 'Crazy Planet' and titled *The Lives and Loves of Wes Spencer*. It was posted a couple of days before Wes showed up in his M&M boat in Corfu.

It had a list of all his 'serious girlfriends' according to the writers, of course, along with a tiny, disgusting story to go with every girl's name. It used to make me want to hurl every time I read it, so I don't.

But at the bottom of the page, I'd added one more.

### 9. The sick girl - Ariadne Demos

We're talking about the stunt girl whom Wes Spencer met while filming *First Sentences* on the island of Corfu. Her relationship with Spencer is said to have been one of the most painful experiences of his life, especially when the brain tumor that threatened her life suddenly started progressing again. Spencer has stated that this period in his life is a time he'd rather forget, and we don't blame him.

A dying girlfriend, that's the last thing our Tristan needs.

It's just fiction, really, and bad fiction at that. But it wasn't intended for anyone else's eyes; only mine. Not even Katia knew about this. They are just a few words jotted down and meant to remind me in a very raw, real way, of what might have happened. What *could* have happened if I hadn't let him go.

To remind me of the kind of pain and drama he didn't need in his life; of the harm I could do. Or maybe of what I am still scared might happen to me.

It was, I see it now, a personification of my fear. Perhaps by writing it, and reading it all the time, I thought it would eventually help me to overcome it, or maybe even let it go.

I can still see it in front of me, although the paper must be pieces of mush buried under the frozen mud by now. It will take a lot more than someone tearing up paper for me to get over this irrational fear.

Of course it does sound stupid if you call it a 'what if' reason. A 'what if' fear. But it's not just that, is it?

This disease turned me into this pathetic, scared person, and I thought that being alone would help me overcome my fears. Become my old self again, or, I don't know, an even better self. Unafraid, indestructible.

*But no one will ever become that, will they?*

People form solid links to each other, and that's how they remain upright when life throws a tsunami on them: by supporting one another.

Images, random memories flash before my eyes. Rosie being lifted in Theo's arms; the glass being shattered in the theater so that clean air would blow in after the fog machine blew up. Pan's students at the concert, looking intently at him for direction. The four guys at that desk on auditions day, joking, laughing, creating art. Distracting Wes from the sight of me walking in.

The truth is, people don't survive alone.

And they certainly don't thrive alone.

But that's what I've been trying to do. I've tried to think that I'll be safer alone. I've tried to isolate myself so that I'll keep myself away from danger. Only it's not working. And it's not working because I'm carrying the greatest danger to myself inside of me. With me. For the first time since the operation, I'm not thinking of my brain or my body as my enemy.

I haven't even thought about it in weeks. Not since I came here, that's for sure.

It's other things that I have to fight. My past is staring me in the face everywhere I go, my mistakes, my choices. My unfinished business. And I can't deal with it like this; not by running away.

It slowly dawns on me that I did the exact opposite of what I should have done if I wanted to stay alive, stay strong, stay myself. It slowly dawns on me that I'm going to need all the help I can get.

Help. Help from *them*. From the people I hurt, from the people I'm scared of hurting again: dad, *pappou*, *yiayia*, Katia, Coach. From the new people who have come into my life, and without whom I wouldn't even be here right now: Ollie, Jamie, Rosie, Matt.

And from him.

Wes.

If he's still willing to give it. I mean, he must be pretty sure I still feel the same about him by now, but I'm not sure he cares. I did see him kiss that girl in front of me. And he was spitting mad at me tonight. Or maybe, not mad, worse: Disappointed.

Plus, he didn't laugh at the 'Tristan' reference.


tumblr.

spencerstumblr

10 steps to overcome addiction

1. Stop lying to yourself
2. Always ask: 'why do I need this?'
3. Stop lying to yourself
4. Stop making excuses
5. Get rid of the people who enable you
6. Get rid of the people who don't believe
you can beat this
7. Stop lying to yourself
8. Find something creative to do. Best cure ever.
9. Don't DON'T quit cold turkey. Never works.
10. Love

Bonus step: 11. Stop lying to yourself

#personal
546,009 notes

# S E V E N T E E N

We arrive and I'm snatched from my thoughts abruptly. *Let's get this over with.*

I pay quickly and slam the door behind me. As I enter the dim interior of the pub again, my eyes start searching for Wes' lean, tall figure, but I don't see him anywhere. I'm about to leave, thinking that he must have left and I was worried about nothing, when I stumble to a stop, mouth agape.

There's someone huddled in a corner on the floor, long, angular body in an unnatural heap. I run over; it's Wes. I can't believe no one is paying any attention to him. Everyone I know is gone; I wonder why.

Wes is absolutely still. His knees are reaching his chin and his head is hanging limply on his chest. Next to him lies his cell phone, still clutched in his fingers, as though his hand dropped and he hasn't lifted it since. He's not moving. Around him people are talking and laughing, oblivious, and my heart shreds to pieces to see him lying there, broken and alone. Heather is nowhere to be seen.

I drop to my knees and take his chin in my fingers, trying to tip his face back, to see if he'll open his eyes.

His head feels heavy. I shake him lightly and it flops back with zero resistance. My heart thunders with sudden panic.

"Wes, hey. . . "

He mumbles something indistinctive; he's not unconscious, at least not yet. I sag in relief, and my back bumps into someone. I turn in their direction blindly. "Would it kill you to take a look around you?" I say to whoever is standing behind me, angrily. "There's a guy falling to the floor here, and no one is. . . "

"Easy there, tiger," a sardonic voice drawls next to my ear, "it's just me."

Pan materializes out of nowhere and thrusts a finger underneath Wes' nose. I turn around and see that he's the 'someone' I bumped into.

"Good, he's breathing," he says coolly. "A little help here?"

He's draped one arm around Wes' shoulders and is trying to lift him in an upright position, but Wes is barely able to stand and his legs are wobbling dangerously. I place a hand under his elbow and feel his weight leaning heavy on me.

Between us, Pan and I half-drag, half-support Wes out into the cold, wet night.

"Where. The. Hell. Are. His. Bodyguards." I mutter between panting breaths.

"Not here, that's for sure," Pan answers curtly. How is he not even breaking a sweat? "He rarely takes them when he goes out with friends. Come on, I'm parked over there." We cross the street to where a shiny black and white mouth-watering MINI Countryman—I mean, seriously? This guy must be loaded—is parked carelessly with the indicators blinking on and off. We prop Wes on the door to catch our breaths for a minute.

"So he called you too, huh?" he asks me with a pleasant smile, as though we're making small talk.

"It's you he called 'two'," I tell him dryly. "He called me 'one'."

He snickers. "Hey, for all I care, he might not have called me at all. Only he lent his driver to that Heather person or something, it was hard to understand what he was saying. He won't shut up about you, you know," he adds with a shrug. "It's irritating. As are you. Hey, *dude!*"

Wes is being sick on Pan's leather boots. I stifle a laugh, and run to open the door so we can push him in before he lands sprawling on the pavement.

"Can I come too?" I ask, feeling suddenly out of place, as Pan slides in behind the wheel.

"No," Pan says, shutting the driver's door softly. Then he rolls the window down and looks over it up to me. "You can come, *one*," he winks.

Letting out an exasperated grunt, I nudge Wes' knees out of the way, and get in the back seat beside him. Pan eases off the curb, and then proceeds to push down on the gas as hard as he can.

"You know, I'm a stunt actor," I say after two full minutes of furious racing around corners and tires screeching in protest, "and I drive like that. . . never."

He's calm as hell. "Do you want to go to sleep sometime before February?" he asks in a bored voice as he turns on the radio.

Wes grabs my shirt and mumbles something against my shoulder.

"What?" I lean down.

"I'm sorry. . . " Wes says, his voice slurring. His head is tipped back, his eyes closed. "I'm sorry about Heathrer, I was confused, alone. . . so alllone. All these pleoples, but alone. I thought. . . I thought you dinwanme, Ars, Ari, Ari *mou*."

Did he just speak Greek? *'Ari mou'* that's what grandpa calls me. *My Ari*.

Something that sounds suspiciously like a snort comes from the driver's seat. I shoot an evil glance at the back of Pan's head and make calming noises, smoothing down Wes' hair. He settles on my shoulder again.

I'd never thought of it like this—that he might need me too. A sudden wave of emotion hits me, and I look for something to talk about.

"You. . . you weren't here before," I say and Pan turns the volume down so he can hear me. "Rosie and I showed for about an hour; then we left. Now everyone's gone."

"I thought Wes and I had decided not to come," he says. "But apparently Spence had a change of mind. I'm not surprised everyone left, he's not a pretty sight when he. . . " he doesn't finish. "I don't drink. Ever."

"Cool," I murmur, trying to hide my surprise.

He flashes a brilliant smile full of teeth at me in the rearview mirror. "Why waste my precious brain cells?" he asks.

"Well, some people. . . " I begin but he cuts me off.

"I didn't say other people's brain cells are anything worth saving. They might as well get drunk."

"You know what, never mind." I settle back. Conceited much?

Wes begins to snore heavily, his breath smelling like a brewery. He's making a sort of gurgling sound with every breath that tears my heart in two.

Pan eyes me through the mirror. "And while we're on the subject," he says as he brings the car to a halt an inch from the bumper of the Ford that's stopped in front of us at a red light, "I would appreciate it if you told your friend Rosie to stop drooling. It's not happening."

I sit up.

"What," I say with dangerous calm, "did you say?"

"Please, you don't need to go all defensive on me. I'm just stating facts here."

"The facts being that you're a jerk."

He bursts out laughing. "As for that Heather thing. . . She's not even in the picture, all right? Just so you know," he goes on undeterred. "She was out of here the moment Wes started yelling at Matt for casting you, even *I* saw that."

"What do you mean even *you*. . . ?" I start asking, my heart beating wildly. "Oh, wait. I don't care what you think."

He laughs harder. "I may even start to like you," he says. "But yeah, basically you broke him."

I don't answer; I can barely hear him. I'm staring down at Wes. This can't be happening.

"Pan," I whisper in horror.

"What?" he asks, whipping around. His gaze meets mine with sudden understanding. For the first time I see a shadow of fear in his eyes. "What?" he repeats, swerving the wheel a bit. "Don't panic, check his airway."

Wes falls on my lap, face down. Then he's absolutely still.

"He's not breathing," I say, fear rising in my voice. I shake him. "Wake up!" I yell, but he just slides away from me and I move quickly to catch his head before it hits the floor. "*Pan*, he's not moving, he's. . . "

"Hey, hey, look at me."

I look up into Pan's eyes, steady and sure, and immediately I calm down. He nods in approval, then turns around, and takes a hard left, cutting into traffic. Horns scream all around us.

"Okay," he says. "Can you do CPR?"

I don't answer, I've started it already. I lay Wes flat on his back and kneel in the space between the front and the back seat, pumping his chest with all my strength. Pan's voice continues in the background, keeping me sane. "Good. You're doing great. It's going to be fine."

He taps on his phone quickly—turning on the GPS. If I thought he was driving recklessly before, that was nothing to how he streams past moving cars now, runs red lights and goes through 'no entry' roads. All the time he doesn't once lose his calm nor does he stop talking to me.

# LOSE ME.

I give Wes my breath, placing my lips on his, tasting the bitterness of alcohol on his mouth, but he doesn't take one breath of his own. We're jostled against the leather upholstery, but I don't have time to think about anything except to concentrate on keeping a steady rhythm pumping his heart, not letting him die. By the time we reach the ER—it might be one hour or one minute—I haven't once removed my hands from his chest. My muscles are cramping up, but there's no way I'm missing a beat. I'm crying so hard, Wes' face is bathed in my tears.

"Be right back, Ari, don't stop," Pan says, leaning a hand briefly on my shoulder as he gets out of the car. Only then does he start yelling for help.

"Come on, Wes, please," I whisper against his chest. My arms are burning, but I press harder, counting in my mind. "I'll breathe for you until you wake up, do you hear me? I'm not giving up!"

A silent scream tears out of my throat as I breathe into his lips.

I pump again and then I'm being pushed away: the paramedics are there. I stumble in the sudden cold and almost fall to my knees, but strong hands support me.

"Don't fall apart on me now," Pan's voice murmurs in my ear. "Just hold on a bit longer, okay? It's going to be fine."

I turn to look at him, tears blurring my vision. He lifts a finger and wipes my cheek. "It's going to be fine," he repeats firmly.

"Is it?" I want to ask, but no sound comes out of my lips.

...

The rest of the night—or rather, the morning— passes quietly, tensely. The doctors buzz around Wes' head, and then clear off a section of the seventh floor and settle him in a VIP room. They stay with him— and me—the whole night, as his manager arrives and makes arrangements for his bodyguards to stand in front of the entrance.

Seated outside Wes' room, I think that she's a bit too much. But in a few hours, just as the sun is peeking in the horizon, I look down from the window and see the pavement flooded with people. Reporters, fans, or just curious people passing by. My breath catches in my throat.

What the actual hell.

It takes forever, but the doctors say it will take him a while to wake up and that his 'vitals are good', whatever that means. I can't stand the wait, the worry. I wonder if Wes felt like this, like his skin was too tight for his chest, while he was waiting outside my operation room, back in New York. When he wrote me that note.

Maybe he felt even worse.

The irony is not lost on me.

At about eight, after the doctors have reassured us that Wes will probably be okay, I call Ollie and tell him most of what's happened.

"Thanks for calling me," he says and then his voice gets all gruff and choked up and he says he'll catch the next flight to London, but it might take him a while to get here. Pan leaves for an hour or two, but Theo comes almost immediately, so I'm never alone.

As the morning progresses and Wes is still asleep, a deep feeling of unease sinks in my stomach. I decide to call dad, too.

"Anything you need, I'm here," he says as soon as I tell him. "Do you want to talk to pass the time?"

"I don't know what I need," I reply. "I'm scared for him."

"But not of him?"

"What?" I bristle.

"Okay, here's the thing." His voice gets all 'dad' and serious on me. "I know we don't choose who we fall in love with. . . "

"Daaaad."

"No, listen, I've wanted to tell you this for some time now, only the time never seemed right."

*And now it does?*

"I don't know what's going on between you two, or even if you are thinking of being with him," dad swallows, and I picture him biting his lip, trying to find the right words. I've seen him do it so many times when he talks to kids' parents, but I never thought I'd be at the receiving end of it. I guess I'm an adult now, though, and that's how adults talk to each other. Carefully. Intentionally. "Wes doesn't lead an easy life. And it's not just the drinking. It's where it comes from. The circumstances in his life that make it possible, and maybe sometimes necessary. Well, not exactly necessary, but they push him to it. You know what I mean?"

"I do, dad," I say quietly. He hesitates. "Tell me what you're thinking." *I need it.*

He laughs. "I'm thinking that you're a grown woman and you don't need your old man's advice anymore. I'm so proud of who you've become, you know. You grew up with no mother, and all I could do was love you and teach you how to kick a ball. Beats me how you turned out to be this awesome person."

"Dad, come on." My eyes are starting to sting. "You know I'm struggling."

"Everyone is struggling, Ari. I have to fight against the instinct to keep you locked up in your room like Cinderella—"

"Rapunzel."

"Whatever, to keep you locked up so that nothing can even hurt you again. No stunt, no sickness, no mistake by your parents, no British boy. . . But I can't do that. I don't want to do that. And, you know what? I don't think I'd need to, anyway. You're strong enough to save yourself as well as others. You don't have to save anyone, but if you choose to, you can. I know you know that."

"I don't," I murmur. "I could barely keep myself alive."

He makes a sound that's half laughter and half crying and I realize he's been crying all this time.

"You'll be fine, sweetheart," dad tells me. I can hear the concern in his voice, but it doesn't make me feel guilty. Not this time. It makes me feel less alone; less scared. "I can hop on the next plane if you need me, but I know you can cope. It's scary right now, but you'll both be fine, I promise."

"I needed to hear you say that," I say quietly into the phone. What I mean is, *I needed to hear those words. I needed you to tell me I'm strong enough when I had the headaches and through all the talks with Spiros and when I was nearly drowning. I needed my daddy to tell me it would be okay.*

"I needed to say it, too," he replies. "You know I may be a poor old guy whose behind you can kick any day at soccer, but I still need to feel like I'm your dad from time to time."

"I still need to be your little girl," I whisper. "And I could wipe the floor with you when I was six. It's not news that I'm better than you."

We laugh and then his voice goes all teary and weird and he calls me 'his baby girl' and I hang up on him.

Two hours later, Pan is back again. He sits down and shuts his eyes, napping; Theo goes downstairs to get us coffee. They keep bringing it to us, but he said he wanted to get some air. Pan gave me a look and I didn't say anything. Something passed between them, a kind of wordless communication I didn't get.

As soon as he's gone, and Pan leans his head back and closes his eyes, earbuds in, it occurs to me that it's just us three and a bunch of managers and bodyguards at the hospital, waiting for Wes to wake up. No family, nothing. My eyes sting with tears. Thankfully, before I have time to think much more, Wes opens his eyes.

It's around twelve.

He wakes up crying.

"Wes?" I whisper, walking up to his bed.

His profile is silhouetted sharply against the harsh hospital lights, and his Adam's apple is working, as a tear slides down his cheek. A golden stubble is visible on his chin. He's staring at the ceiling, not moving, except for his eyes, which are blinking rapidly, trying to stop the tears. My heart constricts.

Wes blinks some more and turns towards the sound of my steps. His eyes find me.

"Not this again," he says. He turns his head away from me and swallows with difficulty.

"What' wro—?" I start asking, but the doctors are on him and they shoo me from the room.

After they're done he sleeps for about an hour more. I think he thought he was dreaming.

Pan sends Theo to get us more coffee, and just sits back, head against the wall, scowling heavily.

"Hey, Ari." I'm surprised by Theo's voice next to my ear in a moment; I might have dozed off.

"Hey," I reply, sitting up. The aroma of strong coffee wakes me up completely. "Thanks. And you are. . . ?"

I do know who he is, of course, but where I come from it's not considered good manners to assume someone's name, even if it's in the papers. You're supposed to pretend you don't know and ask.

He gives me a look that says he knows I'm just trying to be polite. "I thought you'd know who I am. I'm hurt," he says. "I'm Theo."

"Hi, Theo."

"Hi." He flashes me a smile that doesn't quite reach his dark brown eyes.

He stoops down to hand me my coffee—the guy is so tall it's ridiculous. His hands are tapered, but there's an uncertainty in his movements that suggests at great vulnerability. As I take the steaming cup from him I notice that his fingers are shaking.

Pan has popped out an ear bug and he's watching us; no, not us. Him. He's listening to every word we're saying, and not even hiding it. His brow is wrinkled with worry, as if he's scared of what I'll say next.

"*I've* heard all about you," Theo tells me, "although not voluntarily. Some people can't shut up about. . . Well, he needed to talk, let's just say that." He steals a glance towards Wes' room, and then his eyes cut to the floor quickly. Almost as if he doesn't want to look at it for too long.

"Yeah? Like what?"

He shrugs. "Like that you're the girl who lived."

My head snaps up. "What did you say?" I narrow my eyes. Did Wes share *everything* about me with these dudes? "Did you just reference Harry Potter?"

His lips try to smile, but they can't. They're trembling. He's looking at his shoes again. How old is he? Rosie said he's in college, but that doesn't mean he's older than eighteen. Although I think he might be closer to nineteen, from what I've heard. He looks about ten right now.

"I just. . . " His eyes meet mine and I almost flinch at the naked pain and despair that flashes in their bottom. "Why would you want to do that?"

I feel the blood leave my face.

"Do what? Live? Why would I want to *live*?" I ask, horrified. "What are you sayi—why would you ask such a thing? Have you thoughts of—?" I'm so shocked I can't even talk coherently.

Next thing I know, Pan has jumped to his feet, his face ashen. He reaches us in two strides and grabs Theo's arm.

"Teddy, man, you're scaring the ladies," he says, trying to sound light-hearted, but completely failing. His eyes look wild and when he thinks no one is looking he bites the inside of his cheek, hard.

Theo smiles at him. "Sorry," he says to me, sipping his coffee calmly, as though he hadn't just. . . said what he just said. "I'm weird."

"Crazy, you mean," Pan murmurs, tugging him away from me.

Theo snorts. "Got the papers to prove it," he winks at me.

What the—? I open my lips to say something, but Pan sends me a glance over his shoulder, silencing me. Theo slouches into another chair, and takes out a pad from his pocket and starts idly sketching a copy of the Van Gogh on the wall.

In fifteen minutes, they tell us that Wes is properly awake.

After thirty more minutes of the doctors probing him, they tell him he can go home in an hour or so.

"D' you need me to go get your clothes?" Pan asks him as soon as they let us in his room again. "The place is crawling. Not that they'll let you out the front door, but just in case."

Wes looks pale and there are purple bruises under his eyes, but his gaze is alert and sober.

"Is Theo here?" he asks, sitting up.

Pan scratches the back of his head. "Yeah, he... he wanted to come."

"Well, take him home. *Now.*" His eyes meet Pan's and a silent message passes between them. Wes looks tense, almost guilty. "He shouldn't be here," he adds in a lower voice. "Don't let him come in."

"Relax, dude," Pan says, "I'll send your assistant to get your clothes and make sure little Teddy gets home okay."

He talks about Theo as though he's younger than him—which he isn't—and as though he's someone who needs to be taken care of.

Wes' gaze snaps to mine.

"Ari," he says in a hoarse voice. "I want Ari to go."

For once, Pan doesn't make any comment, snide or otherwise; he just lifts his hands in surrender and walks out, nodding for me to follow.

"What?" I ask him, impatiently.

I was kind of looking forward and dreading those precious moments alone with Wes before another nurse comes barging in.

"Talk to one of the guys out there, before walking out the front entrance," Pan tells me. "The crowd will eat you alive." He looks me up and down. "Have enough money?"

I snort. "Yeah, *dad.* I'm fine." He laughs and turns to leave. "Hey, wait. What's up with Theo? Is he okay? Why shouldn't he be in—?"

Pan lifts his eyebrows and his jaw tenses. I stop talking; he has that effect on people.

"Long story," he says, "and none of your business. He... his brother was in and out of hospitals a lot. He was brought home badly wounded."

My heart sinks. Oh no. "Brought home? Do you mean...?"

Pan nods. "Afghanistan," he says, and his lips turn into a thin line. I remember Theo carrying Rosie out of the club, and I wonder whether he's actually the one who needs rescuing. Pan's expression changes abruptly; he places a hand on my shoulder and leans in. "Thanks for keeping Spence alive, Ari." His voice drops and he gives me a rare, tight smile. "You looked like you were pounding through cement when you were doing compressions on him in the car. He doesn't have many people around him who would fight for his life like that."

"He fought for mine," I whisper, but I'm not sure he hears me, because he's gone instantly.

He shuts the door behind him, giving Wes and me some privacy.

Which—privacy—we don't know what to do with.

We just sit there, he in his hospital gown, me in my pajama top and old jeans, and stare at the wall, the ceiling, everywhere but at each other. The monitor is beep-beeping in the silence.

I take a deep breath.

"Did I do this to you?" I ask, not looking at him.

He doesn't answer for a bit, but I hear the rustling of clothes as he turns around. I feel his gaze on me, but I still can't face him. "You destroyed me," he replies slowly. "Ari." My name sounds like a caress on his lips, but his words cut me in half. "Your silence. It destroyed me."

"I know." I inch away from him a bit more.

He sits up. "Come here."

I take one step towards his bed, still staring at my shoes. I take another one. Why is this small distance so hard to cross?

"Come here," he repeats in a raspy voice.

I do. He leans towards me, placing a hand on either side of my face. I suck in a breath. He brings me closer to him, gazing into my eyes. "But of course *you* didn't do this to me. I was the one who did it. I was the one who was stupid and. . . " He lets go of me and his eyes darken—they turn into a deep forest green, like precious stones. "I need you to believe me, Ari," he closes his eyes. "I *need* you to."

"What?" I ask, mesmerized.

"I was clean," he says. "For weeks and weeks. I. . . stayed in rehab back in October, and since then I've been absolutely clean. Of anything. Do you believe me, do you bel—?"

"Yes," I say before he can even complete the question. His tortured eyes light up and my breath catches. "I saw it, Wes. I can see that you're a different person, you've changed, you've grown so much. I could see at a glance that you've left that. . . particular problem behind you. Maybe that's why this happened. Your body was unaccustomed to such heavy drinking after the purge."

He nods silently. "Now what?" I hate the desperation creeping into his voice again.

"Now nothing, you're still clean. You lost a battle, not the war."

He laughs bitterly. "Yeah, right." He sighs and lays back down, looking exhausted. I just want run my fingers through his hair, but just the thought of touching him sends shiver down my spine. "Sorry for dragging you into this."

"No problem," I reply. How much does he remember from last night? He's back to staring at the wall again. "What do you need from home?" He just shrugs. "Anything other than clean clothes?"

He turns his back on me, curling his long body in a ball, facing the window.

"Forgiveness," he whispers against the pillow, shattering my heart in a million pieces.

...

Wes' assistant insists I take a 'car'. Of course, she means a car with a driver. Whatever. I get in and we drive to Belsize Park—the driver, a sweet guy who keeps talking to me about his two kids, a girl and a boy, twins, promises to wait for me and tells me to take as long as I want.

The house is buried in greenery, but as soon as the outer gate slides open, I see a three-storey brick Victorian building, very imposing, with a smaller one attached to it on the side. Wes' housekeeper shows me in. Inside it looks pretty normal, smaller than I imagined; just an ordinary house, like a cute fairytale-like cottage I'd generally associate with the countryside. Tidy, clean. Nothing extravagant.

The housekeeper—Helen—takes me to the third floor, to Wes' bedroom. She shows me his walk-in closet and leaves me to it. I pick up a shirt and a pair of pants that I've seen him wear once before, pressed and folded, fresh out of the laundry, and resist the temptation to bury my nose in his scent. Only just, but I resist it. There's a white dog asleep on his bed, his chest rising and falling with every breath. He has only one ear. *Hook*, I think. A lump forms in my throat as I remember the time he told me about him.

I walk back into his room, and head for the stairs, when something catches my eye. It's on his desk. There's this massive oak office facing the sunlit window, a leather chair pressed against it. Outside, tiny snowflakes keep landing on the ledge—it's snowing again. I walk over, my shoes sinking into the soft carpet.

There's a book open on the desk, a couple of pens with their caps off and a notebook. I press my palm on the flat, sleek surface of the wood, fingering the soft, silken edges of the book. And right there is the thing that caught my attention in the first place: a bright yellow sticky note is pasted to the left page of the heavily-underlined book. I step even closer and lean over to take a look.

A few words are written on it in Wes' neat scrawl.

I read what it says.

Then I read it again, pressure building behind my eyes.

### I also don't judge you guilty.

That's all it says. Underneath it he's scribbled a small reference. I squint down to read it: *John 8:11*. What the heck does 'John' mean? Is it Shakespeare? I don't think it is. I wipe my eyes and glance at the book. One phrase stands out, highlighted in a bright, green color.

It's the same words. *'I also don't judge you guilty.'*

I sit down. The huge desk chair swallows me up; it smells like new leather and Wes. I just stare at the underlined words for a bit, and before I've realized what I'm doing, I'm reading the whole chapter.

The big, black book, it's an English Bible—I've never touched one, let alone read it. It looks less imposing than I thought it would, just a regular, boring book. But this story. . . It's the opposite of boring. The opposite of religious, unintelligible gibberish. It's the story of a ruined, abandoned woman, who is being judged by everyone and. . . Well, not just judged.

Killed. She's being killed by everyone.

It resonates in a way I never thought a story would. It's raw, human, real. It's my story. I've never been abandoned, not in this way, but I have been left. By a mother. I have been judged. I have been guilty. I have been waiting for the other foot to drop, waiting to die. Struggling to stay alive while I was dying.

Just like Wes has been struggling to stay alive. The memory is still vivid, the memory of how I found him, hunched on the floor of that pub, trying to drink himself to freedom. Trying to escape those eyes, thousands, millions of eyes, the world's eyes that are following him everywhere.

This world, trying to kill us all. Succeeding in the end—if you want to get morose. We'll all die in the end. Without one chance at freedom, most of us. But here it is. Someone, finally, who doesn't judge. Someone who is only there to help.

Someone who just is. Imagine that.

I read the story, drinking in every word. I read it twice, while the light slowly fades outside the window.

Wes would be so proud to see me reading right now—and it's not even a script. But for once Wes is the farthest thing from my mind. At some point Hook wakes up and comes to curl himself around my ankles, and I start scratching his neck absently. I read the entire thing through a second time. Then I fold the sticky note and put it in my pocket and go downstairs to thank Helen.

The driver is waiting to take me back to the hospital, true to his word.

...

I find Wes in the same position I left him, legs hugged to his chest, facing the window.

"I brought it," I say. "Now you can go home, isn't that good?"

"Just leave it on the chair," he replies, his back to me. "Thanks."

His voice sounds rough, as though his throat is scraped raw. His accent is more British than I've ever heard it—and, may I add, hella hot. I sit on the bed, curling my left leg under me. Our backs are nearly touching. He's jostled as the bed bounces under my weight, but he doesn't move an inch.

"No," I say. "I brought what you asked me for. Forgiveness." I take out the little yellow note and place it in his hand.

My touch is tentative, just the necessary contact so I can give him the piece of paper. But as soon as my fingers brush his, he grabs my hand, holding it there.

A thrill runs through my body as his warm hand engulfs mine and I want to grab him and kiss away all the hurt I've caused him. Without letting go of my hand, he turns on his back, wincing as though his every muscle is in pain.

Recognition lights his face as he looks down and sees the yellow note. He doesn't open it to read it; he doesn't need to. He knows what it is immediately; he smiles up at me faintly, and butterflies gather in my stomach.

I start to move my hand away, but his fingers tighten around mine.

"You are forgiven," I say, my voice trembling slightly. "You are loved. You know you are." I sit up, my hand still in his. "I read it, Wes. The entire story. How that woman, the hooker or whatever she was, was forgiven; how they weren't allowed to judge her, and the only One that could didn't want to. How she was forgiven. Not guilty." I steal a look at him. He's listening, his brow furrowed in concentration. "I. . . I'm sure it's true for us, too."

He sits up too quickly and his shoulder bumps against mine. The bed's hinges creak.

"Us?" he asks.

"I need to be forgiven as badly as you do, Wes." His eyes are glued to mine, luminous, fiery. His lips are slightly parted. "I want to change, too," I take a deep breath. "I want to change like you did. I see you, and you're so confident and focused, like you've grown up. And look at all the things you've achieved, the things you're doing. . . You've overcome your worst enemy, you're standing up for yourself. I want that too. I want to stop being scared all the time, stop pushing everyone away, stop running away. I want to be brave. To know that when the time comes I can face it. . . face *death* with courage. I want to be able to look back at my life and know I did something good, worthy with it. I mean the stunts are all right, but something to prove that I. . . "

His mouth is on mine and he's kissing me roughly, his lips trembling against mine. I lace my hands around his neck and we drink each other up as though we've been dying of thirst for the past three months. He cups my chin in his long fingers and prods my lips open with his mouth. A rugged sigh escapes his lips as he pulls me to him.

I explore the changes in his body, the bulging muscles on his arms, the lean contours of his back, the sharp jut of his hipbones. He slips a leg on top of mine, roping his hands around my waist and hoists me onto his lap, pressing me to his chest.

"Ari," he murmurs against my lips. "Ari, dammit, I've missed you like breathing."

"I'm here," I whisper, arching my back as he runs his hands up and down.

"You are," he says, releasing me slowly. He ducks his head to meet my eyes, and presses a hand to the side of my face. "You're here," he repeats, as though he's trying to convince himself. "I've missed being this Wes, the Wes I'm with you."

*I've missed who I am with you, too.*

I had no idea before today. Before the familiar feeling of his skin molding to mine, before his lips crushing mine, before his body pressed against mine. I had no idea that we become a different version of ourselves when we're with someone; that we're different when we're alone. I'm different when I'm with my dad, my grandparents, with Katia. Not different as in not myself. Different as in better. A better me. A more open me, a safer me.

Like I'm right now. With him.

*That's* what I didn't know.

We stand still for a second, our bodies tangled up together, just looking at each other. Filling up on each other's sight.

His eyes are hooded, searching mine, his lips swollen from kissing me. He takes my chin in his hand, cradling my head in his other, his fingers teasing the soft hairs at the nape of my neck.

"I hate your wigs so much. So much. All of them. Did you know that? I mean, I don't hate them, but your real hair is just. . . " he runs a hand over my head. A second passes. "Be with me."

That's it. Three words. It sounds so simple the way he says it, looking at me sincerely, his heart in his eyes.

After everything that's gone on between us, it's just those three words and we're back in Corfu again, kissing on his yacht, the inky sea splashing quietly in the backdrop.

But it's not simple. Not at all.

There are lies and hurt and so much time that's passed between us. So many things we haven't said, so many things we should have done differently.

"I'm so sorry." That's all that comes out of my lips.

"So, no?" he says immediately. For the first time since he woke up he looks really scared.

I lick my dry lips. "What I did to you. . . What I did, Wes—"

"Okay, you have to stop doing that," he says, relaxing back. He looks relieved; he can't stop smiling. "Stop thinking of the past."

I get up to give him some room. "I can't."

"Hey," he stands up and comes behind me, placing a hand on my shoulder. "Look at me." I do. His smile is wide, dazzling. "We'll work out what happened, all right? Now just say you want to be with me."

"Heather?"

He looks down and rakes a hand through his hair. "Yeah, that didn't work out. As in, she was sort of into me but all I've been into since September is you. We're not in a relationship, in case you were wondering. That night at Pan's concert. . . It was a mistake, okay? I don't do that anymore, but that night. . . it was hard. I could barely stay in my seat, the mere sight of you made me crazy. You were wearing this dress. . . It was pure torture. You were the only reason I was there. I was sort of hoping for a while that she'd make you jealous, but even that wasn't worth being with someone who wasn't you."

I fling myself at him, and the force knocks him back a few paces.

He's laughing again as he tumbles on his back with me in his arms. I bury my face in his chest.

"Ari? I'm going to need an answer here," he says.

I lift my head so that we're eye to eye.

"I'm in love with you," I tell him. "I'm *still* in love with you. Is that enough of an answer—?"

He's nodding furiously and kissing me again, his face breaking into the hugest smile as his lips meet mine again.

Out of the blue, tears sting my eyes.

His taste, the feeling of his arms tightening around me, the little sound he makes as air escapes his lungs in a relieved sigh against my mouth. . . everything about him is so warm, so familiar, that an ache starts to throb in my chest.

I feel my muscles tense under his fingers.

He notices immediately and stiffens, breaking our kiss. He places his hands on my shoulders and takes a step back, studying my face. "Something's wrong," he says, frowning. "Talk to me."

tweets

**Cathy@triskatfan** @clara456 look made a new gif <3 He is so cute omg @therealwes

**Jon@tww_brrr** Thought I loved @therealwes in TWW but #Peter blew my mind

**Nicgirl@nicolereviews** Do we have a date for #thenewdarcyfilm by @therealwes? #askingforafriend

**Weston Spencer**Verifiedaccount**@therealwes** #thenewdarcyfilm is a wrap

**Nicgirl@nicolereviews** OMG OMG he said it it's official RT @therealwes #thenewdarcyfilm is a wrap

**James Pan@beethoven6th** @therealwes omg you're so cute I love you kisses and hugs

**Weston Spencer**Verifiedaccount**@therealwes** @beethoven6th wanna eff off?

**James Pan@beethoven6th** @olivercromwell @theovan @aridemos send some love to grumpy @therealwes

**Oliver Sikks**Verifiedaccount**@olivercromwell** @therealwes
I'm your biggest fan #triskat #thenewdarcymovie #dyiiiiing
literally

**Teddyteddy@theovan** Just uploaded a new vid remix of
@therealwes @olivercromwell #greyribbon ...bit.ly/...

**Teddyteddy@theovan** check it out everyone ...bit.ly/...
added a moustache to @therealwes

**Teddyteddy@theovan** 3rd video in a row gave a fat suit to
@therealwes so he and @theannadell match

**Oliver Sikks**Verifiedaccount**@olivercromwell** @theovan
lmao dude

**Weston Spencer**Verifiedaccount**@therealwes**
@olivercromwell et tu, Brute?

**James Pan@beethoven6th** @therealwes next time you need
to laugh you come to me

**James Pan@beethoven6th** @therealwes you hear?

**Weston Spencer**Verifiedaccount **@therealwes**
@beethoven6th I hear. Go drink your milk, kid.

**James Pan@beethoven6th** @therealwes switch to dm, kid.

Direct Messages
***James Pan*** *@beethoven6th*
*You ok? Ari got you home all right? Don't piss her off, man,
she's fierce. Also, you're welcome for the trolling. Stay sober.*

***Weston Spencer****Verifiedaccount* *@therealwes*
*Thanks for everything, man. I'm so sorry. No words. I'm
really regretting everything, but you know that already. But
for real, stop mothering me. I'm ok now, going home in a few. I
know how hard it is, but I'm not going to do that to you, all
right? I'm not going to die on you, not me. I know I almost did,*

*but I promise, last time.*
*And I am NOT welcome for the trolling. Bye.*

**James Pan** *@beethoven6th*
*I'll stop mothering you when you stop being an idiot. Hope for*
*Ari's sake it will happen sooner than your 80th bday.*

**Weston Spencer** *Verifiedaccount @therealwes*
*Love you, man.*

**James Pan** *@beethoven6th*
*OMG so do I! Kisses and hugs and farts*

## EIGHTEEN

I can't answer him. I turn my head away and try desperately to swallow my tears. It's not working. He crouches down next to me, and I feel horrible, but how can I tell him what's wrong if I don't know myself?

I gulp down the rising panic, but it's getting harder to breathe by the second.

*'Say something.'*

"Hey, Phelps," Wes says softly. "Did I pressure you into saying those things? This is me, okay? You've seen me at my absolute worst, there's nothing you can't tell me."

I turn my face up to his, letting him see every feeling, every thought in my eyes. Naked. He can see all the way inside me, to the very depths of my heart.

His expression changes; he goes pale, his eyes turning intense and sad at what he sees, but he doesn't let go of my arm. He stands up and sits on the bed. He motions at the empty spot next to him, but I sit on the chair, facing him.

He clears his throat, sighing. "We're starting from the middle, aren't we?" He gives me a tight smile. "I haven't even apologized for the way I. . . for that call."

*Ah. The phone call from hell.* That's how I dubbed those stupid things we both said that day that I decided to follow Katia's dumb idea about 'closure'.

"Wes, after the way I treated you, you have noth—"

"I missed you," he interrupts me. "I missed you so much it hurt to breathe." His throat works as he swallows. "The hope of answering the phone and hearing your voice one day was all that was holding me

255

together. And then that finally happened, only for me to find out you didn't want me."

"I did," I whisper. "I do."

He nods to indicate that he heard, but he's still not done. "That phone call, the way I acted, it was a huge mistake. I was a complete ass. I. . . I was so blind with hurt pride, that I couldn't see. . . I couldn't hear what you were really saying to me."

I'm so surprised by this that I'm jerked from  my thoughts. "What was I really saying to you?"

He shrugs, looking at the floor. "That you needed me. And I was too much of an idiot to notice. I left you alone at the time when you needed me most. I know what you'll say; I know you think you were the one who wasn't calling me or texting or even talking to me. At all." He snorts and I draw away, but his hand snatches mine, pulling me closer. "Baby," he murmurs.

I settle back down, wiping my eyes quickly. His lips move without speaking for a second, but then he goes on.

"I realized it the other day, outside the club. I did it all wrong. I could have waited. I *should* have waited for you. I wanted to, I wanted to wait forever for you, if you needed it, and then there would have been no call, no Heather, no stupid decisions. No picking me up drunk, and doing CPR on the floor of a car."

I shiver. So Pan told him.

"The idea of you all alone, thinking those. . . those stupid, horrible things you wrote on that paper. . ." He shakes his head. "The idea that you kept—*keep* thinking about those things. . . it guts me."

He takes in a sharp breath. His fingers tighten around mine and a thick vein pops on his arm as his muscle tenses.

"The idea of you hurting and me not being there. . . I can't stand it. And to know that I'm the reason you've been hurting these past few days. . . " He shakes his head.

"I honestly didn't know you'd be here when I showed up," I tell him. "No one told me this was your project. I didn't mean to bring up the past. And about that phone call, I just didn't know what to do. A. . . a friend said it was unfair to you to keep you stringing along since I didn't know when I'd be ready to be with you."

He lets out a harsh sound, as though he'd like to throttle said friend.

"She was trying to help," I say quickly. "I made the decision." I pause for a second, thinking. "Actually, even that's not entirely true. *My fear* made the decision. You did nothing wrong. And when I saw you with Heather, I thought—"

I stop.

*When I saw you with Heather, I thought I'd been right. I hadn't been that important to you after all.*

How to say that out loud? But it's true. It's another fear. Another demon I have to fight against. After the worst has happened to you, it's somehow easier to keep expecting the worst. And it's the good stuff you find hard to put your faith in.

# LOSE ME.

I got used to feeling guilty and sad and worried the short time I was with him in Corfu; now I don't know how to enjoy him. Us. Me.

"When I saw you with Heather. . . " I repeat, but still the right words won't come.

But Wes is already nodding with understanding. "You thought you hadn't mattered to me, after all," he says. I swear that dude can see inside my head. My eyes snap to his in surprise. "I know you've been thinking about this from the beginning. I just wish you'd trust me."

He sounds hurt again; I hate it.

"How could I think that a random girl you met on set would matter to you, Wes? I mean, your world is so different from mine, I can't even imagine what kind of life you're living."

He laughs ruefully, repeating 'just a random girl' under his breath. "No, I didn't say you weren't right. All those things that happened with Elle, the stuff I told you not to read in the tabloids. . . You were that important, Ari." He turns me so that we're face to face, so close that our noses are almost touching. His voice is impossibly low and intense. It shakes me to my bones. "You *are*. But basically, yeah, you were right about the kind of life I've been living."

He stops to moisten his lips, and I notice for the first time that he's shaking a little bit. As though he's shaking inside, too. As though this conversation is tearing him in apart. As though I'm not the only one who's feeling like this.

"I *am* that type of person," he repeats. "The person who's been with a million girls, insignificant girls, forgettable girls." He winces. "The person who cares about nothing and nobody but myself. But you made me care. You made me care, Ari, you were the first person who ever did that to me. At first, I cared in spite of myself. I didn't want to care whether or not you died, but I did. I jumped from that deck and I found you in the water and then I forced myself to remember the lifeguarding lessons I'd taken when I was seventeen." He passes a hand across his chin. "I didn't want to care, Ari, you know what I was. Who I was, you saw me, when everyone else saw a movie star. You saw the real me, the sorry, arrogant moron I was. And then I wanted to care. I wanted to be that person, the person who cares about others—who cares about you. You changed me."

"What happened to me changed you," I correct him. "And I'm not sure it was a good thing."

"It was a good thing," he replies. His voice sounds so calm, so sure. I wish I felt that way. "It changed us both."

I stand up, still sniffling like an idiot, and try to straighten my pajama top.

"What if it starts happening again?" I say, looking at the wall instead of him. "I can't stop thinking about that. And being here again, in a hospital, I just. . . I can't. . . " It's getting hard to breathe again. I can't stand this. Why am I still like this?

Wes takes me by the shoulders and turns me to face him. Green eyes shining with concern and pain fill my vision and I notice a lone tear making its way down his right cheek.

"Stop," he says. "Come here." He wraps his body around me and his heat envelops me. I feel his chest suck in. "I need to know two things," he says slowly, but I can hear the urgency in his voice.

"Wha. . . what are they?" I stutter and his face breaks into a smirk.

"Do you still feel anything for me?" he asks.

"I feel *everything* for you," I whisper. Emotions assault me and my voice wavers, but he tightens his hold on me. I feel him shiver against me.

"Yeah, let's not get into the 'everything' right now," he says, rubbing against mine. "Gosh, you're killing me. Even in this ridiculous yellow top that covers you up you're the cutest damn thing I've ever seen. What is this, a bear?"

"Shut up," I murmur, and I grab a fistful of his shirt.

"You shut me up," he answers, and brushes my lips with his, as a challenge. His hand slides down my back, and heat travels through the thick fabric to turn my bare skin on fire.

I'm not ashamed to say I blush furiously. He watches me with an appreciative gleam in his eye, but then he takes a tiny step back, letting a little air come between our bodies.

"Ari." His expression turns serious. "You know I love you," he says, searching my face. "You know, right? I did yell it outside the operation room as you were being wheeled in, although now it occurs to me you were heavily sedated and it might bear repeating."

"I did hear it. I kind of wondered if I was dreaming, but yeah. I heard it. Wes." I say his name the same way he said mine, and, hearing it, he shuts his eyes tightly in relief. "I heard it so many times. I heard it again every time I pressed replay on *'How to finish a boat'* and *'How to pick up a girl'* on YouTube." He takes in a sharp breath, biting his lip. "And yes, it *so* bears repeating."

He cups my neck and brings his lips hard on mine. "I love you," he says against my mouth.

His hands are running down my back, sending a wave of heat all over my body, and right then a nurse comes into the room to tell him his papers are ready and he can go. We part abruptly and as soon as she leaves, Wes pulls me to him and starts kissing my neck.

"If we don't stop right now," he mumbles, his voice muffled against my skin, "we're going to end up on the hospital bed, and that nurse will barge in on us at the worst possible moment."

"End up on the—"

"Do you have any idea how sexy you are in those jeans?" he says in a rough voice.

"I'm wearing half of my pajamas and the cheapest jeans I own."

"You could wear a sackcloth and make me crazy. And this pixie hair. . . I could barely keep my hands to myself that day in the rain. Your wet shirt was pure torture, they way it was peeled to your skin, and the raindrops that were clinging to your throat. . . " he stops to tilt his head against my neck and run his lips all the way down to my collarbone. "I mean," he murmurs against my skin, "how much is a bloke supposed to take?"

"Hey, that tickles," I say, hearing the nurse's hurried steps in the corridor again, and trying to exorcise the memories this particular sound awakens. His mouth trailing against my shoulder helps a lot.

He tips a finger under my top and rubs the skin under it. He lifts his head and takes a rugged breath. I feel his muscles tense beneath my touch.

"You're not. . . Are you. . . . ?" his question trails into silence.

"A virgin? Well, yeah. But you seem about to remedy that." Still he doesn't relax. "I was joking, don't stop," I add as he removes his hand from my sleeve.

"No, I know," he says absently. He stands up and goes to stand by the window. "Ari, what you said before about forgiveness. . . I don't just want to be forgiven. I want to be different. Different to who I was, different to everybody else, if that's what it takes."

"If that's what what takes?"

"I'm not a virgin." He turns to face me, his eyes serious.

"I kind of knew that," I say, smiling uncertainly.

"I'm sorry."

"What? Why are you—?" Now I'm confused.

"You should be the first," he says slowly, as though he's thinking this up as he goes. "You should be the only one. It should be you, us, *this*. Not some girl at the back of a movie set. . . I feel like all the sex I've had before you is something I need to be forgiven for."

He lifts his eyes to mine. They're glistening with tears.

"No," I say, reaching him in two strides. "No, you don't need to explain yourself to anyone, you don't need to apologize. Maybe you're tired. Come on, let's get you home."

"Do you get what I'm saying?" he insists. "I want to fix us first. . . I want to fix *me* before I'm yours."

"I get it." My eyes start stinging again. "I wish. . . I wish I could sort myself first too. But that may take time."

He comes closer and lifts a finger to wipe my cheek.

"Not a problem," he whispers, his voice impossibly tender. "Baby, we've got nothing but time," he tells me, leaning down to press his lips on my temple. "Come with me?"

I nod and he walks to the bathroom to pack his things.

*We've got nothing but time.*

*Time.*

Huh. How about that?

...

The hospital's security guards and Wes' bodyguards escort us to the car. The driver is the same guy who took me to Wes' house. This time around I learn that his name is Archie and that he's got a great-great grandmother on his mother's side who *might* have been Greek.

We chat the whole way, and Wes doesn't talk at all, but he just lies on the seat, his head tipped back, his eyes shut behind his dark glasses. But his lips are permanently curled into a smile.

Once we're at his house, Wes walks in and yells:
"Helen! Get down here, my darling."
Helen comes mumbling down the stairs, but her eyes sparkle as soon as she sees Wes. Wes folds his long body until he's eye to eye with her and leans down to give her a peck on the cheek, proceeding to tell her to take the rest of the day off.
"Go home, feed your kids," are his exact words. Then he turns to me. "Shower?" he asks, raising an eyebrow.

I walk into one of the bathrooms and turn on the shower. Scalding hot water pours over my head and I fumble with the taps, trying to fix the temperature.
The water falls on me at full force, and I imagine it washing the night's sweat and fear away. I close my eyes, letting it seep into my pores. Hot water on cool skin.
I'm lathering shampoo into my short hair and starting to hum a Christmas melody that's been stuck in my head for over a week, when I stop, hand in midair.
*Wes is taking a shower as well.*
*He's somewhere in this huge house, standing naked under the showerhead, his ripped muscles glistening with droplets as the water hits his skin, running down his...*
I stop myself before I finish that thought. Suddenly the water feels so hot on my skin, it's burning me. My knees have turned so weak, I have to lean against the glass door.
*Stop it. Right now. Finish in here and get out.*
I finish washing as quickly as humanly possible, and get out, walking into the other room—yes, the bathroom is actually split into two rooms in this place. Next to the sink, neatly folded in a pile, there's one of his sweaters and a pair of sweatpants that could fit two of me.
*He left them out for me to wear,* I think as I put them on after quickly drying my hair.
*'I hate your wigs so much,'* Wes' words echo in my head.
I look into the fogged-up mirror; there's a different person in there. It's not the Ari with the long, brown hair who's working for the first time in a real movie set, and is scared to meet her own eyes. It's not the Ari with the hollow cheeks and the bald head of the hospital, either.
It's someone else.
But at the same time, it's not.
This person I see in the mirror, this girl with the sharp planes on her face and the fierce look in her eyes; with the muscles in her arms and her short hair that's beginning to fall across her forehead... I know her.
She's been through a lot, but she's becoming stronger because of it.

# LOSE ME.

She's becoming herself.

The pain behind her eyes, the determination in the set of her lips, those words that are waiting to be said in her throat. . . I know them. I know *her*.

She's me.

...

As I walk down the stairs, the aroma of thyme and basil wafts up to my nose. I follow the smell to the kitchen. Wes is over the stove, chopping vegetables into a pan. A red sauce is shimmering in the corner.

He turns towards me, eyes turning into a dazzling green as soon as he sees me. His hair is still wet, and his entire face is transformed by a dazzling smile.

"Hey," he says, setting a wooden spoon down, and walking up to me. "You clean up good."

I was feeling a bit self-conscious in these huge clothes that are drowning me, but Wes doesn't take his eyes off me. He keeps staring at me with that look in his eyes again.

"Thanks for leaving these out for me," I say, trying to tuck that stupid piece of hair behind my ear. It won't stay.

He lets out a long sigh. "You've got to stop wearing my clothes, Phelps. You're going to kill me."

There's naked desire in his eyes, telling me he might have been having the same thoughts as me while he was in the shower.

"There's that blush again," he murmurs, stopping just two paces away from me.

"Sorry."

"I love it, actually."

Laughter bubbles up my throat. He raises his eyebrows in question. He's wearing loose jeans and a simple tee, and going barefoot; he's so gorgeous my chest tightens. "The way you said 'actually' was so. . . British."

The eyebrow climbs further up. "Was it now? And that's funny why?"

"It's not funny, not really." I shrug. "It's just. . . you."

He lifts an eyebrow. "Know what else is 'just. . . me'?"

Before I know what he's up to, he's grabbed me and kissed me full on the mouth. Then, leaving me almost sagging, he asks casually:

"Can you grab the salt?"

The forgotten vegetables are sizzling.

"You're full of surprises." I hand it to him, wiping my lips. "Are you *'actually'* cooking?"

"Well, I'm trying to. Only thing I can make. So far." He flashes me a smile.

"It smells delicious—almost like Greek food."

He laughs out loud, fake-punching me at the shoulder.

"Wow, that *almost* sounded like a compliment."

"It was. You've tasted Greek food. Hey, can I cook these butterfly thingies?" I look longingly at a packet of fancy pasta on a shelf—we call them 'bowtie' pasta in Greece.

"It's *farfalle* and you most definitely can. Okay, here we go."

He brings the large wooden spoon to my lips and waits until I open my mouth to taste the sauce. I make yummy noises but pretty soon it becomes obvious that I've scorched my lips, so he runs into the next room to bring ice cubes.

He puts one between his teeth and approaches me menacingly.

"What are you doing with that?" I ask, giggling.

"Don't move," he says through closed lips. He stands in front of me and presses his lips to mine, passing me the ice cube. He cups my neck as I let it melt against my pallet. "Too cold for you," he murmurs next to my mouth. "Had to warm it up."

Then Hook trots in and I scoop down to scratch behind his ear—and the place where his other ear would be. "Oh, I get it now," I say. "He's 'Hook' like a pirate who's lost his *ear* instead of his hand."

Wes is still smiling. "Looks like I've got some serious competition there."

I don't answer, because Hook jumps up, putting his paws on my shoulders, and I pretend to fall over. We roll around on the floor, and I tickle him all over. He licks my face with enthusiasm.

Ten minutes later, we're both exhausted, our tongues hanging out in tandem, and we flop on our backs on the thick carpet to rest. Wes is standing still, the kettle blowing up a steam behind him, watching us with a curious expression on his face.

"Oh, right," I say. "I was helping you."

"No, don't get up, it's fine," he says in a hoarse voice, picking up a fork. "You look. . . " He has to stop and clear his throat. "Table will be ready in. . . " he glances at his watch. "Ten seconds."

He barely touches his food; I almost say something about it, because he hasn't eaten since last evening, but then I see that his face is beaming, so I don't press him.

Five minutes after we sit down, his phone rings. He looks down, ready to turn it off.

"It's Ollie," he says to me, wincing slightly. He answers it.

Ollie proceeds to yell at him for about twenty minutes full—Wes gets up to go into the next room, but I can still hear my brother's voice through the earpiece. Then Wes tells him that I'm there, and Ollie must ask him to pass the phone to me, because he walks back into the kitchen and sits across from me.

"Ari found me," he says to Ollie, clutching his phone and sending a glance at me, his eyes hooded. "She kept me breathing, she saved my life."

I can't hear what Ollie is saying, except a screeching sound coming from the phone.

"He wants to talk to you," Wes tells me in a second, "although I wouldn't recommend it." He hands me the phone and stands up to give me some privacy, but I lift a hand to stop him. He looks pale again.

"Hey, bro," I say.

Ollie doesn't speak right away. It sounds like his breath is coming short. "Ari, I swear to—"

I interrupt him. "Where are you?"

"I'm landing in an hour," he replies. His voice sounds tortured and impatient at the same time and I wish I was there with him.

"He's fine," I tell him quickly. "He really is. Don't worry, Ollie, the danger's passed. He's perfect now."

Wes bites his lip. "Perfect is a bit of an overstatement," he whispers to me, "considering there's an entire table between us."

I stifle a laugh.

"What did the buffoon say to you?" Ollie asks me. "Just tell him to remember this is my little sister he's got in his lair and to keep his paws off you."

"Real classy, bro." I laugh.

"Sorry," he says. "Just. . . knowing what you must have gone through, and he almost. . . almost. . . Crap, I can't take this."

"We're both okay," I say for the hundredth time. "Trust me, better than okay."

There's silence for a minute as he's processing this.

"I'm glad," he says finally. He sounds calmer; there's even the trace of a smile in his voice. "All right, I can take a hint. Just enjoy your two hours with him, 'cause as soon as I'm there he's getting his ass kicked."

"Wes," I say after I've hung up. "Wes. . . "

"Don't say it."

"What are we doing here?"

He reaches out and grabs my hand. "Okay," he says, taking a deep breath. "Second thing I wanted to ask you. Before we got. . . interrupted. Ready?"

I nod.

"What if you had two seconds left to live? Hey, look at me."

I do. He's watching me, a smile playing on his lips.

"Two seconds," he repeats gently. "How would you want to spend them? Alone or with the people who love you? You have your dad and your grandparents, they'd die for you. You have your friends, and that scary coach bloke who looks at you as though he's ready to take a bullet for you. You have a brother who's coming over here to beat me to a pulp just for putting you through having to save my life. . . Which, thank you by the way."

"Don't mention it," I murmur absently.

He squeezes my hand. "You even have *me* if you want me. Always had me, from the start. You just have to decide if the fear is stronger than the love. That's all."

I just sit there, dumbfounded.

Tears begin to fill my eyes and spill over, dripping into my plate.

Wes' face goes still, like he's holding his breath; he looks at me, horrified.

"Baby," he murmurs, "open up to me. I'm here."

I push the hair out of my eyes and open my lips. Here we go. *Let's do this.*

"Today is not the day I die."

It comes out in this weird, hoarse voice, as if it's coming from a deep, broken place inside of me. Wes opens his mouth, but then closes it again, pressing his lips together. He gets up and comes to kneel next to my chair. He places his hands on my knees and holds me there.

I swallow hard. "That's. . . that's what I kept repeating to myself all this past summer. Trying to believe that it wasn't happening—trying to stay alive by sheer force of will." He shudders. "But in the end I couldn't do it, you know that. You were there. You kept me alive in every sense of the word. But after it happened I didn't know how to exist any more. I didn't want to make you into that guy. . . The guy I needed. But I didn't know that you might need me too."

He looks up at me for a long time, his face upturned, his Adam's apple bobbing, his eyes hardly blinking. He doesn't admit he needs me; there's no need for him to, not after last night.

"Be with me," he says again.

This time there's no hesitation. "Yeah."

I lean down to kiss him, and he wraps his arms around me so tightly I can't breathe.

"You never said you forgive me," I whisper into his neck. He hugs me even fiercer.

"I never said a lot of things I should have said," he whispers back, his chest shuddering against mine. "Like 'I'm lost without you' or '*I'm* the actual, utter idiot.'"

I just shake my head. No need for words, no more need for apologies. This is it.

Us.

Just sitting here, our bodies pressed together until there's nothing between us, finally; his scent in my nose, his lips on my hair, his arms around my waist. Just this.

This sense of familiarity that envelopes me, of safety, of warmth. I know him. And he knows me. I've seen him at his worst, and he's seen me at mine. I'm no longer scared of what's happened to me. I'm no longer embarrassed of who I've been. At least not now, not with him. He saw me fall and he saw me rise. And I saw him.

And, I realize as I bury my face in the crook of his shoulder, I'm planning on seeing more of his future. I'm planning on sharing it. I'm planning on having a future with him.

I'm planning on having a future, period. I'm planning on it.

...

The shooting for Sweet Prince wraps up five days later. Ollie and Theo have already left, and Pan has to go back to school in New York soon.

"Take care of my homeboy," he tells me on his last day, coming to find me as I'm warming up in the wings.

"Get bent," I reply.

"Keep it in your pants," he winks.

"Pan!" Wes' voice roars from the auditorium. "Hands off." Then, although they're not even in the same room, they both burst out laughing simultaneously.

Ugh.


Before I know it, it's time for me to leave as well. The Academy is opening in a bit, and so we spend the last day helping the crew clean up.

"So, are you going with him?" Rosie asks me in a low voice as I'm helping her collect her pins and scraps for the last time.

"Who?" I ask innocently.

"Hamlet," she says.

She's lost some of her bounciness since that night at the club, still she's constantly trying her hardest to cheer everyone up. Let alone that she's probably the hardest worker in here. Except Wes.

I shrug. "I'm not sure."

"Well, you'd better *become* sure soon," she whispers, nudging me and nodding towards the door, where Wes' tall, slim silhouette darkens the opening. He's heard us.

Crap.

I walk towards him, grabbing my coat. Immediately he reaches out a hand and pulls the wig from my hair—it was the pink one today, the one with the cute, uneven bangs.

"Hey!" I protest, but then he runs his palm down the slope of my neck and I shiver with pleasure. "Did you hear what we were talking about?"

Instead of an answer, he lifts an eyebrow. Clean-shaven and rested, he looks almost a different person from the guy I found drunk out of his mind in the club five days ago.

"I want to take you home," he says simply. "Ollie wants to come too, if you're okay with it. What. . . what do you think?"

And that's when I finally realize what kind of home he's talking about.

Corfu.

*My* home.

I start jumping up and down, squeezing my arms around him.

"I thought so," he smiles, his hands coming round my waist. "We leave tomorrow, after the do." Of course there's a goodbye party. They call it 'a do' for some inexplicable reason. I'm looking forward to it only because of Rosie. How I'll say goodbye to her I don't know. "Sounds good?"

I squeal instead of a reply. He takes that as an invitation to start kissing me, right there in the doorway, as students are darting around us, this way and that, packing up the blue lights and the fog machine.

## tumblr.

spencerstumblr

I want to be the one who controls my body.
Not vice versa. Alcohol, anger, girls. . . It's all the same.
I don't want to be constantly forgiven. I want to be doing things right. I want to be someone capable of saving others. Of saving myself. Worthy. I want to be different from what I was. I want to be new.

Be forgiven.
Stay forgiven.

#personal #man_versus_body

701,569 notes

## N I N E T E E N

It's a crisp January morning, two days later.
We're home; we arrived in Athens yesterday evening, and flew to Corfu from there.
The first thing I see when we touch down are thick, dark clouds, painting the horizon a grayish white. The sky is hidden behind them, and they look so heavy, their bellies touching the peaks of Mount *Pantokrator*. The humidity in the air is slicing at my bones and I shudder, breathing in a mouthful of salty sea air.
"Welcome home," Wes tells me, his eyes smiling. "Missed it?"
I shrug. "Haven't been away *that* long," I say and he nudges me, but he doesn't say anything more.
But I have been away that long. He's not talking about being back home in Corfu. He's talking about being home as myself. He can see the change in me already. I can, too.
I have been away for long, for too long. I have missed myself.

# LOSE ME.

Wes squeezes my cold fingers and I can feel his warmth seeping in through my woolen mittens. He understands, even without my having to say it.

It's time to come back. To *be* back.

...

Wes has already booked his old penthouse suite in town, but he drops me off at my house first. Dad hugs him fiercely and then turns aside although it's too late. I've already seen his eyes go misty.

"You'll stay with us," he says to Wes.

"Thank you, not tonight," Wes replies, winking at me. "First thing tomorrow morning, there's something Ari and I have to do."

"There is?" I ask. This is the first I'm hearing of it.

And then he leaves.

A few hours later, after staying up late with dad, talking, I settle into bed.

*I'm finally home*, I keep thinking, *and Wes is here. I can't wait to see Katia, finally. And pappous and yiayia. I've missed this so much.*

I haven't felt like this since I was little and it was Christmas Eve, and I was so excited about all the people who'd come over and the presents we'd open and the games we'd play.

My phone's light blinks.

**Wes**: Asleep yet?

**Me**: not a chance. Remind me again why you're there and I'm here?

**Wes**: Because I'm an idiot.

**Me**: can't disagree there

**Wes**: Tell me you're happy.

**Me**: u know I am

**Wes**: You didn't tell me Corfu winters were so vicious. I'd have stayed in good old England if I wanted to freeze my toes off.

I sit up and groan. Weather? He's talking to me about the weather?

**Me**: srsly? This is what u wanna talk abt right now?

**Wes**: No. What I want right now is to kiss you until neither of us can remember our names. But. . . it's better this way. You need your rest for tomorrow.

**Me**: What's happening tmr?

**Wes**: Trust me?

**Me**: Dude u know I do.

**Wes**: Good girl.

**Me**: you're a good girl

**Wes**: Ok ok sorry.

**Me:** not as sorry as u will be tmr when I kick your ass.

**Wes:**...
**Wes:**...
**Wes:**...

**Me:** having a hard time thinking of a comeback?

**Wes:** Man, you're the best thing that's ever happened to me.

**Me**: oh I know. you're really making me mad saying those things over the phone. Get in yr car and drive over, would you?

**Wes**: You'll be the one to decide. In the morning.

**Me:** decide abt what?

**Wes**: Us.

We stop talking a few minutes later and I try to get some sleep, which proves to be harder than I thought it would. My body is exhausted, but my brain won't stop thinking.

Good things, mostly.

Dad looks good; he hasn't lost weight. He said grandma is trying to fatten him up and he's been fighting her off with a stick. He kept looking at me as though a question was playing at his lips, but he never asked it.

He wanted to know if I was all right.

I hope he got his answer by the time I came up to bed.

I *am* all right. More so than I've even been. The words I read on that book on Wes' desk keep playing in my head.

*'I don't judge you guilty.'*

*Forgiveness should be a synonym of freedom*, I think. A weight's been lifted off my chest; a weight so big I didn't know I was carrying it around before I glanced at that book.

But there's a nagging feeling that won't let me relax. Something unresolved. Something that needs to be faced and conquered.

I don't like leaving things around unfinished; I don't like knowing there's something out there that's stronger than me. I don't like there being things I can't do.

*If only I could put my finger on what it is, I'd tackle it*, is my last thought before sleep finally claims me.

...

The next morning dawns cold and wet, but by the time Wes arrives to pick me up, the sun is peeking behind the clouds and the paved stones of the *kantouni* below my window are quickly drying up. It looks as though it's going to be one of those rare winter sunshine days.

"Nice ride," I say as I see the car he's rented, barely able to contain my excitement. My fingers are itching to grasp that wheel.

"No can do, Phelps," Wes smirks, guessing what I'm thinking. "You'll have a chauffeur today, my lady, whether you like it or not."

He gestures towards the passenger seat with an exaggerated flourish.

"Some chauffeur," I mumble.

I knew he wouldn't prefer to be driven around, given the choice, but this time he's picked a beauty. It's a Ferrari 360 Modena, a ride most of us only dream of even *seeing* in real life.

About five minutes later I'm squirming in my seat, the new-found wonder of the Ferrari forgotten, as I look out the window anxiously.

"We're not. . . Are we going to. . . ?"

Wes doesn't answer, he just looks straight ahead, changing gears as he takes a steep turn carefully.

I settle back. What are the chances of him taking me to *that* beach? *No, he wouldn't. . .*

Wes takes a left. "You all right?" he asks me.

It feels like we're driving to *Pelekas*, as though not one day has gone by since First Sentences.

Suddenly I know. This *is* where he's taking me.

That's the 'surprise' he was planning.

And then another realization hits me: that nagging feeling of something unresolved that was keeping me awake last night? This is it, too. *Pelekas*. The Rubble. The dive.

"Hey hey," Wes reaches over and pries my white fingers from the dashboard. I didn't even know I was gripping onto it so tightly. "Phelps?" His voice sounds clipped, as though he's holding his breath. I turn around and meet his concerned gaze.

"I'm fine." I release my clutch slowly. "Sorry, I didn't realize I was. . . doing that."

"Breathe," he says. "We're almost there."

Fifteen more minutes pass and then the yellow villa peeks in the distance as we take a sharp turn, and my heart slams in my chest. Impulsively I grasp for the door handle.

"No no no." There's a hint of fear in Wes' voice. "What are you doing?" He presses the lock down, and my panic rises. "Give me your hand, I'm right here."

I grab his fingers and press down hard enough to break bones. He bites his lip, watching me. He begins to slow the car down, but then he shakes his head, as though he's having a silent argument with himself, and steps on the gas.

"Let's get there, at least," he says calmly, trying to change gears and steer the wheel with one hand, since his other one is currently occupied. "Yeah?"

I mutter "damn you" behind clenched teeth, but I don't ask him to turn back.

Before I know it, we've arrived at the familiar beach. The Rubble is looming in the distance. Wes gets out and comes over to open my door. I'm frozen on the spot.

*No. No. No.* That's all I can think.

I feel water choking my mouth, the darkness and desperation closing in over my head. I hunch down, putting my head between my knees, my stomach rolling. I hear the driver's door shut quickly and the next second Wes is next to me, his hand warm on my back, waiting for the panic to pass.

In a minute I can breathe again, but then the beeping starts in my head. The heart monitors, the constant soundtrack of the hospital.

*Beep beep beep.*

Sometimes it gets deafening inside my head when I try to sleep at night, but this is the first time it assaults me during the day.

*Beep beep beep beep.*

*Stop it!* I scream inside my head.

*Today is not the day I die. Today is not one of the days I'm sick. Today I'm fine, there's nothing wrong with me. Today and tomorrow and the day after that, there's nothing threatening me.*

"Ari," Wes kneels down beside me. "It's okay if you don't want to get in the water. I'm sorry, I thought. . . But maybe it's too soon."

I lift my eyes to look at him, and I'm surprised so much at what I see that I forget everything else.

"What. . . what are you holding?"

He hands me a piece of long, sleek fabric that almost looks like the costumes on the set of Sweet Prince, I finger the scales-like mesh. It's a black wetsuit with a thin, orange line that goes down the left leg. He's holding a similar one with a yellow stripe.

"Oh," is all I can say.

He bends down to kiss my ear. "You didn't think I'd let my girl dive into the sea in January with just a swimsuit on, did you?" he says playfully, but his eyes are watching me warily. "Even though she's practically a mermaid. So. . . care to give it a go?"

"Hell, yeah." He knew that once he gave me the wetsuit I wouldn't be able to resist it. "Did you plan this?"

He gets to his feet, raising me with him. He looks so smug it's pretty funny. "Went and bought them the day after I got out of hospital."

"I really hate you and love you right now," I tell him and his face beams.

"I aim to please," he says. "Now get your cute little behind over here."

We change in the little white cabins by the fig trees and come out with our lips turning blue with cold. We get into the water and swim to the Rubble. On top of the cliff, the yellow villa is silent, shutters down, terrace empty.

The water isn't so bad, as the sea still retains some of its autumn warmth, and I soon get used to it. It feels so good to swim; I haven't been here since that Tuesday. I try not to think about that day, and focus instead on my strokes and the memories of all the times I trained here with dad or Coach, but still I have a headache by the time I start climbing the rocks.

Just from remembering.

"You okay?" Wes asks. I look at him as he stands there, the wetsuit accentuating his biceps, the soft down of his hair darkened by the water.

"No," I answer. "I'm not okay."

"I know," he says. "This is what today is all about. You have no idea how much I want to fix you, baby, but I can't. No one else can do it for you but you."

"Face your fears and all that, huh?" I mumble, grabbing a rock and starting to climb up the jagged cliff of the Rubble.

Wes follows right below me, carefully placing his hands and feet in the exact spots as me. I'm so proud of him, being smart instead of trying to show off, which is what every other guy I know—including my dad— would be doing right now.

His whole attitude makes me realize that this is not about him. He's just here to support me, but this is not something we're doing together. It's all up to me.

And I'm scared out of my mind.

Fake it till you make it, as Katia says. Well, she was full of bull. I reach the top and look down, getting dizzy. I know it's stupid, and I know I've done this dive a million times, but my brain is certain that if I jump I'll drown.

Like *certain* certain.

"Ready?" Wes says, panting slightly behind me.

Was this thing always so high? I don't remember it being so far above the sea. Wait, maybe the sea receded. Does it do that in this beach? Maybe there's a tide? No, there isn't. And global warming is the waterline rising, not dropping. Right.

271

We're completely alone, no one there for miles. Even the street is nearly deserted.

"Stop being stupid," I whisper to myself.

"Stop being a twit, you mean," Wes says behind me.

I turn around and grab him, kissing him full on the mouth. Before I can take a proper breath, I jump off and free-fall, feet first, into the water.

The cold is nothing compared to the fear that grips me as soon as my body hits the surface. I open my eyes and water gets in my vision, bubbles twirling crazily around me, and for a second I forget to float upwards, opening my lips in a panic and getting in a gulp of water.

Instinct kicks in and, since there's nothing wrong with my legs or my head this time, which is to say I'm not having a seizure or a crippling headache, I rise to the surface and take a big gulp of air.

"You good?" someone yells at me from above.

Wes hasn't jumped after me. He's still on top of the rocks, leaning down, watching me.

I lift my hand in a thumbs-up.

"It was perfect, baby," he shouts, and of course it wasn't, but I know what he means and I smile. "I knew it," his voice, loud and clear, rings all around me. "You can do anything, you're fearless!"

"Get down here," I yell at him.

He extends a leg and does one and a half somersault in the air, shooting like an arrow towards the water. "Show-off," I murmur, but a smile spreads itself across my lips in spite of myself.

I don't have time to say anything else, because he lands with an elegantly small splash right next to me, grabbing my arm and dragging me for a long dive with him. We surface a few seconds later, and he gasps for air against my lips, kissing me at the same time.

"Besides," he pants after a minute or so, when we finally part, "I've got your back."

"I know you do." I want to say everything to him. I'm ready now. "Listen, I never thanked you for saving me those both times and for arranging everything with the hospital and the operation..."

He makes a gesture as though he wants me to stop, but I look at him straight in the eyes and he understands that I have to say these things.

"And the reason I never did," I go on, kicking my legs to keep afloat in the blue-green waters, "the reason I never did was that I didn't truly feel thankful. I know this is a terrible thing to say, but for a long time there didn't seem to be a difference between when I was sick with... with the tumor," I swallow as I say the word, "and when I was sick after the operation. Or sick with fear."

Wes circles my waist and pulls me to him. I rest my head on his shoulder.

"I want to be different too," I tell him. "What you wrote in the note you left me... I read every word, Wes. I know it by heart. I know I have been granted life for a reason. I know that being a walking, taking miracle is a responsibility as well. Surviving is not enough. I want to live. And if you have to fight against your. . . "

"Addiction," he supplies, seeing me hesitate.

"That. If *that's* a constant battle, mine will be a war against the fear that something bad will happen. I don't know if I can ever totally overcome it, but for the first time I'm willing to try. To face it, not to cower away in a corner."

"You already did," he tells me, pressing a wet kiss to my temple. His lips feel like ice cubes.

"Yeah, but it was only once," I reply. "And you're right. We *will* have all the time in the world, you and me, all our. . . lives."

". . . lives," he says at the same time as me and we smile at each other, happiness bursting out of our chests like a current. His chest rises and falls as he gulps in a breath, but before I can ask him what's wrong, he pulls me beneath the surface to kiss me in the water.

"What was that for?" I ask, as he propels us above water in a few seconds. The heady sensation of his lips taking mine is making me dizzy.

"To exorcise one of my own fears," he says. "The memory of almost being too late." He cups my neck and presses my body to his.

"We were doomed from that day, weren't we?"

"Totally," he replies, his face serious.

Theo's tortured eyes from the hospital flash before my eyes, out of nowhere. I remember every strange, tortured word that came out of his mouth, I remember the way his face looked, a mask of pain and sorrow. I know nothing about him; I have no idea what he's going through. But a week ago, my heart had tightened painfully for him and I just wanted to hug him, to make all this pain that was weighing him down disappear.

How does it feel for his friends to feel like that and be unable to help? I remember how Pan looked at him, like a bear ready to pounce on anyone who attacked her cubs. What if Wes had felt like that about me, and I had wrenched myself away from him? Away from everyone who wanted to share my fear, my pain, my sorrow.

I don't want to be that person. The person who doesn't even want to fight for their own life.

'Why would you want to do that?"

'Do what? Live?'

Even after all the pain I have experienced, nothing compares to the depth of suffering I saw in the chocolate-brown eyes of the rich kid who'd been left behind by a brother who went to the war. And yet, I'd been that person for a bit.

I almost gave up.

And I had no right to.

So that's when it finally hits me. What he's been trying to tell me from the beginning, even before he knew what was going on with me.

"I don't regret what happened that day," I say. "Wes, I don't." I repeat it, surprised to hear the words coming out of my own lips. "I don't regret having had the tumor. I used to think of it as that horrible,

horrible thing that happened to me out of the blue, and it was, but now I realize. . . "

Wes doesn't interrupt me. He just floats next to me, waiting for me to finish my train of thought.

"I realize I'd have to have it. I'd have to have it in order to overcome it. In order to become who I am today and who I want and hope to be tomorrow. That girl who thought she was tough because she could kick your ass in soccer and pretty much anywhere else—she wasn't really tough. She had to remind herself not to die every single day. She didn't know how to fight the fights that mattered. And I'm not saying I know how to fight now, but I'm learning to. I'm learning to survive; to live. I'm. . . Is it wrong to say I'm glad this happened?"

It takes a moment for him to speak. "I love that girl who had to remind herself not to die every day," he says, his voice breaking. "I didn't know that was what you had to do at the time, and it would have broken my heart if I did, but I'm so proud of you for surviving the only way you could. That's why I fell for you, head over heels. Your strength, it drew me towards you like a magnet."

He pulls me close and presses his lips to my cheek.

"But what you've become now. . . It's a complete transformation and I can't believe how privileged I am to be witnessing it. I told you I love how this whole thing changed me, what it made me become. And I can't say I'm glad it happened, not in a million years. . . " he sucks in a breath. "But, baby, I am beyond words proud of you and of the woman you're becoming."

Did he actually say 'woman'? I feel a furious blush spread across my cheeks, and duck my head in the water.

He just looks at me and smiles, flipping onto his back and spreading his arms lazily, as though the sea isn't nearing Arctic temperatures.

"All right," I say. "So, I need you to go."

"Huh?" his sandy eyebrows shoot up. I look at his lips longingly; they're red and dripping with water. "Don't do that." His voice is hoarse and I realize I'd been licking my lips. Instead of stopping, I smile, biting them, and look up through lowered eyelashes. "Don't start something you can't finish," he groans, grabbing my waist.

He drinks my lips thirstily and then we tangle our fingers together, starting to sink slowly. I forget all about the cold as the familiar rush of his proximity floods every sense. I could stay like this forever, with his arms around me, his body between me and the freezing wall of water. His hands travel all over my back, ending up on my neck. When the water reaches our foreheads we untangle ourselves and kick to the surface.

"What were you saying before starting this ridiculous come-on?" he rasps, lifting me so I can wrap my legs around his waist. "Damn, baby, when you move your hips like that it makes me crazy. . . no, that's not helping. Stay absolutely still. Hold on a sec, I can't. . . breathe." He runs his hand through his hair, shaking the droplets from his eyes. "So, what was it?"

"Eh? Oh right," I murmur. "I said please leave. I need some alone time with the Rubble, like old times."

He holds me away from him for a second to look at my face with a serious expression. "Leave as in, go sit on top of the rock, or leave as in, get in the car?"

"Leave like go back to town," I whisper as I trace a line of kisses along his neckline.

He starts moaning. "Baby, what are you doing to me?" I feel him go weak beneath my fingertips, and I tighten my legs more securely around his waist.

"I need to do this on my own," I say. "But stay for a little while."

"I'm this close to unzipping your suit," he murmurs.

We stay like this until we can't take it any longer, and then he swims to the shore. He tells me he can't bear to leave me alone, and I plead with my eyes. "What if... um, what if something happens, what if you get tired and I'm not here? Or—?"

"Nothing is going to happen," I interrupt him. His eyes have started to look tormented again, and I can't stand it. I speak matter-of-factly, hoping that just saying things out loud will help scatter both our fears. "I just need to do this alone, that's it. I've done it many times this summer, you know."

"Oh, I saw," he replies. His eyebrow shoots up, and he starts smiling again; I know that smile, it's his 'let's have fun teasing Ari' smile. "I saw you dive. You were *really* good."

So I dunk him.

After that he leaves, reluctantly. I stay in the same spot, watching the splash of his strokes getting smaller as he reaches the beach, then his tall, slim silhouette as he jogs across the sand in his wetsuit. He unzips it and lets the top part hang around his waist—I can understand how he feels hot in the middle of a windy wintry day.

I too feel like I could burst from my skin. But first things first. Taking my eyes off him with difficulty, I start swimming towards the Rubble.

...

And so it finishes, this particular chapter of my life, just like it began.

Just me and the Rubble, the water sparkling in the sun around us. I dive until my limbs feel like they're made of rubber and my lungs start burning. It's from excitement this time, though; not fear.

Behind me, voices.

Dad telling me it was perfect.

Coach assuring me I've got this.

Lee lifting his hand in a salute.

Ollie screaming 'all right!' in celebration.

Katia calling to tell me how lucky I am to have met the pirate in real life, for the thousandth time.

And Wes.

*'Besides, I've got your back.'*

And someone else. Someone else. Calling, calling, calling to me 'I love you.' Visible and invisible in the vast expanse of water at my feet, in the clouds above me.

Blue surrounding me on all sides.

I pause for a second on top of the rocks and take in the familiar view. So much beauty, so much love. I feel as if I can breathe it in, the love that surrounds me. Someone created this world for me to live in. Someone is watching over me right now.

The same Someone who saved my life when I flatlined in that operation room. Because it's true. I may have tried to avoid this realization for some time, because it was too scary, but it is true. Someone saved my life.

I needed saving. And I was saved. I know it wasn't Wes or the doctors, or just luck. It wasn't just one of these random things that happen. I'd be an idiot to think like that.

*'You're a walking miracle,'* Jamie said to me over and over at the hospital.

Well, I want to start living that miracle. Leave all the guilt and fear behind.

*'I also don't judge you guilty.'*

That's the life I want to live. Loved. Unafraid. Forgiven. Transforming, growing day by day. Not alone. Never alone.

I dive and climb and dive again until the water is just water, and the rocks are part of my homeland's soil, and the dive is just another stunt.

I dive with my fears staring me in the face, and I refuse to look at them.

Somewhere in the distance, maybe in the next rise of the road, Wes is waiting for me—I'm pretty sure he didn't go home as I told him, he'll just stay there until he sees me walking up from the beach, covered in dried salt water and exhausted, if I know him at all.

Tomorrow or the day after, *pappous* and *yiayia* will lay down the white tablecloth on the long, narrow dining-room table and we'll all sit down for a huge dinner with dad, and Wes. *Yiayia* will have cooked *spanakopita* and *pastitsada* and her famous bergamot pies that are the pride of Corfu, and she'll make us take seconds of everything, until Wes won't even be able to remember why he ever thought *souvlaki* was so awesome in the first place. It will be nothing compared to this spread.

Maybe Katia will be there too, she's still home for the holidays. She'll tell me how pretty my hair looks and I'll make a face and then she'll have to say hi to Wes, who will tell her he's heard everything about her. She'll blush and he'll explain that I'm always talking his ear off about her and I'll say shut up, I'm not, and Wes will laugh and punch me playfully and Katia will look down, totally swooning inside, but also kind of intimidated and kind of happy. I'll completely feel the same, and I won't be able to wait until she and I are alone in my room to ask her whether she's lost some weight and if she's eating properly in Athens.

Also, what does she think of my brother?

Everyone will pretend they're not watching Wes all the time, but he'll notice. He'll be cool with it though, except maybe for once, when he'll lean down to whisper to me that he can't wait until we're alone. Maybe Ollie will catch a flight from L.A. and he'll be there too, and I'll have everyone I love in the same room to tell them once again how happy I am to be here with them, alive. *Living.*

Then we'll eat everything in sight and fall into that cozy, post-Greek-food hibernation in front of the fireplace, my hand tangled in Wes' fingers, Ollie drooling on my shoulder. Maybe I'll catch Katia's eye across the sofa and she'll smile at me, lifting her new phone to take a picture of the three of us lying there, sprawled like kids next to the Christmas tree.

When Ollie wakes up maybe he'll suggest we go for a game of soccer and Wes will mumble that he didn't know we celebrated Thanksgiving in Greece, cause that sure felt like one heck of a meal, and my grandma will tell him in Greek that this is how we eat every Sunday. He won't understand, but he'll laugh anyway, then run upstairs to put on a pair of my dad's sweats.

We'll spend the rest of the day together, and when the night descends, Wes and I will go for a little walk on the *kantounia*, the moon peeking down at us from dark heavens, and he'll not take his arms from around me for a second, our bodies close, our breaths warming our frozen fingers. He'll grab me and kiss me in the same tiny alley we walked through that night in September, and we'll forget all about the cold.

He'll tell me how he was watching me on those days we trained together on set, how he was conscious of my every movement, and how he was mad that I wouldn't even look at him. I'll tell him I was totally checking him out the whole time and I'll expect him to laugh, but his eyes will go tender and serious and he'll wrap his arms around me and say 'I love you, Ari *mou.*'

The day after I'll come back here, at the Rubble.

I'll do the dive fifty more times, fighting my demons, fighting myself.

I'll do it until I can own it.

And then, when the time comes for Wes to go back home, I may go with him. Or I may go to L.A. with Ollie and meet up with Coach and Matt and start training for another movie. Then Wes might win an Oscar and the world could go crazy around us with paparazzi and interviews and film proposals.

But I'll still be me.

And Wes will be Wes. And he'll be there no matter what, because he saw me at my darkest. He *loved* me at my darkest.

But all of that is one step further. One dive further.

If I can own this dive, I can own the next step. And the next one after that. And so on. Because I can't do this alone. And, the truth is, I don't have to.

So for the rest of the day I dive.

...

As the sun begins to dip in the horizon, I lift my eyes to the road. There's a tall figure walking towards the beach, painted black as the rays of the sun slant behind it.

I lift my hand in greeting and the figure lifts its hand too.

I dive again, shivering from cold and exhaustion, and once I'm in the water I start swimming to the shore. If I stop for a second the cold will catch up with me, so I walk straight up the beach towards where Wes, dressed in dry clothes, is waiting for me, a towel in his hands.

"Okay?" he asks me, wrapping it tightly around me. He leans down to muzzle my ear, but I'm so cold, I barely feel his touch. I burrow deeper in his arms, relishing the draw of my tired muscles and the warmth of his skin. My eyes are stinging from the salt.

"Let's go," I say, putting my hand in his.

**_Peter_ Wins Best Actor At the Oscars! Watch!**

Here's The Acceptance Speech:

[watch in HD]

What a night! _Peter_, the psychological thriller that has been sweeping the big screens across the globe, took home the Best Picture Award as well as the Best Actor Award! The flick, starring British prodigy mega-star **Weston Spencer** and talented child actor **Candice Marks** was easily the biggest surprise of the night. But the biggest winner tonight was hands down the gorgeous pirate of _THE WATER WARS_, Spencer, who wrapped up the Oscars with an emotional speech, thanking the producers and writers.

You can watch his entire speech on video, but here's the press' favorite snippet, which is being featured, as we speak, on celebrity blogs and magazines all over the planet:

'This success does not belong to me. If you know me at all, you're aware that I did my best to destroy myself this past year. Except, someone wouldn't let me. A reporter asked me recently if I've got any regrets about my career so far. Well, let me tell you, I have a ton. But for the grace of God, I wouldn't be here.'

In a gesture that was captured by a million camera flashes, Spencer pointed at his date in the audience, the unknown but stunning Ari Demos, 19, holding up the golden statuette in his other hand [**3:45** min in the video]. Spencer teared up, as he added:

"I wouldn't change anything. Not even the pain."

## Liked it?
## Don't forget to review!

**Did you know how much a single positive review can help an author out?**

If a book has over a certain number of reviews it's automatically bumped up to the retailer's bestseller list!

So just write a few words to show your appreciation for the author's hard work!

The creation of this book would not have been possible without the help of the amazing **tumblr** and **instagram** community. I went to you guys for support and encouragement, and found inspiration. When you said that I wasn't ruined I believed you -that says it all. You are what makes writing the best thing that ever happened to me. I love you and I need you.

Not only this book, but also its author wouldn't be here if it wasn't for someone *—my* someone. You are my constant source of strength and happiness. You know who you are to me and why everything I ever write will be dedicated to you.

**M.C. FRANK** has been living in a world of stories ever since she can remember. She started writing them down when she could no longer stand the characters in her head screaming at her to give them life.

In her books, characters find themselves in icy-cold dystopian worlds where kissing is forbidden (among other things), or in green forests ruled by evil Sheriffs.

Recently she got her university degree in physics and is now free to pursue her love of reading and writing, as well as her free-lance job of editor-in-chief. She currently lives with her husband in a home filled with candles, laptops and notebooks, where she rearranges her overflowing bookshelves every time she feels stressed. She is the creator of The Book Robin Hoods, an online family that connects writers with readers.

She loves to connect with book lovers and other writers on social media. She's found the most amazing friends and readers on **tumblr** and **instagram**, and they are what keeps her going when things get rough.

*Connect with her on social media for awesome giveaways and free copies of her books! She would also love to talk to you about anything writing related.*

Find all of M.C. Frank's books on her website:
**mcfrankauthor.com**

Twitter: **@mcfrank_author**

Instagram: **mcfrank_author**

Blog: **mcfrankauthor.tumblr.com**

Facebook Page: **M.C. Frank**

Goodreads: **M.C. Frank**

Don't miss M.C. Frank's exciting new fantasy
that brings Greek mythology into modern Greece
and mixes fangirls with mermen in a swoonworhty
romantic adventure.

Made in the USA
Middletown, DE
15 September 2020